MASTER OF THE ACADEMY

A novel

By: Marston Moore

MASTER OF THE ACADEMY © Copyright 2012 by Marston Moore. All rights reserved. No part of this book may be reproduced in any form whatsoever, by photography or xerography or by any other means, by broadcast or transmission, by translation into any kind of language, nor by recording electronically or otherwise, without permission in writing from the author, except by a reviewer, who may quote brief passages in critical articles for reviews.

Artwork by Marnie K. Jorenby

ISBN-10: 0-9850926-1-0

ISBN-13: 978-0-9850926-1-0

Printed in the United States of America
First Printing: March 2012

31121 County 8 Blvd
Cannon Falls, MN 55009

www.deerpathbooks.com

To order, visit www.deerpathbooks.com

For Martha Kristen

And the countless others whose

contributions have been blocked by the

Masters of the Academy.

SYSTEMIC DISORDERS

"The cracking of old and famous structures is slow and internal, while the façade holds."

(Barbara Tuchman: A Distant Mirror)

- ACCELERATING COSTS: Between 1999–2000 and 2009–10, prices for undergraduate tuition, room, and board at public institutions rose 37 percent, and prices at private institutions rose 25 percent, after adjustment for inflation. (National Center for Education Statistics)
- STUDENT LOAN DEBT: "The amount of student loans taken out last year (2010) crossed the $100 billion mark for the first time and total loans outstanding will exceed $1 trillion for the first time this year. Americans now owe more on student loans than on credit cards." (Federal Reserve Bank of New York)
- BLOATED ADMINISTRATION: "Between 1993 and 2007 . . . the number of full-time administrators per 100 students at America's leading universities grew by 39 percent, while the number of employees engaged in teaching, research, or service only grew by 18 percent." (Goldwater Institute)
- ADJUNCT FACULTY: "The number of full-time tenured and tenure-track faculty members declined from . . . one-third of the instructional staff in 1997 to . . . one-quarter in 2007." (American Federation of Teachers)
- SPORTS AND ENTERTAINMENT: ". . . 800 million dollars of student tuition and institutional support were allocated to sports and entertainment by so-called 'big time' universities in 2010." (USA Today)
- UNEMPLOYABLE GRADUATES: "22% of 2011 graduates are unemployed and another 22% work in jobs that do not require a college degree." (New York Times)

- EDIFICE COMPLEX: Every college and university continues to construct buildings and stadia that are only marginally related to the academic enterprise. Naming rights to these edifices feed grandiose development schemes that are largely out of control. For example, the University of Colorado recently sold the naming rights of a men's lavatory for twenty-five thousand dollars: the University of Phoenix put its name on the home of the Arizona Cardinals football team – at least, Phoenix avoided the cost and worry of fielding its own football team.

HOW DID IT GET THAT WAY?

These problems and the weakened institutions that result are creations of 'the academy' - the faculty and administrators who shaped them over time. When the rhetorical question, 'Why are academic politics so vicious?' is asked, it is usually answered, 'Because the stakes are so small.'. This popular conception is far from the mark. Academic politics are indeed vicious, because the stakes (for the players) are so large.

Master of the Academy is the story of one political actor, Rich Jessen, who bears much of the responsibility for the appalling state of his University. Rich is a composite of academic politicians the author has known over his fifty years as a faculty member and administrator : in a liberal arts college, a prestigious private university and in a 'research 1' public university. The skeptical reader is advised that every incident reported in this book is based on an actual occurrence.

BOOK I
POLITICAL MAN

". . . if you are ambitious withal, and your spirit
hankers after academic politics;
read, and may your soul (if you have a soul)
find mercy!"
(Francis Cornford: Microcosmographica Academica)

CHAPTER ONE

Acropolis Now

"Scale, not style, is the essential element in good campus design."
(Thomas Jefferson)

Blewett Hall stood on the edge of campus, the public face of Midwest University. A small rise of ground – The Hill – was an appropriate setting for the Greek Temple façade of Blewett. Broad flights of steps elevated those who would enter to the second floor, a prairie style image of the entrance to the Acropolis in Athens.

Midwest University was, however, no Acropolis. While Blewett alone faced the public, other University buildings effectively turned their backs to the outside world. All major campus buildings were placed around the perimeter of a hollow square; the buildings faced inward, their backs presenting blocks of masonry to outsiders. This was what students called 'prison modern' or 'Leavenworth without the fence'. However, the simile was not wholly accurate since Leavenworth actually presents quite an attractive face to its public.

9

Rich Jessen usually entered Blewett directly from its basement garage, through gloomy corridors and cracked marble stairs. But on sunny days like this, he emerged from the garage's outdoor exit and made his way across The Hill to the front of Blewett and approached this educational Acropolis.

During the past winter, Rich had spent many hours reflecting on his status at Midwest and how it might be improved. Being an Associate Professor in the College of Education and Home Economics was a milestone in his ascendancy to the inner circles of the University. When he looked back at the five years that had passed since he came to Midwest, Rich felt that he hadn't yet arrived. The Full Professorship continued to elude his grasp and he mourned his unfulfilled dream. Rich's path was blocked by the fact of his appointment; he was a member of a loose conglomeration of faculty who professed the 'Social Foundations of Education'. This imposing title effectively marginalized Rich; Social Foundations did not enjoy the academic status that could propel him upward as it wasn't even a 'department' in the College of Education and Home Economics. The faculty in Social Foundations included those professing marginal subject matters such as History of Education, Philosophy of Education and the Economics of Education, the latter subject matter the home of Richard Jessen.

As he began to ascend the steps of Blewett, Rich was conscious of the burden of expectation, almost a physical load that slowed his steps through marble columns. He sighed and forced his way through the heavy doors of the Hall. Inside, the Greek theme continued. A three-story atrium drew the eye upward, at first to grimy balconies, then down to bas-reliefs of educational leaders of the past. Here Rich could meditate on the contributions of Pestalozzi, Montessori, Dewey, in addition to numerous educational leaders of Midwest fame. The centerpiece of this display was a larger than life depiction of Ben Blewett, Superintendent of Schools in St. Louis, Missouri in the early 20th century.

Although Rich rarely gave more than a passing glance at these effigies, he did wonder from time to time what had caused the trustees of Midwest to name their educational edifice after Ben Blewett. Had Rich been on the couch of a psychoanalyst, he might have confessed to a measure of envy. He was, however, comforted by the belief that there were no contemporary educators of the status of these august figures. Even Ben Blewett outshone those who now pontificated on the mysteries of schooling at Midwest University.

Rich lowered his gaze to eye-level. On the left-hand side of the atrium, two faux Greek facades, modeled after the Treasury of Athens at Delphi, masked the entries to Men's and Women's comfort stations. The right-hand side of the atrium sported a miniature replica of the front of Blewett - minus the stairs. This was the Office of the Dean of the College of Education and Home Economics, populated by Dean Merton Dunkard and his minions.

This morning, Dunkard was standing in front of the door to his office, a portly middle-aged man with a florid face and receding hairline.

"Hello Rich! Fine day!"

"Ummm . . . yes, I guess so."

"Glad I caught you," Dunkard said as he gripped Rich's upper right arm. "Been wanting to talk with you. Got time to visit for a few minutes?"

Rich pulled free of the Dean and stepped back a pace. "Sure, why not? Nothing special on my schedule this morning." It was, of course, like every other morning; Rich's calendar was filled with blank pages attesting to the pressures of professorial life.

They sauntered into the Dean's Office, concentration on their countenances designed to impress lower-level functionaries.

"Millie," Dunkard ordered, "bring us a couple of coffees!"

The secretary jumped to comply, testimony to Deanly status.

Coffee at hand, the Dean leaned back in his chair and folded his arms over his ample stomach.

"The reason I want to talk to you," Dunkard began, "is related to the changing face of this university. It's been made clear to us Deans that our faculties must be more visible nationally. What this means is that publication is what will be counted by Central Administration."

"I've heard rumors to that effect," Rich agreed. "But what's that got to do with me?"

"I think it opens a door for you. Where you are now in your career, you are caught up in the usual 'teaching, research, service' expectations that bar the door to a full professorship. If there's to be a growing emphasis on 'research', faculty members like yourself will be hard pressed to cover 'teaching' and 'service' requirements."

Rich nodded. "I can't agree more. As it is, I have a tough time getting a couple of pieces into print each year. What with my teaching load and committee service ...," His voice faded as he reflected on an imagined workload and the ever-present need to prevent encroachment of the university on his personal space.

"I know, I know," Dunkard commiserated. "But I think I have a proposal that you'll find interesting. I, too, feel the pressures of Central and badly need help in this office. You are aware that Midwest is changing from the quarter to the semester system and that each college within the university must submit a plan by the end of next year." He looked at Rich for agreement.

"Yes," Rich said. "I'm chairing the Semester Committee of the faculty and . . ."

Dunkard interrupted, "I know, and that commitment takes too much of your time. I can fix that. What I'd like for you to consider is to become Associate Dean where you can shape our response to the semester initiative."

Rich frowned. "I don't see how that solves my problem. That kind of position will just take even more time."

"Bear with me!" Dunkard leaned forward. "Here's the bigger picture. Being Associate Dean means that your teaching load will be greatly reduced. Second, a successful semester plan would put you ahead of the competition for full professor. And, here's the kicker. I can guarantee unlimited travel support so that you can position yourself in the national spotlight at important conferences. How does that sound?"

National spotlight! Teaching reduced! Rich frequently filled conversational space with mental comments, especially when he faced difficult decisions or at those times when he was uncertain about his course of action. This time, mental review helped him pose the key question. "That sounds pretty good, but what does it do to advance me to the professorship?"

"Although I can't guarantee the promotion, I'd say that you'd have a ninety percent chance of a full professorship within about two years. I know that money isn't your primary concern, but you'd get a substantial salary increase as Associate Dean."

Substantial increase! The Dean had said the magic words! Rich was one of the few who knew of the practice whereby faculty in administrative roles not only received an 'increase due to workload', these dollars became a permanent augmentation to salary. As these thoughts raced through his mind, Rich made an effort to control his expression in order to appear the interested, willing servant.

"That sounds very attractive. Of course, I have to think about it. I have students who are at the dissertation stage and . . ."

"Don't worry about them. What I'll do is change your teaching load to advisement and you can meet candidates in this office."

This was an appealing offer. Rich, like many of his colleagues, felt that teaching and other student interactions detracted from serious scholarly work. Looking forward into a future free from students, Rich had nothing to say to the Dean.

Dunkard broke an awkward silence. "Tell you what, let's go over to Tubby's around five today and have a drink. That'll give you some time to think about my offer. OK?"

Rich recovered. "Sure, that'll be fine." Dunkard was a near alcoholic and was noted for making 'deals' at Tubby's, the campus hangout for serious drinkers. "Shall I meet you there?"

"Done!" Dunkard stood, offered his hand and walked Rich to the door.

Back in Blewett Atrium, Rich wandered to the elevator. Reflexively, he entered and pressed the button for the fourth floor. When he arrived on fourth, Rich strode out into a corridor lined with closed office doors. The panel at the end of the corridor had the label, 'Associate Professor Richard Jessen' with a windowed receptacle for 'Office Hours'. Rich looked at this display as he fumbled a key into the lock. *Gotta update these hours!* He knew how important it was for Midwest faculty to post office hours and how rare it was for postings to be honored.

Inside, Rich tossed his briefcase onto a credenza and hung his coat in a small closet. The mirror on the back of the closet door reflected a dark, wavy-haired, rather handsome face. Rich smoothed his hair, attempting to cover the emerging flecks of grey. He closed the door and strode to the window that overlooked University City. Due to the design of Blewett, the window was positioned at shoulder height and Rich was required to stretch his five foot ten frame in order to see the city.

A tree-lined river bent to brush the edge of the campus, defining a boundary between academy and city. Upstream, grain elevators hugged piers where barges collected the commodity that was the lifeblood of University City. A small group of tall buildings defined downtown, the commercial center of the state.

Rich was, from long exposure, well aware of the panorama he viewed. Familiarity provided only a sense of location. There was no appreciation of either social or economic significance of the city. Instead, Rich worried over the Dean's proposal. He knew that accepting the offer would change his life; complete professorial freedom would be exchanged for requirements of office. On the other hand, he would be at the center of College power and he could count on being promoted. Then, there was the money!

He turned his back on the window and sank into his desk chair. Rich sat for a time, mulling the implications of Dunkard's offer. Although he was not at all confused, he had mentally accepted his new status, Rich felt a compulsion to share his situation. Who should . . . ?

Rich had few collegial relationships with Midwest faculty; he had little in common and less respect for those who populated the university. Hank Loras was among the handful of faculty who shared Rich's views, a person who had become a fellow conspirator. He consulted his RoloDex and punched in Loras' number on his desk phone.

"Hank Loras here. How can I help you?"

"Rich Jessen. I'm not looking for help, just want to talk about a conversation I had with Dunkard. You in your office?"

"Yep. Why?"

"I'd like to come over. How's about now?"

"Be lookin' for you." Hank disconnected.

You could count on Hank. No matter how busy he might be, there was always a ready response. As Rich made his way to ground-level Blewett, he reflected on the forces that propelled Loras to his status.

Hank was the most prolific grant-getter in the College; his Center for Community Studies had enviable connections to agencies that funded studies of the handicapped and their journeys toward independence. Hank had been at the forefront of the de-institutionalization movement that had opened opportunity for countless handicapped individuals and the Center was valued not so much for the substance of its studies, rather for the messages it offered to the advocates who supported the movement. As a result, the Center was a bustling place where a dozen or so graduate students delivered on the promises of Loras' research proposals.

Rich exited a side door from Blewett and walked across a busy street to the Center which was located in an old brownstone building - The Annex. This was once the whole of Midwest University, the first building constructed in the early 1900s and now bypassed by development. The Annex showed its age, misleading passers-by as to the level of activity within.

When he entered The Annex, Rich confronted this unaccustomed bustle. The level of noise offended his sense of the silence associated with university life. He was also put off by the familiarity of those students who recognized him.

"Hi Rich! What brings you over here?" a bearded student called.

"Lookin' for how the other half lives?" cracked a buxom blonde.

Rich mumbled responses and threaded his way to Loras' office. He was the rich tourist navigating the gauntlet of street vendors in a foreign country. Eventually, he escaped to the sanctity of Hank's lair. Once inside he closed the door on the rabble outside.

"Whew!" he puffed. "How do you stand it?"

Hank grinned. "It's the sound of money! When it gets quiet, I worry." Loras wheeled his chair back from his desk and crossed his legs. A square face with nose and mouth connected by deep parentheses of flesh gave an impression of confidence. " Now, what's on your mind?"

Rich collapsed into a chair. "It's Dunkard. Here's what he offered." A brief review of the Dean's proposal was followed with two questions: "What do you think of this? And, what's your advice on how I might react?"

"Very interesting. Very interesting," Hank rubbed his chin. "Sounds like old Mert is offering you the professorship on a platter. Almost too good to be true."

"That's what I thought. However, I sure could use a hand up to the next level."

"You're right about the next level," Hank swiveled his chair at a right-angle to Rich. "You've probably noticed how this place works." He paused, expecting no response, and went on to explain. "Universities are the most political organizations in the world. Every decision of any importance is made by the people in power. Everyone else complains and tries to find an angle that might work for them. The common mistake that outsiders make is to think that higher education is governed by rationality," Hank laughed.

"Sure. Sure," Rich agreed. "Now put me and Dunkard in the picture."

"It's simple. Dunkard is Dean and the go-to guy for Central Administration. Right?"

"That's so, I guess."

"But he's hooked on the sauce. So whoever can penetrate the alcoholic fog he lives in can shape the direction of the College. You could be that 'whoever'."

Rich nodded. In Hank's crude assessment of university life, Rich found the confirmation of his own view of Dunkard, and the offer. "Are you suggesting that I should say 'yes' to Mert?"

Hank smiled in a conspiratorial manner. "I would," he said.

"OK. Supposing I do. Have you any advice on how to play the part of Associate Dean?"

Hank put his elbows on his desk and leaned forward. "Of course, you gotta be the 'gofer' on some of the things the Dean doesn't want to do himself. Then you can push your own agenda where it might do you some good."

"Sounds pretty underhanded," Rich mused.

"C'mon!" Hank chuckled. "You weren't born yesterday. Dunkard's handing you the key that'll unlock opportunity. Right?" The parentheses on Loras' face deepened to emphasize this observation.

"When you put it that way, I agree. What's appealed to me about Mert's plan is that I get access to some of his power and some travel money. According to Mert, these will add up to my promotion. My only concern and the reason I'm talking to you is – can I trust him?"

"Now, that's another matter," Hank frowned. "Well . . . no you can't. But, remember the booze. I'd say trust but manipulate. Kind of like Reagan. You remember, 'trust but verify'?"

"Got it!" Rich stood. "Many thanks for your views. I think I'll take Mert's offer."

"Glad to be of help," Hank extended a hand and they shook. Two politicians laying another stone on their personal political structures.

Rich spent the balance of the day in mental exploration of the ways he might construct a political persona for himself. He was not new to a consideration of this nature. Early in his undergraduate years, he was made aware of the political undercurrents that channeled academic life. Although he was rarely affected by these events at that time, he saw how senior professors laid the burdens of the academy on their juniors and, when an underling rebelled, how quickly he or she could be marginalized. Could Midwest University offer larger, more complex versions of collegiate life? Rich concluded that it could.

As five o'clock approached, Rich closed his office. It was time for his appointment at Tubby's. He was aware of conflicting emotions; he didn't want to have a drink with the Dean, but he was eager to begin play in the sandbox of university politics.

Tubby's was in University Village on the far side of the Quadrangle - the enclosure bordered by university buildings. To get to the Village, Rich had to cross a grassy space at the center of the 'Quad'. Exiting the back door of Blewett Rich was, as usual, impressed by the ways buildings spoke of the subject matters they housed. The sciences engaged in their works behind the temple-like entrance to Tesla Hall; humanities held the world at bay behind the blank walls and modest doorway of Lowell Hall; social sciences lurked within the box-like structure of Weber Hall. These buildings accounted for the two long sides of the Quad. The short side next to Blewett was dominated by the Conant Administration Building which, like Blewett, was entered by a flight of steps through marble columns. At the opposite end of the Quad, the Student Center attempted to soften its image behind a flagstone plaza that oozed out to afford a perspective on University City across the river.

Rich navigated the network of paved pathways across the Quad, ticking off political rivals as he went. The social sciences were dismissed as irrelevant, despite the inclusion of political science. So were the humanities, insubstantial players on the stage of power. In contrast, Rich saw the sciences as his primary threat, subject matter substance translated into credibility and ultimately into power. Unconsciously, Rich selected a pathway that avoided proximity to science.

A five-minute walk took Rich to a narrow alleyway between Lowell Hall and Weber Hall where he decamped into the outside world. Wandering students were replaced by bustling traffic. Academe gave way to commerce; dusty meeting rooms to the bright glare of Tubby's.

Rich opened the door of Tubby's and stalked into a dim, yeasty environment where undergraduates stood at a bar watching late afternoon television. Tables near the bar collected other undergraduates in the beginnings of an evening of partying. Toward the rear of the room, a raised area enclosed by a wooden railing, the Quarterdeck, was the gathering place for university faculty.

"Rich! Over here!" Dunkard's booming greeting signaled that the Dean had not waited for Rich before ordering.

Orders were evidently the 'order' of the day as Dunkard continued. "What'll you have?"

"I guess . . . a red wine." Rich sat as Dunkard called for wine, and for another Manhattan.

"Glad you could make it," Dunkard said. "Like to wrap this thing up." He drained his glass and looked toward the bar for the ordered refill.

Rich decided to take control of the conversation; Dunkard was a bit too far into his cups. "Yes. I'd like to talk about the details."

"Sure. Whaddya need to know?"

"You mentioned the possibility that I could attend conferences that might improve my professional standing. Have you any in mind?"

"Hell! That's . . .," Dunkard stopped and looked owl-like at Rich. The question eluded him. "What's that again?"

"Conferences. You know, the kind of gathering where I can identify research topics and make some connections."

"Oh . . . you mean . . . ash hee . . ."

Rich was puzzled. "Ash hee? What sort of conference is that?"

"Don't know that?" Dunkard chuckled. ". . . thatsh . . . Association for . . . what? . . . Study of . . . Higher Education . . ." Dunkard laughed aloud. "Bunch of professors . . . plottin' with their friends."

Dunkard was obviously too far gone for Rich to get any useful information from him. *Ash hee must mean ASHE. Better look that one up.*

Their drinks arrived and Dunkard tried a glass-touching salute with the result that drops of both Manhattan and wine dribbled on the table. "Here's to . . . the future . . .!" the Dean said. "Bottoms up!"

Rich wiped his glass and repeated, "Bottoms up!"

Ten minutes of desultory conversation was all that Rich could stand. He made a show of consulting his watch.

"Gotta run. Promised Muriel that I'd take her out to dinner. You know, to celebrate."

Dunkard frowned. "Hoped you'd make a night . . . take care of the little woman . . . need another . . .," he waved at the bartender as Rich stood.

"I'll see you at your office tomorrow, Dean." He attempted to shake Dunkard's hand, but was unable to capture it as the hand wavered across the table.

Rich left the Dean and Tubby's behind and entered the sanctuary of the Quad. There was still an afterglow of spring evening. Students wandered, free from the bustle of classes. Rich was comforted by this change of pace. He was suspended in an academic matrix that held him fast from the outside world. He strolled – and reflected.

21

A vision of Associate Dean Jessen caused him to straighten his posture. An aura of dignity followed him into Blewett and down the stairs to the parking garage. Confronted by his five-year-old Buick, dignity fled. *Time to get rid of this old beater!* Associate Dean Jessen should be conveyed in style!

Rich sighed and slid into the Buick's driver seat. He wove his way among the few cars remaining in the garage, taking account of those he knew. Loras was clearly still at work and his new Blazer reflected the money that passed through the Center. Dents in Dunkard's car spoke of nights when drink accompanied his journey home. Other cars were examined – most were disparaged – a few were envied.

Rich guided the Buick up the exit ramp of the garage and swung onto University Drive, a broad tree-lined street that followed the river. Ten minutes of early evening traffic put him at the turn into Locust Avenue. Three more blocks and he was at the entrance to his garage. He punched the door opener that hung on the car's visor.

That goofy car! Rich contrasted the staid shapes and colors of academic transport with Muriel's pink Cadillac. Although he disliked his wife's car, he recognized it as a symbol of her success as the state's leader in marketing Mary Kay Cosmetics. The garish Cadillac softened Rich's envy of her income, which greatly exceeded his. Her success had been built on a foundation laid during their years in graduate school at Louisiana Methodist University where Muriel developed her gifts as a leader of Mary Kay teams.

Rich parked the Buick and closed the garage door. The rattle of the garage door operator brought Muriel to a side door that led from the garage into her kitchen.

"Hi!" she called. "You're late. I was beginning to worry."

"Nothing to worry about, Babe. Just a drink with Dunkard."

"You mean 'Drunkard' don't you?"

Rich grinned. "You got that right. But there's news. How about a glass of wine before supper?"

"No problem with that. I haven't started anything. Just waiting on you."

Rich leaned over and lightly put his cheek against hers, a gesture of companionship, not one of love. "Tell you what," he said. "Let's go over to The Chalet. I've got some news that calls for a night out."

Muriel raised her eyebrows. "Something special eh? Good thing I'm still in my work clothes." She patted the dark business suit that was her Mary Kay uniform, the costume that accented her svelte figure and the carefully-groomed blonde hair. She picked up her purse from the kitchen counter. "Want to take my car?" she teased.

Rich laughed, "No, I don't think so. Dunkard might see me."

"OK. I promise not to smoke in the Buick." A major concession, since Muriel was addicted to Virginia Slim cigarettes, especially when weighty matters were likely to be discussed.

The Chalet was on the far side of the river, across from the university. A thick wooden door, framed in field stone, opened into a murky hallway where a co-ed offered immediate seating.

"We'd like the smoking dining room," Muriel said.

Rich nodded and followed the two women to a small dining room whose black-oak beams reinforced the smoking theme. They were seated, drinks were ordered and Muriel lit a Slim.

"Now," she said. "What's this all about?"

Rich folded his hands at the edge of the table and began. "Dunkard has asked me to become Associate Dean. Be quite a change in my workload, but he says that it's the quickest way to promotion. And, there's the money."

Muriel exhaled and focused on the last comment. "What about the money?"

"Well, it'd be about fifteen grand more a year. And that's not all, I get free travel to conferences to build up my vita."

"Sounds good." She toyed with her cigarette packet. No stranger to University practice, she asked, "Do you get to keep the salary increment?"

"No problem with that. Over ten years, that's worth a hundred-fifty K. Plus benefits. The way I figure it, we'd have close to another quarter million in the bank by the time I retire – say around 2010."

This was a familiar discussion centered on 'the bank'. Like many professional couples, the Jessens were constantly aware of money; they measured their accomplishments in dollars and equity. At this point in their married life, they had nearly a million dollars in their retirement and savings accounts, with at least twenty years to go.

A waitress interrupted this pleasant prospect. "May I take your order?"

"Peppercorn tenderloin for me," Rich pointed to the day's feature on the menu.

"And you, M'am?"

"Guess I'm not very hungry," Muriel frowned. "Let's see. Give me a small Chicken Ceaser salad." She closed the menu and handed it to the waitress.

"Babe, you gotta eat more," Rich voiced his growing worry about her weight. "Pretty soon you won't even cast a shadow."

She reached across the table and patted his hand. "Don't worry. I'm just in a kind of phase. Never have much of an appetite." The hand returned and reflexively picked up the cigarette packet.

Rich frowned at the movement. "Thought you were trying to cut down."

"I'm trying! I'm trying!" It was clear, however, that nicotine dependency was trying harder.

As they waited for their order, they lapsed into silence. Rich sipped at his drink and Muriel pulled at another Virginia Slim.

Their entrees finally arrived and small talk accompanied the meal. It wasn't until Muriel lit her 'dessert cigarette' that she raised the concluding question.

"Well. Are you going to take Dunkard up on his offer?"

"Guess so," Rich grinned. "You can put it on the spreadsheet!"

"Wonderful! That'll be a fine addition to my good news!"

Rich sat upright. "What's that?"

She tapped ash from her cigarette. "I've just started ten new Mary Kay teams! Each one looks very good. Should net us at least five grand a team!"

Rich actually applauded. "Keep this up and we'll need a bigger spreadsheet!"

Visions of multi-page spreadsheets motivated conversation for the balance of their stay at the Chalet and throughout the drive to their house. Enthusiasm lubricated the rest of the evening. As midnight approached, Rich hugged Muriel and held her at arm's length.

"Things look pretty good Babe! Right?"

"Sure thing," she smiled. "Tomorrow's the day to do the deal with Dunkard!"

They parted. For the past two years, Rich had slept in the guest bedroom in a far corner of the house. Muriel's morning coughing made it impossible for Rich to sleep; it was she who had suggested the arrangement.

Alone in his room, Rich undressed and slipped into his silk pajamas, bumped his pillow into shape and clicked off the bedside light. Sleep didn't come at once and counting spreadsheets was of no help. He was simply too excited. Eventually he rose, wrapped himself in a robe and sat in the recliner he used for financial studies.

We make quite a team! There was that word again! *Team!* How foreign to life in the academy. Sure, teams worked great for Muriel and she was a master at recruiting others to her business. Despite all the babbling in academic literature, teamwork wasn't a workable strategy. Rich had learned countless lessons concerning the failure of 'teamwork'.

Success in the academy came to those who spoke of teams to their gullible colleagues while at the same time conspired to attain their personal ends.

CHAPTER TWO

Rules Rule!

"Organizational structure, rules and procedures are often best understood as products and reflections of a struggle for political control." (Gareth Morgan: Images of Organization)

Although Rich literally descended when he moved his office from fourth Blewett, insofar as the College was concerned he ascended to the level of power associated with the Dean's office on first Blewett. University movers packed his books and office gear and deposited academic content in the spacious environs of the new Associate Dean. Rich's secretary unpacked and shelved books and hung framed citations of academic achievement. All this was accomplished within the week of Rich's acceptance of Dunkard's offer.

Seated in a comfortable chair behind his new desk, Rich was established as the Associate Dean. On the first day of Rich's residency his secretary, Lois Mueller, appeared and placed a folder in the center of his desk.

"Dean Jessen," Lois advised. "Here are the items Dean Dunkard would like to discuss with you as soon as possible. She opened the folder and assembled several papers for Rich's attention.

Lois continued. "This one is the most important. It's a copy of Central Administration's charge to the College regarding semester conversion. You've probably read it already."

Rich nodded at the familiar statement of Central policy. "Yes," he said. "I'm familiar with the conversion." He was conscious of the responsibility it implied. "What else should I be aware of?"

"There's nothing special," Lois said. "Just some faculty issues that can be dealt with later on. If it's okay with you, I'll sort through things and put them in order for you."

"That'll be fine," Rich said dismissively. "Now I'd better meet with the Dean. Is he in?"

"I'll check."

Rich heard Lois' conversation and the arranging of an appointment within the next hour. While waiting, he opened the College Semester Conversion Committee file and began reading. His own notes as Committee Chair were put aside in favor of department letters and faculty comments – all of a uniformly negative nature. Frustrated by these reams of paper, Rich stuffed wayward sheets into the folder labeled CSCC. With the folder under an arm, Rich stalked into the Dean's office.

"Mert!" Rich said. "I need guidance on dealing with CSCC. I don't see a clear path to successful conversion." With this opener, Rich combined conspiratorial familiarity with the language of collegial problem solving.

Dunkard chuckled. "I see that you're learning the ropes. Getting the faculty from point A to point B is like herding chickens."

Having been raised in rural communities, they both knew how futile an exercise chicken herding could be. They actually paused for a moment, smiling at the simile.

"You got it!" Rich exclaimed. "Can you help me clear out the chicken shit CSCC is shoveling my way?"

Dunkard was favorably impressed with Rich's capacity to apply simile to academic deliberations. "That's a good way of putting it and I agree completely. I'd say that your best hope would be to see if you can shift the blame for semester conversion to Central Administration. After all, they're the ones who're forcing the issue."

"Sounds like a plan, so how do I connect?"

Dunkard pursed his lips and frowned. "Best way is to make an appointment with Waldo Pearson. He's the administration point man on semester conversion."

"Pearson !" This was going a bit too fast for Rich. Pearson was a vice president who dwelt in an ethereal realm removed from the pastoral life of the College. "Now, I wonder . . .,"

"Don't worry," Dunkard grinned. "Waldo is one of us. In fact, he's got a pretty sophisticated perspective on faculty politics. You've met him?"

"Nope. I've only shaken his hand in a couple of reception lines. Can you give me a leg up?"

"Sure," Dunkard said enthusiastically. "Let me make a couple of calls and I'll get back to you soonest."

Rich stood, placed the CSCC folder under his arm and hesitated at the office door. "Many thanks, Mert. Be waiting for your call."

Another lesson in university politics had just been laid on Associate Dean Jessen, namely that responsibility for any action of academic significance had to have an element of deniability so that the 'buck' never stopped on the decision maker's desk.

Rich was somewhat concerned about a meeting with Waldo Pearson. Not only was Pearson the Vice President for Academic Affairs, he was the university's lobbyist at the state legislature. His ability to wander the corridors of government had established the university as a favorite recipient of publicity – and money. Capitol wisdom placed the university as the principal engine of economic development for the state. And it was said at the university that Pearson was the power behind President Melvin Rose. Pearson was known as The Ayatollah, a secretive figure who interpreted the canon laws of the university.

Rich considered these relationships as he stared at his copy of the University Organization Chart which showed the connection to the College to Central Administration and the pathways of control similar to those in other colleges at Midwest.

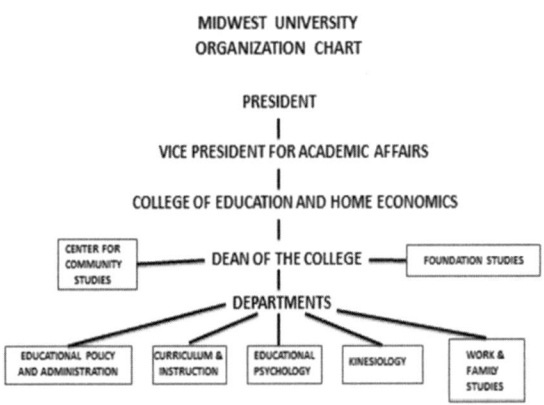

Rich could easily see his position within the hierarchy of the U. He was not only several layers below Pearson, he was also at the margin of the flow of power. His academic home in Foundation Studies wasn't even at the center of Dean Dunkard's administrative concerns. Clearly, a personal meeting with Waldo Pearson was an opportunity to break free of isolation and establish himself as Associate Dean.

Dunkard kept his promise. Rich was to present himself in Pearson's office 'whenever it was convenient'.

Arranging for the meeting was easy, but the walk from Blewett to the Conant Administration Building demanded greater confidence than Rich could easily muster. Apprehensively, he exited Blewett, crossed the Quad and climbed the steps to the Conant entrance. Rich heaved at the weighty doors and slipped onto polished terrazzo. Floor and walls shone with authority. The floor featured the university crest; copies of paintings by Grant Wood and Thomas Hart Benton decorated the walls. Oak doors told of occupants whose titles spoke of power; 'Director of . . .', 'Executive Assistant to . . .', and eventually, 'Dr. Waldo Pearson – Vice President for Academic Affairs'.

Rich checked his fly, straightened his tie and opened Waldo's door. Inside, he was confronted by a martinet who scowled through steel-rimmed glasses and demanded, "Well?"

"Umm..." stammered Rich. "I've got an appointment with Dr. Pearson." He slouched forward. "Is he . . . in?" So this was the lair of The Ayatollah and this woman was his acolyte. Rich felt as if he were summoned to account for violations of holy writ.

"I'll check," the woman growled. She tapped at an inner door. "Man here to see you!"

A muffled conversation was evidently a success and a smiling man rushed out and extended a hand to Rich. "Hello! I'm Waldo Pearson. You must be Professor Jessen. Very pleased to meet you. Please come in."

Pearson didn't look much like The Ayatollah. He was a short, round man with soft, brown eyes that punctuated a smiling face.

Rich glanced at the still scowling secretary and followed Pearson, taking care to avoid her desk.

Pearson beckoned Rich to an armchair on one side of a low coffee table while seating himself. "You should be proud! You've survived the gauntlet! Very few get past Melody!"

Melody! "She is quite intimidating," Rich said. "I imagine that few pass her test."

Pearson laughed. "That's right! She protects my schedule and she's one hell of an executive assistant. I have to take the bad with the good! Now what's so important to Mert that he sent you to me?"

"I'm not exactly sure," Rich said hesitatingly. "I'm in charge of the College Semester Conversion Committee and am having a devil of a time in moving the departments forward. I guess Dean Dunkard thought that you might be able to give me some advice."

"Advice? Hardly. Each college has its own special set of actors who have to be rolled into the conversion. The best I can do is give you a backgrounder on where the conversion came from and what it's really about. Think that might help?"

Rich hesitated. "Don't know. But anything you can tell me will surely be a whole lot more than I know right now."

"OK!" Pearson leaned forward. "What I'm about to tell you stays here. Agreed?" The Ayatollah spoke and the weight of doctrine descended on the meeting.

"Of course!" Rich also leaned forward, a fellow conspirator.

"Here's the scoop. This whole semester conversion thing came out of the state legislature. Barney Kriven, you know that blabbermouth senator from out west, well his kid had a hell of a time transferring from a community college to the U. Seems that the schedules didn't match and our quarter system didn't jibe with the semester courses the kid took. So Kriven, he charges ahead and writes a bill

32

that says that all higher education institutions taking state money have to be on the semester system. And they all have to have a common calendar! He also said, now get this, 'Them books is too fat to be read in a quarter! They take a whole semester!'"

"Sounds pretty typical," Rich said. "But I didn't hear about the calendar. If our faculty finds out that they'll have no control over the calendar, they'll revolt!"

"I know. I know," Pearson commiserated. "That's the politics behind semester conversion. Once we sell the semester idea and get the faculty focused on new courses and programs, the calendar can be slipped in with no opposition!" He sat back in his chair and grinned at Rich.

Rich admired this devious ploy. Here was academic politics worthy of The Ayatollah. And Rich was a player! He took several seconds to savor the opportunity before reaching for the levers of power.

"So you're saying," Rich said. "That I'm carrying the water for Central so far as the College is concerned. Right?"

"Yep, you and the conversion leaders in the other colleges. If Central is seen as forcing the issue, it won't go anywhere. On the other hand, people like you can finesse the conversion. The best advice I can give you is to treat the conversion like a kind of shell game. Put some inducements under one shell, but be sure that you hide the bad pill of the calendar from your faculty. What you have to do is manipulate faculty opinion and focus their discussion on the benefits of the semester system."

"Benefits?" Rich asked. "What benefits?"

Pearson winked. "That's what you'll have to discover. Or make up. I can tell you that your colleagues won't budge an inch unless they can see something in it for them." Pearson stood. "Call me anytime if you have any questions."

The audience was over and The Ayatollah ushered him out of the office. A confused Associate Dean gathered his briefcase and sidled past Pearson's secretary.

The view from Central Administration did little to set Rich's mind at ease. Pearson had effectively passed the buck of responsibility back to Rich. As he reviewed minutes of past meetings of the CSCC, he remained frustrated by the confusion that accompanied every meeting of the Committee. There was no emerging agreement on how to proceed, let alone how the college should respond to Central's demand for a plan to deliver courses on a semester calendar.

The very next meeting of the CSCC was particularly frustrating. Rather than proceeding to plan for the conversion, department heads debated the wisdom of the change from quarters to semesters.

Phoebe Morgan, the Chair of the Curriculum and Instruction Department, was outspoken in her opposition to semesters.

"I can't see the purpose of this change. All we'll be doing is putting old wine into old bottles."

"What do you mean by that?" Rich asked, the biblical reference eluding him.

"Just this," Phoebe spat. "My faculty will take their quarter courses and expand them to semesters. There will be none of the transformation that Central has in mind."

Nelson Wood, Chair of Kinesiology, summed up the opinions of the committee.

"When I came to Midwest," he began, "we were on the semester system. Then, about fifteen years ago, we changed to quarters. Now we're going back to semesters?" The sarcastic question lit a fire of comment.

"That's right on!" Harley Clark (Work and Family Studies) nearly shouted. "Why I'll bet some of the old timers will resurrect their semester course notes and . . ."

Laughter around the conference table confirmed Harley's analysis of faculty behavior.

At that point, Rich could see that there was little purpose in continuing the discussion.

"Let's take the pulse of our faculties so we can better plan how to proceed," he said. "Then we can meet in a couple of weeks and go forward."

This suggestion liberated the members of the committee and they crowded out the conference room door, with one exception.

Carl Mertens, Chair of Educational Psychology, remained seated with his hands clasped, looking at Rich. "Looks like we'll have to come up with a way to move these folks along," he said. "Got any ideas?"

Mertens was, in Rich's eyes, one of the few sane faculty members in the College of Education and Home Economics. He combined intellectual capacity with a sophisticated view of College politics. When he spoke, the Dean and Central listened. So did Rich.

"Gotta tell you Carl," Rich shook his head. "I'm at a loss. There's no cooperation here, only opposition. I met with Pearson last week and he said we have to find some real benefits to bring the faculty along."

"Good point!" Mertens exclaimed. "What's needed is to shift the ground from cooperation to conspiracy. That's the only thing that these chairs understand."

"What do you mean by that?"

Mertens smiled, "We have to lead these mules to a different manger. I've been thinking about Central's charge to the committee. Here, listen to this." He turned several pages and read.

> ". . . credits earned on the quarter system shall be converted to semester credits at the ratio of three quarter credits to two semester credits."

"I read that," Rich growled. "So what?"

Mertens stood, stepped to a flip chart easel and uncapped a marker. "Think about these numbers. This means that students who are now taking three – three-credit quarter courses . . ." He began writing as he spoke. ". . . that's nine quarter credits and . . . that translates to . . . six semester credits."

"Well, OK," Rich shook his head. "I still don't see. . ."

"Hang on," Mertens pointed to the charge and drew a line under the statements concerning the conversion of credits, then returned to the flip chart and proceeded to lecture as he wrote. "Now most of us teach two courses on the quarter system . . . six credits . . . that's the same as four semester credits."

These numbers began to attract Rich's attention.

Mertens continued, "What if we taught one four-credit course each semester! Why that would mean half a load! All we'd need to do would be to expand one of our three-credit quarter courses to a four-credit semester course!"

Rich could easily imagine how that could be done. Wasn't that just what Phoebe Morgan said? Existing syllabi and course notes could be edited over a weekend! "Why, that would cut faculty teaching obligations by fifty percent!" he chortled. "They'd love it!"

"But that's not all," Mertens turned to a clean sheet on the flip chart and wrote in capital letters:

DON'T FORGET VACATIONS: QUARTER SYSTEM : 1 – XMAS 2- SPRING BREAK. SEMESTER SYSTEM: 1- XMAS 2- SEM CHANGE 3- SPRING BREAK. THAT ADDS UP TO - 1 MORE VACATION – AND HALF THE WORK!!

Mertens wheeled from the flip chart, capped the marker and tossed it Rich. "Here, it's your turn to come up with the next steps."

Rich caught the marker and the message. However, he was at a loss as to how to proceed. He stepped to the chart, turned to another clean sheet and uncapped the marker. "Hmmm . . . I wonder." The pen was poised but did not write.

"Think about the different departments," Mertens suggested.

"Yeah, that might work ." Rich began with Phoebe. He wrote:

CURRICULUM & INSTRUCTION: Phoebe Morgan.

APPROACH:

Rich looked at Mertens. "How. . ."

"That's easy. C&I has a bunch of undergraduate classes for teacher training. You've seen them down the hall in Blewett."

Rich nodded. He recalled the many times he had passed the large classrooms on First Blewett and how he had blessed the appointment that freed him from the rows of bored undergraduates. Under Approach: he wrote.

1) Reduce the number of undergraduate classes and contact hours.

Mertens nodded. "Point number two is one Phoebe will think of right away. Remember what she said about old wine in old bottles? Supervision of student teaching carries about six quarter credits. That's four semester credits. When she calculates how many contact hours that involves and finds out that it's a half-load, she'll be a convert."

Rich listed point number two:

2) Reduced load for student teaching.

He stepped back and looked at the chart. "Seems too obvious. Won't the CSCC balk at . . ."

Mertens stood and stretched. "You can see how easy this is. I'll handle Phoebe and my own faculty. You work on Kinesiology, Ed. Policy, and Work and Family Studies. Get them to think about the reduced teaching load and they'll come along."

The next day, Rich tried Mertens' approach with Harley Clark and even went so far as to visit the old Ag. Campus. Seated in Clark's musty office he began his sales pitch.

"Harley," Rich said earnestly, "I think I see a way that your department can benefit from semester conversion."

"Can't imagine what that'd be!" Clark snorted. "Just a hell of a lot of work for nothing. That's the way I see it."

Rich ignored the comment. "Semester courses will give your faculty the time to focus on substantive issues." *Can't believe I'm saying this!* Visions of deadly courses like; 'The Nature of Work', 'Community Education Systems', and 'Vocational Philosophy', derailed his argument. "What I mean is . . .," he paused. Too long!

"See! You can't come up with an argument that'd help me sell this to my faculty!" Clark began sorting the dusty papers on his desk. "Now if you'll excuse me, I have a lot on my plate."

Dismissing me! "That's obvious! I wouldn't want to get in the way of the wonderful progress you're making with Work and Family Studies!" Rich wheeled and left.

InterCampus Bus took him back to Blewett and he strode past his secretary who looked up in surprise.

"My! You're back soon! Wasn't Dr. Clark available?"

Rich covered his anger. "Didn't connect. Better luck next time. Please hold my calls."

Behind the closed door of his office, Rich reviewed his meeting with Clark. Several retorts he might have made were mumbled and rejected. Clearly, convincing his three departments would be heavy going.

It was certainly a blessing that this was Friday and he could (and did) leave his office early. However, the problem accompanied him home and occupied his mind throughout Friday evening and the whole of Saturday.

Finally, Rich could take refuge in one of the Sunday afternoon strategy sessions where he and Muriel discussed developments and prospects that affected their careers. They settled in their customary chairs in the glassed-in porch, Rich with coffee and Muriel with Virginia Slims.

"Well, how did it go?" Muriel asked. "You know. The semester thing?"

"Kind of mixed. I met with Waldo Pearson the, one we call the Ayatollah. He gave me a lecture on how to manipulate the faculty - offer them inducements and hide the pain."

Muriel laughed. "Huh! Sounds pretty devious. Think that will work?"

"Don't know," Rich sipped coffee. "But Carl Mertens, the guy who's head of Ed. Psych., came up with an idea that will work for some of the departments."

"What's that?" Muriel inhaled deeply – exhaled, and coughed.

Rich looked at her. These choking episodes were becoming more frequent. "You OK?"

"Sure. Sure. Just clearing my throat. Now, tell me more about Mertens. What's his angle?"

Rich explained how the semester system could be used to reduce faculty teaching loads and provide more free time. "That's the carrot. The stick is a radical change in the academic calendar."

"Can't see why," Muriel reflected. "That should be no problem. What's so important about the calendar?"

"Really doesn't mean anything. However, everyone has their lives organized around the calendar. Just think! They'd have to reschedule days at the lake . . . foreign travel . . . you name it!"

They mused on these inconveniences. Why they would even have to change their own vacation plans!

"I get your point. So what are the next steps?"

"Lucky for me, Mertens is taking on C&I and Ed. Psych.. That leaves Kineseology, Ed. Policy and Administration, along with Work and Family Studies for me. So far, I can't find just the right carrot for them."

"Hmmm . . .," Muriel paused and lit another Slim. "Aren't those the 'Old Buffaloes' you always talk about?"

"Those are the ones. My problem is that they already have everything the way they want it and I can't think of any incentive that might work for them."

They sat in silence for several minutes, contemplating the stolidity of the Buffaloes.

"Changing these departments is like moving a graveyard!" Rich sighed.

"Wait a minute!" Muriel brightened. "Put me in the picture. Who are the chairs of those departments?"

"There's Bert Parker, he's Ed. Policy; Harley Clark is head of Work and Community; and Nelson Wood is Chair of Kinesiology."

"Got it!" Muriel cried. "Remember that reception Dunkard gave a couple of years ago? The one where he talked about his 'big reorganization' of the College?"

"Sure. But what's that got to do with . . ."

"Wait! Dunkard's message was that new names for Ed. Administration, Vocational Ed. and Physical Ed. put the College in front of University innovation. And, remember how we went home and tried to look up kinesiology in our dictionary? Couldn't even find the word!"

"Yep," Rich smiled. "Another made-up subject matter. But what's your point?"

Muriel waved her cigarette. "Just this. These three departments aren't on the cutting edge; they're way over the edge! So far as the rest of the university is concerned they're a joke. Right?"

Rich nodded. After all, he had been one of the first to criticize the synthesis of these meaningless titles. "I agree," he said. "But what's that got to do with my problem?"

"Just a minute! Suppose you corral these Buffaloes and tell them that semester conversion is a great opportunity for them to show the university how their new approaches fit into semesters. Wouldn't that give them some highly needed academic respectability?"

Academic respectability? Rich recalled the final Doctoral examination of one of Nelson (Nelly) Wood's 'best students'. The candidate presented an overview of his study of the effect of various patterns of sweeping on the velocity of curling stones. A 'stone projector' figured in all of the many tables that proved that broom strokes in line with the stone's direction increased velocity, while stokes perpendicular to the stone's path retarded movement. Each of the Kinesiology faculty members praised the candidate's experimental design and the substantive nature of the findings. Rich was appalled! How could such a meaningless study result in the Degree of Doctor of Philosophy? *Academic respectability indeed!*

"Rich! Are you awake?" Muriel said.

"Umm . . . just thinking about what you said. You're right, these departments need any help they can get. But how . . . ?"

"Here's what I suggest," Muriel stood and faced Rich. "Get the Buffaloes together and talk straight about how they can use semester conversion to develop new courses with fancy names and how that'll raise their status in the university. And, this is important, make sure they know that Central is concerned about their departments."

"You mean make it sound like a threat?"

"Exactly! Since the carrot doesn't seem to work, lay on the stick!" Her laugh turned into a coughing spell. "Guess I'll . . . get a glass of water . . . and lie down."

Rich remained in his chair for the balance of the afternoon, mulling over Muriel's analysis and advice. *Sure wouldn't hurt. And I gotta do something!*

'Something' began Monday morning. Rich waited until nine a.m., then dialed Pearson's number.

"Hallo. Dr. Pearson's office." The voice of the martinet boomed in Rich's ear.

"This is Dean Jessen, College of Education. I'd like to speak with the Vice President."

"Just wait!"

Pearson soon came on the line. "Good morning, Dean Jessen. What can I do for you?"

"Your advice on semester conversion has worked well with several of our departments," Rich began. "However, I'm getting some resistance from others."

"Such as?"

"Educational Administration, Work and Family Studies . . ."

Pearson interrupted. "And I'll bet Kinesiology, right?"

"Yes. Those are the three that are most resistant. I can't seem to come up with any incentives and I'm wondering if you would support me if I implied your concern for the image of those departments."

Pearson was silent for a moment. "Need to take them to the woodshed, eh? Well, I can tell you that there's more than a little questioning of the academic substance behind those names. They are also at the back of the pack on research and publication. Let me tell you in confidence that we'll be putting heavy pressure on the College to move these three programs forward. You can get this message across as best you can without directly quoting me."

"Many thanks. I think I can get the word out and I'll keep you informed," Rich said as they disconnected. *Now what's the best way to proceed?* He considered the options. *Take the three to the woodshed?* This rural metaphor appealed to Rich. By putting the three chairs in the academic spotlight, they might see semester conversion as a way out of the academic woodshed.

"Lois," he spoke through his intercom. "Please make appointments with Professors Wood, Clark and Parker for tomorrow afternoon. Tell them it has to do with concerns raised by Central Administration. And I want to see them here, in the Dean's conference room."

Evidently the mention of Central's concerns cut through any excuses the three might have offered. They were all assembled in the conference room when Rich entered.

"What's this all about?" Wood asked. "I for one don't have a lot of extra time for . . ."

Rich tossed the CSCC file on the table. "I know you are all very busy, but I've some serious news for all of you. I just met with Vice President Pearson and he's raised concerns about your departments and how they are perceived by the academic community."

"Just what does that mean?" Clark asked.

"Hell! Central is always concerned about something!" Parker added.

"Yeah! Wood growled. "I for one don't believe these concerns. Not for a minute!"

Rich glared at the Buffaloes, content in their academic wallow. "Well, I can tell you that this is serious. The sciences, for one, have taken hold of the semester conversion and are putting whole new courses and majors in place." The lie came easily, for Rich knew that any questions the Buffaloes might ask of colleagues in other University departments would elicit comments in support of his assertion. He went on. "Furthermore, Central is looking back at earlier changes." Rich stared at Nelson Wood. "Professor Wood, at our last meeting of the CSCC you mentioned the conversion from semesters to quarters. I believe you said nothing changed at that time. Right?"

"Well, yes. That's pretty much . . ."

Rich continued as if Wood hadn't spoken. "Central is looking back at all our college initiatives such as past conversions, new department names and the like. I expect that we'll see a Graduate School committee in the near future charged with an in-depth review of all departments and programs."

"What the . . . why they can't . . .," stammered Clark.

"Oh yes they can!" Rich raised his voice. "And the College can't afford to have the appearance of lagging behind the sciences." Rich could barely suppress a smile. The Buffaloes were milling – ready to run for cover.

Parker stepped out from the herd. "What do you advise?"

"It's clear that the College must show real initiative on semester conversion. Every department must produce a totally new curriculum with major areas of study that reflect the best theories and practices in their fields. Moreover, Central will be requiring departments and faculty to carry out cutting edge research and to publish the results," Rich gloated.

The Buffaloes nearly wept at these blows. Rich could imagine each of the three counting the days to retirement and the possible escape from the pressures of scholarship. Body language spoke of uncertainty and fear. The cry for help came from Clark.

"Can the Dean give us a hand? This is a pretty tall order…," Clark's voice trailed off.

"Yes," Rich pounced on the request. "Submit a draft of your plans by the end of the week. Dean Dunkard and I will review them and suggest ways you can position your departments so that they can lead the way in the semester conversion process."

There was a collective sigh of relief as the Buffaloes fled the woodshed.

CHAPTER THREE

Organizational Politics

"...(a university is)... a series of individual faculty entrepreneurs held together by a common grievance over parking." (Clark Kerr: President, University of California.)

The next meeting of the CSCC was a demonstration of the effectiveness of academic politics and the efficacy of threats and lies. Every one of the college department chairs presented conversion plans that highlighted innovation, research and publication. Rich was pleasantly surprised at the erudition of the Buffaloes who led the CSCC discussion, pontificating on the academic aspirations of their faculties.

When the committee concluded its discussion, Rich summarized their work. "I'd like to thank all of you for your creative attention to semester conversion and for the productive work of your faculties. Your leadership is evidence of the vitality of the college and I know that Central Administration will be pleased with the results."

The committee left the meeting with many self-congratulatory comments, all except Carl Mertens. When the others were gone, he remained seated. "Now what did you do that brought those old-timers along?" he asked.

Rich smiled. "I just followed The Ayatollah's advice."

"Yeah, so what?" Mertens scoffed. "More peas under the shells?"

"Nope. I called Pearson and he told me that those three departments were vulnerable to the opinions of our academic community. Then I laid on the stick of academic integrity."

"So they got the message. Shape up or else?"

"That just about says it all. You could see how eager they were today."

Rich and Mertens grinned, engaging in a mental 'high five'.

"Got 'er done!" Mertens exclaimed.

Another lesson in the curriculum of academic politics had just been learned. Like other political exchanges, academic debates generally turned on issues of personal and group advantage. And, when advantage turned into credible threat, the most reluctant academician was galvanized into action.

Over the next month the final versions of the departmental semester conversion plans dribbled into Rich's office. These incorporated a narrative section that outlined the 'vision' of the department and went on to specify course descriptions and programs of study. Since Rich was responsible for preparing the college's conversion plan, he was forced to study each department's submission and to shape them into a consistent schema. This Sisyphean task involved rewriting the college plan each time a new departmental effort crossed Rich's desk.

Carl Mertens was a welcome interruption of Rich's labors. "Hi Rich," he called from the office door. "What're you up to today? Looks pretty serious."

"I'll say!" Rich grimaced. "These conversion plans are a real headache. Can't seem to find a way to put them together."

Mertens took a chair across from Rich. "Here. Let me take a look."

They shared plans for several minutes. Finally Mertens said, "You're right. They all sound like C+ term papers. Here's what I suggest. Let's just look at the courses they propose and leave the narrative 'til later."

"OK by me. Here's the Plan from C&I." Rich moved to the side of his desk and their fingers followed the listing of courses.

"Well," Mertens said, "this doesn't look too bad. I wonder just how this plan stacks up against C&I's current courses. Do you have a copy of the recent College Catalog?"

Rich swiveled his chair and picked the catalog from his bookcase.

Mertens took the catalog and opened it to the section for Curriculum and Instruction. "Now, I'll read a course description and you see if you can find something like it in the C&I plan."

Exchanges of description occupied several minutes. When Mertens had finished reading he asked, "OK. What's the score?"

Rich ran a pencil down the C&I plan. "Looks like about . . . twelve . . . new courses. That's . . . let's see . . . only twenty percent! Not much change here."

They repeated the exercise for the remaining plans with nearly the same results.

"Hell!" Rich exclaimed. "There are hardly any new ideas. And I'll bet that the four-credit courses they're proposed are just pumped-up three-credit quarter courses, just like we thought!"

Mertens continued to study the plans. "Short of going back to the committee, the only option I see is to shape some kind of unique narrative that will divert Waldo's attention. Let's think for a minute."

They thought. Shuffling of plans and shaking of heads indicated the enormity of the task.

"No starting point here," Rich said as his finger traced the Kinesiology plan. "Just a lot of exercise-babble."

"Say! You might have something there. Suppose we pull out words and phrases from these plans. You know, language that will sound academic to Waldo."

Rich emerged from Kinesiology. "You mean something like . . .," he re-entered the world of sport, "ergonomics . . . or . . . biomechanics?"

Mertens smiled conspiratorially. "You got it! I'll bet there are a couple of examples in the Ed. Psych plan." He paged through course descriptions. "The usual bullshit, but lots of mention of 'human development'. That could be a banner for our narrative. Right?"

"Sounds good to me. How's this? Ed. Policy says it's into 'intercultural communication'. I wonder what that means."

"Just a bunch of white boys looking for legitimacy!" Mertens snorted. "But it's a keeper for the narrative. We're just about there. Give me the Work Community plan."

Rich slid the plan across his desk. "Pretty thin. This one's the least innovative so far as courses go."

Mertens mimed weighing the plan. "Yep. A real lightweight," he read for a half-minute. "Nothing in the course that I can see. Just a minute! Their Narrative uses three words over and over; 'work','community', 'family'. Good handles for our opening?"

"Hmmm," Rich rubbed his chin. "Yes, I can see how these pieces could be shuffled into a kind of 'think piece'. I'll bet most of the other colleges will emphasize new ideas. What we could do is create a new language for the College, one that would make Waldo sit up and take notice."

"I like it. What say we do a short intro to the College Plan, a kind of 'set up' that'll get Waldo's attention.?"

"OK by me," Rich swiveled his chair and turned his computer on. "How about a title . . ."

Ruminations led to words – to rejections – to possibilities. They each chose favorites.

"Converting to Excellence," Mertens said. "That'll put us level with semester conversion and we're all in favor of excellence. Good enough?"

Rich shook his head. "Conversion is fine, but that sounds like we're short of excellence. What about, say, Educating for Engagement?" He typed the title.

"What the hell does that mean? Engagement?" Mertens snorted. "Sounds too much like a dating service."

"All right, all right," Rich laughed. "I'm sure you're speaking for Ed. Psych. and the prurient interests of your faculty."

More titles were offered – and more rejected. It was Rich that came up with the winner.

He typed briskly and read, "Innovation for the Future. Then we can use a subtitle such as, 'Converting the Curriculum'. Like it?"

"Not bad. Not bad at all. Hard to be against 'Innovation' and Waldo's sure to like the 'Future'." Mertens thought for a moment then rocked forward in his chair. "Get this down. 'The College of Education and Home Economics recognizes that it is the principal interface between the university and the community. Its graduates educate the next generation of state citizens and faculty research informs practice . . . in . . . all the human services.'"

Rich typed briskly. "Sounds pretty good. Now we need a closing sentence. We both know that three sentences are the most that administrators like Waldo can take in at one time." He paused, looking at the computer monitor. "Gotta pick up on 'Innovation'. Here, try this . . .," Rich typed for several moments, trying one sentence, then another. When finished he read, " Accordingly, the College recognizes an imperative for innovation and has driven semester conversion to position itself and the University to address the challenges of the future. Good enough?"

Mertens leaned over Rich's desk and read the complete paragraph. "Great! Now all it needs is explanatory paragraphs to back up the key words. Need any help?"

"Hmmm, don't think so. I'll wordsmith and run it by Dunkard."

"Well," Mertens stood. "I need to get back to herding the Ed. Psych. chickens. Let me know what the Dean thinks."

When the door closed behind Mertens, Rich looked at the screen and shook his head. "Pretty much bullshit! But it's a hell of a lot better than the department narratives," he sighed. "So . . . get to work."

It wasn't all that simple. Language in the several department narratives had to be visible in the final draft, and key department proposals needed emphasis.

Rich picked up one plan after another and wrote for several hours. In each case he wove the statements already written by the departments into his leading narrative. This resulted in emphasis of the words he and Mertens had crafted throughout the final College plan. *Not too bad!*

When he had finished, he signaled to his secretary. "Lois. I'm sending you a Word document. Give it a careful edit and print up a nice-looking copy. When you've finished, see if the Dean is available."

"Will do."

Rich cradled his phone and sat back. He reflected . 'Now, Dunkard carries the ball. Gotta get him to support . . .that way Mert is the front man. If it works, . . .' He thought about salary – promotion – and power. 'And if he fails . . . he's the fall guy!'

Lois interrupted these musings. "Dean Dunkard is on line two."

Rich reached for his phone.

"Mert, I need your advice on the Semester Conversion Plan. Any chance I can have a few minutes?"

"Sure. I've open time now. Come on over."

Rich was not surprised to learn that the Dean was free. After all, most university administrators were only needed at meetings; little actual work cut into their free time. He picked up the department plans and glided into Dunkard's office.

"What's on your mind, Rich?" Dunkard, seated at his conference table, looked up from a thick document that showed no evidence of having been opened at any time recently. "Have a seat," he waved at a chair.

Rich sat across from Dunkard and spread the department plans in a fan in front of the Dean.

"I've managed to get a conversion plan for all the departments. That's the good news. The bad news is that they aren't particularly innovative and the writing is marginal at best. What I need is your advice on how to send this along to Central."

Dunkard glanced through a couple of plans, sighed and said, "I get your point. These are pretty weak."

"Worse than that. For the most part, the departments have merely changed quarter courses into identical semester courses. The result is that programs have been reduced in content by about a third."

The Dean was visibly agitated. "I can't believe . . ."

"Just a moment!" Rich said. "I've come up with an approach that might work. Here's a leading narrative that's likely to get Pearson's attention." He passed his opus across the conference table.

Dunkard read for a few minutes muttering, ". . .innovation . . . research . . . work . . .," and other key words. "Say," he exclaimed. "This is pretty good. Kind of an attention getter." He paused, pencil in hand. "Let's add . . ."

Rich groaned. *Here we go!* The Dean was a notorious editor whose contributions generally weakened the document in question. He waited.

"I think," Dunkard looked up. "Something like . . . academic integrity. What do you think?"

"I agree!" Rich enthused. "I wonder why I didn't think of that! Let me take your idea and I'll get right back to you." He reached out for the narrative, took it in hand and left.

One more sentence! And it's done! Rich gloated as he swung into his office and opened the 'narrative' file on his computer. It took but a minute to write, 'The academic integrity of faculty and staff is the engine that will propel the College into . . .,' *What?* He frowned, then wrote, '. . . a bright future shared with families and communities.'

As he printed his new narrative, Rich was a bit embarrassed by its vacuity. However, he recognized the magic of the chosen words and the spell they would cast on Central Administration.

The spell worked on Dunkard and the College Conversion Plan was forwarded to Waldo Pearson.

Dean and Associate Dean waited, but not for long. Three days later, Dunkard burst into Rich's office.

"You'll never believe this! Waldo loves our plan and wants to use our language to lead the university's publicity on conversion! What do you think of that?"

This was better than Rich imagined. *Waldo copying his stuff!* "I'm very pleased. I hope he didn't read the departmental fine print. That'd make him wonder."

"I worried about that," Dunkard said. "But he didn't say a word! I owe you one for the fine work you did."

Rich smiled – and waited.

The Dean continued, "And I think I've found a way to pay that debt."

Rich straightened in his chair and leaned forward. "Really!" He held his enthusiasm in check. "What might that be?"

Dunkard said earnestly, "I'd like for you to create a first-class higher education program for the College. I think we have the ingredients to make that happen with your leadership."

"Tell me more," Rich said, with a touch of skepticism.

"Think about this. You have the background to lead such a program, especially with your experience in this office. And, there are several professors without departmental homes who could make up a core faculty."

"And who might they be?"

"Well," Dunkard hesitated. "There's Shirley Grimes . . . and Evelyn Howe . . . and . . . Jerrilyn Barnes," he finished confidently.

Rich was flabbergasted. "The Three Witches! You can't be serious! Everyone knows that they are stuck in the 1960's. And . . ."

"I know. I know. But they're under the gun on semester conversion and they have to respond to Central. You're the most likely leader as all four of you are carried under my budget as 'Foundation' faculty. We'll create a new budget line item for a 'Department of Higher Education' to give you salary control over the three. How's that?"

Rich ran a hand through his hair. "That's real heavy lifting! Look how difficult it's been with our departments. I couldn't get cooperation on conversion without the threats from Waldo. I'd also need to convince the Witches that it's a good idea to switch from 'Foundations' to 'Higher Education'."

The issue was now on the table – actually on Rich's desk. The Witches would have to be coerced into the semester system and collected into a sort of 'coven' in higher education. Rich could see himself as the Warlock of the College!

"Well, give it some thought," Dunkard said. "Only thing is, I'd need to get some movement on this real soon. As of right now, your faculty line item and those of the Witches are in budgetary limbo."

When Dunkard left, Rich stood and looked out his window. The bustle of students moving across the Quad were the public face of higher education. Dunkard, Pearson and the conversion were the reality of higher education politics. Rich wondered. 'Could I bring this thing together? What's in it for me?' He realized that the contemplated change was one in name only, he would merely be changing his marginal status in Foundations to one equally distant in Higher Education. And he would need to be careful not to jeopardize his status as Associate Dean.

These questions remained at the forefront of Rich's thinking for several days; they shaped an agenda for his weekend strategy sessions with Muriel. Her conspiratorial advice was the prop that Rich required to bolster his confidence when faced with issues like the Witches.

"Got another problem, Hon," Rich said. They were seated on their outdoor deck in early summer shade. "Dunkard wants me to take on the Witches and shape up a higher education department."

"You mean those three old bags? What do they know about higher education?" Muriel's hand toyed with an unopened cigarette pack.

Rich covered her hand with his. "Not much. What this means is that I've got to convince the Witches that it's in their interest to focus on higher education instead of the outdated 'foundations' crap they are teaching. Pretty tall order."

"I'll say," she paused then repeated the question that was usually at the center of their strategy discussions. "What's in it for you?"

"So far," Rich sighed, "nothing at all. Just an increase in my workload. You see, Dunkard wants to move my salary item, and that of the Witches, off the Dean's budget."

They were silent for some time, contemplating this unreasonable demand.

"I wonder," Muriel said. "Dunkard must feel some pressure on his budget from Central. Probably needs to give the appearance of reducing Dean's office spending."

"I agree. There's been talk to that effect for the last couple of months."

"The way I see it, that's your side of this assignment."

"What's that?" Rich grumbled. "I don't see what you mean."

Muriel recovered her hand – and cigarette pack. "How's about you do a deal with Mert. You know, say you'll take on the assignment but you'll need a salary bump. Think that'd work?"

Rich cocked his head. "Maybe . . ."

"It has to work if you're going to change the Witches into the Stepford Wives!" She laughed, cracked her pack and lit a Virginia Slim.

"I wish you wouldn't . . .," Rich said uncertainly. He knew it was no use; Muriel was still hooked.

Rich mulled over Muriel's advice for the balance of the weekend. He could see the logic that supported a demand for more money. On the other hand, he was uncomfortable with the confrontational approach. Muriel resolved his dilemma on Monday morning.

Following an extended coughing spell, she said, "Now, be sure to lay out your case so Mert can see how he'll benefit. Probably be a good idea to have a number in mind to force the Dean to make a decision on the fly."

"I guess you're right," Rich sighed. "Think five grand is too much?"

"You're talking five K as permanent salary increment, right?"

"Yep. No sense taking on the Witches for any one-time payment."

"I'd say go for it!" Muriel signaled with a raised thumb and slid into her desk chair where she was instantly transformed into a Mary Kay executive.

Monday morning at the Office of the Dean was a time for business as usual so far as Rich was concerned; accumulation of Friday's University 'snowflakes', three 'While You Were Out' messages, and a blank calendar. Nothing that needed his attention, except the strategy that he and Muriel had devised.

The more Rich thought about the strategy, the more he was convinced that a focus on Dunkard's budget was the key to a salary 'bump'. Rich knew that he had but one chance to make his case. If he were to be put off by Dunkard, there would be no second chance. *Solve his problem! Then ask for the money!* He reached for his phone.

"Good morning. Office of the Dean."

"Hi Millie. This is Rich. Is the Dean available for a short conversation?"

"Sure. His calendar is pretty open."

"May I come over now," Rich asked.

"No problem. I'll let the Dean know you're on the way."

Rich stood, more than a little uneasy. He scooped up the CSCC file, wiped his hands on his trousers and strode across the reception area to Dunkard's office.

"Morning Rich. What's up?" Dunkard asked and pointed to a chair.

Rich seated himself and began, "Been thinking about what you said last Friday. You know, the higher education program idea."

"Sure. Did you come up with any ideas?"

"I think so. Your plan for a department of higher education has a lot of appeal to me and, I believe, to Central."

The Dean nodded, smiling at praise for his insight.

"Now, what I'd propose is first, as you suggested, I take on the Chair of this new department and bring it into line with semester conversion. Second, I find ways to position the department on the national scene. That way, I think I can move the Witches along. How does that sound?"

"Great!" the Dean enthused. "Exactly what I had in mind."

"There's more," Rich reached for his mental order book. "We need to take the Witches off the Dean's Office budget and make them, and part of my salary item, stand on its own."

"What a relief that'd be!" Dunkard exclaimed. "Solve a serious problem I have with Central."

Rich leaned forward earnestly. "In order to make this work, I'd need to take on a substantial increase in my workload. I need to give nearly full time to implementing semester conversion and a pretty hefty slice of time to the new department."

Dunkard was clearly taken aback. "Don't know how I can do that. My budget's . . ."

"Wait a bit! There's an upside to what we're talking about, much bigger than moving a few salary items around."

"What's that?" Dunkard asked skeptically.

"It's Central," Rich purred. "We make a big deal of our new University-wide Higher Education Program. This does three things," he ticked them off on his fingers. "First, it puts the college on the map with an example of an innovation that we promised in our semester conversion plan. Second, it gives Waldo something he can point to when the legislators question how the U's plan is coming along. And third, we put the budget items in a department where I can take the management load off your office. How does that sound?"

Dunkard was silent for a full minute, shifting in his chair and rubbing his chin. Then he said, "You know . . . that doesn't sound too bad." Rich could see the flowering of his idea as the Dean began to see how Central would react. "I'll bet Waldo will grab onto this. Might even take ownership. Wouldn't that be ...," The Dean's skepticism faded in the sunshine of optimism.

Rich grinned. "I can see that you agree with me. This is not a problem, it's an opportunity. And, I'll be happy to take on the challenge." He ended without directly asking the salary question.

"I now see your point," Dunkard said. "You'll be taking on a heavy responsibility for the College and I'll need to . . . Say, why don't you shoot me a proposal with a plan for the new department and an estimate of your workload?"

"Consider it done!" Rich crowed. "It'll be on your desk tomorrow."

They actually shook hands, a behavior that rarely concluded academic discussions.

The department plan landed on the Dean's desk as promised. When it had been dispatched, Rich began a week-long wait for a response. Despite his anxiety, he knew that the benefits of academic decision making fell to those whose pleas were last in line.

It worked as he hoped; exactly a week had passed when Dunkard called. "Say Rich, can you come in for a chat? I think I've a solution to our problem."

"Be there in a minute."

The usual coffee and seating arrangements were completed. Then Dunkard began. "I've done the numbers on your plan and I must say that you've made a compelling case. Please know that I'm pleased that you'll take on this additional responsibility," he paused.

Rich filled the empty space. "Why, thank you. It did seem to me that this was something that had to be done."

"Yes. Yes, I know," Dunkard hesitated before moving to the bottom line of Rich's salary. "Well, I think that I can provide an increment to your salary. Given the load you'll be carrying, I think that I can add . . .," The Dean looked at a paper on his desk. "Something like . . . ten K to your salary item."

Rich was stunned. He had expected Dunkard to low ball the offer. *Ten grand!* Those dollars added to his existing Associate Dean salary increment of fifteen thousand. *Twenty-five K!* The number was staggering. *That puts my salary over eighty grand!*

Rich took a deep breath. "Why. . . that's very generous. Your offer makes it possible for me to give this plan my full attention!"

Dunkard visibly relaxed and they continued their discussion of issues that the new Department of Higher Education must address.

As he went through the motions of academic planning, the major fraction of Rich's mind was occupied with salary calculations.

Compensation remained at the center of his attention for the balance of the week, and set the agenda for the Jessens' weekend strategy session. When they had settled on the deck, Rich began the discussion.

"Well Hon, what do you think of Dunkard's offer?"

Muriel blew a perfect smoke ring and tapped ash from her cigarette. "Sounds pretty good to me. In fact, I've got a surprise for you."

Rich was more than a little puzzled by Muriel's statement. She rarely engaged in 'surprises'. As far as she was concerned, 'surprises' took up time and thought that otherwise might be used to economic advantage.

"Can't imagine what that might be. Give me a hint?"

"Come on!" she stood. "You'll see!" She led Rich into the garage and beckoned to the passenger seat of his Buick. "Hop in!" she directed.

Rich's bafflement increased as Muriel drove the Buick through residential University City. "Where're we . . ."

"Just wait! Almost there!" She motored along the Beltway, past familiar midwestern urban sprawl, eventually turning in at Spencer Motors, a vendor of up-scale hardware frequently visited by Rich.

"What?"

Muriel stopped the Buick, smiled and issued a final command. "Out! Follow me!" She wove through rows of shiny, up-scale automobiles. Saabs, BMW's and, finally, a line of Mercedes.

Rich was enthralled by the display of wealth and status, a display that he often visited with Muriel.

"Pretty good looking cars!" she purred. "Now, how's about that black 300?" She petted the hood of a sparkling specimen.

Rich was conscious of a mouth-watering reaction. The beauty of the 300 was almost too much for speech. "Well. . . I must say . . ."

"Come on!" Muriel said. "Out with it! Isn't this just what you've always wanted?"

Was she trying to taunt him? Of course a Mercedes car was an unattainable goal. "Sure, you know how much . . ."

"Brace yourself!" she ordered. "I bought it yesterday! It's a reward for all the work you've done this year – and a way to put the new salary money to work!"

CHAPTER FOUR

Hardball

"What we are discussing here is not political philosophy but practical method. Not why, but how." (Chris Matthews: HARDBALL)

Mercedes and money became the foundation of Rich's dreams, sleeping and waking, for several months. Office hours passed in pleasant contemplation of a future where his political skills charted a path to ever-greater rewards. Even his time spent with the Three Witches was smoothed by reviews of his accomplishments. This sleepy journey was brought to an abrupt halt by one day when Dean Dunkard walked into Rich's office.

"Rich," the Dean's voice boomed, "we need to check signals."

"Sure," Rich said, putting aside a sheaf of papers that evidenced a busy administrative life.

It wasn't more Associate Dean's work. It was more serious than that.

Dunkard closed Rich's office door, sat down in a chair opposite Rich and began. "Rich. We have a problem."

"What's that?" Rich frowned and leaned forward.

"It's Central Administration. They are taking a close look at every program in all the colleges. Seems like they are looking for ways to save a buck."

"So," Rich mused, "what's that got to do with us?"

"You know how much Waldo liked the way we handled the Old Buffaloes? Well, that evidently turned him into a kind of hatchet man, looking for even the smallest cost centers that could be closed. Unfortunately, he's hit on our Higher Education program. Three full-time faculty members plus yourself and not enough students to support them."

"That's probably correct," Rich agreed. "Unfortunately, I've not been able to move those Witches toward anything like a modern program."

The Dean pursed his lips. "It's more than that. He's also looking at research grants and publications. The Witches have nothing to show on the grant side and damn few publications. You're carrying the water on writing but," the Dean raised a warning finger, "none of you has scored on outside funding in the past several years. What I'm saying is that the program, and your appointment, may be at risk."

Holy shit! Rich envisioned the end of a short career. The thought forced its way into the conversation. "But it's not . . ."

Dunkard sympathized, "I know, I know. I've put you on the spot. However, there's nothing I can do to get Waldo off your case. What you must do is make your program conform to the enrollment targets for our college and make some strides on the research and publication of your faculty. Is that possible?"

These novel requirements were expectations that Rich hadn't considered. He had taken his position as Associate Dean as the ultimate insulation from the increasing pressures on faculty to publish and grovel for grants. "Can't say at this moment. How long do we have to deal with Pearson?"

"Waldo told me that he's planning to bring in a higher education guru next spring to take a look at what your faculty is up to. That'd give you 'round six months to shape up your program."

Six months! Why the twelve apostles couldn't ... The magnitude of this blow confused him. ". . . have to think about this," he mumbled. "What say I get back to you with some ideas next week?" Rich drew out his handkerchief as a signal the interview was over. The Dean rose and Rich mopped his sweaty brow.

Rich walked Dunkard out and closed the door. He resumed his seat behind his desk, staring at the bookshelves that framed the entrance to the office. All that knowledge, and not a glimmer of what to do! He had worked assiduously to build a base in the College of Education and Home Economics. Suddenly the playing field shifted and he was faced with the powerful in Central Administration.

"There's gotta be a way," he muttered. Idly he flipped through the old fashioned rolodex on his desk, searching for allies without success. These were the people he had cultivated within the college, a cabal that Rich could manipulate to shape the Dean's decisions. However, they weren't of the caliber required for open combat with Central.

On his second pass through the file of cards, he paused in the middle of the "L's". "Hank Loras! He's the guy!" Why, in a typical year Loras accounted for nearly fifteen percent of the College budget! "After all, he was the one who said I should take Dunkard's offer. . . I'll bet . . ."

Rich reached for the phone.

Loras answered on the second ring. "Loras here."

"Hank. This is Rich Jessen. I'm just back from a meeting with Dunkard where I got the word that Central is on my case. I'd . . ."

"You poor bastard!" Loras interrupted. "I suppose Wrecking Crew Waldo is measuring you for demolition."

"Something like that. What I'd like is to meet and discuss my options."

"Sure. Be happy to talk. How's about a drink at Tubby's, say about five thirty this afternoon?"

Rich confirmed the appointment and left his office on schedule. The journey across the Quad to Tubby's reminded him of last spring's meeting with Dunkard. *That one got me into this mess!*

Loras was waiting at table in a remote corner when Rich entered Tubby's that afternoon.

"Hi Rich! Over here!" Loras beckoned. "Get yourself a drink, it's on my tab."

Rich seldom drank hard liquor, except at important functions. This was important and he carried a scotch and soda to Loras' table. When he was seated, Loras began.

"So what's all this about Waldo?"

"Somehow he's focused on my higher education program. Dunkard says that Waldo is asking specific questions that I can't answer."

"Like what?"

"Well, Waldo has three concerns," Rich employed his professorial manner, raised fingers and counted. "First, my faculty doesn't bring in any grants. Second, we don't publish enough. Third, there aren't sufficient numbers of students in our program. Dunkard says I have six months to shape up!"

"Wheeww!" Loras exclaimed. "That's quite a set of requirements. But I'm not surprised. I've had similar run-ins with Waldo. He laid some of the same on me last year."

"What did you do?" Rich asked.

Loras sipped his drink and looked at Rich over the rim of the glass. "I studied the guy. Found out that he was brought in by President Rose to shape up the colleges so that they could bring in research money and position the U for national status. Seems like he did the same thing on his last job."

"O.K. That explains what I'm up against. But what's that mean?"

"I'll tell you. I asked myself 'What do I have that would make him back off?' The answer was pretty simple. There's a growing national movement to increase access and opportunity for handicapped people. I've got a corner on a slice of the federal money that's supporting work in this area. So, I could argue that I'm doing the grant thing. But I felt that wouldn't do. I needed to put this guy on my side. What I did was to show him how the U was behind the times and at risk of some serious sanctions if immediate action wasn't taken."

"What'd he say?"

"Just tried to blow me off with some general chatter about Central's 'plans'."

"How'd you get around that?" Rich sipped his drink and swirled the ice cubes in his glass. "Sounds like he wasn't listening."

"Exactly! But I found a way to get his attention." Loras chuckled. "I called Waldo for an appointment and told him I'd be bringing one of my staff with me. He agreed – likes to have the lambs find their own way to the slaughter."

"Okay, but . . ."

"Wait! Here's how it went. You know Jim Vandenberg? That guy who's paralyzed by Legionnaire's Disease?"

Rich reflected. "Yep. He's been on several college committees. Poor guy."

"Sure!" Loras grinned. "But he can't get to Waldo's office. Conant Hall isn't handicapped accessible! Well, Jim and I called Waldo from downstairs in Conant and told him we couldn't make it upstairs. He'd have to meet us in the lobby!"

"Bet he was plenty upset about that!"

"Better than that. When he came down and saw Jim in his wheelchair he realized that there was a human side to access. And, after about a half-hour of discussion, he was on our side! He gave me the green light for the Center and pretty much of a free hand to do whatever I felt was needed."

"That's fine for you," Rich growled, "but I can't play a trick like that. Anyway, I don't have access to the kind of dollars you bring in."

"Hang on! The lesson I learned is that it's best to manipulate Pearson. Opposing him won't work. You see, he's into a power grab where he can control the Dean by putting the arm on you. What we gotta do is figure out a way to get Waldo on your side and then . . ."

"On my side!" Rich snorted. "Fat chance of that!"

Hank grinned. "Don't panic." Loras paused, deep in thought for almost a minute. "Here's what I think we need to do. Let's look at Waldo's three demands – one at a time. So what about research?"

"I haven't anything in the works and I'm sure that the Witches aren't playing in that league. No way that I can get something going in the next six months. At least nothing that Waldo will buy."

"Now I wonder," Hank mused. "Just suppose we can come up with a research project that will make Pearson back off. What if you tell him that you've got an interest in handicapped access to university programs and that you've got a proposal in the works to fund a study of major universities?"

"What proposal? In response to what call? Sounds pretty weak to me."

"No problem. There are several categories of federal funding that go to the access issue. Be a weekend's work to shoot off a proposal. But that's not what I would recommend."

"So?" Rich was obviously confused by this convoluted narrative.

"I'm not talking about a real proposal, just the threat of one. When Waldo hears about your research plan, he'll try to get you to back off or delay the study until this place gets its act together. Remember what I said about his reaction to the national advocacy agenda. He doesn't want any hassel on his watch."

"Hmmm . . . maybe. If you're right, that might take care of the research issue. What about the publication question?"

"That's a bit tougher. I suggest that you lay a package of research and publication on him. Say that you're working on a 'think piece' in which you develop a framework for an economic analysis of emerging policy alternatives." Hank smiled, impressed by this recommendation. "In fact, that's such a good idea that I can cut you a slice of one of my recent projects so that you can show a cash flow resulting from your work."

"Now, that sounds better!" Money always got Rich's attention. "On to the last issue. We don't have student numbers and can't produce them out of thin air."

Hank frowned. "I agree – on the face of it. Let me think about that." He stood, stretched and turned toward the bar. "Care for another Rich?"

"No. I gotta be going soon. Muriel isn't feeling so hot and I need to be around this evening."

Hank came back to their table. "Sure hope nothing's wrong. Anyway, we don't need to solve this thing now. Give me a week to think. Meanwhile, why don't you work up a couple of pages that outline how you might study the economics of compliance with handicapped policies? That possible?"

Rich mentally reviewed his calendar. The old blank pages were being rapidly filled by Associate Dean assignments. "Guess so. Meet here again?"

"Same day, time and place next week," Hank agreed. "Give my best to Muriel and don't worry about Pearson. We'll solve that one."

They left Tubby's and Rich walked slowly back to Blewett, his mind preoccupied with the issues he faced. Just maybe Hank would come through. He envisioned the status that 'outside' money conferred and the freedom from teaching that these dollars bought – and the papers that would result. Writing was continually on Rich's mind. It was the other coin of the academic realm, the only other outcome that could be readily counted and factored into salary and promotion decisions.

It did not take long for Rich to disconnect the Higher Education Program from the machinations of Waldo Pearson. At first, Rich did not believe in Hank's strategy – it seemed much too obvious. Surely Waldo would penetrate its thin disguise.

Rich began with a week's worth of study in which he assembled the key words that defined federal policies concerning the access that universities were to afford handicapped citizens. This was followed by a short tour of the buildings that bordered the Quad. It was clear that the University met few, if any, of the many access requirements. All that remained was for Rich to weave these observations into a research proposal.

Writing came easy for Rich. His was a field where content took second place to form; where introductory paragraphs told the reader all that followed in the body of the paper. Two days of skimming through the stack of journals and policy papers provided by Hank gave Rich all he needed to develop his 'research agenda'. It was clear that those who wrote policies in support of handicapped access and opportunity had given little time or thought for the costs of what they enacted. America hadn't been a friendly place for the handicapped, and it wasn't likely to respond to the mandates of government.

Rich's final proposal was ready for Hank when they met for a strategy session at Tubby's. This time, Rich was waiting at a corner table when Hank entered. He waved at Loras.

"Hi Hank. Grab yourself a drink."

Loras followed the suggestion and seated himself across from Rich. "OK, pardner. Let's see what you've written." He held out a hand and took Rich's proposal. After reading for a few minutes he said, "Pretty good start. Now let's add a page on the new direction for your program . . . something to do with 'policy studies' that'll get his attention."

Rich looked puzzled. "I'm not sure what you're driving at. 'Policy studies' sounds pretty fuzzy."

"That's just the point!" Hank barked. "It doesn't mean shit. But Waldo doesn't know that. Remember, you only have to blow some smoke his way to get him off your case!"

"I kind of see where you're going. 'Policy studies' gives me the room to continue to work the Witches without Waldo looking over my shoulder."

"Right!" Hank made several notes and they did some rough word-smithing. "There!" he said. "Give this a good rewrite and it's ready for Waldo. It'll teach him that he isn't the only one that knows how to play hardball!"

"I'll drink to that!" Rich said. "I'll even buy!"

The final version passed across email for the next three days. With Loras' input, the proposal expanded to a full-blown plan for the salvation of Rich and Higher Education. It also marginalized the Witches.

Rich blessed his Rolodex. Loras was indeed a 'pardner'.

And what a pardner! An appointment with Waldo completed the process. Rich sat in Conant Hall across from Vice President Pearson.

"Good to see you, Professor Jessen. What can I do for you?" Pearson asked.

"I thought you'd like to hear of the progress we're making in Higher Education."

"Of course. Of course. Dean Dunkard has been keeping me up to date on your work." Waldo smirked – ready for the kill.

"Well, the basic challenge facing our faculty is to identify a research agenda that will add value to the College's academic enterprise," Rich said smoothly. "One that will bring in the resources needed to strengthen our program."

"Excellent! Exactly what I hoped would happen," Pearson lied. "I know you realize how important the numbers are in these times."

"Well, our numbers are on the upswing. For two reasons. First, my program will shift its focus from traditional studies of higher education to an emphasis on policy analysis. That will give the University the opportunity to define the future of American higher education." Rich paused.

Waldo filled the gap. "Hmmm . . . I see your point. Indeed, 'policy' is the newest idea in academe."

"That's not all. The second aspect of our new design is to capture the initiative on federal policy for the handicapped by studying how universities have responded, with special attention to the resulting costs and benefits." *There! How do you like that pitch!*

Waldo took a mighty swing and missed Rich's curveball. "But, you know . . . we've . . . that's an especially difficult challenge. In fact, I've just estimated the cost of making Conant accessible. Would you believe! That's nearly three million dollars! Money we don't have!"

"I know!" Rich grimaced sympathetically. "That's just what my research proposal addresses." He slid a slim folder across Waldo's desk. "Here. Take a moment to see where I'm headed."

Waldo lifted the folder as if it were a legal summons. He slowly paged through the document, murmuring as he read. "Strong case statement . . . I see that you're positioning this as a national study . . . good . . . I like the summary – shows the real impact on higher education . . . not bad."

"I thought you'd appreciate the wide view I'm taking," Rich smiled. "Here's a chance for the university to shape the response of the higher education community to a major federal policy. Puts us in a position to set the direction of this initiative." Rich relaxed and crossed his legs, waiting for Waldo's summary.

Pearson picked up the folder. "May I keep this? I'd like to show it to President Rose. He's most concerned over this issue and will be pleased to know that the College is taking the lead in responding."

"By all means," Rich said, standing and holding out a hand. "By the way, it would be very helpful if you would write a note to Dean Dunkard to indicate your endorsement of the new directions in my program."

Waldo seized the hand. "Happy to do it!"

The walk back to Blewett was nearly a triumphal march for Rich. He strode along, marching to the music of political success, basking in the light cast by substantive research. "All right!" he exaulted. "Takes two to play hardball!"

Two days later, Dunkard swooped into Rich's office waving a letter. "Congratulations! You're off the hook! Waldo's enthusiastic about your plan for Higher Education. Listen! He says, 'This proposal is precisely what I've been looking for. I know that you're pleased with the fine work of Professor Jessen.' Just what did you do to get him on your side?"

Rich smiled. "It was relatively easy. Policy studies is clearly coin of the academic realm and we can mint it right here!" He marveled at his easy use of metaphor.

Hardball wasn't a familiar game for the Witches. However, they were adept at the leisurely quilting bees of old-time faculty life and most of Rich's hardball pitches were easily fouled off.

Evelyn Howe spoke for the higher ed. bees. "Now Richard," she said in her school-mistress tone, "you need to go slowly with ideas like this." Evelyn flicked a finger at Rich's proposal. "We need to give this careful study."

Shirley Grimes was into more direct opposition. "This kind of stuff belongs in Ed. Psych.. Why, it would be a complete deviation from our focus on the history of higher education." She flashed a scowl at Rich and continued. "It might just be possible to include a bit of your policy concerns in one unit of my course."

As if that weren't enough, Jerrilyn Barnes delivered the final verdict. "I can see that you've been talking with Henry Loras. This is the kind of popular stuff that gives the university a bad name and I don't want anything to do with it!"

These comments summarized weeks of meetings and careful persuasion. Rich never even got to the ballpark. He spent endless hours at his desk, seeking an elusive strategy. Loras' talk of 'hardball' surfaced regularly in Rich's isolated deliberations. One day, over morning coffee, he voiced the thought aloud. "If only there was a way to play hardball with these Witches!" A conspiratorial smile slowly lit his face as he mentally massaged the idea. *But how?* Then Rich recalled Pearson's 'higher education guru'. Had Waldo cancelled the visit? The guru was scheduled for next month. He reached for his phone. *Hold it! Better think this through!*

Rich spent the balance of the day developing a strategy whereby he could use the guru as a relief pitcher to put himself back in the ball game. He sketched an agenda as he spoke. "Now let'see. Waldo arranges for a high-powered guru who has a reputation that will impress the Witches." Rich grinned at a vision of the Witches milling around the guru, chanting educational mantras. "Then the guru paints a dark future for outdated programs." *No problem there!* "The guru lays on a final report for Waldo, one that puts our program in serious risk." *Then what?*

This was the key issue! Rich stood and walked around his office. He stopped and looked out the window – across the Quad to Conant Hall. Would Waldo cooperate? How to get Pearson to . . .? Rich folded his arms across his chest, holding options inside. "Gotta see that Waldo gets the guru to read the riot act to the Witches." *But how?* He wheeled to his desk and sat, staring at the folder containing his proposal. *Dunkard! That's it!* The Dean could be the solution! An umpire to put the ball in play!

Rich collected his thoughts and decided on the approach he would take. He picked up the phone and dialed the Dean' office.

"Dean Dunkard's office, how can I direct your call?"

"Millie," Rich said. "I'd like about a half-hour of the Dean's time as soon as possible."

There was silence for a moment, then she replied, "Can you come over this afternoon about two?"

"I'll be there."

"What should I tell the Dean as to the purpose of the meeting?"

Rich considered. "Just tell him that it has to do with the Higher Education Program."

Rich disconnected. *And the Witches!*

The meeting with Dunkard went smoothly. The Dean agreed that something had to be done to move the Witches into the current century and that the guru might be the lever to make that happen. Dunkard agreed to call Waldo; a call from Rich could follow.

A working plan! Pearson's secretary called Rich the next day to arrange an appointment with the Vice President. Two days later, Rich ambled across the Quad to Conant.

"Hello, I'm Rich Jessen to see the Vice President."

"Yeah. I know," rasped the martinet. "He'll see you now."

When Rich was seated, Pearson began. "Dean Dunkard tells me that you might need some help with your Higher Education faculty. What can I do?"

"I'll start with a question. Have you arranged for a visit of a national expert to take a look at our program?"

"Well, yes. But I've put that on hold. Seems to me that you're making good progress, no need for any expert advice."

"I'm afraid," Rich began, "that it's a bit more complicated. I'm getting a lot of resistance to the ideas you and I discussed. What I need is some authoritative pressure to move my faculty forward."

Waldo chuckled. "I'm not surprised. I understand that your three ladies are a bit long in the tooth."

"That's putting it mildly," Rich sighed. "They haven't had a new idea for several decades. What I'm proposing is not understandable so far as they're concerned and it's quite threatening. So, they are digging in their heels and pulling backward."

"I see," Waldo mused. "What you want me to do is bring in the expert who can put these ladies in the picture - with the implied threat of Central Administration action. Correct?"

"Correct," Rich agreed. "Another way of putting it is that we need to play hardball with these ladies."

"Consider it done! I'll put the machinery in motion. Probably have your guru on tap in a couple of weeks."

Got 'er done! Rich reflected on his way back to Blewett.

It worked! Even better than Rich had expected. Arlan Mose (the guru) arrived on Campus and Rich scheduled appoints for him with each of the Witches. Following a round of interviews, Mose appeared in Rich's office.

"Professor Jessen," Mose said. "I understand that I'm to share my observations with you. Is that right?"

"Yes," Rich said. "Your appreciation of our program will be most helpful as we look to the future."

"Very well, I can be brief. Unless you can greatly change the beliefs and work of your faculty, there will be no future for the program. I have never met higher education faculty that are so far out of date! If I were to leave my recommendations with Vice President Pearson, they would likely result in closure of the program!"

"Oh dear!" Rich feigned concern. "I didn't realize it was as bad as all that! Have you no positive findings?"

"I suppose that I might emphasize my favorable impression of the direction you have outlined. A well-developed policy studies focus could be a valuable addition to the University. However, I must emphasize that such a direction would require a complete revision of the current higher education program. I'm afraid that is the best I can do."

Not bad at all! "As you might imagine," Rich said agreeably, "your conclusions are along the lines of my own thinking. Were you to communicate your findings to Vice President Pearson as you have outlined, they would be very helpful in shaping our future plans."

Mose smiled. "I'm glad that we agree. I must say that my visit has been what I imagine an anthropologist from Mars might experience visiting your program in the early 1900's. In fact, Professor Barnes was extolling the Morrill Act of 1862 and Professor Grimes spoke lovingly of the rise of the junior college movement. I couldn't believe it!"

Rich laughed. "Just what I expected you to find. You can imagine the level of resistance I've encountered from these people."

"Yes, yes," Mose said "That's what I've concluded. I'll be writing a report along the lines we've discussed. Vice President Pearson will be receiving the report by the end of the week and I'll have my secretary send a copy to you."

Rich was careful to mask his glee under a serious countenance. "That will be fine. And I want you to know how pleased I am with your visit and the careful attention you have given to our program."

The promised report arrived. It concluded with Mose's strong recommendation that the Higher Education program either be totally transformed – or else disbanded. Rich read the report carefully and re-read it. *A whole new ball game!*

It was indeed a whole new ball game! Pearson followed through as Rich expected. Dunkard received a formal letter from Waldo that paraphrased Mose's recommendation (with a copy to Rich). *Play ball!*

Dunkard threw out the first ball with a phone call to Rich. "Rich I assume you've received a copy of Pearson's letter. Right?"

"Yes. It's pretty much what I expected. I imagine you agree?"

"Sorry to say, I do. Now what do you advise as to our next steps?"

Rich was ready for this one. "I say an immediate meeting with the Witches where we play hardball. That is, we make it clear that Pearson has them in his sights and that they are at risk."

"Hmmm," the Dean mused, "you're probably right, but that's kind of drastic, isn't it?"

"Sure. But think about it, Grimes and Barnes are both over seventy and might just accept some kind of phased retirement. That would give me room to set the program on the right track. Also, their retirement would drastically reduce the salary load on the Program." *C'mon Mert! Swing for the fences!*

There was a long minute of silence. Then Dunkard spoke, "I think you're right. I'll have Millie get us all together first thing next week. That work for you?"

"You bet! It's on my calendar!" *Hardball!!!*

CHAPTER FIVE

Metaphor

"Metaphorical thought is unavoidable, ubiquitous, and mostly unconscious." (Lakoff and Carlson: Metaphors We Live By)

"Well, looks like your apprenticeship is over," Carl Mertens said as he reached for the maple syrup.

"That's one way to look at it," Rich agreed. Breakfast with Mertens was now a weekly event where larger issues of academic life and personal strategy could be freely discussed. This time however, Rich sensed a different conversational tone. "But what are you driving at?"

Mertens saturated his hotcakes and looked up. "You know that I have a tough time leaving my psychologist persona in my office. Seems that I can't help analyzing our colleagues."

"Yes," Rich smiled. "I remember the time you were actually charting the number of times Evelyn Howe spoke in one of the College committee meetings. Her numbers were off the chart!"

Mertens nodded. "That's a good example. What I discovered was that Howe would engage in long periods of meaningless speech following any question raised by the Dean. When others spoke, she would either say nothing or make a brief comment."

"Sounds plausible. But what does that have to do with anything?"

"Let me back up," Mertens insisted. "What I meant by my comment about your 'apprenticeship' is this. In the past year or so you've moved into the circles of university power and are, in my judgment, poised to be an important actor."

Rich feasted on the prospect. "Sounds too good to be true."

"That's my point. I believe that the only way you'll reap the benefits of influence is to pay close attention to the character of those you'll be working with. Let me give you an example," Mertens slipped into his professorial role. "Take Waldo Pearson. He's an excellent case of a person who uses what I call the 'rational voice' to perfection."

Rich looked puzzled. "I never thought of Waldo as rational. Seems to me he just babbles the Central Administration line."

"Then you haven't been listening. When Pearson speaks it's always in the voice of administrative reason, telling the listener about the facts of university life. And, he's a master at enlisting his audience in the administrative cause of the moment. Think about how he helped you with semester conversion and the Three Witches."

"Come to think of it," Rich rubbed his chin, "that's what impressed me about Waldo. He took my problem and shaped it to conform to Central's goal."

"Yes," Mertens encouraged. "And didn't you come away feeling appreciative of his help?"

"Put it that way, I guess I did."

"Didn't it strike you as odd that Waldo got you to recommend the higher education guru? Wasn't that originally Waldo's idea?"

Rich ground his teeth. *That sly bastard! Why...* He was unable to acknowledge Waldo's manipulation.

"I can see that you get the drift of my argument. Now consider this," Mertens continued the lecture. "Look at Mert Dunkard. What strikes you about his character?"

"That's easy. He's a borderline alcoholic. A classic case!"

"Yes, but didn't he get you to take on semester conversion? And didn't he drop the higher education problem in your lap?"

"Hmmm, hadn't thought of it that way. Sure, I took on his problems, but he came across with money – and the professorship."

"Now don't take this personally. I'd say Dunkard had your number. In effect, he worked you as an apprentice, one who would respond to rewards. What do you say to that?"

Mertens was revealing aspects of university life that Rich hadn't considered. Others were playing their own games – and winning! He felt manipulated, beaten at political exchanges, a naïf loose among the experienced.

"But," Rich mumbled. "I got my way." *Didn't I?* He wondered.

"Sure," Mertens said consolingly. "But you must realize that your way just happened to match Waldo's way and the way Dunkard runs the Dean's office."

Rich was puzzled. "Why are you telling me all this? What's in it for you? And for me?"

"There are two reasons. First, I've been impressed by the way you've fit into university politics. Yours is an emerging generation that's coming of age and will likely shape the future of the U. Second, and this is confidential, I'm moving my salary line item to the Business School. I've had enough of the petty politics of my department and would like to try my hand in the business world."

Rich was stunned! *Move to the Business School!* "Hey! Just a minute! Is that really possible? I mean, your going to the Business School."

"Yep. The machinery is running and I should be at the School for the next academic year."

"Well, OK . . . I guess. But what am I supposed to do with the things you've been telling me. They just don't seem to make any sense."

Mertens poured coffee refills, sipped, and continued with the lesson. "What I hope will come out of this is that you'll begin to study your colleagues and opponents and use their characters to further your own ends."

"Yes, I'd like that. Can you give me another example, say somebody that could be a supporter. Pearson and Dunkard don't fit into that category."

"That's easy. Take Hank Loras. From what you've told me, he's as close to a partner as you're likely to find in the College. What about him?" Mertens went on to answer his own question. "I see Hank as a unique resource. His power base is outside the U and almost totally under his control."

Rich recalled how Loras had used the handicapped student to control Pearson. "Please continue," he said. "Now you've got my attention."

Indeed! There was a remarkable change in Rich's engagement in the discussion. He was transformed from a spectator to a player in the games that Mertens described.

"The simple analysis of Loras would conclude that outside money is immune from the College – or from Central. It's a lot more complicated than that. In order for Hank to succeed, he's got to insulate his funding from the way the U plunders outside money. They usually rip off something like twenty percent of those dollars as 'overhead'. I checked into Hank's Center. His overhead is more like ten percent. Know how he does that?"

Rich considered. "Well . . . kind of. You see, Hank told me how he backed Waldo down by playing the handicapped card. And, he helped me with Waldo in the same way. That what you had in mind?"

"Only partly," Mertens said. "Hank also works with his funding agencies so that they define the parameters of money use. That ten percent overhead is no accident."

"But," Rich asked. "What's in it for the U? Why don't they just shut Hank down?"

"It's the advocacy groups!" Mertens exclaimed. "Not all political action is inside the U. Loras is trading on federal legislation concerning the handicapped; legislation that was put into place by advocacy and that's a force that Central Administration fears. So any way you can connect to Hank strengthens your political muscle."

They were silent for a moment. Then Rich said, "I still don't quite understand why we're having this conversation. Seems to me that there's more to it than you've laid on the table."

Mertens laughed. "You've cut to the chase! Sure there's a bit more, but everything I've said so far is, as I see it, useful to you. The benefit to me is that you and the others we've spoken about are a kind of case study. You see, I'm very interested in how people accumulate power and use it in organizations. My move to the Business School involves just that." He paused.

Rich leaned forward. "So I'm just a research subject! Don't know if I like that!"

"No! That's not at all what I had in mind," Mertens shook his head. "What you've done in the past year or so tells me that you have an important future at Midwest. I'd like to help you make the most of it."

This statement cooled Rich's simmering anger. "OK. Suppose you be more specific."

"The best way I know is to leave this book with you." Mertens leaned over and reached into his briefcase. He drew out a paperback document. "Here, take this. It'll add substance to what I've been saying." He handed it to Rich.

"*Metaphors We Live By.* Sounds like some kind of religious tract. What's it all about?"

"Rich. What I'm proposing is that you and I engage in a joint research project. We'll study university politics from the approach described in *Metaphors*. As we go along, we'll be able to show how universities really function. You know, how academic politicians practice their craft. What do you say to that?"

"Now that's more like it!" he considered for a few moments. "That gives meaning to what you've been saying. Yes, I can see how Waldo and Dunkard could be case studies." Rich considered for a moment and became almost animated. "I will admit that there's plenty of material here at Midwest."

A second pot of coffee was ordered and a research agenda unfolded. Rich agreed to keep notes of his meetings with Midwest's academic politicians and their machinations. "You have a deal!" he announced.

Mertens had the last word. "Just remember, I'm out of the loop so far as the College is concerned. However, you can reach me by phone or email anytime so we can develop our study." He stood and pointed to *Metaphors*. "Give it a close read!"

Metaphors lay on Rich's desk for the next several weeks while he grappled with the Witches. Professors Grimes and Barnes edged slowly toward retirement; Professor Howe was another matter. Rich logged many hours of tedious negotiation with Howe concerning her role in the new Department of Higher

Education. Finally, Rich convinced Howe that her course 'The System of Higher Education' was an excellent centerpiece for the new focus on policy studies.

With the issue of the Witches put to rest, Rich was able to return to the slow-pace of Assistant Deanly work. The resulting 'seat time' began to bring *Metaphors* into focus. Rich was ambivalent. He was intrigued by Mertens' plan for joint research, but offended by the book. Mumbled conversation repeated these themes.

"Who does he think he is?" Full Professor Jessen spoke. "I'm not some graduate student who's dependent on his ideas!"

Rich Jessen, Opportunist, took an opposite view. "After all, I'd be the only College professor with a tie to the Business School. And Carl has always been on my side."

The monologue continued intermittently for many days. Eventually, the Opportunist won out. "Might as well take a look at this thing," Rich said as he opened *Metaphors*. He was immediately captivated by the notion that metaphors provided a structure that shaped human interaction and individual behavior. Rich was especially impressed by the notion that arguments were often framed in the language of war. He read on.

As he applied the logic of *Metaphors* to his life in the university, Rich could see how the behaviors of decision makers could be explained by one metaphor or another. He understood that university decision making occurred under a 'ruling metaphor' where collegial interaction led to rational outcomes, or was supposed to. However, Rich's experience with semester conversion and the Witches convinced him that there was another 'ruling metaphor' dominated by political behavior. This conclusion led him to compare these two metaphors along several dimensions.

During his graduate student years at Louisiana Methodist University Rich had repeatedly encountered the 'four-fold table' of the social sciences. This simple device reduced the complexity of societies and organizations to an array of two variables and four cells. Its acceptance was attested to by countless scholarly articles and many successful products such as the Meyers-Briggs (personality) Type Indicator. This 'four-fold' way of thinking shaped much of Rich's approach to the professorship, and eventually to the mysteries of metaphor.

Rich scribbled his way through an entire legal pad in search of the four-fold key to metaphor. Eventually, he settled on a four-fold table headed by what he considered to be the two 'ruling metaphors'; Political and Collegial. When he had finished with his work, Rich entered the table into his computer, printed the results, and laid the table on his desk.

METAPHOR	POLITICAL	COLLEGIAL
APPROACH	HARDBALL	DELIBERATION
OUTCOME	VICTORY	CONSENSUS

In this simple tabulation, Rich had captured the essential differences between the common speech of collegiality and the reality of university politics. For Rich, the last row of the table was his most significant finding. His experience told him that a political actor enjoyed a significant advantage over rational, conciliatory colleagues. However, the table failed to take the character of university actors into account.

Dunkard now – what about him? For most people at Midwest, Dunkard was simply 'Drunkard' – an alcohol dependent nobody. Was that too simple? Rich wondered. True, Dunkard could usually be made to conform to Rich's wishes, but it was almost too easy. Was there something about Dunkard that he was missing?

As he prepared for his Friday conference with the Dean, Rich decided to explore issues of character. He began by taking charge of the meeting. "What's on our agenda today?" he asked.

"Well now," Dunkard responded. "Let's discuss your progress with the new higher education program."

Don't discuss! That's collegial! "I'm pleased to tell you that we are making excellent progress. And the policy focus is exactly what Mose, our visiting expert, recommended!"

Dunkard looked apprehensive. "I don't know . . . seems to me that 'policy studies' is a concept too far." He smiled at the simile.

"Nope!" Rich said dogmatically. "It's where the action is and any retreat from that direction makes absolutely no sense!"

"Wouldn't it be a good idea if we backed off on the Witches? Seems to me we've come on too strong," Dunkard said pleadingly.

Rich selected an obstinate tone for his answer. "Not at all. We've drawn our line in the sand and we need to stand behind it."

It was too much for Dunkard who conceded, "Well, you know best. Now, I gotta run – an appointment, you know."

"Yes, let's call it a day. See you bright and early on Monday."

Back in his office, Rich gloated over the success of his newly discovered metaphor power. Dunkard had effectively left the field to Rich, the Hardball player.

Now what's next? Rich answered this unspoken question by examining his recent behavior with the Witches. Clearly, he had been dogmatic – carrying the water for Pearson, but probably far too rational in that he had left doors open to the

Witches' arguments. In the future, he would need to be obstinate – a New Buffalo in the university corral.

It was clear to Rich that the character of the actors had a great deal to do with the success of a metaphor. Just as Mertens said; Dunkard's conciliatory approach was tailored to the consensus sought by devotees of the Collegial metaphor, whereas Rich's dogmatic aggressiveness was the key to victory in the political forums of the university. He reflected on these truths, staring at the four-fold table on his desk.

What I need is another line! Rich took a pen and sketched in a 'Character' dimension that showed how he and Dunkard had behaved in their discussion. After several editing entries, Rich switched on his computer and printed a new Metaphor Table.

METAPHORS	POLITICAL	COLLEGIAL
APPROACH	HARDBALL	DELIBERATION
OUTCOME	VICTORY	CONSENSUS
CHARACTER OF ACTORS	DOGMATIC	RATIONAL
	OBSTINATE	CONCILIATORY

Again, Rich was impressed with the meaning contained in this array. He could envision situations where the Political metaphor would easily triumph over the Collegial; triumph due to the juxtaposition of Character attributes. Dogmatic-obstinacy would always win out over the conciliatory – rational. In fact, most university issues were sufficiently clouded that rationality showed no pathway to outcomes. Instead, dogmatically stated positions shaped the behavior of confused faculty and administrators.

These thoughts fueled anticipation for future political engagements. Rich could see years of success ahead – so long as he concealed political machinations under the guise of collegiality.

As he contemplated the use of the Political metaphor, Rich became aware of his debt to Carl Mertens. He took a clean copy of the Table, folded it and reached for a campus mail envelope. *Business School? What's that building called?* Rich couldn't come up with the name and had to consult the university Directory. He turned to the "B's". *There it is!* 'Bunge School of Business'. *Screwy name!* Rich was unaware of the Bunge grain trading company that had endowed the School. He wrote the address on the envelope.

Rich began to slip the Table into the envelope – hesitated – and drew it out. He unfolded the Table and smoothed it on his desk, considering the implications of authorship. 'OK, Mertens gave me the idea about metaphors, but I built the Table.' There was serious academic credit here! *Jessen's Academic Governance Framework!* He crumpled the paper and paged through computer files. *There! Give Carl the old version!* The Table was transformed into a 'four fold' and mailed. *Good!* He actually rubbed his hands.

He speedily cleared his desk and discarded the several phone messages left by his secretary. Scooping up Mertens' copy of *Metaphors,* he inserted the Table picturing his view of the 'ruling metaphors' and turned off the overhead lights.

It was a pleasant perspective that he planned to share with Muriel on the upcoming weekend. Rich was propelled on his homeward journey with the fuel of victory – gained by clever use of his political metaphor. "Muriel will really eat this up!" he said aloud. "Be a real contrast to her 'team metaphor'. Should have a great discussion this weekend!"

CHAPTER SIX

Reload!

"The developmental crisis of generativity vs stagnation raises career and family issues for most middle-aged men."
(Erik Erikson: Eight Ages of Man)

The Mercedes slipped into the Jessen driveway and Rich pressed the garage door control. The door slid up and he parked next to Muriel's pink Cadillac. Waldo Pearson, Dean Dunkard and Carl Mertens faded from his mind. He closed the overhead door, gathered his briefcase from the Merc and stepped into the kitchen.

There were no welcoming smells of dinner preparation. Instead, the room was dark, as were the dining and family rooms. *Where's she got to?*

Muriel was in the guest bedroom. She was lying, propped up by two pillows, an audible wheezing sound with each breath. Rich was stunned. This looked serious!

"What's up Hon?" he asked.

Muriel coughed, a strangled attempt to clear her throat. "Don't know . . . so weak . . . had to lay down . . . can't breathe . . ." She struggled to inhale.

"When? How?" Rich searched for information. *What can I do?*

Muriel answered the unspoken question, "I . . . think . . . better go . . . hospital."

Rich gaped. "Hospital! That bad?"

"Yesss . . . need help."

Rich was stunned! "Can you get into the car? Or should I call 911?"

"I . . . think I can make it. Help me up."

Rich leaned over the bed and folded the covers. Muriel was fully dressed as if she had just returned from a Mary Kay meeting. He put an arm under her shoulders and raised her to a sitting position. "Can you get up, Hon?"

"Help . . .," she gasped. "Lift . . .," she implored.

They staggered through the house toward the garage. Rich folded her into the passenger seat of the Mercedes and got behind the steering wheel. He started the engine and looked over at Muriel. "You O.K.?"

"Nooo . . . not O.K. . . . please . . . hurry . . ."

Rich backed the car down the drive and turned toward University Hospital. The ten-minute drive seemed almost endless – accompanied by Muriel's labored breathing. She shifted restlessly and occasionally bent forward, seeking relief from the pain of inhaling.

At the hospital, Rich guided the car down the ramp to the emergency entrance. An automatic door opened and they passed in.

The car stopped and emergency attendants took over. Rich's responsibility had ended – for the moment. He wheeled the Merc through the emergency room exit and parked in a nearby lot.

'What a hell of a mess! Just when things were going good!' He stood next to the car, leaning against it for support; a pitiful figure, shoulder bowed under the weight of circumstance. Honest concern for Muriel battled with his sense of personal victimhood and he clenched his hands in despair. Finally, he heaved himself upright and shuffled back to the emergency room.

The receiving area was empty, its hangar-like space devoid of people; no evidence of the activity of a few moments ago. Rich swiveled his head. Muriel was nowhere to be seen.

A voice boomed over a loudspeaker. "Mr. Jessen? Please report to Emergency Services as soon as possible!"

"I'm . . . ," Rich began, then realized that no answer was required – only action. Who was this person? Ordering him around! His was the classic stance of ambivalence, legs moving to obey, upper body holding back. Rich's indecision held him immobile.

"Mr. Jessen?" This time a voice came from a nurse who entered the emergency space.

"Yes. I'm Professor Jessen. Have you seen . . ."

The nurse took his arm, gently easing him into a nearby room where curtained spaces enclosed other patients. She led him to an enclosure. Inside a doctor bent over Muriel and nurses worked rapidly to supply oxygen and intravenous drips.

"How? Is she all right?" Rich mumbled, a hand reaching out as if to change the scene.

The doctor turned. "Are you the husband of this woman?"

"Yes, I'm. . ."

"O.K. Be seated until I'm finished. Then we can talk!"

Rich backed into a nearby chair, a spectator, no longer in control of events.

Ten minutes passed, then fifteen.

Finally, the doctor turned away from Muriel and walked over to Rich. "Well, she got here just in time. She's stable now, but we'll need to keep her here for the next several days. Now I need to ask you a couple of questions. This woman . . . what's her name?"

"Muriel . . . Jessen . . . she's . . ."

The doctor paid no attention to Rich. "She appears to be a heavy smoker. Is that so?"

"Yes, about three packs a day," Rich squirmed under the doctor's gaze.

"Thought so," the doctor sighed. "She's pretty far gone. Advanced case of emphysema. And, I'm quite sure that there's a possibility of lung cancer. What I plan to do is schedule her for an MRI tomorrow. Then we'll know."

"She'll . . . be . . . OK?"

The doctor looked at Rich for several seconds. "I have to be honest. If she has lung cancer, we'd have to treat it aggressively and that's no picnic. She'll need care 24-7. Can you provide that?"

Cancer! 24-7! These announcements were a physical blow that embraced Rich in visions of disorder. Years of planning and accomplishment were put at risk. "I . . . don't know. We live alone – no family," he hung his head in despair.

The doctor gazed at the pitiful creature. "Now Mr. Jessen, the hospital can help you. We'll move your wife to an intensive care room and you can visit her briefly. Tomorrow you should make an appointment with our Home Health Care Service. They'll help you arrange for the care your wife will need." He turned to leave.

"Wait! Wait!" Rich lurched to his feet. "What are her chances?"

"I can't say yet. First part of next week I'll have test results and can give you an informed view of her situation. Until then, you should comfort her and try to be optimistic." He left.

Optimistic! Rich sank back in the plastic chair and held his head in his hands. The immensity of Muriel's condition submerged his usual prideful bearing. He was a smaller person; a mote in the refined air of the hospital.

Eventually a nurse arrived at his side. "Mr. Jessen. Please come with me. I'll take you to Intensive Care."

Rich was confused for a moment. *Intensive Care! But I'm not . . .* Then he realized that he wasn't to receive 'Intensive Care'. He obeyed the nurse and followed her.

Intensive Care was a circle of rooms surrounding a central nursing station. Doors were labeled according to the condition of patients; 'BioHazard', 'Radiation Warning', and for Muriel, 'Oxygen Environment'.

The nurse beckoned Rich. "Here's your wife, Mr. Jessen. Please don't stay too long. She needs rest and quiet."

Muriel lay on a partly-elevated bed. IV tubes connected her arms to suspended bottles. An oxygen respirator covered her nose and mouth. Half-opened eyes blinked at Rich and her hand reached out to him.

"Babe!" he blurted. "MiGod! I . . ."

A squeeze of her hand interrupted him and she slowly shook her head. Muriel's free hand lifted the edge of the respirator. "Don't . . .," she mumbled. "My fault . . .," her voice faded.

"But Hon," Rich began, then remembered doctor's orders - 'rest and quiet'. "You'll be OK. The doctor is keeping you here until Monday. Doing a few tests, that's all."

The expression on Muriel's face relaxed. "Good . . . now need sleep."

Rich sat holding her hand for several minutes. Then, as she relaxed, he laid the limp hand on the bed and left the room.

"When can I see her again?" Rich asked the Charge Nurse.

The nurse looked at Muriel's chart. "Hmmm. . . Doctor advises that she should be kept in isolation until Monday. Then he'll let you know when you can visit."

Rich was stunned. "That bad?" He stood, his arms hanging at his side.

"No," the Nurse said. "It's just that she needs quiet so that the medications can do their work. Please don't worry."

The Nurse's advice followed him out of the hospital – into the Mercedes – out of the parking lot – through the return trip - and into the empty house. Rich retraced his path from the garage to the guest room. He stared at the rumpled bed where he had found Muriel. A side table held his copy of *Metaphors* and the agenda of what was to have been a triumphant discussion of their future.

Images of change and uncertainty dominated Rich's thinking throughout that night and the next day. On Sunday morning, he fled the house looking for sanctuary. The Mercedes carried him to the university and the emptiness of his office. He was alone.

Rich sat looking at his telephone. There were no calls from Dean Dunkard, no summons from Waldo Pearson, no friendly sharing of information with Carl Mertens. All was silent. He was alone.

The lack of normal office activity became overpowering. Rich stood and walked to the window overlooking the campus. Even there, little was taking place. Students had escaped to weekend holidays. No scholars marched to academic rhythms. Even administrators had retreated to off-duty lairs.

Silence and isolation became unendurable. Rich wheeled and strode out of his office to the relatively comforting embrace of the Mercedes. It transported him to the familiar bustle of traffic and, eventually, to his house.

Inside, Rich wandered among familiar furniture and settings, once populated by the 'old Rich and Muriel'; co-conspirators in the game of life. Now, he had no confidant. Would she return?

With Monday, came the answer to that question. That afternoon, Rich met with the doctor. They were seated at the central station in the intensive care unit.

"Mr. Jessen, I have bad news," the Doctor began. "Your wife has an advanced case of lung cancer. I'm afraid that I cannot be optimistic. What's needed is a regimen of chemotherapy."

"But how," Rich stammered. "I mean . . . how did this happen?"

The Doctor was blunt. "It should be obvious. Heavy smoking has damaged her lungs and opened the door to the development of cancer. Our only hope is that chemotherapy will halt the growth and prolong her life."

Prolong her life! "Do you mean that she'll . . . die!" Rich gulped. Muriel gone! What about their partnership?

"Yes Mr. Jessen, her prognosis is not very optimistic. What we'll do is try to arrest the cancer and make her comfortable so that she can return home. Now, you must make arrangements for in-home care. We'll help you with that. I've arranged for our In Home Care Coordinator to meet with you this afternoon. Meanwhile, I'll order chemotherapy. That will require hospitalization for the next several weeks. During that time, you will need to visit your wife and support her as much as possible."

Visit? Support! But what about . . .

The Doctor saw Rich's confusion. "I know that this is a great shock and that you'll need to change your work and home life. The record shows that you are employed by the University. Is that correct?"

"Yes, I'm Associate Dean of the College of Education and Home Economics."

"Good. I'm sure the university will be flexible so that you can do what's needed for your wife." The Doctor swiveled to a computer terminal and began entering records and orders.

Rich was left – once again - alone.

He remained isolated until Tuesday when he met with the In-Home Care Coordinator.

A professionally attired woman swept into the room where Rich was waiting at the hospital. "Mr. Jessen? I'm Alice Murphy. I'll be setting up In-Home Care for your wife. I want you to know that we'll make all the arrangements necessary and see to it that you're provided with the staff support that your wife will need. Now, let's get this organized!"

And organized it became! Chemotherapy was carried out as planned. The university gave Rich leave. In-Home Care organized the Jessen's house and employed a full-time nurse who resided in the guest bedroom.

Rich was carried along by these events – as a participant without control. His colleagues expressed sympathy, dodging empathy as a threat to academic life. Political maneuvers faded into the fog of care-giving responsibilities. There was no time for Rich to adjust to the rapid pace of change.

At last Muriel returned home and was gradually able to talk with Rich about their future. She was resigned to her condition and ready to help Rich make the adjustments required. In effect, Muriel became an emotional care-giver for Rich, making decisions that normally would fall to their 'team'.

"Rich, we have to face up to the facts. I won't be able to continue with Mary Kay. We'll have to make arrangements so that my remaining income is protected and," she gulped, "the Caddy will have to go."

No! The pink Caddy, although revolting, was a symbol of Muriel's success. Rich could not imagine the garage without the Caddy. "C'mon Babe," he said. "Let's not go that far. You'll be getting better and . . ."

She shook her head. "No Rich, we must face up to the fact that I won't be getting better. What's best for me right now is to focus on putting things in order so that I won't have to worry about you."

Worry about me! Rich's eyes filled. For a moment, he was the emotional person of their early years. "But Hon, we'll work this out . . . somehow."

Muriel persisted, making financial arrangements that baffled Rich. Earned income from Mary Kay was transferred to Rich. Then one day, the Cadillac disappeared.

When the Caddy had left, Rich stood in the empty stall of the garage. For the first time, he realized the finality of circumstance. Again, it was Muriel whose strength of character set Rich on the path to recovery.

"Rich, you've got to get back on track at the U. I'll be perfectly fine with In-Home Care and you need to pay attention to your future."

For a time, Rich argued against her advice. Eventually, he gave in. His sense of relief was palpable. Muriel had given him an 'escape card' from the clinical environment of their home.

The next morning, Rich dressed in his academic uniform and bent to kiss Muriel's cheek. "Thanks Babe . . . for . . . everything. I'll be back early."

University and the Office of the Dean did not provide the refuge Rich expected. He found that he could not re-enter the political web he had so carefully woven. Although university life had not changed, Muriel's illness created a set of circumstances that confused Rich and reduced his ability to shape Deanly events. He was frequently called by the doctor or the In-Home Care Giver to make decisions for which he had no preparation. Several weeks passed and one such conversation convinced Rich that he must adapt to this new reality.

Rich's phone rang and he answered. "Hello, Rich Jessen speaking."

"Mr. Jessen. This is your doctor. I've reviewed the latest tests on your wife and need your consent for a change in her chemotherapy. Her condition is not improving and I'd like her to return to intensive care for the next few weeks. Would that be OK with you?"

Rich hesitated. "Well . . . yes . . . I guess so. What do I . . ."

"Good," the Doctor cut in. "I'll make the arrangements."

Rich disconnected. *Now what??* He realized that he was locked in a metaphor that required non-political behaviors.

A confused and distracted Associate Dean bounced between academy and hospital during Muriel's second chemotherapy. Dunkard reduced Rich's administrative load so that he had endless hours to contemplate life at the university without 'The Jessen Plan'; that clever strategy with its promise of power and reward. Rich realized that Muriel was no longer co-author of 'The Jessen Plan'.

Rich knew that his approach to university politics was enabled by Muriel's income and support. Without those props, he would need to make his future solely within the bounds of the university. He considered.

The central questions was, 'What was the nature of the future he wanted?' Was he to continue as an administrator; become a researcher-writer; or trudge toward retirement as a lowly faculty member? None of these options seemed especially attractive. Each required its measure of study – and work! There had to be a way!

Associate Dean could lead to Dean and upward mobility into Central Administration. However, this appealing road could only be travelled by those who had personal connections to the more lofty levels of the university. To date, Rich's only such connection was to Waldo Pearson, a connection lubricated by the fact that Rich had delivered on semester conversion, and threatened by the friction his use of hardball may have caused. Not a very appealing prospect.

Research and writing were given serious consideration. Rich knew that he could continue to generate meaningless papers and articles exploring the mysteries of higher education. He could escape this muddle by working with Carl Mertens. Mertens would supply the intellectual direction and access to the business world. Rich would, in effect, follow Mertens' lead, but would rarely receive much in the way of academic 'coin'. He shook his head, there had to be a better way. If only he had the position and money that could elevate him to the higher levels of the professorship and university decision making.

Money! It all came down to that! With Muriel alive, there was a promise of continuing revenue. None of the options he considered had more than adequate money attached to them. And without money, Rich couldn't see a way to acquire position in the University's power structure.

Rich sat rigid in his chair – hands clasping chair arms – eyes focused on his closed office door. Was there no other university actor who could open that door for him? Others he considered were instantly rejected as woefully inadequate as to money, scholarship and power. *Wait a minute!* Rich stood and began pacing around his office. *What about Hank?* Sure! Loras had the power that followed the flood of grant money! And didn't he find opportunity for publication? Finally, Hank had fanned Waldo Pearson with real hardball!

But there was more. Hank and his wife had divorced several years ago and he might be able to offer advice. Rich reached for his telephone and punched in Loras' number.

"Hank Loras here."

"This is Rich. I'd like to talk with you. Any chance I might come . . ."

"You bet!" Hank interrupted. "Tell you what. I've got a proposal to drop off with Dunkard. How's about I stop at your office in . . . say . . . half an hour?"

"That would be fine. See you then." Rich hung up. *Now there's a friend!* Hank was in fact, the only university acquaintance who had bothered to call in support of Muriel's illness. *The only one!*

Later, when Loras swept into Rich's office, gloom left by the open door. Rich came around his desk and shook Hank's hand. "I'm so glad you've come! I . . .," he gulped.

"Say no more, Old Buddy. I know how hard an adjustment you're facing, believe me."

They sat and Rich began. "How did you do it? I just can't seem to get a grip on where to go from here."

Loras sat, leaned back in his chair and sighed. "It wasn't easy. When my wife left me, I knocked around the U for more than a year. Then I hit pay dirt with the Center. Found the money and filled all my spare time with interesting stuff."

"I can see that it worked for you," Rich frowned. "But I can't for the life of me come up with anything like the Center."

Loras studied Rich for a moment. "Listen! I've been thinking about our discussion last year. You know, when we came up with the policy idea. Well, I've been watching the Federal Register and I think that we could roll that idea into a bigger Center, one where you could take a major part. Interested?"

Rich was stunned! "I can't believe that you're serious."

"Yep! Here's what I've in mind. The Feds are planning a policy conference in a couple of months. I've got a spot on that agenda, one where your background in higher education would fit right in. Let me send you some stuff that will bring you up to speed. Then we can talk strategy. OK?"

Rich took the option. "Sounds good to me. Send a packet this way and I'll think about how to reload higher education."

However, it was impossible to slow the process of change. Muriel's condition rapidly deteriorated and she was moved to the local hospice. As the weeks passed, she gradually became comatose. Rich could only sit by her bedside and hold an increasingly lifeless hand. During those moments, he searched in vain for her advice – now badly needed.

The packet from Loras lay on his university desk. Each time he attempted to review its contents, Rich was unable to visualize a pathway toward his future. At home he was immersed in a sea of self-pity, a victim of circumstance who now had no anchor to his only companion.

Emerging from despair was a slow process. Gradually, he realized that he had to renew his professional journey. The now six-fold table gave Rich the framework for his plans. He realized that the two ruling metaphors defined the options he faced. Committing to the collegial metaphor had its costs; endless argument and no guarantee of the benefit of power. On the other hand, collegiality would put him in the mainstream of academic life where publication and participation in university governance would bestow legitimacy.

The political metaphor was a more risky alternative. There would be no overt, academically-sanctioned status consequences. However, astute use of the political metaphor might result in serious influence over both College and University affairs – to say nothing of possible financial rewards.

Political and collegial contested for Rich's attention. While at the hospice, Rich felt an overpowering need to ask for Muriel's advice. Her mute form did not, of course, offer any guidance. At his desk, he studied his Metaphor Table, hoping that its display would enlighten his decision. Clearly, he needed to approach his problem in a different way.

The solution came to him one Sunday afternoon when he sat on the porch – now enclosed for winter and spring. Rich looked across at Muriel's empty chair. *If only ... what would she say if she were here?* He gazed at the Metaphor Table on his lap, focusing on the Character of Actors row. *How about?* "Choose both!" he exclaimed. Rich instantly saw the advantage of this duplicitous strategy. He could give the impression that he was among the collegial, while manipulating his colleagues using political tactics.

Rich savored the benefits. Influence and money, along with inclusion and academic status. He realized that this was what Muriel would likely have proposed. He nodded in appreciation at her empty chair.

What's next? The immediate 'next' followed Muriel's decline. Eventually, there was no hope for her and Rich made the decision to discontinue her life support. Loneliness was his constant companion as he awaited the outcome.

A final call from Muriel's nurse came late one night. Rich fumbled for the phone on his bedside table.

"Am I speaking to Richard Jessen?"

"Yes. This is Professor Jessen , who? . . ."

"This is Hospice calling. I'm sorry to have to tell you that your wife has passed. "

". . . ohhh . . . I guess . . . what? . . ."

"Please don't worry. We'll follow her directions as to all arrangements. If you can drop by in the morning, I'll go over everything with you. Will that by O.K.?"

"Yes . . . sure . . . thanks . . .," he replaced the receiver and sank back on his pillow. So it was over! What a short time! Images of their life together flicked across his consciousness. By morning, all that remained were the blank spaces of 'the arrangements'.

103

The next several days passed in a haze of images where Rich was the focus on unwanted attention. Nurses and administrators at the Hospice provided a kind of 'intensive care' for Rich; 'the arrangements' were managed to conform to the cultural practices of University City.

A memorial service was conducted at a local mortuary where subdued lighting and soft music enfolded Rich along with the few University attendees. Dean Dunkard was accompanied by his wife Evelyn; Hank Loras and Waldo Pearson sat together in the rear of the room; even the three Witches appeared to cast their spells; only Beverly and Carl Mertens appeared to be emotionally involved.

He was required to stand by Muriel's open casket to receive those who wished to pay their final respects to the deceased. Rich's sweaty hand touched that offered by each mourner and he nodded receipt of their comments.

Dunkard and wife led the small procession. "Oh Rich!" Evelyn Dunkard sobbed. "So sudden! And so sad!"

Rich gritted his teeth and reluctantly reached out to the first of the Witches.

It was Jerrilyn Barnes speaking for the coven. "We're so sorry," she burbled. "Anything we can do to help?"

"Thank you. I'm grateful for your sympathy," Rich lied and used both hands to pass the Witches along.

Rich nodded and looked ahead to Hank.

"So Good Buddy, the ordeal's over. Count on me to be ready when you need somebody to lean on."

"Thanks Hank," Rich mumbled. "I know, I know . . ."

Waldo Pearson was next in line. "You have the support of the entire university community. President Rose asked me to convey his sympathy and I'd like to add my condolences."

Rich took the offered hand and responded to Waldo's firm grip. This was a player that held many of the keys to Rich's future. "Thank you, Dr. Pearson. You have been a good friend and colleague. I'm only sorry that Muriel didn't get to know you."

Finally, the two Mertens closed the line of the concerned. "Rich, this is my wife, Beverly. We'd like you to know that we'll try to be of help in any way possible." The genuineness of Mertens' offer stood in marked contrast to the superficiality of the other mourners.

When everyone had left, Rich remained with the now-closed casket. After several minutes, an undertaker emerged. Following the customary routine, the man said, "According to your instructions, cremation will take place today and your wife's ashes will be available to deposit tomorrow."

". . . deposit . . ., " Rich stumbled. ". . . what . . . do you mean?"

The undertaker was puzzled. "Why, our instructions were to carry out the cremation and arrange for deposit of the ashes in one of our Memory Vaults."

Memory Vault! She must have given these instructions! Responsibility was immediately lifted from Rich's shoulders. All he needed to do was follow Muriel's lead. He mumbled agreement, "Of course . . . I'll return tomorrow . . . morning?"

Another arrangement was concluded and Rich arrived at the mortuary the next day. He was received by an undertaker who conducted him to the Memory Vault, a wall filled with gold-doored boxes. To Rich, these looked like old-time post office boxes.

"Here," the attendant said as he pushed an ornate cart along one wall of the Vault. "The location you selected is at eye-level, the better to assist loved ones in reflecting as to their loss." He removed a gold key from his pocket and opened a door. "Now Mr. Jessen, I'll leave you alone to place your wife's ashes in this vault. When you've finished, please report to our administrative office as there's a bit of paper work to complete."

Rich held the key in his hand, watching the retreating form. Alone with the urn containing Muriel's remains, he was unsure of how to proceed. Eventually, he lifted the surprisingly heavy vessel and slid it into its Vault. Closing and locking the door concluded the life he and Muriel had shared. Now everything would be up to him.

BOOK II
ACADEMIC LIFE

"To anyone versed in the intellectual thuggery

of the academic world, the tortuous byways

of (Antarctic) expedition psychology are child's play."

(Roland Huntford: Shackleton)

CHAPTER SEVEN

We got Bahls!

"At the devil's booth are all things sold".
(James Russell Lowell)

For many members of the professoriate, middle-age is a time when reflection and projection produce a belief that one is 'stuck'; there is no higher academic rank to seek nor are there obvious pathways to institutional power. Most of the 'stuck' fall into rigid patterns of behavior that nudge them along toward retirement. Escape from this condition usually takes one of two forms; adventure in love and/or business or, for a few, immersion in 'higher politics'.

The weeks following Muriel's death were marked by a lack of direction and confused consideration of the options facing Rich; he was becoming one of the 'stuck'. He engaged in a continuous dialogue with imagined members of the University community in which alternative futures were proposed, evaluated and discarded. Faculty members and administrative acquaintances served as protagonists for these imagined encounters.

Dean Dunkard advised an administrative path for Rich. 'You'll take my place as Dean of the College, then a move up to Central, probably as Waldo's assistant.' Rich envisioned Waldo's secretary controlling his every move - a miserable option!

Carl Mertens advocated using metaphors to prowl the corridors of University power. A seductive prospect, but there was no obvious point of entry to this journey.

The most appealing scenario involved Hank Loras and his Center; access to money, publication and possible national fame. Clearly this was worth considering!

Over time, these three paths began to come together. *What would Muriel say?* Rich asked himself this question again and again. Gradually, he realized that she would see the promise in each path and she would suggest that he weld the three into his strategic direction. *Take it all!* Rich gave voice to his new strategy, "Continue as Associate Dean. Use Loras' Center to provide the financial muscle. Refine the Metaphor Table so that I can influence . . .," His voice faded as he edited his thoughts. "What I mean is control – not just influence!"

In a roundabout way, Muriel also provided a correct image for the new Rich.

Carl Mertens' wife, Beverly, was assisting Rich in disposing of Muriel's considerable wardrobe. "You know Rich," Beverly said. "Muriel's clothes are very stylish. In fact, I'll bet they're worth a lot of money. Have you thought about what to do with her wardrobe?"

"Well, no," Rich mumbled. "Guess I could donate, say to Goodwill ."

"That would be a waste!" Beverly exclaimed. "Tell you what. Let's take Muriel's things to Second Life Clothiers."

"Who's that?"

"They deal in up-scale, high-quality clothes. Come on, let's give them a try."

Rich was amazed at Second Life. Rack on rack of major name brands offered buyers images of sensuality, success and power. It took only a moment for him to realize that he, too, could acquire a new image. The negotiation took a bit longer. In the end, Rich traded Muriel's wardrobe for a new look for himself, one that was endorsed by the Mertens.

"Pretty sharp," Carl enthused. "Wouldn't believe that clothes could make such a difference!"

"See," chuckled Beverly. "Told you so!"

Beverly wasn't the only one who had something to say that had direct bearing on Rich's strategy. An early morning phone call started the ball rolling.

"Rich? This is Hank Loras. You gotta minute?"

"Sure. What's up?" Rich hooked his right foot on the open lower desk drawer and crossed his ankles. He admired his newly acquired Gucci loafers with their horsebit clasps. How lucky he was to have found Second Life Clothiers! Why, the loafers were actually free!

Hank interrupted these reflections, "Remember how we talked about the Americans with Disabilities Act? Well, there's a big conference in DC next week where the feds are gonna lay out this year's funding priorities. I figure we have to be there."

Rich sat up abruptly. "You think there might be money in it for us? Seems to me that the Act is a little outside our experience."

"That's right, so far as it goes. But the Act is a fairly new federal initiative so there's no history. And, the competition will be wide open."

"So what are you saying? You think we should be at the table next week?"

"Absolutely! We have a connection that could pay off. By the way, your old colleague from Louisiana Methodist will be in charge of the meeting, Mike Bahls. Remember him?"

Mike! Rich recalled the hours when he and Bahls had planned their respective futures while they were graduate students at Methodist. Bahls had elected to focus on education policy while Rich saw opportunity inside the academy.

"Yeah, I remember Mike. Haven't had any contact with him for the past several years. Didn't even know that he was involved in DC."

"He's not only involved," Hank said. "Bahls is the new leader for the Americans with Disabilities program. So he's the one who's likely to set the funding priorities."

A familiar wave of professional jealousy raced through his mind and he clutched the phone for support. Rich hesitated, "Well, I suppose we should attend. What are the dates?"

"The conference is set for the twelfth through the fifteenth. I figure we should fly out on the eleventh, back on the sixteenth. That work for you?"

Rich paged through his desk calendar. "It's a little tight, but I think I can get one of my grad students to cover my classes. I'll need to skip a meeting with the Dean. No problem there, he'll see the trip as a hell of an opportunity."

"OK. Pencil it in and I'll arrange for the tickets. Talk to you later." Loras hung up.

Isn't that interesting! Rich leaned back in his chair, lacing his fingers together behind his head. His mind raced at the prospect of the kind of academic empire that he and Hank could build with federal money.

Louisiana Methodist University had been a latecomer to the 'university club'. Founded as a liberal arts college for the faithful, Louisiana Methodist

College (LMC) evolved in the 1960's into a non-sectarian institution with tenuous religious roots. In a few short years, LMC found that Master's Degrees in Education and the other social sciences served its growing clientele - and made money. As the Directors of what was then still a 'college' noted, market share could be increased by offering a wider range of graduate degrees – including the Ph.D.. It was easy to convince the accreditors that LMC should become LMU.

A nation-wide publicity campaign and a series of faculty lectures at liberal arts colleges produced a steady flow of students for LMU graduate programs. These colleges were often 'bottom feeders', not well known – with indifferent quality faculty and students. When one of the 'star' LMU lecturers came to LECNA College in western Nebraska, Richard Jessen was among the seniors who found the LMU message compelling. Enrollment was ensured when LMU offered Rich a full scholarship for study in the new Economics Department. Now, here he was – reconnecting to LMU – and Mike Bahls.

There was little rest for Rich the night before the Washington trip. He revisited the decision he had made at LECNA. He replayed images of life at Methodist which was dominated by the superior intellect of Bahls and the surpassing beauty of his new wife, Beth. When Rich awoke from these dreams, his pillow soaked in sweat; a fresh pillow and a vow to relax had no effect on his uncertainty

Six o'clock came slowly. When it did, he gave up on attempts at sleep and stumbled through his morning rituals. He worked his way down the stairs into the kitchen.

Coffee! That'll help! The brew was soon ready and Rich sipped at the first cupful. *Damn! Burned my tongue!* Pain triggered self-pity. Should he call in sick to Hank?

No, that wouldn't work. He was committed to travel to Washington, a supplicant, begging for money. Shouldn't Bahls be coming to him? After all, he had the track record of three edited books; fifteen co-authored articles; Associate Dean! Confidence oozed back.

Rich finished his coffee and set his cup in the sink. He opened the hall closet and carefully removed his Pierre Cardin overcoat from its hanger. Again, he blessed Second Life Clothiers for providing the style he deserved. His leather briefcase in hand, he opened the door into the garage.

Rich ran his hand over the sleek outlines of the SL as he passed by. The Mercedes was another symbol of his accomplishment; an object that told other motorists of his wealth and importance. So what if it was used? He backed into Locust Avenue and set off to the airport.

Turns in the drive to the airport were matched by turns of anxiety and confidence. Anxiety prompted tentative turns; other drivers were seen as threats. When confidence took over, the Merc wove through traffic at speed. He was evidently not yet totally ready to be the 'new Rich Jessen'.

The airport ramp entrance ended his mental turmoil for the moment. He drove up the spiral inclines – CLOSED – CLOSED – SPACE AVAILABLE. The Mercedes slid into the first open space and Rich collected his coat and briefcase.

Hank was waiting at the first-class ticket counter. "Hey, Rich! Over here."

Rich followed the beckoning hand. "Aren't you in the wrong line? This is first-class only."

"Listen. If we're gonna come up with a good story line for this conference, we need privacy. Anyway, there's always a few extra bucks in my program for travel."

When they had checked in, Hank led the way to the departure gate. He halted and waved at a seated woman. "Say Rich, you know Felicity Berland?"

A beautiful young woman looked up at Rich with a gorgeous smile. "Oh Professor Jessen. I've been dying to meet you." She leaped to her feet and offered a shapely hand.

Rich was speechless. This creature! Dying to meet him?

"That's right," Hank added. "She's been talking about nothing else since we planned this trip."

Why can't I say something? Rich stood and grinned helplessly. But no words occurred to him. He was mesmerized by the bobbed black hair and brown eyes behind shaded glasses. A beige blouse, cut to show a minute gold chain and . . . his eyes roved over the vision, his mind cataloging attributes.

Felicity gazed at him with interest, waiting for some sign of life.

The impasse might have continued for several minutes, but Hank intervened. "Let's catch a cup of coffee. We'll have plenty of time before boarding."

"Good idea. Come along Professor Jessen." Felicity took Rich's arm and guided him across the concourse to a coffee shop.

"You two grab that table," Hank said. "I'll collect the coffee. Any special orders?"

Felicity saw that Rich was unable to cope with the question. "I'll have a decaf mocha. Would you like the same Professor Jessen?"

Mocha? "Umm . . . well . . .," Rich stammered, "I guess . . . OK . . ."

Overpowered by the image before him, Rich could only sit and gaze at Felicity. His whole being was focused on her face and its frame of glossy hair. He could not help comparing her to Muriel, a quickly-fading image that could not fit into this place and time.

Hank returned with their drinks and joined them. He raised his cup. "Here's to success in DC! May the feds smile upon us!"

The two men drank. Felicity sipped through a straw. Her lips curled sensuously around the straw and her eyes sought Rich. He attempted to speak as he swallowed; coffee and air mixed to produce a fit of coughing and sputtering.

"A little too hot, eh?" Hank asked.

"... guess so ...," Rich gulped.

"Anyway, it's delicious. Don't you agree Professor Jessen?" Felicity said.

"Yes ... it's very good." Rich recovered sufficiently to attempt a conversation. "What are you studying, Ms Berland?"

"Oh, I'm in Higher Education. But I've become interested in your work in economics of education and the importance of your research for public policy."

Work? Research? Policy? Rich riffled through the file drawer of concepts in his mind. It was empty. He could think of nothing he had written that had any relationship to educational practice nor to public policy. He retreated to his usual question-asking as a defense. "Come now, Ms Berland. You'll have to be more specific. After all, there's a lot of ground to cover in that statement."

She was up to the challenge. "I'm referring to your work with Professor Loras on deinstitutionalization of handicapped people. I think it's wonderful that the two of you are taking on this important issue." Her eyes shown in admiration.

This was nearly too much for Rich. He teetered at the brink of incoherence.

"Your attention please. Flight 666 for Washington, DC is now ready for boarding. Will first-class passengers please come forward."

Saved! Rich stood and held out his hand to Felicity. "Come along, Ms Berland. What's your seat number?"

"I'm way back in row 36. I know that you two have work to do, so don't worry, I'll do some reading for my term paper."

Hank and Rich walked away – Rich with occasional glances at Felicity. "How come she isn't in first class," he asked.

"Can't use University funds to buy high-priced tickets for students. She'll be with us in DC. Got a good mind in addition to a great body. You agree?"

Rich had been summing up his impressions of Felicity along those lines. "Roger to that," he said.

Their seats were mid-way in the first-class section with Rich on the aisle. He surrendered the Pierre Cardin overcoat to a steward and settled in his seat. As he reached for his seat belt, Felicity entered the cabin and made her way toward him.

"Hi," she said. "I see that you two are ready for some serious work."

". . . umm . . . yes . . . we'll sure get to it . . .," Rich mumbled as she passed by.

"Guess we got our marching orders," Hank chuckled. "That gal is a real workaholic. Most people can't believe that there's a first-rate mind in that package."

"How did you hook up with her?" Rich asked.

"Came out of nowhere. I thought she was just another eager beaver grad student 'til I read a couple of her course papers. They were so good that I used them as a springboard for a journal article. Funny thing, she caught me at it and suggested that we collaborate on a series of papers on the topic. Best suggestion I ever had."

"You serious?" Rich asked. "I've had a tough time making any use of student work."

"Same with me. But Felicity has the big picture in mind and can predict just what journal editors are looking for."

Rich rubbed his chin and a thoughtful expression creased his forehead. He meditated on this gift. How could he . . . ? Possibilities occupied him until they had reached cruising altitude.

Hank brought him back to the present. "Well, we'd better get goin'. Here's my idea on an approach to the feds." He opened his briefcase and handed a sheet of single-spaced University bond.

'Institute for Community Living: Addressing the Needs of Handicapped Persons.' This title was followed by several paragraphs where Hank outlined how the University was organized to respond to the new federal initiative.

Rich scanned the paper and frowned. "You know this won't sell. The U is very stingy with the 'Institute' label; takes about two years to get one approved. And, the 'Community Living' label is a pretty big mouthful."

"Yeah, I know," Hank said. "But we gotta start somewhere close to where the money is."

"Suppose so," Rich mused. "Another thing, this sounds like you plan to provide direct service to the disabled and handicapped. That right?"

"That's the general idea. I figure that the bucks will flow to those who connect these folks with their circumstances."

"Would you two be having breakfast?" A stewardess smiled down at them, her hand on Rich's seatback.

Rich ignored her and continued reading.

Hank grinned. "Don't think so. But we'd each like a cup of coffee."

"Coming right up!"

"They sure are pests," Rich exclaimed. "They make me nervous with all their questions." For him, people like stewardesses were invisible; functionaries who should do what they were told. There was no veneer of politeness to connect him to the world of service.

"First thing to do is change the name," he handed the paper back to Hank. "We need to come up with a name that sounds good, but doesn't need University approval."

They considered options. 'Program – too common'; 'Initiative – meaningless'.

"Say," Rich said. "What about 'Academy'? Sounds like something academic. You know – bunch of scholars."

"Sounds like a possible. But 'Academy' for what? Doesn't connect too closely to direct service to handicapped."

"That's just it," Rich said. "I can't see how any of us can serve the handicapped population. We'd just get mired down in toilet training."

Hank chuckled. "You just made a joke. But I see your point. None of us has worked with these people. We could be setting ourselves up for failure."

Coffee arrived on plastic trays with linen napkins and airline china. This was as close to 'direct service' they would get. They sipped and stirred for several minutes.

"Be a hell of a note if we got crossways with both University politics and federal policy," Hank growled.

Policy! There was the ticket! "How's this?" Rich asked. "The feds cook up new policies like ADA in response to political pressure, right?"

"Sure, so what?"

"What if we propose to study fed policy and to do research that shows what happens to the handicapped when they try to fit into jobs and the like? Then we're on new territory and I'll bet there's no competition."

"That's right," Hank nodded enthusiastically. "I've been at several DC meetings where there's hand wringing about the lack of research dealing with fed policy."

"Let's try 'The Policy Studies Academy'. That'll make us stand out and we can do most anything under that label."

"Sounds like a plan." Hank placed a blank paper on his seat-table. "Let's see if we can think of a few talking points so we can try the idea out on Bahls."

They considered one-line statements for the better part of an hour. When the plane began its descent into National Airport, they had a short list that included:

Policy analysis for government accountability
Tracking ADA through research
Graduate programming for policy fellows

Rich's eyes focused on the last statement. *Maybe Felicity will come aboard as a policy fellow.* His thoughts ranged over the possibilities that her participation might involve; the research team, graduate seminars, one-on-one advising! Why she could collaborate with him on . . .

"Hey," Hank elbowed him. "What's going on in your head? You're mumbling a mile a minute."

"Oh, just wondering what kinds of things we could do with some real money."

"Yeah," Hank mused. "I'm with you on that. And, I have an idea. Let's run this by Felicity; she can put some meat on these bones. We could even have a working paper by the end of the conference."

Rich snapped his tray table in place and sat back. "Isn't that asking a lot? You know, a grad student and . . ."

"Don't worry about her. She's got a better feel," Hank laughed, "I mean for the substance we'll need in order to get a hearing."

Rich found himself resenting Hank's cheap joke. *Felicity would never . . .*

119

Wheels thumped on runway and reversed thrust pressed Rich against his seat belt. First-class passengers disembarked and they waited for Felicity.

Rich saw her in the throng of passengers where she sparkled with energy and . . . *class!* He experienced an immediate comparison between this youthful image and his last flight with Muriel. Their last year's winter vacation in Acapulco ended with a dreary delay in Houston and an incredible struggle with Muriel's purchases which were distributed among several overhead compartments. By the time they had collected their belongings the plane was empty and they weren't speaking to one another. *How different it would be to travel with Felicity!*

"How was the trip Professor Jessen?"

A picture of Muriel in her Mexican straw hat – adorned with baggage – prompted the answer. "Terrible! I mean . . . it was . . .," he stammered.

"Oh, I'm so sorry! Come, let's collect our bags." She led the way down the concourse.

"Whaddya mean terrible," Hank asked. "We had the first-class treatment and got a lot done."

"Nothing . . . just thinking about a different trip, I guess." Rich watched the sway of Felicity's hips as she found a path through the oncoming passengers.

Bags in hand, they hailed a cab. Felicity took the center of the rear seat, between the two men. It was a medium-sized car and Rich instantly felt the heat of Felicity's thigh against his.

Sexuality hadn't been a major item in his recent life. The final version of Muriel just wasn't a turn-on. For some people, sex was sublimated and folded into other strivings. Others simply forgot sex and shaped their lives without it; Rich was one of these. The small movements of Felicity began to awaken old drives that further confused his emotions. He attempted to avoid these distractions by looking out the cab windows.

"This the first time you have visited DC?" Rich asked.

"Oh yes!" Felicity gushed, looking out one side window and then the other. As she swiveled, her shoulder and breast brushed against Rich – a sensation from his past.

The passing landscape blurred, distorted by proximity and heat. He was silent, enjoying these new sensations.

Soon the cab pulled up at the entrance to the Mayflower Hotel. A uniformed bellman opened Rich's door.

"Welcome to the Mayflower," he said. "Please proceed to the registration desk. I'll arrange for your luggage."

"Oh my!" exclaimed Felicity. "Just like the movies!"

"Yes, it's pretty fancy," added Rich.

"You ain't seen nothing yet," said Hank. "This is a classy place. Just the kind of setting Bahls would choose for the conference."

They checked in and Hank led them to the Mayflower dining room. When they were seated, he set the ground rules. "This is a working lunch so I've got the check. Order whatever you wish. You go first Felicity."

"Thanks, I'll have the Waldorf Salad and black coffee. How about you, Professor Jessen."

"I . . . guess the same for me."

"Boy, you two are really big spenders," Hank moaned. "Anyway, I'm for the New York Strip."

The meals arrived and Hank began the 'working' side of lunch. "Here's what we need to get done today and tomorrow. First, we need to agree on our objectives. Second, we need to leave an Executive Summary of our ideas with the feds. So, let's get goin'. Rich, you outline our basic idea for Felicity."

This was more like it. He fell into his pedantic teacher role. "We believe that the feds make policy in response to advocacy, usually without a sound policy analysis."

Felicity nodded. "I agree. There isn't much serious research behind most legislation."

"Correct. Now, we think that a Policy Studies Academy with a research focus would appeal to the administrators who have to carry out legislative mandates."

"Why, that's a wonderful idea," Felicity smiled and took a small sip of her coffee. "It's especially true for the Americans with Disabilities Act. I looked through all the major journals and the Congressional Record and found little of substance."

Rich returned this verbal volley and the academic game was on. Comments concerning basic research, policy analysis, public policy, and university capacity flew between Rich and Felicity.

Hank worked at his New York Strip and mumbled contributions between mouthfuls. "Sounds like you have the ideas we'll need for the feds. Felicity, you think you could work them into a short concept paper by tomorrow?"

"Sure, no problem. In fact, the term paper I'm working on is along these lines."

"Tell you what," Hank folded his napkin and pushed back from the table. "Rich and I will hit the reception tonight. If you can put something together, we can meet for an early breakfast. OK?"

Rich was appalled at the idea that Felicity should work while they partied. "I wonder if . . ."

"Nope," Hank broke in. "Don't think about working on the paper. You and I need to connect with Bahls and get his attention."

They left the restaurant and watched Felicity into the hotel elevator; another job passed on to an eager grad student.

The reception was in a third-floor suite where the sounds of cocktail party dominated the hallway through an open door.

"Sounds like a good time," Hank observed. "Hope there's some booze left."

"You pretty sure Bahls will be here?" Rich asked.

"Yep. I emailed him and told him that you would be coming along. He wants to hear what you've been doing."

Rich reviewed several opening comments. 'Hello, Mike. So nice to see you.' Too formal. 'Hi Mike. How're things in DC?' Too familiar. *What should?*

Bahls was standing at the entrance to the suite, cocktail in hand. "Hi Hank. Who's the distinguished gent with you?" He held out a hand to Rich.

Six foot one! Rich still looked up to Bahls – as was always the case at LMU. *Slender!* Rich took an unconscious deep breath to ease the pressure against his belt. *Those clothes!* He noticed Mike's glance at his shoes. *Thank God for Second Life!*

"Well, hello Mike. It's great to see you after all these years."

"We've both covered a lot of ground. I see by the journals that you're one of the leading lights in economics of education."

"Maybe," said Rich, "but we're a long way from the center of things out at Midwest."

"Let's see if we can fix that," Bahls took his arm. "Come on in. There are some folks you need to meet. Hank, you know the drill. Get Rich a drink and help yourself."

Bahls moved smoothly away, the crowd seeming to part for him and his smile.

Rich watched while Hank poured two scotches – envious of the attention Bahls was receiving.

"Sure is popular," Hank observed.

"He was always that way," Rich said. "Back at LMU Mike was our leader and the darling of the faculty."

"Seems like he parlayed that into a cushy job here in DC."

"What exactly does he do?" Rich asked.

Hank swirled the liquor in his glass. "Far as I know, he's the one the Department looks to as translator of congressional mandates. What I mean is that Bahls decides who gets what level of support."

Jealousy nearly overcame Rich. Here was a person who wasn't stuck. Far from it. Mike had his hands on the federal spigot and would be careful how he directed the money flow. *God! How I hate that guy!*

The object of hate approached. "Sure happy to see you Rich. Beth and I have missed you and . . . your wife. Lot's of good times at LMU. Right?"

Rich clinked glasses with Bahls. "You bet!" The lie was concealed behind the rim of his highball glass. "Unfortunately, Muriel just passed away."

"I'm so sorry to hear that!" Bahls commiserated. "That will shock Beth. Please accept our sympathy." He drank and resumed his 'fed' manner. "This conference is very important and I hope you'll be able to give us your ideas."

"That's why we're here," Hank said. "We'd sure like to connect our policy studies group to the ADA agenda."

"What's that?" Bahls asked. "I haven't heard of your group. Tell me more." He looked at Rich.

"It's like this," Rich responded. "Hank and I have developed a Policy Studies Academy at Midwest. What we hope to offer to ADA is the capacity to examine policy from all angles; political, social, economic."

Bahls was clearly taken with the idea. He began to speak. "That's marvelous, why..."

Hank finished the thought. "What we need to do is share a concept paper with you before we go too far. We'd like to meet for dinner tomorrow after the conference. Would that work for you?"

Bahls considered. "Umm... I guess so. Ask me tomorrow morning and I'll confirm." He moved off in the direction of the bar.

Rich stared at Mike's back. "Sounds like a turn-off. I thought we had him interested."

"Possible," Hank observed, "but we have no meat on those conceptual bones. If he pressed us, we might blow the opportunity to tap into his money."

"OK, I hope you're right." They headed to the bar for a refill.

The balance of the evening was taken up with casual conversations between Hank and other attendees. Rich was an observer, impressed with a new language, one that described the barriers facing the handicapped in various social and employment situations. The longer he listened, the more convinced he became that he and Hank had no contributions to make to the ADA. Depression settled in and Rich hovered around the bar for the balance of the reception.

Retirement to his room brought no relief. Rich passed the night comparing images of himself with the luster of Mike's persona. He was, in a word, stuck! Dawn brought no new light and he dressed slowly. Then, reluctantly, descended to the breakfast meeting Hank had scheduled.

Felicity and Hank were already seated in the Mayflower dining room. She looked up as he approached. "Oh, Professor Jessen. I'm so happy to see you and to hear your ideas about the Academy."

Academy? What . . . ? He slowly seated himself and opened his napkin, considering how he could begin. "Let's see what you have developed. Then I can fit my ideas into your framework."

"Good idea, Rich," Hank said. "Felicity has some fine concepts that need only a little tweaking. Go ahead, show Rich your paper."

She moved her chair around to Rich's side of the table. "Well, it's twelve pages so maybe we should start with the Executive Summary." She held out a single sheet of paper.

Rich scanned the document. The opening paragraph: 'Public policy is usually focused on a specific problem or social group. Policies are designed to impact a limited set of indicators through a simplified model of cause and effect.' The paragraph went on to argue that this was a linear approach to human systems that were infinitely more complex.

"I like that paragraph. It gets the reader's attention. In fact, it's pretty much along the lines I've been working on." Rich smiled mendaciously. "Now let's see where you're taking it."

"I thought it would be useful to say something about the kinds of things the Academy might address." Felicity pointed to the next paragraph. 'The Academy pursues two parallel research agendas. The principal focus of Academy research has to do with the experiences of those affected by policy initiatives.'

Hank was following along. "I think this will catch Mike's eye. Especially if we can emphasize the idea of 'experiences'."

"Yes. That's what I had in mind. If we can give voice to the disabled, we'll be unique." Felicity said.

"Give voice to the disabled?" Rich nodded. "That would be a very different approach to research. Is it feasible?"

"Could be," Hank said. "We need to be different. And, this plays into the advocacy basis for the ADA."

"OK. So what's the other agenda," Rich asked.

"This one's a bit more complicated." Felicity read from her paper. "Policies address systemic problems, thus relevant research must be similarly constructed."

"Sounds sensible, but what does it mean?" Rich looked puzzled.

Felicity responded. "The way I see it is that the Academy needs to develop models of policy systems that are fully identified."

There were too many new ideas in this sentence for Rich. *Systems? Models? Fully identified?* He clearly needed a professorial question to regain control of the conversation. "You're articulating an idea I have in mind. That is, we must present an innovative approach to policy studies. These two sentences do it well. Focus on the disabled and the social system to identify policy models." He sat back with a smile.

"Oh, I'm so pleased that we agree," Felicity returned the smile.

"Well," Hank said. "Seems like we have something for Bahls. Felicity, would you polish the Executive Summary so we can take it to Mike at the end of the conference?"

"Sure thing. I can skip the afternoon conference and have it ready on time."

They were all smiling now; intellectuals who had feasted on a conceptual meal.

The conference agenda delved into the five Titles of the ADA. This dreary journey taxed Rich's attention. Every few minutes he shifted in his chair, struggling to keep his eyes open. At the same time, he attempted to connect the ideas in the Executive Summary with Bahl's description of the Act.

"He or she has a physical or mental impairment that substantially limits one of more of his/her major life activities," Bahls droned. "You all can see how wide ranging the catchment is for the Act."

Catchment? Mental impairment? Work on the ADA wouldn't be at all like real educational research. Especially the way Felicity put it. Why, Mike didn't have a clue . . .

Every one of the five Titles challenged Rich's understanding. He was stunned by the requirement for employers to 'restructure jobs', 'layout workstations', 'modify equipment'. This was a dose of reality for the disconnected educational researcher. *How the . . . ?*

The flood of new ideas continued for the balance of the conference. During the breaks, the three gathered to polish Felicity's paper. It was ready 'on time'. Felicity left in mid-afternoon of the last day to print the final version.

Rich and Hank sat together as Bahls was summing up. "I'm happy to say that several of you have come up with innovative ways to help us make this important policy a success. In the months ahead, we'll be requesting proposals for research and development projects. I'll be looking for your input."

As they filed out of the meeting room, Bahls was waiting for them. "Rich, Hank told me a bit about your Academy this morning. I'd like to hear more so I hope we can do drinks and dinner."

"Well . . . sure," Rich grappled for a response. "We have an Executive Summary of our Academy that we can share with you."

"Great!" Bahls clapped him on the shoulder. "Knew I could count on you Rich! I've a few things to clean up here. Then I'll meet you in the lobby bar. In a half-hour or so."

Hank waved a hand. "We'll be there."

They followed the crowd to the mezzanine escalator. "So, how do we play this?" Rich asked.

"I think it's time Bahls met Felicity," Hank said. "As you might have noticed she makes a hell of a favorable impression. Let's have her walk Mike through her paper. You can chime in to add some of your 'academic integrity' stuff where it's needed."

At the bottom of the escalator, Hank led the way to the bar. "Better get a table, Rich. I'll call Felicity and have her join us. We've got a couple of hours before we need to catch our plane."

Rich forced his way through the post-conference bar crowd to the dining room. He was surprised to find Bahls waiting for him.

"Hi Rich. Where are your partners?"

"On their way. We'd better get a table. We only have a couple of hours until plane time."

"That's too bad," Bahls signaled to the maitre de. "I had hoped we could go into your Academy idea in depth."

They followed the formally-dressed host to a corner table. A waiter was instantly hovering and drinks were ordered.

"Bring me a dry martini with two olives," Bahls said. "What's your pleasure Rich?"

"I think I'll just have a cup of coffee. I don't like to drink before traveling."

"I'm glad we're alone," Bahl's said. "I'd like to lay out a proposal for you. If your Academy shapes up along the lines you suggest, I think I can assure you of substantial funding."

"But what about peer review of proposals?" Rich asked. "The competition will be pretty tough if this conference is any sign of interest."

"Sure," smiled Bahls. "But I control the purse strings and can structure reviews to get what I want."

"Sounds good. We can put money to good use and probably do your program a good turn."

"All that's fine, but I am interested in a quid pro quo."

Rich frowned. *Quid pro quo?* "I'm sure we'd be happy to help in any way we can."

"OK, here's what I want. I'm pretty sick of the scene in DC and am looking to move to a university position. So here's my question. Can you deliver an appointment?"

Rich reflected for a moment. Sure, he could manipulate Dean Drunkard to do most anything. But what did this all mean? "If Midwest would work for you, I can almost guarantee a post. Why, we have a faculty slot opening this fall and . . ."

"I'm not talking about some junior rank," Bahls rejected. "What I want is full professor rank and some significant budgetary control."

"That's tough. We don't . . ."

"Let me finish. I know that you're unlikely to have the dollars. That's why we need to deal on the Academy. I'll fund it and you get me the position. What say?"

Rich's mind raced. *Money! Real power!* But Bahls would be calling the shots. Well, without Mike, there wouldn't be any shots to call.

"It's a deal," Rich said. "I can get our Dean to come along if there's federal money."

The martini and coffee arrived. They raised glass and cup to cement the deal. They drank and smiled.

"Hey! What you two grinning about?" asked Hank as he swept toward the table, Felicity in tow.

"Just reminiscing about old times," Bahls said.

"This is Felicity Berland," Hank said. "She's a member of our Academy Team."

Bahls gaped at the package. ". . . pleased . . . to meet you!" He stood, grasped the offered hand and held out a chair for her.

"Oh, thank you Dr. Bahls!" Felicity purred. "I've followed your work on ADA and, I must say that I'm impressed."

They sat, ordered and dinner proceeded rapidly; the kind of pleasant social event Rich remembered from LMU. Bahls was the raconteur of old, keeping everyone involved and laughing.

At the end of the meal, Bahls leaned forward and looked at each of the three Midwest representatives, one at a time. "Since you've got to leave soon, I want to be sure we're all on the same page. I like your Academy concept. I can tell that it's not a fully-developed idea. However it has the features I've been looking for. In the next funding cycle, we'll have something like ten million for support of policy research. I think a good chunk of that could come your way."

Ten million dollars! A good chunk! Rich barely resisted licking his lips. Clammy hands gripped one another under the edge of the table.

"Sounds like exactly what we need to give the Academy national visibility," Hank said.

"I agree," Rich added.

"What about you Ms Berland," Bahls asked. "How do you see this working out?"

"It seems to me that your support would help us give voice to the handicapped. We could connect their experiences and concerns to the policy initiatives that drive organizations." She smiled at Bahls. "Everyone wins with the right approach."

Bahls' attention focused on Felicity. "I like the sound of that! 'Voice to the handicapped'; I can see that you have the big picture. If there are more grad students like you at Midwest, there's no end in sight to what might be accomplished."

"An accurate observation," Rich said. "We have the talent and the training to conduct first-rate academic research."

"I know, I know," Bahls said over his shoulder. "Now Ms Berland, tell me more about this policy system idea."

Rich began to raise his hand to signal a new contribution. "I . . .,"

Hank's foot connected with his ankle and the sentence died.

The two men were silent listeners to a dialogue between Felicity and Bahls. It was much like a verbal tennis match where first one then the other would serve up a concept for the other's return. Despite Bahls' expertise, Felicity held her own and, so far as Rich was concerned, came out the winner.

Hank finally intervened. He waved their airplane tickets. "Say, we need to call this off. Our flight leaves in two hours and we need to check out pronto."

"I'm sorry to hear that," Bahls said. "This has been a very interesting conversation." He seemed not to realize that Hank and Rich were only bystanders.

"I agree," gushed Felicity. "I never thought policy folks were so well informed."

Bahls laughed. "We're not all old buffaloes."

Hank tried again. "Well, we need to shove off. I hope we can be in touch as your project moves along."

"No problem," Bahls said. "I'll be sure that you get any RFPs that will work into your Academy."

"We'll appreciate any information you can send our way," Hank shook hands with Bahls.

"Rich," said Bahls, "I'm glad we could connect again. If everything works out, we may be able to collaborate on one of our policy studies. Please give my best to ... your wife." He obviously had forgotten that Muriel was dead.

Rich extended a moist hand to Bahls. "Good to see you. I'll be looking forward to the future." He released Bahls' hand and was chagrined to see Mike wipe his hand on his trousers.

Felicity was saved until last. "Ms Berland, this was a very pleasant evening. I know we'll find ways to continue our discussion."

Rich watched her face light up. *Shit! That guy!* He savored various comments he might make. Well anyway, Felicity wasn't staying in DC.

The trip to the airport was a blur of lights. There was little conversation as each was engaged in a review of the conference and meetings with Bahls. Check in and boarding were extensions of the cab ride; three individuals in cocoons of thought, waiting to break out with new professional opportunity.

Hank and Rich were again in first-class where Rich waited for Felicity to board.

She came down the aisle. When her eyes met Rich's, her face lit up as it had for Bahls. "Thank you so much, Professor Jessen. This was a wonderful experience and, I hope, the beginning of some productive work." She passed on to the second class cabin.

Once in the air, the cabin lights dimmed and passengers relaxed. Rich replayed the trip over and over. Content gradually disappeared and the image of Felicity sharpened. Would she ask to become his student? Could he soften his style so that she might be attracted to him? What if she was?

These questions preoccupied him for the better part of an hour. He smiled at possible answers. There were no dangers in the possibilities as he saw them. Then, the grinning image of Mike Bahls worked its way into his consciousness.

Half-asleep, Rich shrank from this apparition. An image of Bahls was joined by Felicity. Both pointed toward him, wide grins on their faces. Rich twisted in his seat. There was no escape . . .

"Ladies and gentlemen. We are beginning our descent. Please place your seat backs in their upright position and stow your tray tables. We will be on the ground in ten minutes."

Rich pressed his seat button and sat up. He looked across at Hank who was chuckling as he scribbled in his pocket notebook.

"What's so funny?"

"Oh, I was just summarizing our meeting," Hank said. "Here take a look at this." He handed Rich the notebook.

Rich turned on his overhead light and read.

WHEN THE FEDS SEND OUT

PROPOSAL CALLS

WE DON'T WORRY CAUSE

WE GOT BAHLS!!

"Say that's pretty good!"

CHAPTER EIGHT

Go Fish!

"A bad day fishing beats a good day working."

Unlike his colleagues, Rich Jessen didn't get spring fever. His daily routines varied scarcely at all. He taught his course (1), advised his student (1), served on College and University committees (10), and fulfilled the minimal expectations for Associate Dean. His interaction with others followed the pattern established over recent years; powerful mantras, supercilious comments, pontifical statements, all designed to keep others at their appropriate distance.

Until this spring, when the events of the week in Washington occupied ever-larger slices of his day. Felicity was always at the center of his thoughts. When he saw her on campus, he made detours to accompany her, once actually waiting outside the ladies room in the Student Union. On the occasions of her visits to his office, he gloried in her presence and in what he perceived to be her admiring glances. In this budding relationship, Rich's behavior was completely out of character. Gone were scheming, intimidation, self-righteousness and those related attributes that defined Professor Richard Jessen.

Instead, he was respectful, an understanding counselor and academic mentor. That is, when he could tear his thoughts away from Felicity's fresh presence. When he reviewed their meetings, he would take pride in his ability to amaze her with his superior knowledge and he would agonize over the adolescent errors that crept into his conversation. On the whole, he was excited by the ideas and perspectives Felicity presented. He became committed to shape his behavior to the image he believed she held of 'her professor'.

Thoughts of Mike Bahls were a strong competitor for Rich's mental attention. The prospects of funding, national visibility and academic fame were focal points for his new-found energy. Gone was the sense of being 'stuck' in his career. Despair had vanished in the bright light of opportunity shining out from Washington. Continual phone calls from Hank Loras kept the light burning.

"Hey Rich! I just got off the phone with Bahls. We need to move fast if we're gonna land him at Midwest. He told me that he's already got two offers from other universities and he has to respond pretty quick."

Lose Bahls? Rich sat up in his chair. That would be a disaster for all his plans. "So what can I do to help?"

"I've been thinking about that. You know the Faculty Fishing Frolic is next week, right? Well, that's when we can put the bite on old Dean Dunkard for a special appointment."

"You know how I hate the Frolic," Rich said disgustedly. "The last time I went, the Dean was half in the bag and the rest of the faculty were drunk."

"Yeah, I remember," Hank laughed. "You and I spent most evenings out in a canoe – away from the party. But this time's different. We're under serious pressure and the Frolic is the only time we can get the Dean away from his office."

"But Hank," Rich pleaded, "I was planning to use the break to work on a paper with Felicity and . . ."

Hank cut in. "Forget that. There will be plenty papers if we get Mike here. And there'll be money to support grad students. So let's get together and strategize how to get the Dean to do what's needed. You on for lunch?"

Rich flipped open his desk calendar. "Yeah, I don't have anything on this afternoon."

"OK, I'll meet you at the Campus Club 'round 11:30."

Rich heard the buzz of disconnection and replaced the receiver. *There go my days off!* He paged through the calendar to the mid term break. There, five days were blank except for a lightly-penciled F that reminded him of Felicity. Now that one F would be replaced by three Fs – Faculty Fishing Frolic.

Rich knew that spring fever took on a special manifestation in the College of Education and Home Economics. Around mid-March, male faculty met at lunch and in their offices to discuss the Faculty Fishing Frolic. This was an annual event that coincided with the state fishing season opener. It was welcomed by students, since Dean Dunkard decreed that there would be no classes for five days during which time course papers could be written and examination preparations made. The students weren't, of course, fooled by the decree and they proceeded to make their own 'frolic' plans.

Faculty were of two minds about this event. Men anticipated three days of partying (plus two of travel). Women were relieved by the disappearance of their male colleagues. Thus the Faculty Fishing Frolic – or F3 as it was called – had an appeal for nearly everyone in the College. Since Merton Dunkard had risen to the Dean level of incompetence, drink was the center of F3, resulting in many College tales that featured Dean Drunkard. Nearly every member of the College faculty enjoyed these stories, except for a few like Rich whose self-image didn't include wild partying and heavy drinking. For Rich, the Frolic was something to be avoided. *Not this spring!*

Rich looked at his watch and groused. *Already 11!* He arranged his calendar on his desk and placed the Journal of Higher Education in its proper place at the center of the blotter, open to his recent article 'Economic Returns to Degrees in Veterinary Medicine'. Rich had hit upon these props and an open office door to give any passer-by the impression that Professor Jessen was engaged in scholarly pursuits. He also found that the open door to an empty office gave him complete freedom to wander the campus or to spend the day at home, undisturbed by university life.

He stood and donned the leather jacket he had purchased at Second Life Clothiers. Rich caressed the leather and cocked his Greek Sailor's Cap at a jaunty angle. This treasure was the result of an extensive hunt through the ad pages of the New Yorker and the Atlantic. He developed the new campus image of Rich Jessen after careful thought, considering how Felicity would see him. The reflection in his closet mirror confirmed the wisdom of his creative use of haberdashery.

"Lois. I'll be out at a meeting for a few hours. Please take any messages."

Rich stepped out of Blewett, pulling up his coat collar against the April wind, and set off toward the Student Center; the Associate Dean on his way to a conference. *Why couldn't they put the Campus Club in some other place?* This familiar lament arose every time he made the two-block walk to the Club.

What was normally a walk, became a trudge against knots of students – blown toward him on gusts of wind . Rich was not in the best of humor when he reached the plaza in front of the Campus Club. In disgust, he turned away from the crowds of students and walked to the railing that defined the edge of the plaza. He stood with one hand on the railing; Greek Sailor's Cap atilt; leather coat collar framing his craggy face; peering across choppy waters of the river.

The wind shifted, wafting the odor of the Budweiser Malting Plant on the far bank into his face. He was transformed from the Captain of the Achilles Cruise

Liner to the impoverished owner of a Greek fishing scow. Rich turned away from the railing and concentrated on recapturing his mental image of himself.

"Professor Jessen! Professor Jessen!" Felicity's voice penetrated Rich's cloud of gloom. He swiveled his head, searching for her in the crush of students. Felicity was weaving her way across the plaza, her hair trailing in the wind; a classic Greek maiden, hurrying to meet her lover returned from the sea.

Rich drew himself to his full height, sucked in his stomach and peered out from under the bill of his Greek Sailor's Cap. "Well, Hello Ms Berland. This is a pleasant surprise. What brings you out on a day like this?"

"Oh, I just had lunch. I'm on my way to my mathematical modeling class. It's so exciting."

Mathematical Modeling? What . . .? Rich speedily recovered from this confusing input. "That's a wonderful course. I'm sure that you'll be able to use modeling in your thesis."

"I just knew that you would approve of my schedule. It's so rewarding to have an adviser who is up to speed on the latest methodology."

"Now, Ms Berland," Rich said patronizingly. "All professors are expected to know how the field is evolving."

"Well, I have to run. See you soon!" She hurried off into the Quad – followed by Rich's eyes. The Greek sailor was now safe in port.

He strode off in the direction of the union, imagining himself in an Athens market square. Student chatter, modulated by wind, sounded as Rich imagined it would; an amalgam of Mediterranean languages. Inside the union, the press of bodies blocked his way to the elevator.

"Excuse me please." "May I pass through?" *Get out of the way, scum!* His size and forbidding scowl cleared a narrow pathway and he pressed the 'up' button of the elevator. He entered the cage and the door shut on the awful confusion outside. Rich was alone with his desires and schemes.

Sweeping upward, Rich experienced his customary disconnection with the undesirable aspects of university life. He was leaving students and colleagues behind, transported to the realm of academic politics where leisurely dining and conversation charted the course of the academy. Here was the arena where he could arrange for a future that included both Felicity and Mike Bahls.

The cage stopped and the door slid open. Rich was faced with a panorama of University City visible through the circle of windows that enclosed the Faculty Club. Many tables were already occupied and several acquaintances nodded in recognition. Rich removed his jacket and cap and smoothed his hair into its neat waves.

"Rich! Over here!" Hank beckoned from a table near one of the windows. The table was in an alcove, shielded from other diners.

"Sit down, Old Buddy," Hank said. "We've got a lot to talk about."

Rich sank into the appointed chair. "Guess you're right. I've been racking my brain to find a way to sway the Dean on a position for Bahls. So far, no luck."

"Me too," Hank shook his head. "It's going to be tight, but we have to come up with the right package or else we lose our hold on the bucks."

The enormity of their challenge kept them silent through most of lunch. Pike fillets, garlic mashed and chardonnay disappeared as they sat, enveloped in solemn thought. When the waiter had cleared their table, Hank set the agenda.

"Now. Let's move to Tabaccy's and have a smoke."

"Suits me," said Rich as he pushed back from the table.

Tabaccy's was the faculty answer to the campus-wide smoking ban. Located just outside university property, the cigar store was a cross between the traditional English men's club and a cloistered setting where weighty intellectual issues could be discussed. The atmosphere lent a tacit approval for many political schemes and decisions; actions familiar to both Hank and Rich.

They stopped at the cigar counter and each selected his favorite smoke. Hank chose the middle-class Antiono y Cleopatra; Rich reached for a higher level with a Flor de Oliva. The found a pair of chairs in a secluded corner and lit their cigars.

"Well," Rich began. "You seem to think we can use the Frolic to work our magic on the Dean. How so?"

Hank blew a perfect smoke ring at the ceiling. "Don't know for sure. Probably the best way to proceed is for us to plan the schedule for the Frolic day by day. Then we can see where opportunity lays."

"Suits me. Where do we start?"

"First of all," Hank said earnestly, "how are we going to get to the Frolic. Should we drive or go with the college bus?"

Rich was filled with horror at the prospect of six hours in the college bus. *All those faculty from Work and Family Studies! And Kineseology!!* The college Directory passed through his mind. *Nelson Wood! Bert Parker!* Each possible seatmate was quickly rejected.

"No way! I couldn't be civil for six hours with any of our colleagues!"

Hank laughed. "Thought you'd say that. Guess that means we'll have to drive. Just you and me?"

"Suppose so. When should we leave?"

Hank though for a moment. "I've been at more Frolics than you and, believe me, we should skip the first night. Too much partying. For sure, the Dean will be loaded and in no shape to discuss anything. I'd say we leave early the second day and arrive at the Frolic just after lunch."

"Sounds good to me," Rich agreed. "Then what do we do?"

"Seems to me," Hank reflected, "that we have a big bone for the Dean to gnaw. All we need to do is to make him see the benefits."

They sat and smoked; exhaled puffs spun a grey cloud around them. Other faculty passed by, avoiding their serious demeanor. Minutes ticked as each weighed and rejected approaches. Ideas surfaced at the same instant.

"Say! . . ."

"What about . . ."

Looking at one another, they smiled.

"You thinking what I'm thinking?" Rich asked.

"Bet I am. You're remembering the Dean's presentation of the College budget, right?" Hank said.

"That's it," Rich confirmed. "When he laid out the budget in the last faculty meeting, I had the sense that he was hiding something. But what?"

Hank tapped the ash from his cigar. "The College is facing a heavy assessment from Central Administration to make up university-wide shortfalls. The state legislature has vetoed our request for tuition hikes and reduced their level of general support. This means that the U needs to find serious savings."

"Mert hasn't clued me in on that," Rich said. "If Central takes the College to the woodshed on this, there's no way the Dean can resist. He has zero clout with Central."

"Hold on! What about Waldo Pearson?"

They reflected on the recent Pearson cost-cutting initiative for a moment.

"You may have something there," Rich said enthusiastically. "Waldo could help us if we can show him how our Academy – and Bahls – would help to bail the U out of a jam."

"You haven't been at the last couple of Frolics, but I gotta tell you, Waldo is a real party boy. He lets it all hang out and is, I think, vulnerable when he's on the sauce."

"I think we've got it!" Rich exclaimed. "We can fill in the blanks on our way up north. By the way, where's the location of the Frolic?"

Hank levered himself out of his chair. "It's at the Knotty Pine Resort on Little Pickerel Lake. I'll pick you up at your place next Friday, around six a.m.. That should get us there a little after noon."

Afternoon sun dappled the Quad with shadows of hurrying students. With the wind, now a breeze, behind them, Hank and Rich strolled back toward Blewett Hall.

"Place don't look so bad, once spring comes," Hank observed.

Rich walked along without comment. His eyes roved over the flow of students, seeking a chance sighting of Felicity. *Class should be over by now.* His was, however, an ambivalent search as he was not ready for any encounter with mathematical modeling.

Hank held the door of Blewett for Rich. "After you, Herr Professor. Sorry, but I can't speak Greek."

Rich grimaced, not so much at Hank's comment; he had the same feeling whenever entering Blewett. It just wasn't proper for Rich Jessen to have to work in such a low-class building. He should, by rights, be housed in one of the science halls.

The next several days were a monotonous extension of Rich's professional life. There were no important university committee meetings and, hence, no opportunity for him to exercise his political skills. In fact, he found himself actually looking forward to the Faculty Fishing Frolic.

Friday didn't come soon enough to suit Rich. At five forty-five a.m., he was standing in front of his garage, shivering in the weak light of the April sunrise. He began to pace restlessly, glancing occasionally down Locust while looking at his watch. At exactly six, Hank's Chevy Blazer swept around the corner of the block and into the Jessen driveway.

Hank's head popped out of the driver's window. "Hi, Pardner! Ready for the Frolic?"

Rich waved a hand, opened the passenger door and glanced into the back of the Blazer. The rear seat had been removed and the resulting space filled with cases of beer and liquor. "What have we got here? The delivery truck for the Ajax Liquor Store?" He lowered himself into the seat.

"Bout right," Hank answered. "The Dean called me on Wednesday and gave me an order on the entertainment budget."

"Evidently, there's no short-fall on that account," Rich laughed. "He must be expecting quite a crowd."

Hank backed the Blazer into the street before answering. "Yep. By my count, there must be at least thirty of our colleagues at the resort. And, they'll sure be anxious for us to arrive!"

Not much was said for the next few miles. Then Rich could no longer contain his feelings. "I don't much like the idea of us being errand boys for the Dean. Seems to me he could use one of his fellow drunks for this assignment."

"Aw, don't let it bother you," Hank patted Rich's knee. "We do the Dean a service and start to set him up for the big hit. Now, let's talk a little about what we're going to do."

Rich remained somewhat rebellious and asked. "I suppose we've got to drink and carouse. You know, be one of the boys?"

"No, that's not the way to look at it. What we'll do is continue as good guys and see that everyone has plenty of booze."

"What good will that do? The Dean will just see us as flunkies."

"Probably. That is, until everyone is plastered. Then we can plant our ideas in the right place."

Rich thought about this for several miles. The idea of working against the weakness of the Dean and the rest of his colleagues appealed to him. Maybe Hank had the right idea. Their strategy matured into Folic tactics and specific targets were identified.

"Now, you be sure to get Waldo Pearson aside and whisper sweet nothings in his ear." Hank advised. "Try to find out just how much the College is in the hole with Central."

"Can do. You going to work on the Dean?"

"Betcha. I'll know where he's planning to cut the College budget and how much each department will have to pony up."

The last hours of the trip were taken up with variations on these two questions. Each offered Frolic scenarios where answers could be sought. Drink was the only imponderable in their plan; drunken behavior could render Pearson and Dunkard insensible – alarming prospects for which no plans could be made.

Finally, they arrived at Little Pickerel Lake where a signpost showed the way to the Frolic.

KNOTTY PINE RESORT
3 MILES

Three miles of sandy dirt road led them through scrub oak and scraggly evergreens that scraped the sides of the Blazer. Weaving through this tangle challenged their sense of direction and it wasn't until the road tipped down that they could see the lake and the cabins of the resort.

"The College has the whole Resort," said Hank. "Every one of those cabins has a pair of our colleagues in it. The Dean and Waldo are holed up in Cabin Number Three."

"How did you find that out?" asked Rich.

"Nothing to it. I suggested to the Dean's secretary that she work up a housing chart. Wanted to be sure that we were somewhere near the center of things." Hank pulled the Blazer to a stop in front of the central lodge. "Now let's see how it's going." He opened the rear gate of the Blazer and pointed to two large aluminum coolers. "Take one of those, I'll get the other. The boys will be glad to have a cool one on us."

They muscled the heavy coolers through the front doors of the lodge. An explosion of enthusiasm greeted them.

"Look! It's the rescue team!"

"BiGod! On time for once!"

"It's Miller Time!"

Hank and Rich were nearly trampled in the rush for the coolers. Eager hands competed for brews. Friendly jostling created a kind of whirlpool around the coolers where lucky fishers holding beers were cast out to enjoy their catch. Soon, every Frolicer was holding a beer and toasting the rescuers.

It took less than a half-hour to empty the coolers. Cries for sustenance reached a second climax.

"This all there is?"

"Hey Hank! Fill 'em up!"

"Rich! This one's dead!"

The rescue team returned to the Blazer and hauled the remaining beer and liquor into the lodge. Coolers were replenished and ice was procured. Revelry went on throughout the afternoon.

Sundown signaled the 'Barbecue Bust' served up by the resort staff. Yellow bug lights were festooned on an arbor, keeping clouds of mosquitoes somewhat at bay. Rich was amazed at the endurance of his colleagues, who continued to pop beer cans throughout the Bust. Evidently, solid food served to absorb some of their alcoholic intake as they returned to a semblance of sobriety.

After the Bust, the group returned to the Powwow Lounge where circular tables and chairs were in place for the evening's poker party. Poker was more than a ritual for the Frolic; it was the preferred recreation of a large fraction of the male faculty. So much so, that a college newcomer could expect to be judged by his card-playing interest and skill.

Rich had been able to avoid being rated on this scale by defining himself as one who was prevented from playing by unknown forces. These were assumed to be of a religious nature by his colleagues and hence immune from criticism. On those occasions when he found himself in a poker setting, he assumed the role of observer – commenting on play from a neutral perspective. He also absorbed the structure and play of the popular games. The Frolic was such an occasion.

Each table in the lounge seated six players with sufficient room for both play and drinks. Whiskey was the beverage of choice for most players since it allowed for long periods of seated concentration without the restroom breaks associated with beer. Games varied according to the whims of dealers as did the stakes. Small amounts of money did change hands, but not enough to inconvenience or anger the players.

Hank was a player, not an observer. He was seated at a table where the Dean and Waldo Pearson held forth. Rich noticed that Hank was drinking a Coke and that he appeared to be a good deal more alert than his companions. Play began with the Dean's deal.

"Five card stud. Deuces wild. Fifty cents to play."

Everyone tossed the required number of coins to the center of the table. And the Dean dealt the first cards – face up.

"Ten of spades. Three of diamonds. Ace of clubs. A lucky opener, Hank."

The Dean continued. "Five of clubs. Queen of hearts. Pretty symbolic, Wally."

"Dealer takes a . . . Jack of diamonds. Ace of clubs is high card. Your bet Hank."

"Hows about a buck?" Hank tossed the bill into the center of the table.

Other players looked at their face card and stole surreptitious glances around the table. The silence was too much for those holding the five of clubs and three of diamonds. They folded.

The dance of play continued. Cards fell. Bets were placed. Winners were declared. Losers moaned. And whiskey flowed.

Several hours passed with short breaks. At ten o'clock, resort staff wheeled in a table with coffee and desserts. This gave players an opportunity to converse and to change the composition of tables. Hank was careful to stay with the Dean. Rich was deputed to watch Waldo.

Play went on toward midnight. By that time, many of the players were well on the way to insensibility. Waldo Pearson was, by any measure, the most seriously afflicted. He had considerable difficulty in holding his cards and following the sequence of play. Others made efforts to accommodate his disability, but it became impossible and the evening of poker drew to a close.

Frolicers gradually dispersed to their cabins. Hank and Rich were left with Waldo and the Dean. Both were collapsed on their respective tables, heads down on outstretched arms.

"Guess we're stuck with these birds," Hank grimaced. "If we don't put them to bed, they'll be here all night."

"Yeah, you're right," Rich said. "Come on. I'll see if I can get Waldo moving."

Some fifteen minutes passed before the two helpless men were safely in their cabin and Rich and Hank in theirs.

"That was a real failure!" Rich exclaimed. "We didn't make any progress on our agenda. Why, those drunks are likely to sleep until noon!"

Hank nodded agreement. "We'll just have to see what tomorrow brings. Meanwhile, I'm ready for the sack."

Another fifteen minutes and they were in the twin beds of their cabin. Disappointment stifled any further conversation and soon both were asleep.

Although asleep, Rich's mind was a whirl of problems, opportunities and pleasures. He found himself to be the Dean – confronted with gallons of red ink and a frowning Waldo. Then he was in Washington, trying to tell Mike Bahls how their plan had failed. Felicity strolled into Mike's office. She sat on Rich's lap, her arms around his neck.

The office chair was unable to support their combined weight.

CRRAACK! A clatter of breaking glass!

Rich sprang out of bed – fully awake.

"Jesus Christ! What the Hell's that?"

Hank was by his side. "Look! The window's smashed. Some drunk must have . . ."

149

"Fuckin' drunks!" Rich exploded. Over the years, he had purged his vocabulary of all his adolescent curses. However, they surfaced whenever he was frightened or helplessly angry. "Goddamn loonies. They tryin' to kill us?" He switched on the table lamp.

"Watchit!" Hank said. "There's glass all over the floor. Better get some clothes and shoes on then we can go after this bastard!"

They dressed in record time and raced out of the cabin. Their heads swiveled right and left.

Rich caught a movement at the window of the next cabin and a flicker of matchlight.

CRRAACK! A clatter of breaking glass!

Then, he saw a stumbling figure totter down the path that led to the lakeside cabins.

"Hehehehe," the figure cackled. It wavered on and stopped at the window of the next cabin in line.

Rich could see its hand reaching into a trouser pocket. "Hey you! Knock it the fuck off!"

Hank ran past him and grabbed the man. "Sonofabitch!" he blurted. "It's Waldo! Get hold of him, Rich! We gotta get him outta here!"

They each siezed an arm and marched Waldo to the cabin he shared with the Dean and opened the door.

Rich looked over his shoulder. He could see milling shapes back on the path; shapes that were beginning to resolve into running men. "Hurry up! Let's get this guy under cover!"

Waldo was shoved into his cabin and the door was slammed just in time. Other Frolicers raced around the corner of the next cabin.

"You catch him?"

"Where's the fucker?"

"Just missed him," Hank said ruefully. "Had a hold on him, but he wiggled away. The last I saw him, he was running down toward the lake."

Rich picked up on the ruse. "Let's fan out! If we cover the area, we'll be sure to get him!"

"Good idea!" Hank shouted. "Rich and I will check the back of the cabins. He might be hiding there!"

The Frolicers raced off, scattering across the lakefront.

"Way to go, Rich. Now, let's see what we can do with damage control."

They entered the Dean's cabin and switched on the light. Waldo lay, passed out on the floor, firecrackers spilled out of his pocket.

"OK," Hank said. "Help me hoist this meat into his bed."

Grunting and maneuvering, they rolled Waldo's heavy body on his bed.

"Should we cover him?" Rich asked.

"Let the bastard lay. Some cold air might sober him up." Hank reached for the light as they faced the door.

"Wait a minute!" Rich bent and retrieved one of the firecrackers from the floor. "The goddamn idiot was shooting M80s! These babies are illegal. If the cops find out, he could be in serious trouble!"

"BiGod! You're right. The 1966 Child Protection Act makes possession of these puppies a federal offense. We got a real problem on our hands." Hank thought for a moment. "Tell you what. You stay here with Waldo and I'll get up to the lodge and see if I can keep a lid on this. Better turn the light out."

When the door closed on Hank, Rich sat in the dark. Events of the night were reviewed in flashes of light and explosions that recalled surprise and fear. He remembered a time in high school when he was climbing the stairwell to get to his second floor class. The vision of a falling, sputtering object dominated his mind –

he heard the **CRRAACK!** of the explosion and his fear intensified. The principal accused him of setting the blast and he was expelled for a week. It took him nearly a month to identify the pranksters and to plant M80s in their desks. Their expulsion lasted for the balance of the school year. He smiled at the cleverness of his vengeance.

Would something like that work here? His mind raced at the prospect of Waldo and the Dean in debt to him. *How could he pull this off?* It depended on Hank.

He opened the cabin door and stepped out. Cries and noises of searching came from the lakefront. All was quiet around the cabin. He closed the door and turned the light on. Waldo and the Dean were sunk in drunken sleep. He knelt and scooped up the scattered M80s. Then he saw a box on a nearby table with other salutes in it. The box was labeled 'Real M80s' and it was addressed to Waldo Pearson! He pocketed the box and turned the light off.

Rich sat and gloated. *Now it's up to Hank!* He leaned back in his chair and listened to the ragged breathing of his wards.

An hour later, there was a scratching at the door. "Rich, you in there?" It was Hank.

Rich opened the door and stepped out. "How did it go at the lodge?"

"Not so hot. They're really pissed off. I had a hell of a time keeping them from calling the police. Finally, they backed off when I said the Dean would handle it and pay for any damage."

"Good for you!"

"It's not over yet. They want pictures of each cabin and we have to clean up the mess before we take off."

"Think about it," Rich said. "If we can put the pictures together with these," he held up the M80 box, "then we have all the evidence we need."

"Could be. Now, let's get back to our cabin so nobody connects this escapade with the Dean."

The balance of the hours until sunrise were spent devising a strategy that would give them the leverage they needed to pry concessions out of the Dean. It was Rich who summarized the plan.

"So here's what we'll do. We use the resort camera to take pictures of the damage. By the way, can you get a second film so we can have copies?"

Hank reflected. "As I remember, there were several new films in the camera bag at the check-in desk. Should be able to get our hands on one."

"OK. We get copies of all the damage and some pictures of the M80s. Then we sit down with the Dean and lay out our case. We can show that Pearson is way out on a limb and that we can saw it off at any time."

"That's right, but I have a better idea."

"Let's hear it," Rich commanded.

"We go ahead with our meeting with the Dean. But we don't come on strong. Instead, we show how we've avoided a major scandal. Then we give the Dean copies of the photos to use as he sees fit."

"I see. I see. That would put him in major debt to us. But what does it do for our problem of the Bahls appointment?"

"Two things. It does delay action by the Dean. On the other hand, it opens the door for ever bigger things."

"Such as?"

"Well, we want the Policy Studies Academy, faculty rank for Bahls, and this is the big one, control over any of the money that Bahls sends our way."

Rich tossed the M80 box in the air and caught it again and again. Then he said, "Can't see why the Dean would give us free rein on the money. The College is broke and he needs the money to satisfy Central."

"That's the beauty of it," Hank crowed. "We tell the Dean that we're the only ones who can manage the federal grant. If he wants to funnel some of it to Central, he's got to give in to us on all sorts of things like office space, consulting freedom and the like."

"I like it." Rich thought for several moments. "How's this for a twist? We take the photos this morning. Then we meet with the Dean and tell him the story about how we smoothed over problems with the resort. We save the M80 stuff for later."

"Why's that?"

"The way I see it is that we're just good boys now. We wait until our copy of the film's developed. Then we ask for a meeting with the Dean where we come in all worried about a big scandal. You know, the M80s are illegal, and so on. That should really soften him up."

It was Hank's turn to 'like it'. "Sounds much better to me. We're helpful now and worried later. When he leaves here, the Dean will think all's well. The pictures and the legal issue will really put him in our corner."

Rich stood. "So let's get going. The light's about right for pictures so we can get them done before the Dean wakes up."

Pictures were taken of each of the damaged cabins. Hank exposed several frames for every cabin, including indoor flash shots of glass shards and other breakage. The process was repeated for the second roll of film – the one to be taken back to the University for developing. On this film, Rich positioned the opened M80 box on a table along with several salutes.

"That about does it," Hank said. "I'll take the camera and the resort's film back to the Lodge. Why don't you see if you can entice the Dean out of his nest."

"I suppose I have to," Rich growled as he walked off down the path.

Their plan couldn't have worked better. When the Dean emerged from his cabin, his mind was still clouded by drink. Rich toured the wreckage with him pointing out the damage, emphasizing the danger of flying glass. By the time the tour ended, the Dean was quite sober and alarmed at the magnitude of the problem.

Hank met them on his way back from the lodge. "I see that Rich has put you in the picture, Dean. Kind of an exciting night."

"I . . . just can't believe . . .," the Dean stammered. "Waldo would . . . . He must have been drunk."

"You can say that again," Rich said. "I've never seen anyone so out of it."

"It's the results we need to worry about," Hank added. "I've been talking to the resort owners and they are plenty mad. They are talking about calling the police!"

"The police!" the Dean screamed. "They can't do that! Why . . ."

"We have to face reality," Rich pronounced. "They have every reason to call in law enforcement. The damage to property will be quite costly and is likely to disrupt business."

"But. .. but. . .." the Dean sounded like a dying outboard motor and his face had the appearance of a feeding carp.

Hank came to his rescue. "Don't panic! Here's what we did. Rich was able to get Waldo in your cabin before anyone else saw who did the damage. Then I talked with the resort owner and convinced him not to call the police. However, I had to promise that the U would pay for any damage."

The Dean sighed with relief. "That's a load off my mind. What do you think I should do now?"

"First, be sure that you muzzle Waldo," Rich said. "Then you ought to go with Hank and make amends with the resort."

155

"OK," the Dean said. "But what about the faculty? How do I keep them out of the problem?"

"They believe that the prankster was somebody from the area. If the three of us hold to that view, they shouldn't connect the fireworks to Waldo." Hank took the Dean's arm and gently led him up the path to the lodge. "Now, we should see how to handle the damages. Rich, you might want to check on Waldo."

Rich watched the two until they entered the lodge. Then he walked downhill to the Dean's cabin. Inside, Waldo lay on his back, snoring his way toward sobriety.

Later that day, Hank and Rich met in their cabin to compare notes. Hank led off. "Well, the deal's done. The Dean agreed that the resort could add the cost of cabin repairs to the bill for the Frolic. Should add a good bit to the College's shortfall!"

"I think we're OK with Waldo," Rich said. "He doesn't seem to remember the Mad Bomber episode. It'll be quite a surprise when he sees the evidence. Sure hope the films turn out."

"Me too. If this works out, they'll have to change the evening card game at the Frolic from poker to Gin Rummy."

Rich smiled. "No, a better game would be Go Fish!"

CHAPTER NINE

Liar's Poker

"Here politics is the craft of permanent mendacity".
(C.W. Ceram: Marginalia)

Room 110 Blewett Hall was a special place for Professor Rich Jessen. The number '110BH – Office of the Associate Dean' mapped Rich on the landscape of the university where he was surrounded by the academic shrine he had created. The walls of his office were covered with bookcases filled with all the appropriate authors and titles. Economic subjects were treated by Samuelson, Friedman, Hayek and Keynes; Education by Dewey, Montessori and Pestalozzi. Other subjects were similarly represented so that visitors could marvel at the wide-ranging intellect of Professor Jessen.

On the days when he was not roaming the political arenas of the university, Rich was seated behind his desk, facing the door. Few of his colleagues had hit upon the power of this setting, where the professor was framed by knowledge. Rich frequently tested the visual impact of his environment by swiveling his chair to let his eyes range over his library.

The Monday following the Faculty Fishing Frolic, Rich was in his office at 8 o'clock; a great surprise to the Blewett Hall janitor, who considered calling University Security to deal with a suspected intruder. Luckily, the janitor recognized the leather-coated figure as 'that asshole, Jessen' and went about his business. Rich set his attaché case on his desk, twirled its combination and opened it. The case contained a single item – the M80 Salutes box addressed to Waldo Pearson. Rich put the attaché case aside and studied the M80 box. He fondled the box and gloated over the power it gave him; power to influence Central Administration!

Over the years, Rich had accumulated tidbits of information that were equally powerful. These were hoarded, but rarely used in any direct way. Instead, Rich used the knowledge represented by the items to shape his political agendas. Waldo Pearson could be easily persuaded to follow Rich's direction, not because Rich would make any direct threats; just the fact that Rich 'knew' gave significant weight to his suggestions.

Rich turned his chair with the M80 box in hand. He stood, walked to the office door, closed it and moved to the Philosophy section of his bookcase. His fingers traced the alphabet of authors to the H's; Habermas, Harding, Heidegger, Husserl. These authors concealed a secure hiding place for Rich's treasures, safe from the prying eyes of fellow scholars who, like Rich, avoided these deadly tomes.

Every time he faced the H's, he recalled his preliminary examination for the Ph.D. Degree at LMU. Candidates were required to pass an examination in a foreign language; Rich had selected German as he found it easy to master. One of the exam questions had to do with a quotation from Heidegger to the effect that "Die welt weltet." This meaningless phrase could be loosely translated as "The world whirls." Rich offered this translation as his examination response along with a reference to the soap opera 'As The World Turns'. He was pleasantly surprised when the exam paper was returned with a mark of 'Excellent'. Rich often used this experience to remind him of the intellectual poverty of much of philosophic thought, and to confirm his cynical approach to the life of the mind.

Rich slid the books from the shelf. In the opening behind the books, there was a small metal box. He took the box to his desk and opened it. The first thing that he saw was a green woman's glove. *Felicity!* Rich had found the glove on the floor of the cab they took in Washington. Rather than return it, he kept it as a memento of that first encounter. Rich lifted the glove and held it to his face, savoring the faint odor of Felicity's perfume. He laid it aside. The balance of the contents consisted of a collection of index cards, bound by a rubber band. Rich took the rubber band and slid it over his wrist. He thumbed through the cards.

There is was! The card was covered with dense writing on both sides. It was labeled: 'The Dean's Lap Dance'. Under the heading was a kind of citation of the setting of the 'Lap Dance'. The citation read: 'American Educational Research Association' – 'Annual Meeting' – Boston, Mass.'. Next, the card listed: 'Participants' – followed by names of University faculty and administrators – 'Dean Dunkard, VP Pearson, Harley Clark, Nelson Wood'. Then the narrative. 'Following the University open house, the Dean suggested we all visit the bars near our hotel. Selection wasn't great – only a few seedy clubs. Clark chose the 'Gentlemen's Dream' in response to its garish lights and the promise of 'Girls! Girls! Girls! After several rounds of drinks, Nelson Wood bought the Dean a Lap Dance from 'Lover's Climax' – an overdeveloped blonde. Dean obviously loved the Dance. At the end, Wood went offstage with the Lover. Soon back. Didn't have the cash for the Climax. Had to borrow it from the Dean. Finally got the group back to the hotel. Dunkard passed out in his room.'

Rich smiled at the recollection of this tidbit. He remembered how the Dean had waltzed around the incident the next day at the conference where Rich said nothing. And, how clever he had been; to let the Dean worry about Rich's knowledge and what would occur if the incident became known back at the College.

He laid the card next to the box of M80s and considered how they might be used to bring Mike Bahls to the University. Rich realized that the political worth of these two items was infinitely greater if they remained hidden. By keeping the secret of the Dean's Lap Dance, Rich had become a confidant of the Dean – if not a friend. Maybe the box of M80s could play a similar role with Pearson. Rich weighed the items, one in each hand. What about the College budget? Might that be an opener for a discussion with the Dean?

Rich reached for the phone and entered Hank's number.

"Hello, Hank Loras speaking."

"Hank, this is Rich. Got time for another lunch at the Club?"

"Sure. What's on your mind?"

"I have an idea that might get the Dean to spring for a position for Mike."

"Great! How's 11:30?"

"Suits me. See you then." Rich hung up the receiver and turned his attention to the box and the card. 'Now, let's see. Central is short on cash.' He placed the box of M80s at one side of his desk blotter. 'The Dean needs to contribute a big slice of the College's budget to Central.' The Lap Dance card went to the opposite side of the blotter. Rich took a blank card and wrote the word 'Budget' on it. This card went to the center of the blotter. He smiled at the juxtaposition of the three items, drawing mental arrows from Lap Dance and M80s to Budget. Rich took another blank card and wrote 'Bahls – Bucks' on it. This card went to the top of his blotter with a mental arrow down to 'Budget'.

After studying this array for several minutes, Rich gathered the cards and snapped the rubber band around them. The deck of cards and the box of M80s went back to their hiding place. Rich arranged the philosophers carefully so that their bindings were level with other books on the shelf. Back at his desk, he spent the remainder of the morning considering how best to engage the Dean in their plan. Positioning was everything!

Walking across the Quad to the Campus Club, Rich couldn't help but be excited by the prospect of cornering both the Dean and the Vice President. Imagine! He and Hank were about to influence decisions that would normally be made by Central Administration and the College! There was a spring in the gait of the Greek Captain.

Rich's eyes roved over the waves of students, looking for a sighting of Felicity. Today, there was to be no appearance of the Greek Maiden. Disappointed, Rich sailed along, eyes on opportunity.

Seated with Hank in the usual alcove, their luncheon conversation skirted around the topic that drew them together. Enthusiasm occasionally forced comments to bubble to the surface.

"Think we got 'em?" Hank asked.

"Suppose so. Be hard for the Dean to forget how we bailed him out of the soup," Rich observed, concentrating on his Greek salad.

Hank smiled and looked out of the window; the university theirs for the taking!

After lunch, they rushed to Tabaccy's, where the next level of the plan would be forged. Cigars were purchased and lit, comfortable chairs arranged for intimate conversation.

"Well, here we are," Hank stated.

"Yes. By the way, did you get the Frolic photos developed?" Rich asked.

161

Hank pulled a packet from his coat pocket. "Here's your copy. Take a look. You won't be disappointed."

Rich opened the Kodak envelope and drew out the sheaf of pictures. He examined them one by one.

Hank watched his expression. "Good pictures, eh?"

"They are only excellent," Rich enthused. "These shots of broken windows make the resort look like a war zone."

"Yeah, and what about that view of the M80s?"

The picture in Rich's hand showed Waldo Pearson's address on an open box of 'M80 Salutes' with scattered crackers around the box. "This will sure settle Waldo's hash! Why this photo . . .," he stopped.

"I know what you're thinking," Hank said. "We could easily talk the resort owner into taking this thing to the local police. With these photos there's an open and shut case against old Waldo."

Rich shook his head. "You're right, but that takes away our leverage. Think about it. We're a much greater threat just knowing about the M80s. You agree?"

"I kind of thought about it," Hank confessed. "You mean we have more influence if we say nothing about the Frolic?"

"Right! Remember the Dean's Lap Dance at AERA? Well, he became an instant friend of mine just because I said nothing about that night."

Hank frowned. "So . . . what you're saying is that our case is stronger if the Dean and Waldo are buying our silence. That it?"

"In a sense, our knowledge puts them in debt to us. So long as we don't bring it up, they'll fall over themselves to help us out."

"I like it," Hank chuckled. "We kind of become their partners in crime."

"Something like that. Now, we need to decide how to get our Bahls proposal in front of the Dean. Got any ideas?"

Rich hesitated, ". . . I guess these pictures are a place to start. What say you call the Dean and tell him that I just got them from the resort owner?"

"Good opener, then we can let him figure out how to use the pictures with Pearson; sort of a second step in a chain of influence that will connect Waldo to us through the Dean."

Rich put the pictures back in the Kodak envelope and stood to leave. "Good plan." He shrugged into his leather jacket.

"Try to hold out for a meeting so both of us can be there when he sees the photos," Rich said.

"Will do," Hank gave a thumbs up and left.

Leaving the Student Union, Rich examined the groups of students on the Quad. Still no sighting of Felicity. He shrugged and turned into Blewett. There were no messages on his voice mail and no message from his secretary. He closed himself into his office and retrieved the metal box from its hiding place. The pack of Kodak photos joined the other treasures in the box. He closed and locked the box, returning it to its philosophical guardians.

Waiting for the consequences of political plans was always difficult for Rich. Although his predictions were usually correct, the delay between his actions and the desired outcome was a time of anxiety. Two days passed with no word from Hank. Finally, the phone rang on the third day.

"Hank here. We have an appointment with the Dean at two this afternoon. Can you make it?"

"You bet!" Rich blurted. "Come by my office at quarter to. Say, can you look up that Child Protection Act. Wouldn't hurt to have a fulcrum for our lever."

"I get it!" Hank said. "The better to pry some action out of the Dean. See you at one forty-five."

163

Rich hung up with a satisfied grin on his lips. He loved to hear others respond to his metaphors. When they used them appropriately like Hank, he was confident that thought shaped action. Now all that would be needed is to find the right metaphor to use with the Dean.

He considered various approaches, recalling a particularly effective instance early in his career at Midwest when the faculty in Curriculum and Instruction (C&I) developed a graduate program for Native Americans interested in teaching at tribal colleges. Rich was opposed to this initiative from the start. After all, tribal colleges weren't 'real colleges' and program candidates could never meet university requirements. The debate became heated when C&I faculty proposed dropping one of the university admission requirements – the Miller Analogies test – on the grounds that it was culturally biased. Rich's concern for academic standards was virtually powerless as he faced accusations of racism. Metaphor came to his rescue when he hit upon the old military label 'walking wounded'. Repetition of this metaphor finally wore down C&I advocates and the tribal college program disappeared. Metaphor had won the day!

Repeated use of 'walking wounded' had gradually lost its power as few could visualize a WWI soldier, covered in bandages and gore, in search of first aid. For a time, Rich was puzzled by the blank stares that followed his use of the metaphor, especially among younger colleagues. He slowly came to the conclusion that in order to be effective, a metaphor had to be anchored in the experience of those whom he wished to influence. Consequently, he replaced 'walking wounded' with 'two bales short of a load' when dealing with admission to agriculture programs and the use of "Elvis wannabees' for music aspirants.

These lessons made Rich a master of the use of metaphorical language. He listened carefully to the common speech of his colleagues, seeking those words and phrases that embodied a general meaning or emotion. He looked for nodding of heads and/or laughter as signals of possible metaphors. These became candidates for experiments where he tested their effect on individuals and small groups. Concepts that passed these tests went into his repertoire of politically useful discourse. They gave meaning to his Metaphor Table and enabled him to finesse a melding of Collegial and Political metaphors.

The problem he now faced was one that challenged his stock of tested metaphors. Rich needed to invent a metaphor 'on the fly', taking a risk of serious failure. The problem was mulled over again and again. Possible scenarios of the upcoming meeting with the Dean were reviewed in attempts to abstract elements of conversation that pointed to useful metaphors. Every candidate metaphor seemed to Rich likely to raise the Dean's anger and prevent a positive outcome to the meeting.

In despair, Rich turned his attention to the Frolic. Was there something in Waldo's escapade that might be useful? 'Faculty Fireworks' drew a laugh from him, but was likely to further embarrass the Dean. 'Frolic Fandango' was less a metaphor than a label of the incident. He shook his head. *There's no hole card in this deal! Hole Card! Poker!* The game was the center of the Frolic activity, a manipulation of shared images and the foundation of a common language. Rich leaned back in his chair and closed his eyes, transporting his thoughts to the poker game he had witnessed at the Frolic. He mentally reviewed the turns of cards, banter and bets. He recalled Waldo raising the Dean's bet by tossing a blue chip on the pile of counters in the center of the game table. *Wait a minute! Blue Chip!* Here was a metaphor that had nearly universal meaning. Now how could it be used?

Better call Hank – so we're on the same page. He picked up the phone.

"Hank Loras."

"This is Rich. Did you get the info on the Child Protection Act?"

"Yep, it's very specific on the powerful fireworks. As far as I can see, that aspect of the Act was driven by M80 accidents."

"OK, that takes care of Waldo. How do you see handling the Dean?"

"I'll open with the pictures and the Act. That way, the Dean will see that Waldo is in the soup."

"Fine. My guess is the Dean will panic so we need to sooth the savage beast with our full cooperation."

"Right! But then what?"

Rich hesitated for several seconds. "I'll tell him that these are the only pictures and he can share them with Pearson if he wishes. You can tag along by raising the College budget and how Waldo owes us a favor."

"Hell, the Dean will just say that he has to cut the budget. That won't help us."

"Oh yes it will. You can bring up the Bahls connection to show the Dean that there are big bucks in the offing."

Rich could almost see Hank nodding. "That's the ticket! Well, it's time for us to see the Dean." Hank hung up.

Dunkard was waiting for them and beckoned them into his office. "Let's gather around the table and hear what you boys have in mind," he said.

A large, round table filled the end of the Dean's office. It seated six in comfortable oak armchairs, all with padded seats where participants discussed weighty academic matters. In the center of the table, a smaller version of the university crest was displayed in multi-colored splendor. Two griffons (rampant) held a sheaf of wheat (resplendent) against a background of wheat fields (receding). The university motto was inscribed surrounding this image – 'As Ye Sow' (base) – 'So Shall Ye Reap (elevated). These words were generally taken to mean "Abandon Hope All Ye Who Enter Here'.

They seated themselves and waited for the Dean's secretary to bring coffee. When their cups were filled, the game began. Rich followed the play eagerly; developing the metaphor in his mind.

"So what can I do for you?" Dunkard asked.

Rich began a mental narrative: *What's the game today?*

Hank took a Kodak envelope out of his pocket. "It's really about what the College can do for Vice President Pearson. Take a look at these photos."

Liar's Poker!

Dunkard spread the pictures on the table and scanned the layout. "So? There's no surprise here. I'm sure Waldo agrees that his prank caused some problems, but they've all been solved. Thanks to you boys."

"The picture of the firecrackers is the problem," Rich said. "M80s are illegal and Waldo could be in serious trouble for buying and using them." *That ups the ante!*

"Come on," Dunkard said. "Nobody is going to make a fuss about a few firecrackers." *Bluffing!*

"That's what we thought," Hank said in a judicious voice. "But we remembered something about M80s in the Child Protection Act of 1966. I looked it up when we got back to campus and found out that possession and use of M80s is a federal offense." *Jokers wild!*

Rich cut in. "If the resort owner takes this to the cops, Waldo is in a world of hurt. It's lucky we have these photos rather than the police." *Raise you two red chips.*

Hank followed Rich's lead. "We thought you should have the pictures so you could decide how to let Vice President Pearson know that the College is protecting him." *Make that three reds!*

Dunkard studied the pictures. "So you think these photos give the College leverage with Central." *Dean throws in three red chips and calls.*

"I don't see it quite like that," Hank said. "The pictures just set the stage for a discussion with Waldo. It's important that he doesn't see them as a threat." *Hank's three fives beats the Deans pair of aces!*

The Dean looked puzzled. "What kind of discussion might that be?" *Let's play another round.*

Here was the opening Rich was waiting for. "Seems to me that there might be a way to make everyone a winner." *OK, the game is Liars Poker – winners split.*

"Explain that," the Dean said. *Whaddya mean 'Split'?*

Rich went on. "The budget is the issue we are all dancing around. Central needs a sacrifice from the College and we need to ease the pain." *It means two best hands split.!*

"How's that possible?" Dunkard asked. "Seems to me that Central and the College are both bathing in red ink." *Not enough chips to play the game!*

"Here's where we can help," Hank enthused. "Rich and I recently attended an ADA conference in Washington where we met an old classmate of Rich's, a guy named Michael Bahls. You may have heard of him." *New stacks of chips for everyone!*

"Yes, he's quite well known, a guru for the handicapped as I recall." *Maybe I'll play another round!*

Rich seized on the opening he had been looking for. "Bahls is a real Blue Chip scholar! Why, he's probably the leading researcher in the field!" Rich thumped the table for emphasis. "And there's a chance we could land him at Midwest!" *Time to bet the Blues!*

"I don't see how," the Dean looked puzzled. "We have no open items and are unlikely to get any from Central in the near future." *He's fondling his chips. Can't decide whether to bet.*

This time Hank followed Rich's lead. "That's exactly what we think could happen. Bahls would like a university appointment and he's able to bring significant funding with him! That's where the College and Central could capitalize on this Blue Chip opportunity!" *Another Blue Chip in the pot!*

"Sounds interesting. Tell me more." *He's ready to bet a Blue!*

Hank raised a finger to emphasize opportunity. "Bahls told us that he could guarantee something like ten million a year if we would develop a policy studies program. Rich and I think we have the people to do that. All's that's needed is a position for Bahls." *Hank bets the whole stack of Blues!*

"That's just a dream," Dunkard said skeptically. "There's no way that the College can come up with a position in the near future. Don't you agree Rich." *He's ready to fold!*

"That's absolutely correct. If we aren't creative, this opportunity will pass us by. I think that it's critically important, both for our budget and for our academic excellence that we try to land this Blue Chip scholar." Rich sat back. *There! Do you want to play or don't you!*

Blue Chip scholar! Money for the budget! Help out Central! Little beads of sweat formed on Dunkard's forehead. "I agree Rich, but I can't see how we can move this along. Have you any ideas?"

"Let me think this over. I feel that there may be a way to do this that won't involve year-long faculty meetings." This was the time to leave. Rich and Hank stood at the same time. *Time enough for counting now! The dealing's done!*

Hank and Rich left the Dean's office. Rich beckoned to Hank and led the way into his office. With the door closed, the game continued.

Hank sank into a chair and exhaled. "Whew! I think we have him hooked. But how can we get a spot for Mike in the next couple of weeks? You heard the Dean, the budget's frozen."

"Sure, if things proceed as usual. However, I think there might be a path through Central that would give us what we want."

"How so? Central's just as short of cash as the College"

"Put the money aside for the moment," Rich advised. "If we get Mike, we get the money that helps both the College and Central. Agreed?"

Hank nodded. "That's right, but the position . . ."

Rich held shook his head. "Wait a minute! The position is a roadblock if it goes through the normal faculty channels. Those idiots would take a couple of years to come up with a position and it would be a hodge-podge of departmental wants. Not at all what we need."

"But what . . ."

"Let me finish. In my reading of the history of the university, I came across an item in the Charter that gives the President the power to appoint a University Scholar. It's only been done one or two times in the past, but I can't find anything that would prohibit the President from designating a 'Policy Scholar' position. How's that sound to you?"

"Amazing!" Hank's expression captured the comment. "But how can we get President Rose to . . ."

Rich interrupted again. "Old Melvin will do what Waldo tells him to do. Our next step is to go back to the Dean with the idea of a 'Policy Scholar' and help him sell it to Waldo."

The reference to 'Old Melvin' brought a smile to Hank's face. Melvin Rose had recently been appointed President of Midwest after a failed national search. His Texas roots and the alliteration of his name resulted in many short ballads – all beginning with – 'I'm Melvin Rose of Texas and my friends all call me Tex.'. Unlike the defenders of the Alamo, Rose was easily manipulated by astute political actors at Midwest. The most influential of these was – Waldo Pearson.

President Rose had established an image of the 'good fellow' rather than that of the 'academic leader'. His approach to collegial life involved oversized cigars and pancake breakfasts for faculty and staff in university parking lots. Rose was always surprised by anything that related to the business of education, and ready to be led into the cloisters of academe. For all practical purposes, the university was managed by Vice President Pearson, a Blue Chip administrator.

"Here's what I think we should do," Rich proposed. "Dunkard will call us in a couple of days to let us know what Waldo has to say about our proposal. More than likely, he will point to the university-wide freeze on new positions."

"I suppose you're right. So how does your idea get around the freeze?"

"The Presidential Scholar; listen to what the Charter says," Rich swiveled his chair and took a slender volume from the bookcase. He paged through it and read. "In order to foster the development of the University, the President shall – on his own authority – appoint Presidential Scholars who can strengthen strategic areas of study. Such Scholars shall enjoy all the rights and privileges accorded the members of the University faculty."

Hank was amazed. "It's almost as if we wrote that. Clearly, the President can make a regular faculty appointment on his own. Colleges, departments and faculties have nothing to say."

"That's the way I read it. So what we'll do is wait for the call, then get the Charter in front of Pearson, he'll do the rest. By the way, this is item 22 in the Charter."

"MiGod – Catch 22. In reverse!"

The call from Dunkard came two days later. "Rich, this is Mert. I've met with Waldo. He's sympathetic to your idea, but he says there's no way a new appointment can be made with the position freeze on."

"That doesn't surprise me. However, there is a way that gets around the freeze. I've been studying the University Charter and would like to show you some language that's on point. May I come over?"

"Of course, how about right now? Please bring Hank Loras along if he's available."

Rich disconnected and entered Hank's number.

"Hank Loras."

"Mert called. It's on now. See you in the Dean's office."

Dunkard was suitably impressed by item 22 of the Charter. "Reads like presidential permission to make an appointment whenever he pleases." He closed the Charter and reached for his telephone. "I'll see when we can meet with Waldo, OK?"

Hank and Rich nodded and the call was completed. A meeting was arranged for that afternoon.

The three-person delegation marched across the Quad to Conant Hall. There, Hank heaved the entry half of the bronze gateway ajar and offered Rich and the Dean entry. The effect was, Rich thought, much like pictures of the Reichskanzlei in 1933 Berlin.

The three men clattered down the hallway to the side office of the Vice President. The martinet ushered them into a conference room where an oak table and leather chairs were dominated by a floor-to-ceiling fireplace.

Pearson was standing at the mantle, holding a cup of coffee. "Hello Rich. Hi Hank. Good to see you." He held out his free hand. "Always a pleasure, Dean. Please sit down. Would you like coffee?"

They refused the offer, and waited for Waldo to begin. "Well, Mert tells me that you have a line on federal funding. As you know, it would be most welcome, but I'm afraid we can't give the College a new salary item in these times."

That's what I told Rich," the Dean said. "However, he has an interesting proposal that you should hear."

Pearson looked at Rich. "Well Rich, shoot."

"It's really quite simple," Rich explained. "The University Charter gives the President the authority to appoint what the Charter calls "Presidential Scholars' any time he sees an area in need of new ideas. We believe that President Rose could appoint an 'Educational Policy Scholar' to give Michael Bahls a home at Midwest."

"That's a provision of the Charter I haven't seen. Have you a copy with you?"

Rich opened the Charter book to Item 22 and slid it across the table to Pearson. "You'll see, Waldo, that the language is very clear. Also, I've reviewed the history of this item and found that it has rarely been used. What Item 22 means is that Presidential Scholars can be appointed without the usual search process. You'll notice that the Charter specifies that Scholars 'enjoy all the rights and privileges' of regular faculty. That means that Scholars are on a tenure track."

Pearson continued to read. He paged to the front of the Charter to determine the intent of the items. Then he looked to the final pages where changes and amendments were discussed. "Giving this a quick once over, I think you have something Rich. Tell you what, I'll run this by the university attorney. If he gives his OK, I can lay it on the president's desk."

Hank shifted uneasily in his chair. "We recognize that the President must act within the legal framework of the Charter. But that takes time and our connection to federal money is on a very short timeline. Do you see any way that the decision making process can be moved along quickly?"

Pearson laughed. "The legal mill grinds slowly, but I think I can turn the crank on the attorney."

"Sounds good to me," Rich said. "Michael Bahls is a Blue Chip scholar and it would be a shame to lose him – to say nothing of the money involved."

"I've heard of this guy," Pearson said. "Maybe we should get him out here for a visit while we explore possibilities. That make any sense?"

Hank nodded vigorously. "Sure does! My research program could invite Bahls to make a presentation on the Americans with Disabilities Act. The President could meet him and take his measure."

Pearson considered this proposal for a half-minute. "OK. Go ahead with the invitation, but be sure that you don't make any commitments as to possible employment."

"Will do," Hank said. "May I coordinate his visit with your office?"

"Sure thing," Pearson said, then he murmured. "Blue Chip. I like that."

On the walk back to Blewett, Dunkard enthused over the prospect of a Presidential Scholar. "I'd say there's a high probability that Rose will go for a position for Bahls. That makes his visit extremely important. We must try to determine how likely it is for him to deliver the federal funding."

"That's right," Hank agreed. "Even though we need to dance around the appointment, Bahls has to come away with an understanding of the arrangements we are working on."

"I'll second that," Rich said. "When we met with Bahls in DC, we talked about a Policy Studies Academy here at Midwest. If we could give that idea some substance before his visit, Bahls will make the connection between funding and our R&D potential."

They walked along past the Library. At the door to Blewett, the Dean paused. "Why don't you two work up a plan for Bahls' visit? When you have it in place, let's get together and discuss the details. Sound OK?"

Rich nodded and held the door for the Dean and Hank. Inside, Rich confirmed the assignment. "Will do. Hank and I can have it on your desk tomorrow."

"And don't forget to put some words around that Academy," Dunkard admonished.

"Consider it done!" Rich enthused.

CHAPTER 10

Peer Review

". . . the persons most qualified to judge the worth of a scientist's grant proposal . . . are precisely those who are the scientist's closest competitors."
(Horace Judson: Journal of the American Medical Association)

Bahls' visit to Midwest was an example of the stagecraft of academic politics. Rich assembled a majority of the faculty of the College of Education and Home Economics in the atrium of Blewett. A promise of wine and cheese ensured that the usual afternoon exodus of professors would be postponed until Bahls had finished his speech. With Hank's assistance, Rich programmed Dean Dunkard's remarks and arranged for suitable post-speech questions that would illuminate Bahls' intellect.

Bahls swept into the Blewett Atrium dressed in Mafioso style; black trench coat worn as a cape over a black three-piece suit. A dark shirt and tie completed the image. He was about to make an offer that couldn't be refused!

Dean Dunkard did the introduction. "It is my great honor to present Doctor Michael Bahls to our College. As most of you know, Dr. Bahls has emerged as one of the most important leaders in the U.S. Department of Health and Human Services. In fact, the Americans with Disability Act is, in no small measure, his doing. Today, we have the opportunity to hear how the Act will shape the future of American education. Please give Dr. Bahls a Midwest welcome!"

As Bahls proceeded to detail his view of the Americans with Disability Act, Rich followed the speech and made mental notes. Key comments were filed in Rich's mind – to be explored in depth later on.

". . . it is essential that we educators realize the significance of ADA," Bahls said as he looked at the audience over half-glasses. "There will be a realignment of funding with ever greater emphasis on services to the handicapped . . ."

Funding! That got Rich's attention. *Realignment!* With Mike's influence some of that money would be 'realigned' to Midwest – and to Rich!

Another nugget fell from Bahls' narrative. ". . . a key element in our view of ADA is policy research. Leaders in H&HS are eager to know how ADA alters the opportunities of disabled Americans."

Policy research! Here was confirmation of the plan Rich and Hank had devised. With Bahls at Midwest . . . !

As the speech drew to a close, Rich's body tensed and he straightened on his chair. *C'mon Mike! Make the pitch!*

As ordered, Bahls summarized. "My personal commitment to ADA is to ensure that substantive policy research is carried out in a timely manner. Accordingly," Bahls paused and took a sip of water, "I am hoping that Midwest will develop into a national center for policy studies. And," he looked around the Atrium engaging the eyes of individual professors, "you can be sure that I will do everything in my power to provide the support and resources necessary."

Support! Resources! These were the words that moved professors and administrators! Rich glanced at his colleagues. He could see that Bahls' message had hit its target.

The balance of the visit to Blewett went according to Rich's plan. He reinforced Bahls' message in an aside to the Dean. "Well Mert, what do you think of Dr. Bahls?"

"Pretty damn impressive," Dunkard concluded. "He's just what we need, but we're gonna have some issues with Central on funding for the position."

"I know, I know," Rich commiserated. "It's my hope that Bahls can come with enough money to make the case."

"That's the way!" Dunkard exaulted. "Money talks with Central!"

At the same time, Hank was introducing Bahls to College leaders. From what Rich could see, they too were impressed. All in all, the visit was shaping up very well.

Rich was surprised to note that Carl Mertens was among the attendees. His puzzled frown drew Mertens to his side.

"So Rich, this is the guy we've been hearing about. Is he for real?"

"Of course. Dr. Bahls is a candidate for a position in the College. Probably will work under Hank Loras.

"C'mon!" Mertens chuckled. "There's a hell of a lot more than that. I hear that Rose is likely to make Bahls a Presidential Scholar. Kind of an end run around the appointment process."

The implied question confronted Rich and he stumbled in response. "Well, I guess . . .,"

"Don't come with that!" Mertens said. "I see your hand in this. And, I have to congratulate you. I would never have thought of the Presidential Scholar gambit. In fact, it sounds made to order for us in the Business School."

For God's sake! Rich imagined ranks of Presidential Scholars, all competing for Rose's attention. Rich laughed heartily. "It isn't all that simple. I'd suggest that you go slowly and see how we make out with Bahls."

"I get your message," Mertens said, clapping Rich's shoulder. "Well, gotta go back to the School. Keep me informed, any advice on how we should proceed will be welcome. And don't forget to send me notes that we can use in our metaphor papers."

"Sure thing!"

That evening, it was time for the three conspirators to agree on approaches that would build on Bahls' presentation. Tubby's was not the place for a discussion of this magnitude. Instead, the three adjourned to a table in a secluded alcove at the Chalet.

When drinks had been served, Rich began. "OK. That went well. Now what's next?"

Bahls swirled the ice in his Martini. "Here's what I propose." He took a long pull at the drink. "I'll stay over another day and work with you to develop a proposal that will bring the money to Midwest."

"Hmmm . . .," Hank mused, "that's all well and good, but my experience with H&HS funding suggests that the best we'll be able to do is a six-month turn around."

Bahls chuckled. "Sure, that's the usual. But I've got a line on a special appropriation that's focused on ADA policy. The turnaround on this is only a couple of weeks."

"So," Rich said skeptically. "What's the assurance that we'll be in line for the money?"

"Leave that to me!" Bahls boasted. "All that's needed is the right language and I can help put that in place." He waited while the other two digested this assertion. "Just give me a day with that grad student, you know the one that was with you in D.C.."

Grad student? Rich was puzzled by the request. "You mean Ms. Berland?" he asked.

"Yes," Bahls smiled. "That's the one. She appears to have a view of policy research that fits into the new RFP. She available?"

"Well . . . I suppose," Rich hesitated. "Let me see what I can do."

"Why not give her a call now," Hank suggested. "Here, you can use my cell phone."

This was moving too fast for Rich. Inviting Felicity to work with Bahls was asking for a new dynamic. One more actor confused the political alignment Rich had crafted. However, he had no option. He reached for Hank's phone.

He punched in Felicity's home number. *Maybe she won't . . .* He hoped – but she was!

"Hello Hank. What's up?" Felicity's caller ID pointed to Loras.

"Ms. Berland. This is Professor Jessen. I'm meeting with Dr. Bahls and . . .," *And what . . .* he waited for inspiration . . .

"So happy to hear from you," Felicity said expectantly.

"What I called for . . . is . . . to see if you might be available to work with Dr. Bahls and myself tomorrow," Rich found his direction. "You see, there's a new RFP that H&HS will be posting and our Center might be in line for favorable consideration."

"How exciting!" Felicity said enthusiastically. "Of course I'd be happy to help. Where will we meet and at what time?"

Rich put his hand over the phone. "It's OK with her. Shall we meet at the Center?"

Hank nodded. "I'll set up a work space – say for nine a.m.."

"Ms. Berland, we'll meet at the Center at nine. Will that suit you?"

"I'll be there!"

"Good job Rich!" Bahls praised. "Now you two need to understand just how this is going to work. Best if Berland isn't in the loop on the back story. What I've done is to limit the RFP to a couple of university groups like yours. I'll see to it that the grants are spread around but, here's the kicker, the bulk of funding will go to your Center."

"Wow!" Hank said as he raised his glass. "This calls for another round!"

"Better make it a light one," Bahls said. "We'll need to have our wits about us tomorrow."

Money, Bahls, the Center and Felicity roamed the hallways of Rich's mind on his way home and as he attempted to sleep. Again, circumstance confused his careful plans. It was almost as if Bahls was already at Midwest. *Why did he have to bring her into this?* Like many other nights, he slept fitfully and awoke not quite prepared for a new alignment of actors.

The Center was already filled with secretaries and students when Rich arrived the next morning. Bahls was standing, coffee cup in hand, talking with an attentive Felicity.

"Morning Rich!" Bahls called. "Ready to go? I've put Felicity into the picture. C'mon, let's get cracking!" He used his free hand to guide Felicity toward the Center conference room.

Felicity! He called her Felicity! This was familiarity that Rich had planned for himself – in the future! He trailed along behind the pair. *Gotta get control . . .*

That wish proved to be impossible. When they were all seated, Bahls took charge of the meeting. "Here's what we need to do. Rich, you and Hank work up a budget that has about," he made several notes on a legal pad, "five million in total! How's that sound?"

"Wheew!" Hank wheezed. "That's a lot of green! You sure about that number?"

"You bet!" Bahls said confidently. "What you and Rich need to do is to apportion the dollars to staffing, travel and the like. By the way, what's the indirect cost level here?"

Indirect cost? Rich was unable to respond, lost in contemplation of the immense size of the grant. *Five million dollars!*

"Central takes ten percent of my grants as indirect cost," Hank said.

"Pretty low number," Bahls pursed his lips. "We'll need to work on that in the future. Now, Felicity and I will do the body of the proposal. Rich, I'd like for you to look over our work and match the outcomes we develop to the budget numbers. Everyone OK?"

The work groups separated; Rich with a longing glance at Felicity as she disappeared with Bahls.

"Let's get goin'," Hank beckoned from the door to his office. "Grab a cup of coffee and close the door."

Rich followed direction and seated himself at Hank's conference table. "So what's next?" he asked.

Despite his wide knowledge of university politics, Rich had virtually no knowledge of the mysteries of grant writing. The idea that two small work groups could access a flow of money in a half-day was confusing – and exciting.

"So," Rich asked. "Where do we start?"

"Watch!" Hank stepped to a white board on an office wall where he drew a simple matrix. Columns were labeled as 'Program Activities' with blanks for the results of the Bahls-Felicity team. Rows were entitled; 'staff', 'travel', 'supplies', 'contracted services', 'indirect cost' and other less familiar labels. He then drew a box in the lower right-hand corner of the matrix. Standing back, he pointed to the box. "See! Here's where the five million goes!" He inked in the figure. "Now, we work up from that number to distribute the bucks. First, we take off Central's ten percent." Hank wrote '$500,000' on the 'Total' column of the 'indirect cost' row. "Tell you what," he said. "Take a yellow pad and keep score."

"Keep score?" Rich looked puzzled. "What do you mean?"

Hank frowned, facing the newcomer he said, "We just spent five hundred grand of the five million. There's four and a half million left. Get it?"

"OK . . . I guess. But I don't see . . ."

"Hang on pardner! I'll show you how we spend money! The big one here is 'staff', that's Mike with some of our time thrown in. It's also grad students like Felicity. It's also where we have to do some creative computing."

"By 'creative' you mean?"

"For instance, if Mike comes here his university salary and benefits are likely to be in the range of a hundred-fifty K. Assuming the grant is for three years, that eats up another four hundred fifty grand."

A hundred and fifty a year! Why that's fifty more than I make! "Isn't that a little high?" he asked.

"Nope. Don't think so. We ain't gonna get Mike for peanuts. Remember, investing in Bahls is on the come. He's the one that can open the money tap!"

Rich noted the impossible sum. The five million was reduced to four million fifty thousand. The figures were blurry markers of higher education finance.

"Guess . . . that's OK," Rich said resignedly. "Now, what about us?"

"Good thinkin pard! I'd say we put in for half time each. No, that won't work. One of us has to be Principal Investigator for the project. I'm already pretty well loaded up, so I guess it's gotta be you."

Principal Investigator! Rich envisioned a revised resume where his new role would receive star billing.

183

"Think the Dean will go for that?" Hank asked. "I mean, can you cut some slack in the Associate Dean budget?"

Rich reviewed his work load. *Teaching has to go!* He smiled. No more Saturday classes! No idiotic term papers! "Yes, I'm sure Dunkard will release me for this kind of money. Remember, I've already moved my salary item to Higher Ed.."

"So let's put you at round a hundred a year. That close enough?" Receiving a nod from Rich, Hank continued. "So you cost the College three hundred for three years. Half of that is one fifty K. How much we got left?"

Rich made the necessary notes. "Looks like three million nine hundred thousand."

"Now, I'll take fifty of that for some of my time," Hank paused for several seconds. "Nope, this isn't working. Let's go back and put all three of us at the same level." He penned the resulting figures at the side of his matrix. 'Mike - full time -$450,000; Rich - half time - $225,000; Hank – half time - $225,000. "Now that's better," He looked at Rich. "You got that?"

Rich didn't answer. He was gaping at the salary figure for 'Rich'. He had just received a fifty percent salary increase! Without doing anything! With a trembling hand, he did the sums.

"Way I see it," Rich mumbled as he wrote. "We've given Central five hundred K and spent . . . ummm . . . nine hundred on 'staff' . . . that leaves . . . three million six hundred thousand left." Rich stared at these impossible figures. So that's what grant writing was all about!

A tap on the conference room door interrupted calculation. The door swing open and Felicity was framed in the opening.

"Professor Jessen," she said. "I recall reading your plan for a study of the response of colleges and universities to ADA. I told Dr. Bahls about it and he would like to see if it can serve as the centerpiece of our proposal."

Rich saw the connection at once! He, the Principal Investigator, could claim the project as his own! "That's very interesting, I've just been thinking along those lines," the lie rolling easily off his tongue.

It did not, of course, fool Hank who looked askance at Rich. "Not a bad idea! Say! I'll bet I have copy here." He wheeled his chair to a file cabinet and where a moment of search produced the document. "Here Rich. This is it, right?"

Yes! Higher Education Institutional Response to ADA! Rich admired the paper as he passed it along to Felicity.

"Oh thanks! This is exactly what we need!" Sweeping out the door, she waved the trophy.

"Now, that's very interesting," Hank said reflectively. "You see where this is going? Suppose that your paper is the key to the project, then we can funnel the money to support appropriate research."

The Principal Investigator took possession of this suggestion. "Yes . . . that's very much in line with my thoughts. We can use a considerable slice of the money to do on-site visits of a sample of institutions, and ..."

Hank cut in. "We could send teams of grad students to do inventories of the extent to which higher ed. is complying with ADA. Let's try that on!"

The balance of the budget developed quickly. Hank created column headings for; 'interview protocol development', 'interviewer training', 'campus visits', 'consultation' and 'data analysis'. As these activities received their share of the grant, Rich envisioned himself at the center of a web of activity. *This was real research!*

"OK Old Buddy," Hank said as he capped his flip chart pen. "Here's how I think it pans out. We gotta remember that the load's gonna fall on you and me. We'll have to find the grad students and work them through the whole research process. You ready to put in some overtime?"

For Rich 'overtime' meant anything beyond a half-day. It now appeared that this definition would be significantly rewritten if the grant came through. Evidently, this wasn't 'free money' – he'd have to earn it! However, the magnitude of reward was such that Rich was a ready volunteer.

"Of course," Rich said confidently. "I can use some of the Dean's time if need be. One thing though. I'll need a full-time grad assistant, somebody that is up to speed on ADA and higher ed.."

"Bet I know what's on your mind," Hank chuckled. "You're talkin about Felicity. Right?"

Caught in what he thought was a deceptive generality, Rich could only nod.

Hank accepted the agreement, uncapped his pen and added the amount of a hundred thousand to 'grant administration'; taking money from each of the program areas. "There! That'll do it! Now let's see how the deep thinkers are doing.

They crossed the Center workspace to the other conference room where Felicity and Mike were in earnest dialog.

"Hey you two!" Hank said. "How's the proposal comin? We got the numbers as we see them." He laid the matrix in front of Bahls.

Rich glanced at the table. *Why! There's nothing written!* He couldn't believe his eyes! The budget matrix lay next to Rich's research proposal. There was nothing else. *What had they been doing?* Waves of jealousy washed over his mind. He finally found his voice.

"I see that you've been studying my research proposal. Think that we can use some of those ideas for this grant?"

Bahls waved a hand. "It's right on! What we've been doing is figuring how we could use site visits to test compliance with ADA, and . . ."

Hank pointed to the matrix. "Exactly! We're on the same page. So how do these numbers work out?"

Bahls ran his finger down each column. "Good enough for now. You agree, Felicity?"

"Looks fine to me. There'll be no problem connecting Rich's proposal with these numbers," she turned a dazzling smile toward Rich. "Your proposal is exactly what the feds are looking for!"

Rich's legs nearly buckled under the glow of that glance. *She called me Rich!* The love-stricken professor gradually gave way to the Principal Investigator. "I'm pleased you see it that way. You'll notice that we've provided for a stipend for you as Assistant P.I.."

This was a gambit Bahls couldn't match. "Good move," he said reluctantly. "You'll have to make sure that I don't appear anywhere in the proposal. What you can do is to indicate that the project will be posting a position to recruit a person with ADA expertise."

"Thought you'd say that," Hank observed. "The proposal will have to fly on the wings of Rich's and my resumes."

"No problem!" Bahls barked. "I've got a peer review committee in place. These are people with sound ADA credentials and they owe me big time! I see that you've provided money for 'consultation'. We'll use most of that to bring some of my review committee into the project. That way, everybody wins!"

None of those involved in this parody of scholarship questioned their actions. They readily accepted the formalisms of academic integrity to further their narrow, highly personal ends. All this was made possible by a kind of 'academic canon law' that provided a structure into which individual work was to fit and a mechanism whereby status could be conferred on the most adroit academic lawyers so that money could be funneled to friends of court. This was the 'real research' that Rich would direct.

They stood around the table for some time, contemplating their work. Agreements were made as to next steps with Rich and Felicity detailed to produce the final draft. Hank was assigned to 'make the numbers work'. Bahls was released to return to Washington where he would receive a draft of the proposal for editing.

Work proceeded smoothly and the draft was emailed to Bahls. His comments were incorporated into the final document which was ready to move through university grant-submission channels.

Rich, as Principal Investigator, was responsible for meeting university requirements and for securing the final signature from Waldo Pearson for transmittal to H&HS. The entire political strategy hinged on Pearson's signature. His approval of the grant would include an offer of appointment to Bahls, endorsement of realignment of Rich's position (and salary) and support for a Policy Studies Academy within Hank's Center.

"Well Pard," Hank said seriously. "Now the rubber meets the road. How we gonna get Waldo to buy the package? You know, it's gotta be everything – or nothing."

"Yes," Rich squirmed. "That's a fact. The way I see it, the key is the Bahls appointment. Without that, we don't get the money and the whole Policy Studies thing is a washout."

"Time to play the M-80 card?" Hank asked. "Can we scare Waldo into our corner?"

"No, I don't think that'll work. Waldo gets pretty defensive when he's attacked. What we need is a carrot for Central to get him to sign."

Hank reflected. "Got it!" he exploded. "Indirect cost! Remember what Bahls said? The U isn't taking as big a slice of grant money as other universities."

"You may have something there. Let's see . . . the U gets ten percent of our grant," Rich paged to the budget page of the proposal. "That's five hundred K. I'd say that's pretty big."

"Sure seems like it," Hank agreed. "But I've checked on other university indirect cost levels. The U is way at the bottom. What we can do is jockey the figures and up the ante." He reached for the proposal and moved his pen across the budget matrix. "Suppose we give the U twenty percent. That's an even million. Take the extra money from . . .," he made several entries, ". . . 'data analysis' and 'consultation'. I don't think that'd weaken the grant. What say?"

"Well, I don't know," Rich grimaced. "Seems like the U's getting a lot for nothing." He felt the grant dollars slipping from his fingers. "I don't see why . . ."

"Think about it! You gotta realize that this is the way the game is played. We buy Waldo's support, Bahls gets the appointment and we get more than enough money to do our thing."

Rich stacked these blue chips and proceeded to bet the pile. "I suppose . . .," Uncertainty nearly withdrew the wager. He hesitated, then the size of the pot ruled. "OK, I guess. Who gets to lay this on Waldo's desk? I suppose it's me," he said ruefully.

"Yep. Gotta be you. You're the Principal Investigator. I'll send it to Pearson in campus mail and you can see him in a day or so."

It was an easy sell. Waldo was all smiles when he received Rich. "Glad to see you Rich! This is a very interesting proposal. Sounds like it could put Midwest on the map! C'mon in!"

Hank had been correct. Indirect costs were the key to Pearson's support. It was the first item on Pearson's agenda.

"I see that you've upped our indirect cost percentage," Waldo observed. "What's the rationale for the change?"

"It was Dr. Bahls' idea," Rich lied. "He feels that the university isn't covering its costs with the current percentage. In fact, he's able to guarantee that the new percentage will apply to all future grants."

"I'd say that makes the deal," Waldo shoved the proposal across his conference table. "I'll approve an appointment for Dr. Bahls and sign off on your proposal, contingent on your assurance that you'll do your best to land this Policy Studies Academy."

Rich muffled a sigh of relief. *The whole enchilada!* On his return to Blewett, the Quad seemed to him to have the bright glow of springtime. Rich floated on the bustle of students; several who knew 'The Prof' were amazed at his friendly greeting. He wafted into Hank's Center and marched across the workspace to Hank's office.

"I can see that you have good news!" Hank said. "Grab a chair and tell me all about it!"

"Couldn't believe it!" Rich gloated. "Waldo bought the whole package. Now all we have to do is to get the Dean to send Mike an appointment letter!"

"Good work!" Hank praised. "And get that proposal in the mail! I'll give Bahls a heads up on the proposal and you can work Dunkard on the appointment. You know, peer review works best when the peers are your friends."

CHAPER ELEVEN

Grantsmanshop

"... (grantsmanship requires an)...understanding of the pivotal role relationships play in grant seeking..."
(University of Missouri: PUB AF 8832)

"Hey Rich!" the voice on the phone was clearly that of Mike Bahls. "Got the good news!" Bahls continued, "The appointment was just what we planned. All the thanks goes to you!"

"Well, yes," Rich said. "I just received a copy of the appointment letter in campus mail. Looks good to me. So, are you coming?"

"You bet! This is exactly what I've been looking for. Working with you and Hank will be a real pleasure. And, I've got some good news for you. Your grant request has been approved for the whole five million! How about that?"

Rich exhaled a long sigh of relief. "Wonderful! That makes the deal!" He sat back, and smiled; picturing a three-year run of plenty.

Bahls interrupted this reverie. "You still there?"

"Umm... yes, just thinking how happy Dean Dunkard and Vice President Pearson will be with the news. After all, they're the ones that we had to convince in order to get your letter in the mail."

"Well, you did exactly what was needed. When I get on board, I'll fill you in on what happened at this end and what it all means for the future."

"Glad to hear it. Now, what can I do to help?"

There was a slight pause. "Not much I guess. If you could scout out housing opportunities, Beth and I would be grateful."

"No problem. When will you be coming out to University City?"

"Not for a few weeks, but Beth will be there next week and would sure appreciate getting your perspective on the U. Possible?"

"Sure. Just let me know . . ."

"Fantastic!" Bahls interrupted. "She'll be coming in on flight 666 next Wednesday. Hope you can meet her. Anyway, I gotta go now. See you in a couple of weeks."

The connection was broken and Rich stared at the silent instrument. Here was the beginning of the plan he and Hank had masterminded. Mike! And money! Why wasn't he happy?

Master of Arrangements! Rich grimaced. "It'll all be better when Mike gets here," he mumbled unconvincingly.

Flight 666 was on time and Rich had no difficulty in identifying Beth Bahls. *She looks just like she did in grad school!* He was struck by the difference between the radiant Beth and dead Muriel. The foursome that dominated the social life of LMU was now a threesome.

"Over here, Rich!" Beth called.

Rich obeyed and opened his arms for her greeting. "So good to see you again Beth. Just like old times."

"Oh Rich! I was stunned to hear about Muriel. Such a tragedy!"

"Yes, it's been tough. Anyway, let's get your bag and I'll introduce you to Midwest."

Once in the Mercedes and free of airport traffic, Rich began his travelogue. "We're coming into the city on Riverside Drive. It'll take us past the U and I can point out Blewett Hall. That's where Mike is likely to be located."

A smiling Beth participated in the tour, comparing the peaceful scenes with Washington. "Rich! This is fantastic! I've been waiting for this kind of setting. D.C. is all hustle – nothing like this."

The tour continued through residential areas of the city where Rich located faculty homes. He saved the President's mansion for last. "There's where President Rose hangs out. He'll want to welcome Mike as the first Presidential Scholar."

"Yes," Beth mused. "Mike's told me about that. One thing you need to know is that he's very ambitious . . .," A long pause followed.

The anxiety in her voice got Rich's attention and he pulled the Merc to a parking spot. He faced Beth and noticed lines of worry. "What do you mean? Is there a problem?"

"Not something to be overly concerned about, but Mike's always looking for the next rung of his ladder. That usually works out OK; however, there have been times when his expectations drive him a bit above reality."

He frowned. "I don't understand. Are you telling me that there are problems ahead?"

"No, not exactly. What I'm trying to do is tell an old friend to be aware of a kind of unbridled enthusiasm that can push Mike ahead of the pack. Usually, that's worked well for him. He has the wit to shape opportunity. If there's a problem it usually has to do with bringing his colleagues along."

"Can you be a little more specific?"

Beth reflected for moment. "Take the grant you just received from H&HS. Mike has kept me in the loop on this since it's determining our future. Well, in order to seize that opportunity, Mike has had to do some serious manipulating of his review committee. Normally, there's a lot of that sort of thing in D.C.. In this case, I know that he's promised some payback to several on the committee."

"Are you talking illegal?"

"No, that's not the way it works. What I mean is; if you and Mike hope to land grants in the future, you'll need to follow his lead on how to work the system. Don't worry, he's a master at this sort of thing. I guess the reason I've spoken frankly, is that he'll need your guidance on how the University works."

"That's easy!" Rich said with a relieved sigh. "We're pretty simple here."

"OK," Beth said, patting Rich's shoulder. "Just remember what I said about Mike's ambition."

Rich started the Merc and delivered Beth to her hotel. Her comments about Mike were forgotten and Rich's next several days were given to the search for housing. He was somewhat surprised to find that his suggestions were cordially rejected in favor of more expensive options. Beth eventually agreed on a Georgian two-story on Riverside Drive – a significant step up from the Jessen home.

When Beth was settled, Rich began planning Mike's reception at Midwest. As President Rose's first 'University Scholar' Bahls already had the attention of Central Administration as well as key faculty members of the College. These made up the list of those to be invited to an up-scale version of the 'wine and cheese' that passed for a formal reception.

In order to put his plan in motion, Rich needed to involve both Dunkard and Pearson. Two phone conversations were all that were needed. Rich's first call was to the Dean.

"Mert, this is Rich. As you probably have heard, Dr. Bahls has accepted our offer and will be arriving next week. I'm working with Central on a suitable reception," Rich paused to let the lie speak for the importance of the reception. "Would it be possible for our office to invite College department chairs?"

"Of course!" Dunkard boomed. "We'll help give Bahls a Midwest welcome. He's a real Blue Chip!"

A few additional comments were exchanged and Rich disconnected. "Blue Chip!" he said aloud. "That was a real game changer!"

Rich was able to off-load reception planning to President Rose's office. A reception at the Presidential Mansion was arranged to support Rich's agenda.

These arrangements met with Bahls' enthusiastic approval upon his arrival in Rich's office a week later. "Great job Rich!" he said as he pumped Rich's hand. "Beth and I are so pleased at your warm welcome!"

"Glad to do it," Rich responded in a somewhat hesitant tone of voice.

Bahls looked at Rich earnestly. "Now, you can tell me what Rose is likely to say and how I can best respond."

"I've thought a lot about that," Rich said reflectively. "Since you're his first Presidential Scholar, Rose will lead with his view of the position and how important your appointment is for the future of Midwest. He'll follow that up with some of the usual stuff about the opportunity our faculty will have to work with you. The rest will be welcoming boilerplate," He paused for emphasis. "What I suggest is that you focus your remarks on the Policy Studies Academy and how it'll put this place on the national map."

"That's easy," Bahls said. "All I need to do is to give a repeat of some of the comments I made on my last visit. Then, I can get everyone's attention by announcing the new grant. Think that'll do it?"

"Yes, that's the basic stuff. You might also throw a few bones to the department chairs; you know, how they are likely to get a slice of the pie."

The reception was a success! Midwest faculty and administrators glowed in the reflections of Bahls' brilliance and the shine of federal dollars. Rich could see that everyone left the Mansion immersed in mental calculation of self-interest.

The next morning, Bahls flopped into a chair opposite Rich's desk. "Well, that was great and now it's time we get to work. You and I need to meet with Hank to plan how we'll work the new grant, and we have to set the grant-getting machinery running."

"I understand the first part," Rich said anxiously. "But what's this about the 'machinery'. Didn't we just land the big one?"

"Steady Old Timer!" Bahls chuckled. "I know this kind of money is a bit of a shock. Get used to it! There's more on the way! In fact, there's a Request For Proposal coming out in a couple of weeks and I think we should take a shot at it."

"But . . .," Rich hesitated, "don't we have a full plate with the new grant? I can't see how . . ."

Bahls cut him short. "Sure, we'll have the bases loaded, but the only way to deal with the Feds is to keep the money tap flowing."

The mixed metaphors confused Rich. "I think we'll have a tough time meeting the deliverables on the current grant. Why . . .," he reflected for a moment, "there's at least, let me see, three major research reports due by the end of the year."

"That's right!" Bahls proclaimed. "And we'll have them in D.C. ahead of time! All we need to do is set a group of grad students to work on each deliverable. Then we can sit back and monitor what they do. Believe me. I've been on the receiving end of these sorts of reports and I know how overloaded D.C. grant offices are. If a report has the right bulk and a good Executive Summary, it gets the green light."

As Bahls developed this theme, Rich imagined a balding, shirtsleeved worker inundated by stacks of paper. A rubber stamp descended on the cover of a report and the worker placed it in a basket marked 'Approved'. The image brought a grin to Rich's lips. "OK, if you say so. But what's this about another RFP?"

"It's a big one!" Bahls smiled. "The feds are planning to fund what they are calling a 'Policy Studies Academy'. You'll recognize this as the seed we planted when I was in D.C.. They're throwing millions at this initiative and I think we have a good chance of landing the grant."

"Well now," Rich mused. "That's sure worth …"

Bahls cut in again. "You bet! So the three of us are gathering at Hank's place on Saturday. You know, the place where his ex wife used to board horses."

Rich nodded. He did indeed know of 'Almosta Ranch' and recalled the earthy Mrs. Loras. There was a measure of envy when he thought of the Ranch and how Hank seemed able to live in the horsy world – without Mrs. Loras.

"Probably a good idea," Rich agreed hesitatingly. "I suppose we need to plot some strategy."

On Saturday morning, 'strategy' was the organizing concept. When the three were seated in the glassed-in Almosta gazebo, Hank opened the discussion.

"Seems like we've made some real progress. You heard President Rose, we've got permission to move our agenda along. Now we need to come up with a plan to do just that."

"Permission doesn't exactly capture what the president is saying," Rich grumbled. "He's laying out something like marching orders!"

Bahls laughed. "Makes no difference whether it's permission or orders, we have just what we need. So let me tell you the way I see the national scene and you two can put me in the Midwest picture. So far as H&HS is concerned, there are two money spigots and I think we can turn both on."

"Whaddya mean two?" Hank asked. "I've made the Center work with typical research grants. Is there more than that?"

"You bet!" Bahls said confidently. "Yes, one pipeline delivers cash for what I'd call policy research. That's money we can depend on. However, it's not where the real big bucks come from."

This was the kind of talk that got Rich's attention. "Tell us more," he commanded.

"It's a little complicated," Bahls warned. "So pay attention. What you've been doing Hank, is following the standard formulae for grant writing and research reporting. Right?"

"Yup. I am an enthusiastic follower of APA. Works for me!"

APA! Rich was a believer in that particular canon. He religiously followed the format developed by the American Psychological Association in every so-called 'research paper' he wrote. "Yes," he added. "APA's the way to go."

"You got that right!" Bahls exclaimed. "But let me tell you how it really works. First of all, research proposals that aren't following APA guidelines don't even get a reading from my reviewers. In fact, I've got one nut from upstate New York who only studies the citations; I've seen him reject perfectly good proposals if they have commas in the wrong place!"

"Wondered about that," Hank groused. "One of my best ideas came back with plenty of red marks on the citation pages. Not one mark on the content!"

"That's lesson number one!" Bahls said. "On any of what we'll call 'research papers' we follow APA to the letter. To make sure that happens, I'd like to hire my secretary from H&HS to do the formatting and proof-reading. OK?"

Hank and Rich nodded.

Bahls went on. "Now for the big money! Back in D.C., I elaborated on your Policy Studies Academy idea; to the tune of twenty million for a national effort in that direction. Now, we just might be able to land all of that money for ourselves. To do so, we'll need to follow the lead of Vocational Education."

"Vocational education!" Rich sputtered. "Why, that's . . ."

"Calm down, Old Timer," Bahls said soothingly. "We won't become 'Vokies'. What I'm saying is that their National Center for Research in Vocational Education is the model we'll follow."

"I've heard of that," Hank said. "But just how is it a model for us?"

"The way H&HS does it is to contract with a university to disperse the bulk of the grant to other universities for specific projects. Then . . ."

"Just a minute!" Hank said. "That means we do the work and other universities get the money! Doesn't seem like much of a strategy to me!"

Bahls took a sip of his coffee, leaned back in his chair and continued. "You're missing the point! I've put the model in place in D.C. and we're on track to be the National Center for Policy Studies! How about that!"

Certainty always comforted Rich. "All right," he said, "but how does it actually work?"

"Simple. We get, let's say, five million a year for three years. That gives us a hell of lot of leverage on policy makers, to say nothing about our fellow educators. Why, I'll bet that our papers will breeze through peer review and, of course, we'll put a big slice of the dough on our plate."

"So, what do we need to do here?" Hank asked.

"Yeah," Rich seconded. "How do we get organized?"

"I've thought about that," Bahls said authoritatively. "We'll need to reconfigure your Center, Hank. It has to reflect our capacity to focus on policy studies. I'd say that's possible, given the studies you've done on the education of the handicapped. Further, we'll need to show a robust education and training effort that's fully supported by our College. Finally, we'll have to keep Central in our camp."

The other two contemplated the assignment. Finally, Rich responded. "Sounds sensible, but it's a pretty tall order. Got any ideas as to our individual responsibilities?"

Bahls was ready for this question. "Yes, Rich. You're clearly the one to take on the education and training effort. Can you work this along with your Associate Dean role?"

"No problem there. Dunkard will be relieved to know that my salary item is off his budget for good."

"What's that mean, actually?" Bahls asked.

"Well, the research grant we've already received pays for half of my time. The rest is covered by our new Higher Education program."

"Hmmm," Bahls frowned. "That may need to be changed. How's about renaming Higher Ed.. Maybe that's a place for the Policy Studies Academy. Whaddya say to that?"

"Not a bad idea," Rich said approvingly. "That'll connect graduate students to the new Center. Remember, I'm PI on our last grant. And the new name will," he smiled, "put Professor Barnes on the margin." He visualized the last Witch attempting to cope with federal mandates.

"OK," said Hank. "Now what about the Center?"

"That's more complicated." Bahls stood, walked to a window and gazed at the landscape, then he turned. "I think that I need to be in the background. Won't do for H&HS folks to see the new Center as my baby. Hank, you'll need to be the P.I. on this project. I can be listed as the University Professor of Policy Studies. That way, I can take charge when the money arrives. You see, the feds will want the University to contribute my time. That's already in place from the President's office."

"Sounds like a plan," Hank pronounced. "All that remains is to cook up the actual application. Remember, our current grant has you on the budget. Any guidance on that?"

"Yes," Bahls hesitated. "What's needed is essentially a three – part application. The usual way this is done is to develop the conceptual foundation for the grant, then the work plan flows from that. Lastly, the budget is driven by the deliverables in the work plan. That's the usual way." He stood and went to the sideboard for a fresh coffee. Full cup in hand, he faced the other two. "This time, we're gonna turn this on its head."

"Whaddya mean?" Rich sounded puzzled.

"The way I've got this wired," Bahls said, "we know what the budget will be – almost to the dollar. What we have to decide is how much of the money will come directly to our Center and how we'll allocate the balance to other universities."

"Sounds familiar," Hank nodded. "That's the way we did the last proposal; focus on the money."

Rich had no problem with focusing on the money. He was, however, confused by the reverse logic of grant construction. "But, how do we construct an argument that makes any sense? Seems to me that we'll have a tough time connecting the dots."

"Good point," Bahls said with a rewarding smile. "Here's how it'll work. I've got a pretty good idea as to the deliverables and how much each will cost. My connections at H&HS will make it possible to increase the U's indirect cost rate. That'll put us in solid with Central. The grant will actually be paying for my time." He paused to let this important political maneuver sink in. "I'll work with

Hank to make sense of the work – budget connection. What you'll do Rich, is to write a few pages that describe policy studies and how the grant will inform ADA policy and, if possible make life easier for the disabled."

Rich was overwhelmed by the scope of this task. "But, I really don't have a grasp on disability research ," he shook his head.

Bahls walked to the back of Rich's chair and clapped him on a shoulder. "Nothing to it! What you do is lead with a revised version of the narrative you used for the grant you just received. Then, develop a section where you lay out how the proposed research informs policy makers. I can give you a hand on the ADA literature."

"So," Hank said. "What's the timeline?"

Bahls held up a finger. "Number one Hank, you and I meet tomorrow and cook up the deliverables and lay out the budget. We'll also get on the phone to a couple of people I know in the ADA field to get some letters of endorsement for the proposal." Bahls raised a second finger. "Number two Rich, try to get us a rough draft of the narrative by day after tomorrow. Possible?"

Although this was an impossible assignment, Rich realized that they had moved from the realm of rigorous scholarship to that of the superficial - an area of academic work with which he was familiar. "Of course, just give me a lead on each of the deliverables."

"No problem. Here," Bahls slid a paper on which there were three handwritten statements.

- Extent of implementation of ADA –
- Impact of ADA on educational institutions –
- Research to inform policy makers

"Hmmm," Rich pretended to study the paper. "Are you saying, in bullet two, that we can do surveys of school districts and universities to see what's been done to date?"

"Exactly," Bahls praised. "All you need to do is create a foundation, you know, with some references that will support studies that can produce a deliverable report on the impact of ADA."

"Got it," Rich said confidently. "Well, let's get to work." He assembled his collection of papers and left Bahls and Hank.

Enthusiasm rode with him on his return to the university. It lightened his steps out of the Blewett parking garage to the door of the office of the Associate Dean. At that point, enthusiasm deserted Rich, leaving an awareness of the magnitude of his assignment. He sat in his chair and laid Bahls' handwritten bullets on the desk top.

Several minutes passed in review of approaches he might take. He was not inspired; his usual ability to transform simple ideas into extended narrative deserted him. There was, however, a way out.

Felicity! He reached for the phone and entered the familiar number.

"Hello Professor Jessen," the melodious voice said. "Good to hear from you."

Rich was puzzled as he had not been introduced to the mystery of caller ID. "... ummm ... hello, Ms Berland. Have you a minute to talk?"

"Anytime. Go ahead."

"Well, I'm working with Dr. Bahls on an important proposal for H&HS and I'm wondering if you'd be willing to give me a hand with the narrative."

"I'd be delighted!" Felicity exclaimed. "What's the proposal all about?"

"It's too complicated to explain over the phone. Might you be available for a short conversation this evening?"

Without hesitation Felicity said. "Of course! Shall I come to your office?"

"No. Tell you what, why don't we meet for a drink . . . say . . . around seven?" The mental struggle between scholarship and infatuation turned hesitation into conversational full stops.

Felicity hesitated. ". . . I guess that would work. Where shall we meet?"

Tubbys? Rich quickly rejected that option. It wouldn't do for the Associated Dean to be seen with a young student at the campus hangout. Instead, it had to be . . . "How about the Chalet? We can get a booth where it's quiet enough to lay out . . . the work assignment."

The phone was silent for a long half-minute. "I guess . . . OK. I'll meet you there." She disconnected.

A first date! Or just a professional meeting? Rich's behavior testified that the upcoming meeting was an adolescent dream. During his drive home he screen-tested scenarios where professional bonds were transformed into intensely personal relationships. He gave meticulous attention to appearance and costume, all the while actually humming the few romantic tunes he could recall from his youth.

Rich arrived at The Chalet a good fifteen minutes ahead of schedule, secured a private booth and arranged the setting for the upcoming conference. He sat facing the doorway where Felicity would enter, ordered a glass of wine and positioned Bahls' list of deliverables in the center of the table.

Felicity arrived at exactly seven. She breezed through the doorway, a vision of youth and energy. "Oh Professor Jessen! I hope I'm not late!"

Rich stood and held out a welcoming hand, cloaking himself in dignity and understanding. "Not at all! I just arrived. Please be seated." The hand moved to assist Felicity, but did not touch her.

"Do you have a preference for wine?" Rich asked, beckoning a waiter.

Felicity shook her head. "Since we're working, I'll just have a black coffee."

Reluctantly, Rich gave the order and took his own seat. This wasn't off to exactly the right start. Replacing wine with coffee didn't promise the romantic outcome he hoped for. He sighed. "Well, we'd better get going."

Rich outlined the purpose of the proposed grant. He was encouraged throughout by Felicity's enthusiastic response.

When he had finished, she asked, "So. What can I do to help?"

"Here," Rich slid Bahls' list across the table. "This is the framework for the narrative that needs to be finished tomorrow." He waited while she skimmed the list. When she looked up, he asked, "How does that strike you as an outline? And, would you be interested in working with me to put the narrative in place?"

"Certainly! I'd say this is pretty easy. For instance, we can morph your paper on university responses to ADA into a comprehensive research agenda. With a little tweaking, that can serve as the model for a general assessment of ADA implementation."

"Great!" Rich praised, raising his wine glass. "That takes care of two of the three requirements. What about number three."

"Let me think," Felicity tossed her hair and wrinkled a smooth brow.

Rich nearly spilled his wine, his whole body weakened by her loveliness. Felicity did not notice.

"That requires a bit more work. Offhand, I'd say that we could do a meta-analysis of existing policy research."

Meta-analysis? Rich was, as usual, baffled by what was evidently an emerging methodology. Nevertheless, he was ready with his customary response. "Just what I thought! I'm pleased that we're on the same page!" The wineglass was now under control. "So, let's outline the writing task."

Felicity looked at a glittering watch on a slender wrist. "I'm kind of pressed for time," she looked up brightly. "But I can get to this on the Internet later tonite and meet you early tomorrow morning."

Rich was crushed! There would be no lover's tryst. No 'getting to know one another'. No --- whatever! "I thought, maybe . . .," he shifted from evening to morning time, "I suppose . . . that will be fine."

"Great!" Felicity stood, holding Bahls' list in hand. "May I keep this? I'd like to study it more closely."

"Of course! Of course!" Rich rose, his napkin sliding to the floor. As he bent to retrieve the wayward cloth, agility of youth won out over age and she handed the napkin to Rich.

"Thank you so much for including me! This is so exciting!" She waved a hand and disappeared.

Rich was left with the dregs of his wine and the memory of his companion; memory that accompanied him home. By morning, memory had faded in the light of anticipation and he arrived early at his office. Today would be different!

He was the first to arrive at the Dean's suite of offices. After opening his own office, he set the coffee brewer in motion and arranged the Dean's conference room for the upcoming writing exercise.

The first bubbles of the coffee maker played background music to the tap of Felicity's heels. She wafted in through the suite's outer door.

"Good morning! My, that coffee smells good!"

"Yes, good morning Ms Berland." Rich pulled out a chair, mesmerized by the shining hair.

"Thanks," she said. "Now, if we're going to work together on this, let's get on a first-name basis. Would that be OK?"

First name! Finally! "Why . . . absolutely! You may call me Rich if you wish."

"Great! Now, if you'll pour us some coffee, we can get down to work."

The balance of the day followed this pattern. 'Felicity' and 'Rich' worked as a team. Draft followed draft. The office printer hummed. Enthusiasm multiplied.

Shortly after the Dean's office closed, they stood over the printer as the final draft emerged.

"Isn't it exciting!" Felicity burbled. "What an opportunity! I hope this goes forward!"

"No problem there," Rich said. "Dr. Bahls feels that Midwest is the front runner for the grant."

"I'll keep my fingers crossed!" Felicity promised. "Let me know what I can do to help." She assembled the papers on the desk into a neat pile and handed them to Rich, gazing directly into his face.

Rich beamed. "You'll be the first to be involved! I'll see to that!"

BOOK III
MANTRA

"<u>Some of mankind's most terrible misdeeds have been committed under the spell of certain magic words or phrases</u>" (James Bryant Conant)

CHAPTER TWELVE

Academic Integrity

"Many wear the Robe, but few keep the Way."
Kipling (Kim)

Winslow Pyke had been Rich's favorite graduate student for the past two years; his sole doctoral student and intellectual confidant. Pyke's superior intellect and incisive logical mind constituted the substance of most of Rich's recent writing. Publications in *Economical Education* and *Explorations in Economic Thought* – ostensibly authored by Professor Jessen – were largely the brainchildren of Winslow Pyke.

This unacknowledged arrangement was mutually beneficial. Rich plundered Pyke's ideas to produce the papers and articles that brought the Professor fame and salary increases. Pyke trolled in the Professor's wake as collaborative author in order to attain a measure of name recognition. Whenever he thought about Pyke, which wasn't all that often, Rich saw himself as an intellectual priest educating a willing acolyte.

When Felicity became Rich's second doctoral student, there was a new relationship among these three persons. Pyke's access to Rich declined and Felicity became the source of Rich's papers and articles, to say nothing of her involvement in H&HS grantsmanship. There was also a fundamental change in the area of the Professor's scholarship. Economics faded in the light of Rich's new interest in federal policy.

Being an astute observer, Pyke saw that his academic future was at risk and that a change in intellectual direction was indicated. He also began to notice Felicity and to draw her into one-on-one discussions of policy issues. Their increasing interaction transformed Rich from the center of their academic attention to a peripheral observer.

At first, Rich had a benevolent view, glorying in the evident competence of his graduate students. However, as weeks passed he became increasingly concerned; jealous of the time the two students spent with their heads close together in the student work space he had provided in the Dean's Office.

The dynamics of intellectual discussion became an issue for Rich one evening when he returned to his office after a late dinner with Bahls and Loras. Pyke was seated at a table in the outer office where he was displaying something on his computer monitor. Felicity was standing behind Pyke's chair, one hand on his shoulder, her bobbed hair brushing the side of his face. They drew apart and looked up at Rich in the office doorway.

"Oh . . . hello Ri . . . I mean . . . Professor Jessen," Felicity said. "We didn't expect . . . that is . . . we were just remarking . . . about . . . this new policy model that Win has developed."

Win! She called him Win! What's going on here! "I hope I didn't frighten you," Rich growled. "I saw your light and stopped by to see what's up."

Pyke beckoned at his computer. "Here Prof. Take a look at this model and tell us what you think."

Here Prof! Just like a fucking dog! Rich gritted his teeth to keep the angry retort locked inside. "Sounds interesting. Let me see what you have there." He moved to Pyke's other shoulder, standing as close to Felicity as possible.

The screen showed a spidery circle with words in boxes connected by arrows.

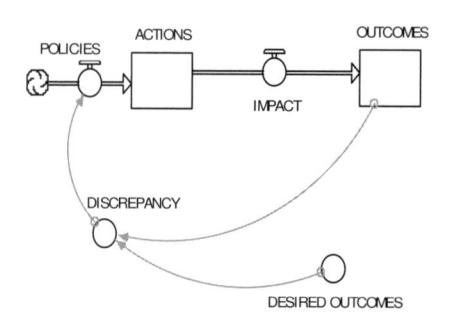

BERLAND-PYKE POLICY MODEL

POLICIES → ACTIONS → IMPACT → OUTCOMES
DISCREPANCY ← DESIRED OUTCOMES

Rich was stunned! *Berland-Pyke! Like they're married!* He was unable to speak for a long moment. "Why, that's . . . very interesting. The words seem to make sense, but I don't follow your reasoning Winslow." *That should put the little snot in place!*

"Oh, it's quite simple," Felicity smiled. "You see, policy is always based on the discrepancy between what the feds want and what exists in the way of outcomes."

212

"I can see that, of course!" Rich feigned understanding. "What I don't see is how this sort of drawing has anything to do with our policy research. For example. . .," Rich looked into Felicity's glowing face. *For example! What example?* Another momentary lapse provided him with an appropriate response, ". . . our funding agency would want to know how this helps them take timely actions."

"I'm glad you asked," Pyke enthused. "Look at this graph!" He pulled up a colored chart containing confusing wavy lines.

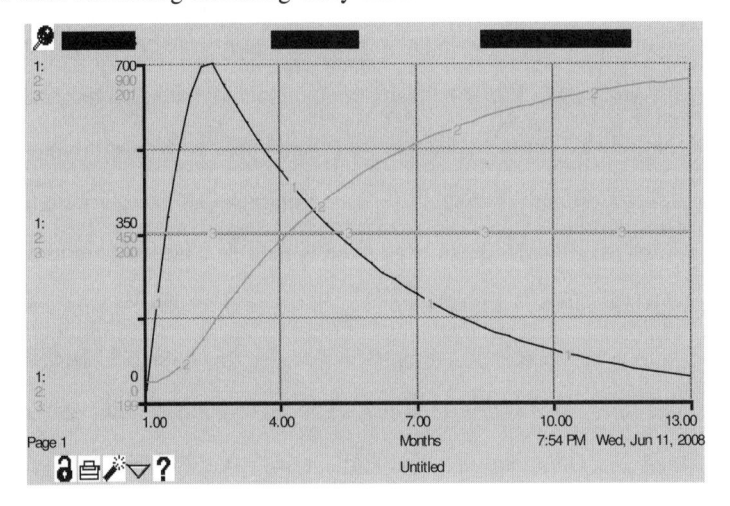

[Graph showing curves over Months 1.00 to 13.00, with y-axis values 0 to 700, dated 7:54 PM Wed, Jun 11, 2008]

"Isn't that wonderful!" Felicity exclaimed. "Just look at how Actions and Outcomes overshoot what's desired!"

"I don't follow!" Rich blurted.

"Simple Prof," Pyke lectured. "Suppose the feds want – let's say 450 clients in a program. The system starts with 50; that means that new Actions are needed. But Actions don't take effect right away, so more Actions are called for. The model shows the typical fed response to a need."

Rich couldn't help himself. "What's that?" he asked.

213

Felicity took over the lesson. "They keep on throwing money at the problem! And they overshoot the goal. Look! Outcomes end up way above what's wanted!"

Pyke provided the conclusion. "She's absolutely right! All, or nearly all, policy systems have this feature. They are characterized by delays and policy makers have imperfect understandings of how their actions play out."

Rich could see that the lesson was over as far as he was concerned. The two students looked at him with a mixture of pride (Felicity) and expectation (Pyke). They reminded him of the traveling salesmen who called on the family hardware store so many years ago. Order books were in hand and open for business.

"Wouldn't it be great if we could fold Win's policy models into our research Professor Jessen?" Felicity asked. "I've been thinking about an addition to the proposal we have been working on. You know, the one where we are looking at the effect of ADA policy."

Rich shook his head as if to empty his brain of this heretical idea. *Win's model in our project! No way!* "I'm sure we should consider it, but remember we're working on a short deadline," he said coldly. "We'd have to renegotiate the RFP. It'd be pretty risky."

"Anyway," Pyke said. "I'll work something up for you Prof. Should have it on your desk tomorrow."

"Fine," Rich grunted. "I'll give it a look. Now, I better be on my way. What about you two. Anybody need a ride home?" He looked expectantly at Felicity.

"Oh! Thanks! But Win and I have a bit more work to do on the model. Don't worry, we'll be sure to turn out the lights and lock up."

They looked like a pair of adolescents; eager to put the father figure to bed so life might take a more interesting turn. There was nothing Rich could do.

If emotion could take visible form, there would have been a black cloud hovering over Rich's head as he stomped down the stairs to the garage below Blewett Hall. All his fantasy life with Felicity was obscured by gloomy thought. *This is serious!* Rich had visions of an emaciated Winslow Pyke fondling a luscious Felicity. He gritted his teeth in anger.

Mood intensified on his drive home; tires on his Mercedes squealed their complaint on each corner; the car nosedived in response to heavy breaking at each stop sign; repeated curses at fellow drivers. "C'mon!" "Out of the way!" "You dumbass!"

Once in his garage, Rich sat rigid in his seat, hands clutching the steering wheel. He wrenched at the wheel – images of Pyke's neck swam in front of his eyes. Gradually, the spasm passed and he sunk in the seat, drenched in sweat. He finally became aware of his surroundings; the Merc, the garage, the door to the kitchen. Thoughts of Felicity gave way to the possibility of life without Felicity. He opened the car door and stood. His normal routine required the prop of his attaché case, but it had been forgotten at the office. Rich seemed puzzled by the empty seat where the case normally sat; a man without the scaffolding of his profession.

He skipped his usual solitary supper and resigned himself to an evening of television. The mindless dramas and adolescent commercials offered no refuge for his interest; the face of Winslow Pyke appeared on heroic actors while beautiful actresses all looked remarkably like Felicity.

Gradually the emotional strain of these contrasting images exhausted his remaining energy and he fell asleep. Dreams took control. A new life began to take shape; Pyke faded into the background. A smiling Professor Jessen was closeted with Felicity, they were collaborating on important academic work. There was even a sailboat where Captain Jessen looked forward to a windblown Felicity. The slideshow played throughout the night.

First light of morning worked its way across the room and fell on Rich's face. He struggled awake, stretching cramped muscles. He wiggled out of the embrace of his recliner and bumbled through shave, shower and dressing.

Downstairs, he skipped his morning coffee and stumbled out of the kitchen into the garage. Rich was about to enter the Merc when he heard the kitchen phone ring. "What the Hell?" He raced to the kitchen door and caught the phone on the fourth ring.

"Hello. Professor Jessen."

"Rich. Mike here. Can you come by and pick me up? My car's on the blink and Beth's got the other car."

"Guess so." Rich did a quick mental calculation. "I was just leaving. Should be at your place in about fifteen minutes."

"Great! And thanks!"

Rich continued to be preoccupied with thoughts of life with Felicity during his drive to Bahls' house. He wove his way through morning traffic, avoiding other drivers in a reflexive manner.

Bahls was waiting on his front steps as Rich turned into the driveway.

"Looks like he's in a hurry," Rich mumbled. "Wonder what's up."

Bahls opened the rear door of the Merc and tossed his briefcase on the seat. Another smooth move put him in front next to Rich.

"Hello pal! Good to see you!"

"What are you so happy about?" Rich grumbled. "Seems like today's just like all the others." He backed the car into the road and drove off.

"Got a great phone call early this morning," Bahls said. "Feds are gonna come across with the big one! However, we need to put some more meat on our study of the impact of ADA. That should do the trick!"

Momentarily, Rich was distracted from his woman problem. The sound of money invariably focused his attention. "That'd be great! Any idea as to what they are looking for?"

"Just the usual. Couple of new legislative initiatives in the works that need some serious study. Nothing we can't deal with. In fact, I've been working on some notes that I need to shape up for Hank. So let me do a little scribbling while you drive."

Rich nodded and allowed his mind to wander. Bahls' mention of policy study refocused his musing on Winslow Pyke. Was there any way he could use Mike's connections to take Pyke out of the picture? He smiled at this pleasant thought. *But it's gotta be done right!* Rich continued to develop a Pyke-Removal Strategy for the balance of the commute to the University.

The abrupt downward plunge into the underground parking lot jolted Bahls out of his RFP planning. "Hey! We here already?"

"Yep." Rich climbed out of the car. "Say, you got any free time later this afternoon? I've something we've been working on that might fit into the new RFP."

Bahls recovered his briefcase and stood, looking over the car. "That's sounds interesting. Sure, I can come to your office around two. That OK?"

"You're on. See you then." Rich watched enviously as Bahls trotted up the stairs toward the campus exit. "Still the athlete!' he mumbled as he pressed the elevator call button. Inside the cage, he reviewed his plan. *Hope Pyke is his usual early bird. Got to get him focused – on what? Some kind of policy model . . .*

Rich was in luck. Pyke was hunched over his computer in the outer office. He looked up as Rich entered.

"Morning Prof. Nice day."

Rich imagined how easily an evening with Felicity would produce a 'nice day'. "Yes indeed." He unlocked his office and ran through the usual morning ritual; turn on desk light, shuffle papers, open and close file cabinet. Then . . .

"Winslow, can you come in here a minute?"

A beaming face was instantly framed in the doorway. "Sure thing. What's up?"

"I've just been informed that there is a new policy studies RFP that sounds like it's right up your alley."

Pyke plopped into a chair next to Rich's desk. "Golly! That's interesting! Tell me more."

Rich looked away to avoid the eager, youthful grin. "Seems to me that the model you were working on last night might be developed into a more complete view of some of the legislation being considered by Congress. I was especially impressed by your use of feedback loops."

"That's the key Prof! Felicity and I think we've hit on a unique approach to policy analysis."

Felicity? Nothing doing! "Well, yes . . . but the way I read this RFP you'd have to take the lead. The proposal readers won't take kindly to a pair of grad students." Rich turned his chair to face Pyke. "What I'd advise you to do is change the title of your model to something like 'Policy Study System'. Or something like that."

Rich could almost see the synapses connect in Pyke's brain. "What I have in mind for you is a possible Washington internship where you could develop the

218

model and make some important professional connections." *Now let's see if he cuts Felicity out of the picture!*

Pyke's eyes actually dilated at the prospect. "... Prof ... I ... what ... should I do? How ..."

Rich leaned back in his chair and folded his hands behind his head. "I think there may be a way for you to test this idea. Professor Bahls is coming over here this afternoon to talk about the new RFP. If you had a new model ..."

Pyke leaped to his feet. "I'll get right on it. I'm sure ...," His voice faded as he rushed into the outer office.

Rich smiled as he heard the clatter of Pyke's keyboard. *Now we'll see how far he goes!*

Keyboarding and mumbling continued in the outer office for the balance of the morning. Around noon, Pyke appeared in Rich's doorway. "Prof, can I show you what I've come up with?"

"Of course," Rich said in a syrupy voice. "I'll come right out."

The display on Pyke's computer was even more confusing. Boxes, circles and arrows swam in front of Rich's eyes. However, the title of the model was changed. It now read, 'POLICY ANALYSIS MODEL'. There was no mention of Felicity!

"Well, what do you think?" Pyke asked.

"It's very compelling. What you've produced is surely breaking new ground."

Praise was exactly what Pyke wanted. He visibly expanded and, Rich was surprised to see, appeared to gain in height. "Say! Thanks! I wonder what Professor Bahls will say?"

"I can't predict his reaction," Rich said. "Tell you what. Print me a copy of the model and take a lunch break. I'll study your work and set up your presentation with Professor Bahls."

Pyke stretched and rolled his head to relive tension. "That'll be great! I'll run over to the Student Center. What time shall I come back?"

Rich pretended to study his desk calendar. "Hmmm, he'll be here around two. Why don't you plan to come back then. I'll work you into our discussion as soon as possible."

Pyke bounded off. Rich rubbed his hands like a sly merchant who had just completed a particularly advantageous bargain.

The deal was in the bag! All Rich had to do was introduce Pyke and Bahls. When Bahls arrived, the two spent several hours looking at Pyke's version of the Policy Model. Every question that Bahls raised resulted in a modification of the Model and an erudite explanation of its behavior by Pyke. When Pyke's tutorial concluded, Bahls came into Rich's office.

"Rich! You have a winner there! I've never been able to visualize how a policy effects organizations and their clients; Pyke has shown me a way that is sure to impress the folks in D.C.!"

"I'm glad Winslow could put you in the picture," Rich said silkily. "As you can see, he would be a wonderful asset to the policy people on the Washington end."

"I couldn't agree more!" Bahls exclaimed. "I'll make a few calls and Pyke can pack his bags for the big time!"

No sooner said than done. In less than two weeks, Pyke was on his way to D.C. with Bahls' promise of endless career opportunities and Rich's genuine sendoff.

Pyke's departure for Washington was, for Rich, an occasion for celebration. Winslow had chosen wisely, connecting the 'Policy Model' and the federal RFP. Now the only rival for Felicity's attention was gone! Rich was free to concentrate on re-establishing his mentorship of Felicity and re-creation of a fantasy world where she would become a true companion.

There was however, an unanticipated consequence that Rich had not considered. Felicity did not revert to the enthusiastic graduate student of the past semester. Instead she would sit for hours in the outer office at the desk where she and Pyke had created the Policy Model. Sighs and aimless paper shuffling gave the impression of a lack of focus, confirmed by mediocre performance in Rich's seminar. This was not the Felicity who starred in Rich's fantasy.

Several weeks passed before Rich could force himself to raise the issue with Felicity. By manipulating the order of presentations in his seminar, he succeeded in keeping Felicity engaged in discussion until all the other students left.

He opened with a formal approach, "Well Ms Berland, how are you coming along with your thesis?"

"Professor Jessen . . . I . . . don't know how to say this. I'm so disappointed . . ."

"At what?" Rich asked eagerly. *This could be the opening!*

"Well . . . I thought that I would be included in the RFP and that I might have a chance at a Washington internship. You know how much that would mean to me."

Hadn't thought of that! Rich gnawed at this unpleasant thought. Getting rid of Pyke . . .

"But Fel . . . Ms Berland . . . you would be wasting your time as I see it."

"Just how do you see it?" she asked as she stood and snapped the catches on her attaché case. "Do you mean that Wins is more qualified than I?"

Rich was stunned by a voice he had never associated with Felicity. Frustration and anger shaped her every word and gesture. *What the Hell did I do? And what the Hell can I do?* Mental exhortation resulted in a plausible – if halting – response.

"Nono. . . not in the least! In fact, I have been thinking . . .," *what?* ". . . that . . . you would be a fine candidate . . . for a position here at Midwest."

Now it was Felicity's turn to be stunned. She fell into the chair she had just vacated. "What do you mean? What position? When . . . ?" Her questions crowded one after another – each requiring an answer.

Encouraged by her interest, Rich began to construct a scenario that featured a higher education faculty led by Berland and Jessen. All he would need to do is have Dean Dunkard approve a new faculty position for the Academy. No problem! Just a phone call away!

"You see," he began, his voice strengthening, "the funding we have in place for the Academy provides a foundation for ongoing research and development that would position the Academy as the leading policy research operation in the country." *That should do it!*

It did! Felicity offered a tentative smile that turned into a grin. "Oh, Professor Jessen! That's so much better! I know that the four of us can make a significant impact on all aspects of state and federal policy!"

Her enthusiasm bubbled into ideas and plans so that Rich was overwhelmed by the effect he had created. Finally, he was able to bring the discussion to a close with a promise.

"Well, Ms . . . Felicity. I'm so pleased with your interest. You can depend upon me to see this through."

Felicity turned the full force of her smile on Rich. "Thank you Rich! I can hardly wait to hear what's possible!"

They were back on a first-name basis. Pyke was now a distant and, Rich hoped, a fading memory.

Early the next week, Rich called for an appointment with Dean Dunkard. As usual, he was moved to the top of the Dean's agenda.

"Hi Rich! Good to see you!" Dunkard extended a hand and bestowed a benevolent smile. "Come on in. Coffee?"

"No thanks. Just a short meeting about staffing the Academy."

The Dean frowned. "When I talked with Hank Loras last week, he indicated that your group could handle the work. What do you have in mind?"

Rich folded his hands on the conference table. "Since then, Professor Bahls has a line on additional funding. When it comes through, as we believe it will, we'll be short on faculty time. What we need is an additional line item."

Dunkard frowned. "This comes at a very bad time, Central Administration has just put a lid on new faculty positions in the College. There's no way I can authorize a position."

The magnitude of this pronouncement shoved Rich back in his chair. "That's not good news. Why, we wouldn't be able to perform on the new contract. Are you sure there's no slack from Central?"

"No slack there, but there may be a solution to your problem." Dunkard reached into a file drawer and pulled out a thick folder. "Shelia Solvay has indicated an interest in transferring her faculty item from Work and Family Studies to your Policy Studies Academy."

Rich became rigid at this prospect, forcing his chair back from the table. "Shelia Solvay! Why... she's ... just not ...," he sputtered.

"I know, I know," Dunkard said. "She's not my idea of the perfect faculty member. However, she is a hard worker and has some excellent connections to our community colleges. That would, it seems to me, be an asset to the Academy."

The prospect of any relationship between the Academy and these second-rate institutions was . . . "Solvay would be a disaster," Rich gritted. "What she calls 'research' is just a collection of war stories about two-year colleges. She would weaken the academic integrity of the Academy!"

The Dean shuffled papers on his desk. "That may be, but you know the rules of the University. If a faculty member asks for a transfer of item to another department, the receiving department must consider the request and act on it. I have no choice and neither do you. The Academy faculty must meet and vote on Solvay's request."

Trapped by the rules! Rich had been the chair of the committee that wrote the transfer policy for the University. Now he would have to arrange for the Academy faculty – Bahls, Loras and himself – to give serious consideration to Solvay.

As if he were reading Rich's thoughts, the Dean said, "Rich, you need to be very careful to do this right. There can be no question of bias in your consideration of Solvay."

"I know," Rich sighed. "Remember, I wrote the policy."

The Dean nodded. "Here's what I think you should do. I'll recommend two faculty members from other College and university departments. That way there can be no complaint of unfair treatment from Solvay."

"OK . . . I guess. You must have somebody in mind."

"Yes, I do." The Dean opened a folder and flipped through several papers. "I'll ask Roxanne Graves from Psychology and Arlene Thomas from Curriculum and Instruction to work with you. They are both highly regarded, but aren't especially close to Solvay. They will see to it that job's done right."

The discussion continued for the better part of an hour. Solvay's vita and collected papers were examined and a plan for the review of her record was put in place.

When Dunkard stood at the end of their meeting, he extended a hand to Rich. "I'm sorry Rich, but this is the only possibility for augmenting your faculty. I know I can count on you to make the best of it."

Rich took Dunkard's hand. It was moist and shaking. *Bet he's in a corner on Solvay!* This observation lit a glimmer of possibility for Rich and he shook the Dean's hand and looked into his eyes. "You can count on me, Mert."

"Good," Dunkard said. "Here, take Solvay's materials. You can begin to share them with your committee."

Rich received the box of papers, holding them away form his body to avoid contamination by their junior college content. The papers seemed to gain weight on the walk back to his office. He was actually perspiring as he thumped the box on his office credenza, a sound that drew Felicity to his door.

"Oh, Rich. Have you any news for me?"

The beautiful face with its expression of enthusiasm nearly drove Rich to his knees. "We had . . . a productive meeting . . ." *Resulting in what?* "I have nothing concrete to report as yet . . .," *And maybe never will!* He experienced a lump in his throat; impossible words forcing their way to vocalization.

Felicity sensed his discomfort. "Please excuse me," she said brightly. "I know that these things take time and I'll try to be patient."

She kept her word and resumed the role of a gifted graduate student, worshiping at the feet of her Professor.

The next day, Rich began the rituals associated with the review of Professor Solvay's request. He called each committee member; set a date for a meeting; copied Solvay's vita and papers; circulated them and informed Dunkard of progress. Rich's mental state emptied these activities of their academic meaning; their only significance was as obstacles to a position for Felicity.

Reading Solvay's papers was the most trying of experiences. Their topics: Transfer Policy; The Role of Adjunct Faculty in Community Colleges; Technology and the Future of Work, reminded Rich of a mundane world that surrounded the University, where insignificant people engaged in trivial activities.

Nevertheless, it was Solvay's papers that suggested a solution to Rich's dilemma. One evening he was reading 'Transfer Policy' when he happened to notice a similar title in Solvay's vita. He ran a finger down the entries on the vita, mumbling as he read. "Hmmm, her thesis is Transfer Policy . . . then . . . she published a monograph on . . . Transfer Policy . . . isn't there a copy?" Rich flipped through the box of papers. "Here it is . . .," He placed the two Transfer Policy papers side by side and read along. "Why! She uses the same language word for word! And she makes no mention of the first paper in the second one!"

It was as if a neon sign flashed on the wall of Rich's office. ACADEMIC INTEGRITY! *What was it? Something about plagiarism?* His mind raced. Where had he heard . . .?

Rich relaxed in his chair and folded his hands in his lap; a posture that he used effectively to enhance recall. As usual, it worked! "Max Werner!" he shouted and jumped out of his chair. "The University Handbook!" Rich strode over to his bookcase and withdrew the slender volume. Anxiously he paged through its entries: Conditions of Employment; Tenure Code; Academic Integrity.

He returned to his desk and skimmed through the section on Misconduct. "Here it is," he whispered and read half-aloud, 'Academic Integrity is founded on the originality of scholarship. Accordingly, all forms of plagiarism are prohibited and will be dealt with severely by the Committee on Academic Standards.' "Sounds pretty threatening," he said aloud, "but not very clear . . . hmmm . . .," he mused for a time, then reached for his University Directory where he found 'Werner, Max – Professor of Law 5-5452'

Rich lifted the receiver on his phone and entered the number. "Hope he's in . . ."

"Professor Werner."

"Max. This is Rich Jessen. Remember when we were on the Revision Committee for the University Handbook?"

"Yes, quite a project. So what's on your mind?"

"It's the section on Academic Integrity, where we deal with plagiarism. . ."

"Just a minute," Werner interrupted, "let me get my copy."

There were muted sounds of paper shuffling, then Werner returned. "So . . . I have it . . . page 38 . . . right?"

"Yes that's it. You see where it says 'all forms of plagiarism'? Well, I seem to recall that we included something about plagiarizing one's own work. That right?"

"Yes. We included 'self-plagiarism' as one of the deadly sins," Werner guffawed. "Why do you ask? Been using that old paper too many times?"

Arrogant old fart! "No, but I am on a Review Committee for a faculty member who has clearly used a substantial portion of text in two published papers."

Werner thought for a moment. "Does the second paper site the earlier work?"

"No. That's what raised the question for me."

"That doesn't sound too good. Tell you what. Send me copies of the papers in question. And, send me a copy of the faculty member's vita. I'll give it a look and get back to you.'

Can't wait on that! "Better yet. If you have a moment, I'll bring them by. Shouldn't take but a minute. Looks pretty clear to me."

"Well... OK. Try to come as soon as possible." Werner hung up.

Rich stifled his customary complaint about the behavior of a colleague. After all, he needed this guy!

The session in Werner's office was brief and to the point. Solvay's papers were placed side by side along with her vita. Werner scowled at the text through steel-rimmed glasses.

"Pretty weak stuff! If I had written this sort of thing, I sure wouldn't advertise it!" He continued to read and highlight identical passages in the two papers. "You know Rich. This kind of thing is done all the time. It's especially prevalent in the social sciences where a typical paper is rarely read by more than a half-dozen readers."

Rich smiled. "I know. But the question remains. Is this self-plagiarism?"

"Clear cut case," Werner bundled papers and vita on his desk. "Shouldn't be too much of a problem. Give the lady a warning and scare her."

"I think it's more serious than that," Rich said. "She's trying to use these papers to enhance her status in the College. Plans to move from one department to another."

"Now, that's another matter." Werner stroked his chin. "Kind of depends on your committee. If they are hot on academic integrity, they could use the Handbook to make this a disciplinary case."

"That's what I thought," Rich said. "I recall our deliberation when we wrote this section. Seems to me we used the 'all forms of plagiarism' language to guarantee academic integrity. Am I correct?"

"Yes, I believe that's right." Werner stared at Rich. "Just what are you driving at?"

"Professor Solvay has a history of tacking pretty close to the wind here at Midwest and she's been quite successful. I think we should make every effort to raise her plagiarism to the highest level, to set an example for others."

Werner scowled, "Supposing you are correct about her past behavior, we could make a case for serious sanctions."

"Might that include dismissal?" Rich asked hopefully.

"That would be possible unless, of course, the Faculty Senate advocated for Solvay. Is that likely?"

"Possibly, the case would have to be presented in the strongest terms."

"The best way would be to have the Graduate School Committee on Academic Standards make a recommendation for dismissal. I chair that Committee and we've been pretty tough on all forms of misconduct."

What a break! "That makes sense," Rich said. "Now what's the best way to move this case to the Committee?"

Werner took off his glasses and polished them on his tie. "The usual practice is for the issue to be raised to your Dean – it's his choice – discipline or dismiss. If he chooses to remove Solvay, he can forward her case to our Committee."

So it's up to Dunkard! Now we'll see if the Dean remembers the M-80s! Rich stood to leave. "I'll leave these copies with you and convene my Review Committee. They are pretty strong on integrity so it'll be up to Dean Dunkard."

It took Rich another week to set up the meeting with Solvay's Review Committee. First, he shared her work and his discussion in Werner's office with Bahls and Loras. They proved to be reluctant to make an issue of Solvay's work.

"Seems pretty rough," Bahls said. "Hell, everybody gets mileage from articles. I've seen this plenty of times on federal proposals.

"I agree," Loras added. "Solvay is sure a bitch, but I can't see firing her for something as chicken shit as this."

Rich was not surprised by this reaction. He knew that both Mike and Hank were probably guilty of self-plagiarism. "Think about this, you guys. The Dean's gonna work hard to transfer Solvay. How'd you like to work with her as a full member of the Academy staff? You like that idea?"

"Hell no!" exclaimed Hank. "I tried to involve her in a project last year. She nearly had me for lunch!"

"You gotta point there," said Bahls. "Wouldn't do to bust up our team now that the money's flowing."

"Thought you'd see the light," Rich concluded. "Now, I need your help on the Review Committee to bring the two other members along. And remember, they will only be swayed by the academic integrity argument."

They all nodded and Hank added, "So long Professor Solvay!"

Rich scheduled a meeting of the Review Committee for the next week. In the intervening time, he decided to see if one of the outside members could be persuaded to present the plagiarism case. Arlene Thomas was an easy reject as she represented a field that was notorious for disorganized content. On the other hand, the Psychology faculty prided itself on its robust research; often under the leadership of Roxanne Graves.

The next day, Rich arranged the Solvay files on his desk, straightened himself in his chair, wiped his hands on his pants legs and reached for the phone and punched in the number for . . .

"Professor Graves." The authoritative voice boomed in Rich's ear.

"Roxanne. This is Rich Jessen. The Dean tells me that you are a member of the Review Committee for Professor Solvay. Has he had a chance to confirm that?"

"Yes," Graves growled. "Waste of time! Shouldn't need a Committee to do a simple departmental transfer."

"I agree," Rich said. "But there's an issue in this case that I'd like to share with you privately. Would that be possible?"

"Well . . . I suppose so. Send me the papers and I'll take a look."

Rich hesitated. "There's a short timeline on this. It would be much better if I brought the papers to you and showed you what's involved. Could you spare a half-hour today?"

There was extended grumbling, then Graves spoke. "I've a few minutes now. Bring them over as soon as possible." She hung up.

Just like Werner! The arrogant bitch! Rich crammed the Solvay papers into his briefcase and hurried out of his office. Forgotten was his Greek fisherman costume. This was too important! Psychology was located in the Freud Memorial Building across the Quad; effectively disconnecting that subject matter from education. Rich forced himself to think positively about this demonstration of intellectual superiority. "It's all a matter of academic integrity," he said to himself.

Graves added to the irritants by keeping him waiting for fifteen minutes – a not to subtle reminder of his inferior status. When he was finally called into her presence, he saw himself groveling at Graves' feet.

"Good to see you Rich," Graves said, in a comment devoid of meaning. "Let's see what's troubled you."

Rich laid Solvay's vita and papers on Graves' desk. He pointed to the citations on the vita and to the paragraphs he had outlined on the two papers.

"As you can see," he said. "A substantial portion of the papers are identical."

"Yes I can see that. So what?"

"Here, take a look at the page I've marked in the University Handbook – where it states the policy on plagiarism."

"I'm familiar with that," Graves barked. "But I don't see how it applies."

"I wondered about that too," Rich lied. "So I checked with Max Werner in the Law School. He was one of the authors of the policy. When the policy was written it states 'all forms of plagiarism' which was meant to include self-plagiarism."

Graves looked up. "I seem to have heard of that concept. What exactly does it mean?"

Rich explained. "According to Werner, any repeated use of one's own work without appropriate citation is the same as any other plagiarism. Solvay has used her work repeatedly and violated the academic integrity of the University. As Chair of her Review Committee I feel that I must ask the members of the committee to take this issue most seriously."

The mention of academic integrity did the trick! Graves face was a study in scholarly resolve. Here was a person of little account who was, after all, only a Vocational Educator; threatening the very fabric of the University! Graves instantly changed from Professor to prosecutor.

"I get your point. Behavior like this must be punished!" Tiny drops of saliva define the corners of Graves' mouth. "I will see to it that the Review Committee deals with this transgression!"

I'm sorry to have had to bring this issue to your attention," Rich said, "but it really does cut to the chase on integrity."

Graves nodded vigorously, "Now, when can we meet to move this along?"

Rich stood with his hand on the back of his chair – the pose of the Assistant District Attorney. "I'll call a meeting for next week and see to it that Solvay's papers are circulated at once."

"That will be fine," Graves pushed the Solvay file aside and began to read from a scholarly journal. Rich was to find his own way out.

He accepted this affront with glee and almost skipped back to his office. It was wonderful how a mantra like academic integrity could align the political forces of the University!

CHAPTER THIRTEEN

Misconduct

"... plagiarize, plagiarize, plagiarize -Only be sure always to call it please 'research'."
(Tom Lehrer: Lobachevsky)

Despite appearances, Rich was not all that much of a scholar. The books and journals that lined his office remained in their unopened state for the most part. Envy overpowered whatever intellectual curiosity he may have had during his undergraduate years; what others wrote detracted from the fame that rightfully belonged to Rich. While this explanation accounted for much of his academic life, there was a more fundamental concern that had to do with the intellectual poverty of his field. For Rich, education was an orphan in the university community where sciences set the standards of scholarship.

There was, however, one topic that Rich followed closely – that of cognitive science. Ever since Carl Mertens introduced him to the work of George Lakoff, Rich had read widely in cognitive science; there he discovered insights into political discourse in the academy. Metaphors, mantras and models were powerful concepts that showed Rich the pathway to power over his colleagues. He found the metaphor of the academic poker game to be a useful way to shape conversations where decisions were made; he often played his 'Blue Chips' to cover the bets that competitors offered. Rich was also the master of the mantra, a statement that could not be questioned. His repeated use of the academic integrity mantra fed his appetite for the power of language.

All of these ingredients came together in a model of higher education that was shared by the faculty and administrators at Midwest. This 'standard model' was one where peers controlled access to position, publication, funding and, ultimately, to power. Of these, publication took first place in the university; promotion, tenure, and salary all depended upon production of peer-reviewed papers and articles. This was a model that Rich had encountered in his early years at Midwest when he struggled to understand its workings. Now, with the aid of cognitive science and his Metaphor Table, Rich was rapidly becoming a master of the mantras that empowered his use of political hardball.

Thus it was quite natural for Rich to reflect on the relationship between the 'standard model' and his Table as he prepared for the Solvay hearing. He did this by working with a set of note cards at his desk, behind a closed office door. The cards contained words or short phrases that Rich had found useful in conversations and meetings. He worked with the cards, using his poker game metaphor to help him decide how he would introduce mantras and model-defining concepts in the upcoming meeting.

As Rich played the game, he mumbled aloud, a running commentary on the anticipated flow of events.

"Let's see now. There's likely to be three phases . . .,"

He constructed a mental division of his desktop to represent the agenda of the Review Committee.

"Charge to the Committee," he read from a card. "That's phase one. What's said there's pretty important to the outcome of the hearing."

Rich sat back and shuffled through his cards. ". . . 'transfer of appointment' . . . takes away from the real issue." He continued to study the cards, rejecting several. ". . . 'highest standards of scholarship'. . . Now, that's more like it." He placed the card on the left of his desk.

Continued application of this process built a small stack of cards in Phase One. Rich laid them in a column:

Phase I

Highest standards of scholarship

Academic Integrity

Research I

Faculty Handbook

It was easy for Rich to see how his opening Charge to the Committee could be fashioned around these concepts.

"Now what about Phase Two?" The challenge Rich faced involved moving the attention of the committee from a simple 'transfer of appointment' to the issue raised by Solvay's papers. Clearly, a new set of concepts had to grow out of 'academic integrity' in order to empower the Committee in its dealings with Professor Solvay. It was almost too easy:

Phase II

Peer review

Self-Plagairism

Tenure

Promotion

Rich's desk now held two small piles of cards and an empty space that seemed to wait for its share of cards. "The Committee has to conclude. . .," he mused, ". . . with some action that will stand up to any legal challenge Solvay might make."

He tossed the remaining cards on the desk and picked up the Faculty Handbook. Rich knew from long experience that his colleagues had a very short attention span when it came to committee service. If they were to be engaged, professors had to share a simple view of the topic under discussion; it would do no good to attempt to lead them through the complex card game he was playing. Rich needed a concrete foundation for the case he was building.

Paging through the Handbook, he returned several times to the section that outlined the specifics of Misconduct; a word that caught and held his attention.

"OK, Solvay asks for a tenure review and submits her work. We read the papers and find evidence of 'self-plagiarism'. Then I point to the Misconduct section of the Handbook."

Rich copied Phase III words from the Misconduct section:

Phase III

Committee reports misconduct to Dean

Dean decides to discipline

Dean forwards the case to U's Discipline Committee

That says it all!

Two days later Rich convened the Review Committee. When all members were seated, he began. "Thank you for assisting in evaluating Professor Solvay's request for tenure review. As you know, she is also asking that her appointment be moved from Work and Family Studies to Policy Studies. While it is customary for the receiving program to decide on the appointment request, I am deferring the decision of my Higher Education colleagues to await the results of this Committee's work."

Rich paused and looked around the conference table at the other members of the Committee; Hank Loras, Mike Bahls, Arlene Thomas and Roxanne Graves. "I have asked Professor Graves to chair our meeting. May we proceed Professor

Graves?" *Come through for me, Roxanne Baby!* The incongruous thought nearly brought a smile to his face.

Graves came through! "Thank you Rich. I have reviewed the materials submitted by Professor Solvay and feel that there is a question as to her academic integrity."

Rich checked off these key words in his mental construct of the meeting. *Off to a good start!*

But it wasn't to be all that easy! Professor Thomas straightened in her chair. "Just what does that mean?" she asked. "I didn't see anything amiss in the materials I read."

"Oh, but it takes a bit of analysis," lectured Graves. "If you read her papers carefully, as I have, you'll see that she has some serious problems with self-plagiarization."

Rich struggled to keep a serious look on his face, a mask hiding his growing exultation. He cast a meaningful glance at Hank Loras, moving his eyes to connect Hanks gaze to the papers on the table.

"Yes, I wondered about that," Hank said. "Seems to me that Solvay has used the same piece of work several times without attribution."

Rich made the connection. "Yes, I think it's a very clear repeated use of the same material to make the case for tenure."

Bahls was quick to support this line of reasoning. "I see it as a clear-cut instance of plagiarism, blatantly used as evidence for a tenure decision. That impugns the academic integrity of this University. We must take this very seriously!'

Rich reviewed the cards on his mental desk. The major key words were now in play all that remained was . . . he opened the Faculty Handbook to the place he had marked . . .

"The Handbook is very clear on that point," he proceeded to read. "This is an instance of faculty misconduct. Here take a look at the paragraphs I've marked." He passed the Handbook to Thomas.

As she read, Rich could imagine how she might be processing University rules. *I bet she can hardly wait to paw through her own papers and articles to see how many times she's self-plagiarized!* He made a mental bet that Thomas would …

"Hmmm," she mumbled, "sounds serious. Let me see the papers in question."

Professor Graves slid the offending documents across the table. "Here, I've marked the paragraphs. You can easily see that Solvay has used identical materials without attribution."

Rich had forgotten 'attribution' a powerful keyword in this context. He made a mental note to insert this concept when opportunity occurred.

The committee read the offending documents, quietly shuffling pages, heads swiveling to compare passages. Several minutes passed. Rich watched with approval at the evident seriousness of the work in progress.

Professor Thomas assembled her packet of papers and looked at Graves. "I can see what you mean. Solvay has clearly made multiple use of her thesis research. What I'm not clear about is how the University views this kind of behavior."

Rich caught Professor Graves' eyes and shoved the Handbook across the table. "The section I've marked . . ."

"I know. I know," Graves barked. "The Handbook makes a special point about plagiarism. That includes multiple use of an individual faculty member's work without attribution. That's self-plagiarism!"

"That sounds like the letter of the law," Thomas said. "But we need to be sure that Solvay's work rises to that level."

This was the opening Rich was waiting for. "Professor Thomas is correct. We really must give Professor Solvay the opportunity to explain her work." Rich was confident that Solvay would dig a deeper hole for herself if she were given the opportunity to talk to the Committee.

"Sounds like fair play," Loras said.

"Yeah," Bahls seconded, "let's get her in and hear her side of the story."

Professor Thomas looked around the room, evidently surprised by the proposal. "I know she's waiting outside. Shall I call her in?"

Four heads nodded in agreement and soon Solvay was seated at the end of the conference table.

Graves began the interrogation. "Professor Solvay, you are aware that this Committee is charged with examining all aspects of your professional life as evidence to be used in coming to a tenure decision. Is that your understanding?"

"Of course," beamed Solvay. "I'm very grateful to all of you for taking the time to consider my tenure review."

"Very well," Graves said. "We have studied many aspects of your work, paying special attention to your published papers and articles. As a result, we have some questions concerning your work on Transfer Policy."

Solvay nodded enthusiastically. "Yes, that's my major contribution to the field. I've written several pieces. In fact, I have a new paper that's been accepted by the Community College Transfer Digest. Here are several copies for the Committee." She opened her briefcase and handed copies of the new paper around the table.

"Let's all take a few minutes to review this new paper." Graves looked around the table, her glance emphasizing the comparison assignment.

Rich watched his colleagues bend their heads to their work. All were clearly embarrassed by Solvay's hole-digging behavior, with the exception of Professor Graves, who was obviously enjoying the hunt for plagiarism.

When Graves had finished her reading, she looked up. "Now Professor Solvay, I find that each of these three papers contains a large section taken from your Doctoral thesis. Am I reading them correctly?"

"Oh yes. My transfer findings are at the core of these papers," Solvay exclaimed proudly.

"But," Graves said, "you have at least three pages of identical text in each paper; text that is taken directly from your thesis."

"Yes," Solvay frowned, "but that's just the message I'm trying to send the field."

The Committee watched these exchanges as if it were a cross examination. Rich was amazed at the prosecutorial manner of Graves. *I'd sure hate to have that bitch on my case!* This time however, Graves was on his side.

Graves opened the Faculty Handbook. "Are you aware of the University policy on plagiarism?" she asked.

"Of course," Solvay stated. "Everyone knows that."

There was a shuffling of papers as Graves turned to the reference section of each Transfer paper. "I see that you have not referenced your other writings in any of the papers – despite using identical text material."

Solvay was puzzled. "What's wrong with that? Each paper draws out new implications for transfer policy."

"Just this," Graves thundered. "Repeated use of identical materials without attribution is self-plagiarism! It is viewed as misconduct by the University. What have you to say to this?"

"Why ... why ... I didn't ... everyone does that. Isn't that so?" Solvay looked at each member of the Committee. Nobody met her questioning gaze. "Well, isn't it common practice? Come on!"

"I'm afraid it's all too common," Professor Thomas said. "But that doesn't make it right. The University is very clear on its condemnation of self-plagiarism."

Solvay stood, red spots of anger on her cheeks. "I can't believe what I'm hearing! Is this the kind of treatment given to every candidate for tenure? Or am I a special case?" She clutched the back of her chair, her knuckles white and arms shaking.

Rich could see a shouting match developing. He set what he believed to be a soothing expression on his face. "Please, Professor Solvay. This is only a preliminary study of your record. The Dean has the final word; we only try to establish the facts . . ."

"Facts!" Solvay exploded. "Why you . . .," she wiped her mouth with the back of a hand, then spoke in an artificially controlled voice. "Very well. The Dean will be hearing from my lawyer!" She shoved her chair violently against the table and stalked from the room.

"Wow!" Loras said. "We really stirred up a hornet's nest!'"

"You bet!" Bahls added. "Now what can we do to cool this off?"

"We must not be swayed by Professor Solvay's reaction." Graves said in a level voice. "She is obviously ill-informed as to academic standards and seems to have little respect for this Committee. We should follow the Handbook's procedures carefully and inform the Dean of our findings and conclusion."

It was clear to Rich that Graves had heard Solvay's threat of legal action. "I agree with Professor Graves," Rich said. "Let's all take a close look at the evidence and take a vote on our action. Does that sound right?"

Everyone nodded agreement – except Professor Thomas who attempted to avoid the implication of a misconduct conclusion. "Aren't we coming down a little hard on Solvay? After all, we don't want to force the Dean's hand, do we?"

"I don't see it that way," Rich said. "The Handbook makes it clear that any action is the responsibility of the Dean. All we're supposed to do is to decide if there has been misconduct."

"Yes," Graves ruled, "this new paper makes the case! Solvay has done it again! We have no choice but to recommend that Dean Dunkard consider our conclusion of misconduct!"

And so it was. A reluctant Professor Thomas was persuaded that the Committee was 'forced' to forward a report of misconduct to the Dean.

Professor Graves closed the meeting. "I will report our findings to the Dean and make it clear that we take a very serious view of self-plagiarization."

Rich was, of course, pleased with the outcome. He was also amused at the committee members' rush to leave the meeting. He could envision empty file folders and a significant increase in the volume of recycled paper in the days ahead as Committee members destroyed evidence of self-plagiarization.

Two days after Graves' report appeared in Rich's mail box, he received a call from Dean Dunkard.

"Rich. This is Mert. I have the Review Report on Professor Solvay on my desk. I'd like to talk to you about it. Can you come over?"

"Of course. I'm on my way."

The Dean was seated at his conference table when Rich arrived. Solvay's file was opened in front of him and Dunkard was reading the committee Report.

"Sit down Rich. I need some help in understanding the Report. A charge of misconduct is pretty serious and I don't see clearly what's called for."

"We had a tough time in the committee," Rich lied. "All of us noticed that Solvay used the same material in several of her papers. That didn't surface as a problem until we took a close look at the Faculty Handbook. Here, I've brought a copy of the Handbook where I've marked the relevant section."

The Dean studied the Handbook for several minutes. "I can see how the committee came to its conclusion, but I must confess that I have never heard of self-plagiarization."

"It's rarely discussed," Rich said. "I myself hadn't given it much thought so I went to the source."

"How's that?"

"Well, Max Werner, he's on the Law School faculty, wrote that section so I took the Solvay issue to him. He saw her work as a clear violation of the Misconduct section of the Handbook."

"Really!" Dunkard exclaimed. "I didn't think it was so serious!"

"I didn't either, until Werner pointed out that this kind of behavior threatened the academic integrity of the University."

Dunkard rose from his chair and began pacing the office. "Integrity! If the word gets out that this College can't manage the behavior of our faculty, we'll be in deep trouble with Central!"

"That's just what the committee concluded. The College must respond to Solvay's behavior by following the Handbook to the letter!" It required all Rich's self-control to keep his enthusiasm for inquisition in check.

Dunkard halted in his wanderings and leaned a hand on his desk. "What do you think I should do?"

"Unfortunately, this thing has the potential to get out of control. Solvay was very angry at our meeting. She even threatened to take legal action!"

"No!" The Dean was shocked. "Why . . . that would . . ."

"Yes! This must be handled carefully. There's no way this offense can be overlooked. It must be dealt with quickly – with appropriate punishment."

"But," protested Dunkard, "I can't just fire her! That would bring the faculty Senate down around my ears. There must be another way!"

"Tell you what I'd do," Rich offered. "I'd get the University Attorney's office involved right away. They could work up a settlement that goes something like this. Solvay agrees to resign. The U offers a severance package and agrees that her record won't show her plagiarism."

"Won't that be terribly expensive?"

"Sure. However, it'll be a good deal less than a court case; especially where something as soft as self-plagiarism is the core of our argument. Better to buy her out."

Dunkard shook his head. "You're probably right, but I don't like it. You're sure there's no other way?"

"'Fraid not. You could, though, get Max Werner to support you with the Attorney. That would help to make this a University issue, rather than one of our special problems. Also, that approach would very likely shift the expense to Central."

"OK," Dunkard nodded. "I'll meet with Solvay and see if I can get her to cooperate."

"That's it! The committee was confident that you'd be able to handle this in a humane way." Pinocchio-like, Rich rubbed his nose. Were these lies changing his profile?

For once, the bureaucratic mills of the University produced their grist quickly. A relieved Dunkard called Rich a week later.

"Rich, I'm happy to report that the Solvay case is closed. She took your deal and it's all signed off!"

"Now that's very good news! What did you say to make her agree so soon?"

"She was ready to go to the mat on the plagiarism thing. Then I asked her to think about what might happen if she were to persist. You know, she couldn't return to Work and Family Studies and it wouldn't be likely that you folks in Policy Studies would welcome her. When she compared this to the attractive settlement I got for her from the Attorney, she caved in. Rich, I have to thank you for taking this on and coming up with a solution!"

"Happy to do it," Rich said. "Anytime."

The 'time' came around two weeks later. Then it was Rich who called the Dean and made an appointment.

Before he entered Dunkard's office, Rich twisted his face into a mask of tragedy.

Dunkard stared at Rich. "Whatever's the matter Rich? You look worried!"

Rich slumped in a chair. "You bet I'm worried. I've done the numbers over and over and there's no way we can cover all our research and instructional commitments."

"Tell me about it."

"The way I see it, Bahls and Loras are now overloaded with existing and pending federal contracts; they need help from a competent researcher. On the instructional side, I'm responsible for most of the higher ed. classes and all graduate advising. It's a no-win situation." He looked at the Dean as a dog might plead for a bone.

Dunkard was moved by Rich's whining. "What can I do to help?"

"Here's the best I can come up with," said Rich. "Remember Solvay's request to transfer her position to Policy Studies? Well, that position is now open.

If we accept the transfer and mount an immediate search to fill it, we can guarantee the viability and academic integrity of our program."

The Dean rubbed his chin. "It's true that Solvay's position is effectively open. The only problem is that Central is quick to capture such positions; it's unlikely we can save it."

"I've thought about that. Would you agree that Waldo Pearson owes us for saving him on the M-80 incident?"

"Sure. But we can hardly use that as a club."

"I agree," Rich thumped a hand on the table. "It's more subtle than that. We can use the Solvay settlement as our opening card. Waldo has to be pleased with the way you've managed to keep the U out of legal trouble. M-80's are only in his mind, we never need to mention them."

Rich marveled at his clever juxtaposition of events. There was always something in his files that could be used to sway decisions. Trump cards that need not be played.

"I can see where you're going," the Dean nodded. "It just might work; especially if it's presented as a way to ensure quality and academic integrity." The Dean was learning! Even the most obtuse administrator could recognize the power of knowledge when it was used to lubricate the wheels of bureaucracy.

They sat for a moment, each shaping a strategy. Finally, the Dean concluded.

"Let's give this a try. Write me a short memo outlining your program and research needs and I'll get it on Waldo's desk."

Rich stood and handed an envelope to the Dean. "I've anticipated your request; here's an analysis of our situation. It includes the numbers I think you need to justify retaining the Solvay position."

Most decisions in higher education involved endless committee meetings and procrastination. However, when the planets of power were in alignment, action could occur at light speed. This was the case for what Rich thought of as 'the Solvay caper'.

With the stroke of a pen, Vice President Pearson gave the College permission to initiate a search for a tenure-track professor to replace Solvay. He also approved Rich's request that the position be lodged in Policy Studies. The M-80s exploded without being ignited!

Dean Dunkard was also under the influence of M-80s. He constituted a search committee with Rich as Chair, Bahls and Loras as members.

"Be sure you do this right, Rich!" Dunkard admonished. "There can be no shortcuts!"

Giving this advice to Rich was like telling Lyndon Johnson how to run the Senate of the United States. Rich had manipulated countless position searches - using the mantra of 'academic integrity' to select the 'blue chip' candidate he favored.

Felicity was the first to know of the new opening. She was working at her computer in Rich's outer office when he called to her.

"Felicity will you please come in for a moment?"

"Of course Rich." She appeared in the doorway.

"Close the door. I have some good news for you."

Her smile anticipated the news. "Is it . . .?"

"Yes," he returned the smile. "The Dean has created a tenure track position in Policy Studies. I'm chairing the selection committee and I hope you will apply."

"Oh Rich! That's just what I want. Of course, I'll apply. I only hope that I can be a successful candidate."

Felicity was a gifted observer of the politics of higher education. There was no need to plot the manipulation of the selection committee; Rich would take care of that. All she had to do was participate in the search as if it were a fair competition. Their smiles signaled a bond of understanding that need not be verbalized.

Rich's smile was also one of anticipation. Felicity would be his colleague! They would produce endless articles! Win lucrative grants! Become famous! And they would shape the College to realize their political ends!

An ad in the Chronicle of Higher Education produced the expected flood of applicants; members of the multitude of Doctoral graduates who were pursuing ever-scarcer positions. Rich took a perverse pleasure in culling the few 'blue chips' who met his standards from the dregs of the unemployed. 'White' and 'red' chips were quickly discarded – judgments based on whatever flimsy evidence Rich could muster. When he had collected a small stack of 'blue chip' candidates it was time to share them with his selection committee.

Felicity's file was on the top of the stack, followed by several candidates whom Rich believed would gravitate to Ivy League universities. Other files were added to create a semblance of competition. He wasn't worried.

Committee deliberation conformed to Rich's expectation – almost.

Two hours of discussion reduced the stack of files to three. Rich set the 'charge' to this committee, "Let's each take one of these files and summarize the strengths and weaknesses of the candidate. I'll take Ms. Berland. Who would you like, Hank?"

"I'll go for this Hispanic guy – Horatio Fernandez. You know, the one from Arizona State."

"How about you, Mike?" Rich asked Bahls.

"I'm left with Nancy Feldt, graduate of Southern Illinois. But I'd like to replace her with another possible candidate."

"Who's that?" Rich said.

"Well, I'm wondering if another of our own graduate students might fill the bill. I'm thinking about your old advisee Rich, Winslow Pyke."

Pyke! Rich tried to compose himself. "That might be a good idea, but we don't have an application from him. Our deadline has passed. If we tried to bring him in at this point, the Dean would have a fit!"

"I see your point," Bahls said. "It's just that I can't support the Feldt woman. Her Degree is in Educational Administration. Besides, she only has an Ed.D.."

"You got that right," Loras said. "That kind of vita would weaken our grant applications. Can't imagine what she has to offer."

These were the comments Rich had hoped for when he brought the Feldt application forward. *Imagine! An Ed.D. in our group!* "I could see no other course of action," Rich said. "She is among the best qualified on our criteria." Rich having weeded out others with stronger records - 'blue chips' in another game.

"Well, at least we have two strong candidates," Loras said. "Either Berland or Fernandez would be a great addition to our group. I'd put them as dead even. Fernandez has the more impressive publication record and Berland has the ideas and experience that we need."

Fernandez! Rich gulped, then spoke with less than his normal assurance, "Are we then agreed that I'll put these three on the Dean's table?" Heads nodded. "Do we want to prioritize them?"

The three conspirators looked at one another. Eventually, Bahls said, "Well, I'd put Feldt at the bottom. The other two are kind of . . . you know . . . tied."

"I favor Felicity," Loras picked up her folder and leafed through it. "She's a keeper!"

"I'll second that!" Bahls said.

Rich collected the three files. "OK. I'll tell the Dean that these are our best candidates and that we have them in the order of Berland, Fernandez, and Feldt."

"Rich," Bahls admonished, "you gotta remember how hot Dunkard is about adding minorities to the faculty. He's likely to go for Fernandez.'

"That's right," Loras pursed his lips. "We could end up with a guy who's off on his own publishing kick. That'd play hell with our operation."

"You're probably right," Rich paused, considering his options. "Let me think about this. There may be some way we can . . ."

Loras and Bahls could see that Rich had the message. Their faces showed the confidence they placed in Rich's manipulative skills. They actually smiled as they stood, looking down at their seated Rasputin.

When the two had left, Rich remained – deep in thought about what he might do to save Felicity's future. 'Can't leave the Fernandez file out. Dean might go through the whole pool.' He leafed through the Fernandez file. 'Let's see. Great publications. Outstanding teacher. Active in minority rights.' *Minority rights!* Rich leaned back in his chair, eyes glazed. "What does that mean?" He returned to the file. *There!* He pulled a newspaper clipping. 'Professor Fernandez sues University for discrimination.' The clipping had come from an anonymous source; one of the devious ways recommenders submitted their real opinions about candidates.

Rich nearly jumped out of this chair. He hastily assembled the three files and swept out of the room; on his way to the Dean.

Dean Dunkard was in and available. Rich laid the files on the Dean's desk. "Here are the three candidates the committee recommends for consideration. We have them in priority order. Feldt is in third place. Fernandez and Berland are tied for first."

Dunkard paged through the files in a desultory manner. "Anything the committee said that could help me decide?"

"Yes. Feldt is the best of the remaining, rather weak, pool of candidates. We are especially concerned about her Degree. It's an Ed.D.. And, she's another community college person. Just like Solvay."

"I'll accept that," Dunkard said, moving the Feldt file aside. "Now what about the other two?"

"Each has a very strong vita. They differ in emphasis. Fernandez is a nationally-recognized writer. Berland is an upcoming, creative researcher."

Dunkard placed the two files side by side. "Hard to go with one of our own graduates; especially when the U is emphasizing publication and national visibility."

"Take a look at this newspaper clipping," Rich advised. "It came in along with Fernandez' recommendations."

Rich nearly laughed as he watched the Dean's face. Interest gave way to concern that transformed into anger. "Not another Solvay!" Dunkard shouted. "There's no way I'll expose the College to any kind of legal problems. Why, Central would . . .," Anger left facial space for dejection.

"Let me make a suggestion," Rich offered. "Why not offer the position to Berland and keep Fernandez on hold? Then if there's any problem with Fel . . . I mean, Berland, you can always turn to Fernandez."

"It's the only way!" the Dean blurted. "She's a very strong candidate and will be a great addition to our faculty!"

"With your permission, I'd like to let Ms Berland know of your decision. As you know, she's my advisee and I'm very proud of her accomplishments." Rich positively glowed.

"I see no problem with that. Just be sure that she doesn't say anything until she receives my appointment letter. You can also write all the other candidates – except Fernandez – and close their files."

Rich nodded repeatedly, fidgeting in his chair, eager to convey the news to Felicity.

The tightly-knit world of the academy was held together by a kind of extra-sensory network that linked key actors in webs of understanding. Those in the know were instantly aware of plans and decisions that might affect them.

During her years as a graduate student, Felicity became a node in the College rumor network. She was waiting in Rich's outer office when he returned from the Dean.

"Hello Rich. You seem very cheerful. What's new?"

"Greetings, Professor Berland," he crowed.

She put her hand to her mouth. "You mean . . ."

"That's right! The Dean will be sending you a letter of appointment to a tenure track position in Higher Education. Let me be . . ."

Felicity leaped to her feet and ran to hug Rich. "Oh Rich! I'm . . . now . . . we can work together!"

Rich held her closely and looked over her shoulder at the future.

The academy was selective in choosing the misconduct to be punished!

CHAPTER FOURTEEN

Naming Rites

"Once a donor has given money to the University, they are presented with a correspondingly long list of naming opportunities - $5,000 can give you the right to name a faculty office, $200,000 gets your name over a 200 seat classroom. Once you get up to the $2+ million level, you start to be able to name entire facilities." (Virginia Commonwealth University)

One of the characteristics of an accomplished academic politician is to be ever on the alert for new opportunities whereby power can be increased. Rich was a master of this aspect of his craft; however, he had little opportunity to move beyond the petty triumphs of daily academic life. That was about to change.

The change agent was Mike Bahls who presented Rich and Hank with a hitherto unknown arena where outside money sought immortality. The meeting was held behind the closed door of Rich's office.

"You guys," Bahls began, "I gotta tell you what I heard in D.C. on my last trip."

"I suppose there's another federal grant on the way. Ain't we got enough on our plate?" Hank moaned.

"Second that!" Rich said. "I for one have more than enough to do."

"Stop whining!" Bahls commanded. "This is about free money that we might be able to bring to Midwest. Here's the way it works. You know how universities have always named buildings after donors. Well, the name of the game today is to sell naming rights to everything on campus – including the faculty."

"So what?" Hank asked. "Doesn't seem to me we have anything to sell."

"He's right!" Rich seconded. "Besides, all of our buildings already have names. Take Blewett for example . . ."

"That's just it!" Bahls wagged a finger. "The U didn't get a dime from Ben Blewett, they just picked his name out of a hat. What would happen today at many universities is that buildings like Blewett would be renovated and renamed after a donor who coughed up a couple of million."

"Sounds like a good idea," Rich said. "But I'll bet the U wouldn't go along with that. Besides, I can't imagine anybody with that kind of money laying it on this old barn."

"Listen up!" Bahls said. "I'm not finished. Buildings are only the big ticket item. Some universities will get five K donations for donor names on gymnasium lockers. And, it doesn't cost a bundle to get your name on a room. Why a donor could even get the naming rights to your office."

Rich got the point. He could imagine coming to work each morning and opening the door to the Budweiser Malting Memorial Office. He shuddered at the thought. "Isn't that going too far? If you're right, Blewett would be filled with brass plates on each room."

"You win the prize!" Bahls licked his lips and continued. "I've done a few numbers and I figure that the College could raise a couple of million bucks from its alumns. All that's needed is a little creative marketing."

"I'm not convinced," Hank said dubiously. "Give me an example."

Bahls thought for a moment. "O.K., take Blewett. When I came here last year and gave that talk in the atrium it was hard for me to concentrate. The place was dirty; it hadn't been redecorated in years. Even Ben's statue was grey rather than white. Suppose the College were to set up an alumni task force to plan the renovation of the atrium. I imagine it would cost a couple of hundred thousand."

"Hold it!" Hank interrupted. "The alumns raise two hundred K, renovate the atrium and get a label. Don't see what that does for us."

"The point is this," Bahls responded. "We help the College pick projects that will appeal to alumni. Then we set the fund raising goal well above actual cost. The money comes in. The job gets done. And the fund balance is there for the College to use as it sees fit."

Rich followed this mental arithmetic. He could see that Bahls had put his financial fingers on that segment of graduates who felt that they needed to give something back to the College.

"I take your point, but what's all this got to do with our work?" Rich asked.

"That's where it gets a little complicated," Bahls admitted, ticking off points on his fingers. "Here's the way I see it. First, we get the grants and do the work. Second, Central takes our indirect costs and skims the lion's share. Third, the College gets the balance to distribute to the departments. Finally, we need to break into the indirect cost cash flow. I think that what I call the 'naming rights strategy' is the way to do it."

"I can see where you're going," Hank commented. "But I think this 'naming rights' thing is way too complicated."

"Sure," Bahls agreed. "If things go along as usual. Suppose that we shake up the whole business. All we need to do is to set up a kind of 'naming rights test' in the College and show Central how to bring in the bucks. Then indirect costs get lost in the blizzard of donations, to say nothing about some of the extra dollars coming our way."

"Sure. Sure," Rich mumbled. "I still don't see how the 'naming thing' gets off the ground."

Bahls was instantly transformed from teacher to consultant. "You both heard me use the atrium example. Suppose that each of you try to come up with something similar that alumni might want to support. Give it a try."

They adjourned. Bahls strolled out of the Associate Dean's office, exuding confidence. Hank followed, a perplexed frown on his face. Rich remained sitting at his desk, looking into an empty mental bag of alumni goodies. He finally gave up in frustration, stood, turned out the light and left.

Nothing occurred to him that evening and he came up empty of ideas for the morning meeting in Hank's office. It was impossible for him to give any mental time to the 'naming thing'. The only name he was interested in was Felicity, his new colleague. Rich gloried in her attainment of professorial status. As usual, his enthusiasm for collaboration was tempered by worries about her tenure and continuation of appointment. *Endowed chair!* Would this new source of money work to support Felicity?

Rich was enamored by this possibility. However, when he calculated the level of contributions needed for an endowed chair, he realized that there were few donors who would provide the million dollars needed. Back to the drawing board!

Rich's drawing board was the old recliner on his enclosed porch where he and Muriel had woven the tapestries of their futures. Now, he only sat in the porch when he was burdened with weighty political issues. This evening was one of those times. It did not take much reflection for Rich to realize that Bahls' proposal was much larger in scope than just money for Felicity. What he needed for the

257

upcoming meeting was a fund-raising concept that had the potential to attract the attention of Central Administration.

He sat gazing across the darkening lawn – into the past. They were young then, enthusiastic couples at LMU. Those were good days. *LMU!* What had he recently heard about LMU? Something to do with fund raising! Rich leapt out of the recliner and raced into his home office. He wheeled his desk chair to his computer and connected to the Internet.

Rich typed 'Louisiana Methodist University' and worked his way to 'Giving to LMU'. There it was! 'LMU Legacy Fund' He read the description with growing interest.

THE LEGACY FUND

Become a part of the LMU Legacy by donating to your University. The Legacy offers many attractive opportunities to memorialize your experience at LMU and your commitment to its future.

Rich read this message several times, enunciating the key concepts aloud. ". . . memorialize . . . attractive opportunities . . . commitment . . ." He sat back and pronounced his verdict. "That says it all! Legacy! That's what Mike's really talking about!"

Here was his chance to transform Bahls' idea of 'naming rights' into a university-wide movement. Rich could see that a few successful legacy gifts to the College would be political gold in Central's counting house. He began to type furiously.

He opened his proposal with a version of the LMU Legacy description. Mindful of the penalties for plagiarism, he was careful to mask the source of his idea with references that would appeal to Midwest alumni. The final version was, he thought, a masterful foundation on which Midwest could build its Legacy. He printed three copies in bold face type.

THE MIDWEST LEGACY FUND

The Legacy Fund affords members of the Midwest community many opportunities to memorialize their experiences as students and provide support for the future of Midwest University.

Contributing to the Legacy Fund gives donors the opportunity to name facilities and programs that have special meaning for them. In that way, the Fund is a living memorial to the on-going relationship between Midwest and those who wish to strengthen their bonds to this institution.

Rich read the two paragraphs. Sure, it was heavy with emotional content, but that was the way to get the money! He slipped the three copies into his attaché case for the next morning's meeting. He slept well that night.

When the three gathered in Rich's office, Bahls began the discussion. "I can see the light of money in your eyes! Why don't you start off Hank? What's your idea?"

"Well, I ran through my list of College grads who are making it big time. There are two that I know personally and I think we could persuade them to ante up."

Rich was interested. Hank might have something for the Legacy Fund! "Who might that be?" he asked.

"You remember Sally Tofte, Rich? You know, the one who worked with me five-six years ago on facility planning for disabled clients?"

"Guess so. Isn't she the one who owns Disability House?"

"That's the one. Now, get this, she's worth something like ten million! And, I'm still connected with her as a member of the Disability House board."

"Sounds promising," Bahls said. "Any ideas as to what she might be interested in?"

"Thought about that," Hank mused. "I think she'd plunk for a million or so to have her name on my old building."

"Looks like that's one for the money," Bahls said. "So Rich. What's your idea?"

"I've though a lot about what you've said. As I see it, the problem is that the College doesn't have a whole lot to sell. Hank's building is the only one that hasn't been named and we can hardly label the Ben Blewett statue with a donor's name. Seems to me that we're sort of selling out of an empty warehouse." Rich sat back, satisfied in his use of this business metaphor.

"Well, I suppose you've got something there," Bahls looked puzzled. "Got any ideas on what we could do about it?"

"Yes, take a look at this," Rich passed out copies of his Legacy paper. "What I suggest is that we use the idea of naming rights to set up a University-wide 'Legacy Fund'."

There were several minutes of silence as Hank and Bahls studied Rich's paper.

Hank looked up. "You know, I kind of like this. Legacy. That has lots of appeal. I certainly could use it with Sally Tofte. She'd plunk for her 'legacy' in a minute!"

"Think so?" Bahls asked. "So, suppose donors like the legacy idea. What does it do for us?"

"Here's what I think we should do," Rich paused. "First, we'll need to sell the Legacy to Dunkard and Central. Next, we show how it works with a big gift – like Tofte. Finally, we set up the details of how the fund works and how colleges split the take with Central."

"Pretty big order," Bahls frowned. "I don't see . . ."

Hank cut in, "I, for one, think Rich has something. I'll bet that Tofte would up the ante if she were to be the first Legacy donor. We figure out how to get Dunkard and Central on board and I'll guarantee the lead donation."

Rich smiled. "Exactly what I had hoped! Without a demonstration, Legacy would come up empty."

Bahls was interested, if not convinced. "This is way beyond what I originally proposed, but it would be some feather in our caps if we could pull it off. Let's start the ball rolling. Rich, how do you suggest we approach Central."

"I'd say we lie!" Rich blurted. "We go to Pearson and tell him that Hank has been approached by a big-time donor who wants naming rights on the old Annex Building. We tell Waldo that we think this is an opportunity for the U to put the Legacy Fund in place. That possible Hank?"

Hank considered. "I'd have to lie to Tofte to start. It's a big risk and we need to be sure that Central will approve the Legacy." He grimaced. "Pretty fast footwork!"

"But you're a pretty good dancer!" Bahls laughed. "How's about this. Hank, you talk up the idea with Tofte. Rich can test the water at Central. I think he's right – Waldo will eat this up."

"Meanwhile," Rich added. "I'll work up a short paper for Waldo that lays out more detail on the Legacy."

The ball rolled. Within a week, Hank reported that Sally Tofte was excited about putting her name on the Annex. Rich completed several drafts of the Legacy Fund concept and they were ready for Pearson. The three decided that Rich and Hank should make the case at Central

They were, by now, familiar visitors to Waldo's secretary. "So it's you two again. Comin' over here pretty regular. Suppose you wanna see him." She flicked a switch on her intercom. "Boys from Education here," she rasped.

Pearson's response was audible to the visitors. "Send them in!"

At least Waldo was friendly, Rich thought. Quite a contrast from the outer office.

"Hank, Rich," Waldo said. "What's this about a fund raising strategy?"

"We've developed an innovative approach to fund-raising that I believe you'll find interesting." Rich handed his proposal to Waldo. "If you'll just skim the introductory paragraphs you'll have a good idea of what we have in mind."

Pearson picked up the proposal and spent several minutes reading and re-reading the first page. He looked up, "I've heard of this approach at other universities. I must confess that I haven't considered how we might apply a 'legacy fund' at Midwest."

"That's what we'd like to talk about," Hank offered a single sheet of paper. "Here's an example of what's possible in the College."

Rich and Hank watched Waldo closely as he read the paragraphs describing how Sally Tofte might provide a leading gift in support of Hank's program. They were quietly elated at the broad smile that possessed Waldo's face.

Pearson exclaimed, "This is fantastic! I didn't realize that the College had alumni of this caliber."

"We believe that Tofte is only one example among many who would be interested in contributing to a Midwest Legacy Fund," Rich said persuasively.

"And we hope that Central will support this idea," Hank added. "Give us the green light and we'll try it out."

Waldo laughed. "Not so fast! This is a great idea that I'll need to run by President Rose, and the university attorney. Give me a couple of weeks. In the meantime, I'd advise you to go slow, but try to come up with other examples."

The balance of their visit involved discussion of the features of the Legacy that Rich had outlined. Waldo added suggestions that Rich noted for a next draft of the Legacy proposal. Although Hank was attentive, he was engaged in mentally exploring a list of Legacy donors to add to Tofte's name.

"One more thing," Waldo said as he held out a farewell hand. "Give me an idea of how the Legacy might be organized and how monies might be disbursed. And, don't forget to give us at Central a cut!"

"This calls for a drink!" Hank concluded as he and Rich left Conant Hall. "Let's stop in to Tubby's for a bump!"

Rich agreed and they were soon seated in a corner of the Quarterdeck. Drinks arrived and Hank took the toastmaster's role.

"Here's to the Legacy Fund, Good Buddy!"

"I'll drink to that!" Rich exulted. "I do, however, have one question. Just how can we organize the fund so that we don't lose control of the money? Central's 'cut' worries me."

"Me too," Hank said. "The Legacy has to be structured so that we don't have to fight with Central on every gift. I've done a little background work on that issue and I believe the answer lies in 'fund accounting'."

"How's that?"

"According to Carl Mertens, you know the Ed. Psych. guy who went to the Business school, most universities use fund accounting to keep track of monies that have special purposes. For example, if Tofte springs for a million to renovate the Annex and support its operation, the U has to put that money in a fund account. Now, here's the kicker! The money can't be used for any other purpose!"

"You mean that Central has to spend all of her donation on the Annex? That's exactly what we need!"

"I'll say!" Hank said. "This calls for another drink!" He stepped down from the Quarterdeck and returned with refills. "Now," he said, raising a full glass, "all we have to do is write this up for Waldo."

"Not quite," Rich cautioned. "There's more. Suppose we have a donor who can't find anything to put a name on. That money would go into the Annual Fund where Central's in full control."

Hank frowned at this detestable news. "We'd for sure get nothing out of that! Why, we'd be raising money for Central!"

Rich grinned. "Thought of that. So – what if we folded the Annual Fund into the Legacy where we'd have our hands in the till?"

"Sounds good, but how . . .?"

"All we have to do is to give that part of the Legacy a 'purpose' so we're in the loop when spending decisions are made."

"I can buy that, but what sort of 'purpose'?"

"How's about this," Rich said in a prideful tone. "We put all the 'non-naming dollars' into an 'innovation fund' with a College committee that decides what sort of 'innovation' is worthy of support. What do you think of that?"

The other patrons at Tubby's were startled when Hank's fist thumped on the table. "Bigolly! I can see it now! You, Bahls and I are the 'committee' and . . .," He was unable to continue, overpowered by the innovation stratagem.

Often maneuvers of this scope came up against significant roadblocks. This was no exception and Rich identified the problem they faced. "Dunkard's the fly in this ointment. The first thing Waldo's going to do is to consult with Mert and get his approval for the Legacy. We've got to be sure that Dunkard's on board before that happens."

"Pretty tall order. Mert is the last person I'd nominate as an innovator!"

"That's right on! So here's what I propose. Remember, I'm the Associate Dean. I go to Mert and tell him that Pearson has asked me to develop a proposal for the Legacy. Then I work on Dunkard so that he thinks the whole thing is his idea! How's about that?"

"Think it's possible?" Hank asked skeptically. "I know that Dunkard is a couple of quarts low." He laughed at the notion that the Dean might be a bit short of a full mental crankcase.

"No problemo!" Rich promised. "I'll start the ball rolling tomorrow. Meanwhile you can work on the Tofte donation."

"OK, but what do we do about Mike? After all, the whole thing was his idea."

"That's right," Rich sipped at his drink and grinned. "But what if we move Dunkard out and put Mike in as Dean?"

"Holy shit!" Hank sputtered. "How the hell . . ."

"Easy does it!" Rich leaned forward and spoke in a confidential tone. "The annual fund is the way. So far as College alumni are concerned, Dunkard is the face of the U. They don't know about his problem with booze. He's seen as the father figure of the College; the one who can make the 'ask'."

"Hadn't thought of it that way," Hank reflected. "But I see where you're going." He paused. "It might work if there's a way to get Mert to buy it."

"Let me work on him," Rich summarized. "I think we have the right spin on the Legacy and I'm confident that I can bring Mert along."

"So what's next?"

"We need to meet with Mike as soon as possible. If he doesn't agree with our plan, we're back to square one." He paused. "Any suggestions?"

"Well . . .," Hank considered, "we've got the good news from Waldo and your scheme for the Legacy Annual Fund. I think that's enough to get started. I'll give him a call this evening. Let's meet for breakfast – no – for an after lunch smoke at Tabaccy's. OK?"

Rich agreed, they paid and left Tubby's. That night Rich slept well – covered with political cloth.

The next afternoon was evidently a busy day at the U and Tabaccy's was nearly empty when the three convened after lunch.

Cigars were purchased and lighted. Then Hank began the discussion. "Rich," he said. "I've put Mike into the picture and he has a couple of questions that I'm sure you can answer."

Bahls tapped the glowing ash from his cigar. "Rich, I really like your concept of the Legacy. Especially the way you're planning to use fund accounting. What I can't get my arms around is the idea of putting Dunkard in charge of the Legacy. Shouldn't one of us take the lead?"

"Yes, that seems like a good idea," Hank said. "But that would leave Dunkard in charge of how College money would be spent."

"OK," Bahls nodded. "I agree that we have to control things at the College level. However, with Dunkard head of the Legacy wouldn't he be likely to shift money to other colleges?"

"Sure. That's possible," Rich concurred. "However, with Waldo in our camp, I think Mert will be on a short leash. Now, here's the big question. Mike, would you be willing to take the Dean's place at the College?"

Although Bahls knew of this option, he was a bit taken aback when it was presented as a choice. He hesitated for several seconds. "Well . . . I guess so.

Wait a minute! That would take me away from the Center. I don't see how . . ."

"Wait!" Rich commanded. "We have to think bigger here. Let me ask you this, Mike. Would control over Central be more or less desirable than continued grants from H&HS?"

That alternative was even more stunning to Bahls. He appeared visibly disturbed, stumbling through a response. ". . . control . . . over the U? I don't see how . . . we . . .," he stopped.

Rich took over. "I admit it's a long shot. The way I see it, we gain big time by putting the Legacy in place. If the alumni buy it, as I think they will, it means a steady, large flow of funds into the U. That outweighs grant revenue. Then, we have Mike's foot in the door for other administrative roles, while we control the Legacy through Waldo."

Bahls was easily convinced. The carrot of 'other administrative roles' fed his appetite for advancement and he instantly became an advocate for Rich's Legacy scheme. "I see where you're going Rich. The Legacy is a great way to build on my initial idea. So let's divide the work and get going!"

"Fine!" Rich enthused. "Here's the way I suggest we proceed. As I said Hank, you should begin – carefully – to explore Tofte's interest with special attention to the notion that she could be the lead Legacy gift. I'll take on Dunkard and see to it that he accepts our plan as his own. I'll write the proposal and circulate it to you. Then Mert can carry it to Pearson. What I'd like from you Mike, is a list of the kinds of naming rights we see in the College. How's that for next steps?"

Heads nodded all round. Cigars were stubbed out and they exited Tabaccy's.

The confidence Rich had exhibited at Tabaccy's lasted through the first draft of the Legacy proposal. It turned out to be a fickle supporter when he considered his approach to Dunkard. Rich realized that the Legacy concept was an easy sell; it was the movement of Mert to Central that might be resisted. The only way to set his mind at ease was to lay the idea on the Dean's table.

Legacy proved to be a compelling idea insofar as Dunkard was concerned. "Why Rich! This is exactly what I've been thinking about." Dunkard lied. "I've been considering how we can tap our graduates to support the work of the College. The Legacy will do it."

"I'm glad to hear it," Rich said. "And I'll be willing to work up your ideas into a proposal for Vice President Pearson."

"Great. Just keep me in the loop." Dunkard began to rise to conclude the meeting.

"There's just one more thing we need to discuss. I've been thinking long and hard about leadership for the Legacy. Pearson is concerned that we use our very best talent to lead this important venture." Dunkard wasn't the only one who could make use of lies.

The Dean sank back in his chair. "I agree that leadership for Legacy is crucial, but where does the College come in?"

"It's my recommendation that you move your position to Central and take on this important assignment. There's nobody better suited to appeal to the many alumni who see you as the embodiment of the U."

The shock of this announcement silenced the Dean for several long seconds and he seemed to Rich to deflate in size. Finally, Dunkard spoke. "That's . . . a very interesting idea."

Interesting! Rich fastened on that word. If Dunkard was 'interested', then Rich was nearly at his goal. All that remained was to fill in the thought with detail.

"I'm glad you see it that way," Rich said soothingly. "In order to go ahead, we'll need to think about our approach to Pearson. Along that line, would you be comfortable in carrying the Legacy proposal to Central?"

Another moment of silence. "I . . . suppose so," Dunkard said. "If I'm going to explain the Legacy to Waldo, I'll need to discuss the proposal with you at length. Can you meet his deadline? What was it? Two weeks?"

"No problem," Rich promised. "With your help, I should be able to produce a draft by the end of this week." He knew that the draft was already in Waldo's hands. All that had to be added was the argument for transforming the Annual Fund.

Meeting closed! Draft produced! Dean edited! Rich was well prepared for the Dean's visit to Pearson. There remained only the issue of Legacy leadership. How was Waldo to be persuaded to select Dunkard? Rich knew that he needed to meet with Waldo.

Another meeting at Tabaccy's was called for. This time, Rich splurged for a box of Partagas Robustos and had them waiting on a table in one of the smoker's alcoves.

Hank was the first to arrive. He sat and groped among the Robustos. "These are pretty fancy; you didn't have a baby, did you?"

"No, Dummy," Rich snorted. "This celebration is for Mert Dunkard, the new Director of the Midwest Legacy Fund!"

"You mean that? Mert bought the package?"

"The whole nine yards! Looking at him, you can see that he's already deciding what kind of office he'll need!"

At this point, Bahls entered. "Robustos! Allright!" He clearly knew quality and he scooped up a small handful of cigars that went into his blazer pocket. "So, what's to report?"

"We've got Mert where we want him," Rich said. "He's going to carry the Legacy Proposal to Waldo. What we have to decide is how to set up that meeting so Waldo buys the entire Legacy; and chooses Dunkard as Director."

"You know," Hank said reflectively. "I think I can help. I've had a couple of conversations with Sally Tofte and she's hot to be the lead donor for the Legacy. In fact, she's likely to sweeten the pot with another million!"

"Holy shit!" Bahls exploded. "Are you serious?"

"You bet. Sally's already working with her attorney on the language of the gift. And that language will ensure that the money goes to the Annex and our Center. That should get Pearson's attention."

"I'll say!" Bahls said. "I can't match that. The best I can do is this list of possible naming opportunities." He handed copies to Rich and Hank. "You'll see that it focuses on buildings and objects. However, I've taken Rich's innovation idea and worked up some language." Another set of pages was shared.

Cigars gradually disappeared as Rich made notes on the Legacy Proposal. Bahls' innovation narrative was folded into the Legacy Fund and Tofte's lead donation was used to lend weight to the document.

"I think we're ready," Rich said. "I'll get the final version to Mert and set him up for his meeting with Waldo."

"Meanwhile," Hank grinned. "We'll keep our fingers crossed!"

At the end of Pearson's deadline, Rich forwarded a copy of the Legacy Proposal to the Vice President's office. It resulted in a phone call from Waldo.

"Congratulations Rich," Waldo said. "This is a very impressive document. You'll be pleased to know that President Rose is enthusiastic about the Legacy; that lead donation went a long way in convincing him as to the merits of your proposal."

"Why, thank you," Rich said humbly. "It's an idea whose time has come. By the way, do you agree that Dean Dunkard is a good choice to lead the Legacy?"

"That caught me by surprise, I must say. However, the lead donation shows that he has name recognition among alumni." Pearson paused. "I'm a little puzzled as to who might succeed him as Dean. Aren't you the logical choice?"

Rich was ready for this question. "Yes, it would seem so. But there's a much better candidate. I hope you'll consider Dr. Bahls for the position. Having a Presidential Scholar as Dean would help to enhance the reputation of the College and attract donors."

Pearson ruminated for several seconds. "Ummm . . . yes, I see where you're going. If we appointed Bahls, would you stay on as Associate Dean ?

"Of course, if he wishes me to do so."

"OK. Send Dunkard over and I'll see what I can do."

Rich sensed that he had just finished a conversation with an expert on university politics. He mentally reviewed the results. Legacy Fund. Lead donor. Legacy Director. Dean Bahls.

The review was correct in all four dimensions. The Legacy Fund (including the old Annual Fund) was established under Mert Dunkard's leadership. Sally Tofte's lead gift of two million set the hoped-for standard. And Mike Bahls was named the Dean of the College of Education and Home Economics.

These were real naming rights!

CHAPTER FIFTEEN

External Review

> *"College and university administrators, confronted by revenue shortfalls, usually 'retrenched,' that is, a centralized team made 'hard decisions' about who stays and who leaves."*
> *(Edward St. Carl: National Higher Education Journal).*

National and international educational developments were often unknown at Midwest. Academic news was routinely ignored as irrelevant for university life in the midlands. On those infrequent times when the outside world penetrated the academic culture of Midwest, intense debate energized the political forces that controlled the university. Such was the case when the College of Education and Home Economics was subject to an external review.

As a senior faculty member, Rich had been involved in selecting representatives of colleges of education from universities thought to be Midwest's peers. He had worked closely with the new Dean Bahls and other professors in their attempts to shape the final product of the external review. They were surprised and angered when the reviewers submitted their report.

This morning, Rich was in his office at seven a.m. studying the report. It was no casual perusal. The Graduate School was to receive the report this very afternoon, and Rich was to be the bearer of the bad news it contained. He uncapped a yellow marker and began highlighting the points made by the reviewers. Each stroke of the marker was accompanied by a vocal response from Rich.

'In preparing this Report, the reviewers have taken care to support their conclusions and recommendations with data collected by examining university records and conducting interviews with key informants.' As the marker squeaked over this sentence, Rich exploded. "Bullshit! It's that bastard Gherke at Tallahatchee!" Louis Gherke was Dean of the College of Education at Tallahatchee State University and one of the competitors Rich confronted at ASHE meetings. Rich had resisted appointing Gherke as a reviewer, but was over-ruled by the Graduate School Dean at Midwest. "Now we're stuck with that sonofabitch!"

Rich's vocalizations continued; increasing in volume as the highlights multiplied. *'College faculty appear to have little sense of mission and are often engaged in activities that are at cross-purposes.'* Rich squeezed the marker, hands clutched as if to strangle Gherke. "Where the hell did you get that stupid idea? Generalizations! It's all generalizations! A first-year grad student comment!"

'Scholarship has a low priority among senior faculty who do not engage in substantive research nor is there a high level of publication.' "What the fuck!" Rich spat. "What about the Policy Studies Academy? What about that?" Gherke did not, of course, answer these questions.

The monologue went on through the thirty pages of the report. Rich's tension grew into a palpable ache in his neck and shoulders. He swiveled his head in a futile attempt to relax. Then he slowly turned to the Conclusions section of the report.

A series of bullets listed the shortcomings of the College. The statement that focused Rich's anger said: *'The large enrollment of able graduate students is not well-served in either coursework or advising.'* This bullet went directly to the heart of the academic corpus of the College. Like many of his colleagues, Rich blamed the victim. "How can they expect us to teach these idiots! If they had interviewed students, they'd find out how really dumb they are!"

The final recommendation was stated in a single sentence. *'The Reviewers are in unanimous agreement with the recommendation that Midwest University close the College of Education and Home Economics in an orderly manner so as to minimize the effect on students.'* "Close!" Rich shouted. A passing student obeyed, closing Rich's office door. "What the hell kind of a recommendation is that?" He stood and hurled the marker at the closed door. Anger fought with fear for domination as he marched around his office. *Those rotten! . . . Will I lose tenure? . . . They can't do. . .*

Each circuit of his office magnified the problems he would be facing at the Graduate School. Clearly, there were no easy rejoinders to the issues raised by the external review. Even his most powerful mantras would be illuminated as empty rationalizations in the light of the scheduled inquisition.

How many times had he sat in judgment of other units of the U? Frequently, a single word or phrase from Professor Jessen had swayed Graduate School decisions. When coupled with Rich's considerable knowledge of academic canon law, his words carried an unassailable message of academic integrity. Now others could use a similar approach to hasten the demise of the College – and his future.

He spoke aloud. "There has to be a way to . . .," He stopped pacing. "Mike!" Rich reached for the telephone and dialed the Dean's Office.

"College of Education, Dean's Office. How may I direct your call?"

"Millie, Rich Jessen. I need to talk to the Dean. Is he in?"

"Just arrived. I'll put you on hold."

Rich lowered himself into his desk chair and opened the report to the 'Conclusions' page. *Look at this shit!* He raged. . .

"Rich, this is Mike. What's up?"

"Have you read the reviewers' report?'

"Yes. Looks pretty bad for the College. You have quite an assignment this afternoon."

"You can say that again," Rich snorted. "Those bastards from the science faculty will devour the report like fresh meat!"

"So what can we do?"

"You and I need to talk as soon as possible. I need to have some sort of bone to throw to the Graduate School, or the College will be put on a short leash – possibly closed."

"Don't like the sound of that. Better come right over. I'll clear my calendar for the rest of the morning."

Rich hung up and did a quick mental search of his files. *Have I got any ammunition to fire at the Grad School?* He could think of no hard data. Nor had he copies of other evaluations of the College that ended on a positive note. *Nothing!* He spun around in the chair and started to rise. *Wait a minute! The budget!*

Rich wheeled his chair to a file cabinet and pulled open a drawer. He flipped through a section marked University Reports to a Budget folder. There he had arranged documents summarizing university operations for recent years. The current year was at the front of the folder. He took that Budget Report from the file and wheeled back to his desk.

It took only a few minutes for Rich to confirm his suspicion. *The Grad School is in deep shit!* "Let's see . . . they are short about . . . two million!" It was as if a complex theory had been confirmed by research! "No wonder the

Reviewers' Report is so important! Close the College – take the money – and save Central Administration's ass!"

"Missouri State! Wasn't there something about advising?" Rich opened another file drawer and pawed through files of clippings from the Chronicle of Higher Education. It took him less than five minutes to lay his hand on an article entitled; "Missouri State Focuses on Student Advisement". The content was as Rich remembered; MSU had indeed focused on student advisement by instituting a policy of 'thesis advisement credits', which were incorporated in student programs of study – and in their tuition bills. Here was a possible way to use the Review to the benefit of the College. Rich backed this hunch with a cursory perusal of catalogs from other universities; charging for thesis credits was clearly a cash cow!

The Budget, the Chronicle article and the Reviewers' Report went into Rich's briefcase and he strode across to the Dean's office.

Mike was waiting outside his office. "Rich! Come on in. Millie, we'll need a pot of coffee. Please hold my calls."

Coffee cups and copies of the report were positioned on the Dean's conference table. Rich and Mike alternated coffee sipping with aimless paging through the document. Neither was eager to begin the discussion. Finally, Bahls cleared his throat.

"Well, Rich the reviewer's haven't said anything favorable about the College. Right?"

"It's the bullets in the Conclusion that shoots us down. I have to say that I can't come up with any evidence that refutes what's said here."

Bahls removed his glasses and folded his hands on the report. "Neither can I. What that means we have to find a way to take the Grad School minds off these statements."

Rich pushed his chair back from the table and crossed his legs. "This morning I went through my files. The only thing that has any promise is the University budget. The way I read it, the GS is short a couple of million."

"That's news to me," Bahls said. "But the whole university is feeling legislative pressure to cut expenses. I imagine the Grad School Dean has nowhere to go to find new money."

They contemplated this happy state of affairs for several minutes; each searching for a way to use the Grad School's misfortune to defuse the report.

Rich broke the silence. "Think about this. The Conclusions all point to a possible closure of the College. Now, what would happen if we could take a couple of the Conclusions and use them to arrive at solutions to the Grad School's problem?"

"That'd be great, but I don't see how any of the reviewer's comments have anything to do with the GS budget."

"Not directly," Rich agreed, "but take, for instance, the bullet that says, 'The large enrollment of able graduate students is not well-served in either coursework or advising.'. What if we said that we totally agree with this observation and . . ."

"Hold it!" Bahls shook his head. "We don't want to agree with the Report."

"Mike, you and I know that this is a true statement. We don't like it, but the more I think about it, it's right on. So bear with me. Right now, we advise our grad students when we feel like it. The good ones get some time, the others may take years to finish their theses."

"OK. I agree, but . . ."

"Let me finish. I checked the catalogs of some of our peer universities. Several require students to register for thesis credits and they charge tuition! Suppose we told the Grad School that we are recommending this practice and that we'd split the tuition take between the GS and the College."

"Sounds interesting. Let's see how the numbers might work." Bahls stepped to a white board on his office wall. "Now, we have about . . . fifty doctoral students a year. Each would take . . . how many credits?"

"The other universities range from a quarter to a third of student programs," Rich said. "That would be something like twenty-four credits for us."

Bahls did the arithmetic. '50 x 24 = 1200' "We charge . . . $400 per credit." '1200 x 400 = $480,000' "Nice piece of change, but not enough."

Rich frowned and penciled numbers on the back of his copy of the Reviewer's Report. He reported, "At the last Grad School graduation exercise, the College finished about . . . an eighth of the grads. So multiply the four-eighty by eight. That'll estimate the total take across the U."

Bahls wrote. '$480000 x 8 = $3,840,000' He circled the total. "Holy shit! That's more like it! The only problem is that other grad programs need to go along or it won't work."

"If other division chairs and deans see these numbers and we talk about a split with the Grad School, they'll sign on just like that!" Rich snapped his fingers. "Every one of them is in a budget bind and – get this – nobody gets any reward for advising now. With this scheme, there is a payoff for everyone."

"Except the students," Bahls observed. "They'll be mad as hornets."

"Don't think so. Most students complain about our advising. This way, they pay for service and we are motivated to deliver." *And, that'll teach the fucking students not to bad mouth us!* Rich admired the political finesse of this solution.

"You know," Bahls said, "we can put some icing on this by suggesting that concentrated advising will improve our research output."

"Now that's an interesting idea. Kind of a medical school model; collaborative research, right?" Rich went on to answer his own question. "Yes . . .

that's the real secondary benefit," he beamed. "Faculty will be able to ride along on student research. More publications, visibility, and students too will . . .," Rich contemplated the personal pay-off of the idea. *Why I can get a couple of publications out of my best students.*

Bahls resumed his seat and picked up the Report. "Let's for the moment, go with this approach. "You meet with the Grad School committee and get them to focus on the Conclusions section where you agree with the reviewers that . . ."

"What do you mean?" Rich erupted. "We agree? That'd sure cook our goose! We're only talking about agreeing with a couple of the bullets."

"Don't think so. There's no way we can counter these accusations." Bahls waved the Report. "Instead, you tell them how serious we are about developing a productive response. You know, the Dean of the College has formed working groups to address each issue."

"But there aren't any such groups."

"Don't worry, there will be by the time you get to the GS. I'll phone two or three professors and ask them to form working groups. They'll be meeting with you and me in the next weeks to develop a strategy for the College."

Rich swirled his coffee cup. "What about our tuition scheme? Shouldn't we reveal it now?"

"No, we don't want the Committee in on this. What we'll do is develop the concept and get our working groups to believe that they thought of it. Then, we can lay it on the lap of the Dean of the GS."

"What good will that do?" Rich asked.

"Look. The GS Dean will make the decision about the future of the College. What we want is for him to see that we are a money machine that he needs. That way, the Committee can babble all it wants. We'll put this thing to sleep!" Bahls tossed the Report at his wastebasket. Perfect three pointer!

That afternoon, Rich had an uncomfortable sensation in his stomach and a film of perspiration on his forehead – much like his reaction to an upcoming proctological examination. His mental health wasn't improved when he entered the conference room at the Graduate School.

Members of the Academic Affairs Committee were already seated around a long table. An empty seat at the foot of the table was obviously reserved for Professor Jessen. Rich's eyes roved over the assembled.

Shirley Jackson, Professor of English; Franklin Shelby, Professor of Political Science; Nelda Lange, Assistant Dean of the Graduate School; Nancy Utoft, Professor of Mathematics; Professor Edward Menes, Professor of Physics and Chair of the Committee. All heavyweight scholars with national reputations!

"Professor Jessen, we are pleased that you will be discussing the Report of the External Reviewers with us." Menes scowled through thick horn-rimmed glasses. "I'm sure you know all of us and that you'll be able to help us understand the implications of the Report." He nodded at the empty chair. "Please be seated and we'll begin."

Rich slid into the empty chair and placed his copy of the Report on the table. He rolled his shoulders, hoping to reduce tension. Sweat trickled down his sides and he could feel his face redden.

Menes cleared his throat. "Now, you all have read the Reviewer's Report and the Conclusions it offers. Let me set our agenda by suggesting that we should take our guidance from the external review of the Department of Education at the University of Chicago which concluded, and I quote,
'The external report pointed to several problems, including "uneven" faculty research, isolation within the division, and "low expectations." Evaluating the self-study's renewal plan, the second team concluded that . . . the prospects for

rebuilding the department to the standard of quality expected in the University and the division are not good." ."

Rich was stunned. *Jesus! If Chicago can't support a Department of Education, how can we? So much for Mike's strategy!*

Menes continued. "It seems to me that our College of Education and Home Economics has all these attributes. Professor Jessen," he stared at Rich, "you have frequently announced your commitment to academic integrity and to the high standards it requires. What do you have to say?"

What have I to say? Rich was stunned by the tone of Menes' voice. In past GS meetings, they had often been on the same side when other university units were being interrogated.

"Professor Menes, you have identified the key issue in this Report." Rich's response was an attempt to pour verbal oil on the troubled waters of the meeting. "Each of the attributes you mention is identified by the reviewers. Let me direct your attention to their conclusion. It provides a framework for my response."

Each Committee member paged through a copy of the report and raised eyes expectantly.

Rich cleared his throat. "Hem . . . now, as to the College's response to these issues. Dean Bahls has named a working group of College faculty to address each major issue. For example, the Dean is leading a group that is considering how the College can improve faculty research focus and productivity. Also . . ."

"Wait a minute," Menes barked. "That kind of committee work assumes that the College will continue to exist. What we want to hear is a reaction to the reviewer's proposal to close the College."

Nancy Utoft shifted her bulk in her chair. "Yesss," she hissed, "this Report is an indictment of the academic integrity of the College. What about that?"

"That's precisely my point," Rich shaped each word in his most pontifical style. "Academic integrity requires that we study this Report and assess the validity of the reviewers' recommendation. To accept it without question is irresponsible."

"I quite agree," Nelda Lange came to his rescue. "All of our past reviews have led to in-depth studies by the unit involved. I think we need to give Professor Jessen the opportunity to tell us what the College has in mind."

Rich nearly smiled as he thought of the gift of thesis credit money the Grad School would receive. His optimism was, however, short-lived.

"Very well," Menes sighed. "Continue with your response, Professor Jessen."

"As to the study group I just mentioned, we believe that research productivity can be greatly improved by conducting collaborative studies of major educational policy issues such as . . ."

"Sounds like a graduate student seminar," Menes interrupted. "That kind of collaborative research just reduces quality and allows for free-loading by weak faculty."

"I don't agree," Franklin Shelby said. "My work with the Policy Studies Academy has convinced me that research by College faculty is likely to influence federal legislation. That's the kind of research that defines the mission of a college of education."

Thank God we involved Shelby! Rich scanned the faces of the Committee. He could see the division clearly. Menes and Utoft salivating for closure; Lange and Shelby advising caution. Where was Shirley Jackson? She hadn't said a word.

"Huh!" Utoft thrust out several folds of chin. "Professor Menes is right. This Report is an indictment of the College and it requires action by this Committee."

"Well," Jackson said. "I for one won't support any recommendation for closing the College without a careful internal study. After all, what do we know about the reviewers? Wherever is Tallahatchee State?" She smiled at the name and grinned at Rich.

"Well, it's not exactly a peer institution, more like a four-year community college." Rich looked down at Tallahatchee State from the academic heights of the University. "Nevertheless, we must take these criticisms seriously and take steps to examine them and address any shortcomings."

"Fox in the chicken coop!" Utoft snorted. "Be a miracle if you find any support for these recommendations."

There were several seconds of silence, then Nelda Lange spoke in measured tones. "I propose that we table the Report and request a formal response from the College."

"I'll second that," Shelby said.

"Me too," Jackson added.

"I don't like it," Menes grumbled. "But I can see that Professor Utoft and I are outvoted."

"That may be," Utoft agreed. "However, I hope the Committee will agree to setting a deadline for the College's response, say three weeks?"

Heads nodded. "OK by me." "Good idea." "I'll support that."

"Then we agree," Lange said. "Professor Jessen, please tell Dean Bahls that the Graduate School will expect a formal response to the Review three weeks from today."

Rich relaxed. "I will do so." *Dodged a bullet!*

Menes and Utoft left the room with scowls and mutterings. The other three committee members remained.

"Looks like you're still on the hook," Shelby chuckled. "I wouldn't worry though; Bahls will come up with some creative ideas."

"I sure hope so," Jackson said. "If he doesn't, Menes will surely make this a University-wide issue."

"I want to thank you both for your support," Rich looked at the two faculty members. "I agree that this is serious business and I know that Dean Bahls will see to it that the College doesn't let you down."

Finally, Rich was alone with Nelda Lange. She gathered her papers and placed them in an accordion file. "Rich, this is more of an issue than you realize. Shirley Jackson was right. Menes has been circulating the Report around the University and has a lot of support in the sciences and the medical school. In fact, the Dean of the Grad School is leaning in the direction of closure of the College. You'll need a very powerful argument to save the College."

"Yes, but remember how the College got legislators behind us the last time this kind of thing happened. Why, the University nearly lost . . ."

"That won't work this time," Lange said sternly. " President Rose has told the Grad School that he won't stand for any political involvement in the affairs of the University."

Rich groaned and shook his head, "Well, I guess I'd better share your concerns with Dean Bahls." He stood to leave.

Lange caught him at the door, putting a hand on his arm. "Please understand Rich, we at the Grad School are hoping the College can diffuse the allegations of the Review."

"Thanks . . .," Rich escaped.

His journey from the Grad School to Blewett Hall was a confusing kaleidoscope. Fleeting images of campus life were in unequal combat with his sense of impending disaster. Outside air cooled his sweat-soaked body so that he was shivering when he opened the door to his office.

Even that familiar space didn't provide the usual sense of sanctuary. Rich closed the door and slammed the Report on his desk. "Goddamn stupid jerks!" He roved around the room; anger warmed him and he began to sweat.

Gradually, his agitation abated. He removed his jacket and shirt, tossing them on the floor behind his desk. His soaked tee shirt followed and he used a towel from his gym bag to dry himself. A fresh tee shirt and turtleneck sweater came from a corner cabinet and Professor Jessen was superficially renewed.

Three weeks! There was no way that he and Bahls could come up with a strategy that had any prospect of placating Central. Finding money for the Graduate School was a major accomplishment, surely a step in the right direction, but would it be enough? Ruminations were interrupted by a knock on his office door.

The door swung open and Felicity swept in. "Oh Rich! Please excuse me but I just had to come by to thank you."

"Glad to see you, but thank me for what?"

"Just this! I received a letter from the Dean of the Graduate School. I'm now an Associate Professor! With tenure!" She beamed at Rich. "And you're the one who made it all happen!"

"But I . . . ," Rich was unable to respond to this kind of praise. He was accustomed to his quantum of academic reward; however, in all his years at Midwest he had never experienced anything like Felicity's enthusiasm.

He stood and held out his hand. "Professor Berland," he said with academic solemnity. "Please accept my congratulations."

Felicity lunged past Rich's hand and threw her arms around his neck. "Oh! Thank you!"

Rich's arms went around her shoulders and he held her closely.

Her emotions were those of a young person who had climbed a major rung of her professional ladder. His were those of a middle aged man without a companion. He looked over her head toward a life with new and exciting dimensions.

It was Felicity who broke the spell. She released her embrace and stepped back, eyes shining. "I still can't believe this. And I owe it all to you."

Rich let his arms fall to his sides, letting her escape for the time being. New images raced across his mental vision: Felicity his partner; their academic life; a life without the College?

Felicity frowned. She could see evidence of preoccupation in Rich's face. "What seems to be the problem, Rich? Have I said something to upset you?"

"No, no. You just caught me at a bad moment. You see, I spent the afternoon at the Grad School trying to defend the College from our External Review."

Her glee was instantly transformed into concern. "Come, let's sit down so you can tell me what happened." She motioned to chairs at Rich's small conference table.

"Now," she said, "what did the Reviewers say that caused all the trouble?"

Rich slid the Report across the table. "Here, read the Conclusions and you'll see why I'm upset."

She paged through the Report. Sharp intakes of breath punctuated the bulleted points offered by the Reviewers. Shakes of her head negated the allegations in the Report. When she confronted the final recommendation, she exploded in uncharacteristic anger.

"Why! This is completely ridiculous! Close the College? This Report is way off base!"

"Yes. I said the same thing to the Grad School Committee. All I got was a reprieve – on a three to two vote."

Felicity quickly reverted to her analytic self. "Where's the opposition? Who are they and what do they want?"

"It's the usual suspects. Menes from physics and Utoft from math. That's bad enough, but Nelda Lange at the GS tells me that the President is leaning toward closure of the College. What a mess!"

She considered this news for a moment. "Any ideas that might sway their opinions?"

"Well, Dean Bahls and I found a weakness in the Grad School budget that could be plugged by charging tuition for doctoral advising credits."

"Students won't like that!"

"No, I suppose not. But what about the alternative? No more College and no more degrees."

"I see your point," she sighed. "But I don't see what this does to weaken the opposition."

"The way we see it, all doctoral programs will leap at the opportunity to increase revenue. And the Grad School could be bailed out of its budget problem if the new money is split between colleges and the GS."

"Neat!" she marveled. "It might just be possible to convince students that they will get their money's worth, especially if they can demand advisement. You know that access and support is really variable across faculty."

They contemplated the scheme for a time. Then Felicity spoke. "This might take care of the bullets in the Report, but I don't see how it plays against the recommendation for closure of the College."

"Me neither," Rich said. "I thought we had a reprieve at the end of the meeting until Lange told me about the President. We have nothing to combat that kind of threat."

Felicity stared out the office window, obviously searching for another political gambit. "Here, give me the Report."

Rich watched her as she leafed through the document, her hands caressing the pages, hair falling forward. This image took possession of his mind and he was unable to focus on the issues at hand.

"I think the answer to our problems is right here in the Report," Felicity said. "Take a look at page ten." A slender finger pointed to the second paragraph and she read, "*'The College suffers from an amalgamation of disparate units. Curriculum and Instruction, Kinesiology, Child Development and Home Economics represent various disciplines that weaken the mission of the College.'.*"

"Sure," Rich agreed, "that's quite true. Many of us disagreed when the University put all these departments under one tent. But I don't see what you're driving at."

"Think about this," she said. "What if the Dean continues with his strategy of agreeing with the Reviewers and offers to close one or more of these departments? Wouldn't that satisfy the President and the science people?"

Rich was transfixed by the cleverness of this stratagem. *Why that would get rid of those cooking classes! And even programs in weight loss studies!* He could scarcely contain his enthusiasm.

"Professor Berland! You may have hit on a solution of our problem. If we sacrifice whole departments, Central Administration will surely be impressed."

Felicity blushed. "Well, I wouldn't go that far, but it's a thought that might be worth discussing with Dean Bahls. Anyway, I have to run. Celebration time you know." She stood and waved as she left the office.

Celebration! Rich shook his head. Celebration could wait. Now was the time for serious political machination. Sighing, he laid a yellow legal pad on his desk and began his usual monologue.

"Closure of departments is probably the right idea," he mumbled. "But we can never get the College faculty in line on this in three weeks." He wrote 'Closure' on the pad, stared at it and crossed it out. Images of the faculty in targeted departments resulted in a row of X's on the pad. "Gotta be a way."

A half-hour of blind political alleys revealed no exit. The three-week deadline was simply too short for any of the customary academic gambits. "Buy some time," he mused. "Accept her advice and agree with the Report." Rich wrote the word 'Agree'. "But spin out the response." The word 'delay' was added.

Looking at these two words, Rich began rifling through strategic options. *The Report!* He turned to page ten, following a mental image of Felicity's finger. "Amalgam of disparate units," he read. "Sure got that right!" He resisted the temptation to initiate plans for closure. "Start closing units and Central will shut the College down."

Rich was back to square one. "Wait a minute!" he commanded himself as he circled 'Accept' and 'Delay'. "Need a simple idea that grabs Central." He knew that a powerful word could easily determine the outcome of complex issues in Central Administration. Now he was on familiar ground.

"The idea has to reflect the important issues raised by the Report and carry the day on our response." More words filled the pad. 'Study' 'Convene Experts' 'Graduate Input' All were rejected as typical academic strategies. Was there no guidance to be found in his political model of the University?

"Retrenchment!" he said in a loud voice. "Of course!" Here was a word that conveyed serious College action in the face of the Report. If it was supported by proposed actions, 'retrenchment' would become the mantra that would sway

Central and preserve the College - so long as it was stated dogmatically. It was a relieved, and confident, Professor Jessen that left his office that evening - on his way to Retrenchment!

Replacing 'closure' with 'retrenchment' was, however, more than a change of terminology. To make this occur, Rich realized, there would need to be concrete actions in response to the External Review. Mike and Rich worried over this bone for several days, searching for conceptual meat to cover the wounds of the Review.

It was Rich who proposed the solution. "What if we changed the name of the College?" he asked. "Wouldn't that hide most of our problems?"

Bahls frowned. "Whaddya mean by that?"

"Just suppose we put a new label on the College. That would give us the freedom to retrench our weakest departments. You know, put them with stronger units. That way, Central wouldn't be able to force closure."

"Hmmm," Bahls pursed his lips. "You may have something there. I'm pretty sick of carrying the water for the Old Buffaloes, to say nothing of the embarrassment of that 'Home Economics' label."

"Let's give it a try," Rich said. "I'm sure we can come up with a name that will do the trick."

They worked at this for several days. Rich searched the Internet. Titles flew to and fro over email. Bahls tested labels with his Washington contacts. Not surprisingly, the result was confusion; there was no obvious candidate.

Rich agonized over this roadblock. Although he remained committed to 'retrenchment', he was unable to translate his new mantra into action. Alone in his office, he muttered, "What we need is a paradigm change!" *Paradigm change!* Rich repeated the thought, "Paradigm change! That's it!" He suddenly realized that their search for a new name for the College was blocked by the mounds of intellectual baggage associated with 'education'. Every university had its college of education, nothing new there. And wasn't the Ed.D. the laughing stock of the sciences!

It took Rich only a half day of yellow-pad scribbling to come up with a name for the 'retrenched' College. He stepped to a white board and wrote in bold capital letters:

COLLEGE OF HUMAN SCIENCE

Stepping back, he could see at once that this new 'college' would acquire instant stature. Science would replace education and home economics and cover weak departments with a cloak of respectability.

Dean Bahls was an enthusiastic convert; one call to D.C. convinced him that the new College of Human Science would open funding opportunities. Why, the National Science Foundation might even be interested!

Rich and Bahls wove the new label into a tapestry that glowed with optimistic responses to the External Review. Even Professors Menes and Utoft reluctantly approved the College's plan. And Central backed off on plans to close the College. All due to the hard work of Associate Dean Jessen and by replacing the recommended 'closure' with the euphemism 'retrenchment'.

This linguistic ploy was so successful that Rich used his computer to print it for his office bulletin board:

RE<u>TRENCH</u>MENT

Underlining was used to focus on the 'trenches' occupied by the faculty whose departments were at risk of closure. Rich's political mantras were not usually so obvious, but he gloried in the notion that certain faculty members would be popping their heads 'above the trench' only to be shot down by the Associate Dean. Surely nothing could spoil his enjoyment!

CHAPTER SIXTEEN

Adult Supervision

"Education: the inculcation of the incomprehensible into the indifferent by the incompetent."
(John Maynard Keynes)

Incessant ringing of Rich's desk phone penetrated a month-long aura of 'Retrenchment'. He had a premonition of trouble.

He picked up the receiver. "Hello, this is Associate Dean Jessen."

"Rich, this is Mike. Can you come over now? I need your help."

"Sure, I guess so. What's on your mind?"

"Tell you when you get here. This one's right up your alley." Bahls chuckled as he hung up.

Right up my alley! I'll bet! In the past month, Rich's relationship with Dean Bahls had undergone changes that weren't all that appealing. The mantle of authority seemed tailored for Bahls and he swung it in ever-widening arcs as he took control of the new College of Human Science. Gradually, Bahls was changing from friend and fellow conspirator to academic administrator; a change that weighed on Rich's mind.

"Well, better get going. Doesn't sound too promising." Rich positioned several papers and books on his desk to give the message of serious intellectual activity. These props did nothing to dispel Rich's apprehension; his steps dragged a bit as he crossed to the Dean's office.

Bahls' greeting reinforced Rich's premonition. "Hello Rich. Am I ever glad that you're around when problems like this come my way." He grinned and gestured to a chair at the Dean's conference table.

Rich slid into the indicated chair and tried to look distinguished as he asked, "Sounds serious. Personnel problem?"

"Well . . . sort of," Bahls steepled his fingers and gazed at Rich. "Ever since Carl Mertens left Ed. Psych. that department has lacked leadership. Currently the department is short a Chair. I hope that you will agree to act as Chair for the balance of the year. Any problems with that?"

Rich was stunned by the offer. *Chair of those nuts!* "I hardly think that I'm the right one for the job."

Bahls smiled, "I disagree. You have the experience and knowledge of the University that Ed. Psych. lacks. So how about it?"

Rich could see that there was no way out of this assignment. "Well, OK . . . I suppose so. Just so long as it's only until the end of this term."

"I can live with that," Bahls nodded. "What I'd like for you to do is to identify the faculty member most qualified to take on the Chair for next fall. You know that's a tough assignment as Mertens had real problems with his colleagues."

"I know, I know," Rich shook his head. "Carl and I often met for coffee and he invariably spent the time talking about the weird behavior of his faculty. Nevertheless I'll try to get an in-depth reading on them and let you know what I think."

"Great! Now, I've scheduled an Ed. Psych. faculty meeting for next Wednesday. Can you free up your calendar to be there?"

This was moving too fast for Rich. However, there was no escaping Bahls' intense gaze. "I . . . guess so."

"Fine! That's settled." Bahls left the conference table and moved to his desk where he began sorting through a pile of telephone messages. Rich, the Acting Chair, was sent on his way.

Back at his office, Rich opened his desk calendar and marked the next Wednesday for a meeting with his new colleagues. He outlined the day with heavy dark lines. "Black Wednesday!" he said and sighed at this interruption in his carefully-planned life.

It seemed like no time at all and he and Bahls were seated in the Ed. Psych. conference room. The room was scarcely larger than Rich's office. Walls were covered by dilapidated bookshelves where collections of psychology journals were stacked randomly. On one shelf a small space was set aside for some kind of vine – which was clearly dead. Another shelf displayed award certificates earned by the faculty; Outstanding Life Coach, Brain-based Learning Institute, Certificate of Appreciation.

What a dump! Rich leaned back in his chair and let his eyes take the measure of his new associates as Bahls introduced each.

"Hello everyone," Bahls began. "As you know, this Department needs to identify new leadership. I've asked Associate Dean Richard Jessen to work with you as Acting Chair to assist you in this important task. To get us started, I'd like each of you to give a short overview of your work as an introduction to Professor Jessen. Let's begin with you, Professor Emmit."

A skinny, mousy woman leaned across the table and stared at Rich through thick soiled glasses. "Dean Jessen, I'm Dr. Jerrilyn Emmit. I teach the introductory psychology course every term. My research has to do with the social psychology of sex workers in University City. I've been able to identify the roots of prostitution in our secondary schools!" Emmit's eyes dilated at this academic tidbit and she wiped her mouth with the back of a bony hand.

MiGod! "Why. . . Professor Emmit . . . that's most interesting. I'll look forward to reading what you have to say." Rich's surprise at this line of scholarly inquiry allowed the lie to escape his usual disinterest in the works of others. He actually blushed at the thought of Emmit leaning over his shoulder to point to pornographic pictures in her most recent article.

Bahls swiveled his chair and motioned to a stocky, red-faced man seated next to Rich. "Professor Klein, why don't you take it from there?"

Rich twisted his head to gaze at his seatmate. He saw a caricature of a nineteenth-century Prussian officer. A clean-shaven bullet head was supported on a thick neck with folds of fat on its back. *The Mark of the Beast!* Rich was transported to a seminar room in a German university where Professor Klein was about to lecture.

A wayward sunbeam wove through ascending dust motes to glint off rimless glasses. "Ach, ja! I am Ulrich Klein. I vas trained in Vienna and am an eggspert in Freudian analysis."

This observation was punctuated by a snort of derision offered by Professor Emmit.

"Dere is no need to make light of the verk of the Mawster," Klein glared. "He vould be greatly amused at the scholarship of sex. Proof of his insight into the subconscious. Yes?"

"I'm sure he'd be interested in the work of Karen Horney!" Emmit grinned at her pun.

There was a long pause, then Klein responded in Vienna style. "Den zertainly you know Professor Horney's views on the zublimation of zechsual drives in middle-age vimmen."

This zinger drew the remaining color from Emmit's face. It was as if her blood drained directly into Klein. Rich watched gleefully at the increased reddening of the roll of fat on Klein's neck. Germanic will was about to score another triumph over the untermensch!

"I'll have you know!" Emmit shouted. "That I'm the Program Chairman of the Midwest Queer Studies Group! We're taking the study of sexuality way beyond outdated Freudian . . ."

Reference to the 'Mawster' threw verbal gasoline on the smoldering embers of Klein's argument. "Zo!" he sputtered. "Dot goes to show da lack of intellectual background to your verk!"

Unfortunately, Rich wasn't able to enjoy the unfolding of this drama. Bahls had seen enough of dysfunctional faculty. "Let's move along. How about you, Professor Singer? Can you give Dean Jessen a snapshot of your work?"

The plump female figure in Rich's peripheral vision sat upright and chirped. "I'd be happy to do so! Why, my work is sooo interesting! I'm applying qualitative analysis to the child-rearing practices of single fathers in . . .," Her voice droned on – and on.

Rich's mind wandered. He recalled an undergraduate chemistry class where lab sessions were directed at the process of qualitative analysis. *I wonder – suppose she is taking samples of the school lunches prepared by single fathers in search of their chemical composition – or maybe it's simpler than that -she's just looking for a husband!* He stared at her, imaging possible sexual behaviors of this rotund woman. He smiled.

Singer took the smile as indication of interest. "I'm glad you are pleased at my work, Dean Jessen. We'll have some very interesting chats when you're Acting Chair.

This invitation brought Rich back to the present setting. "Umm, yes. I suppose that . . .,"

Bahls nudged his foot under the table. Rich struggled to engage the meeting. "Yes! This is most revealing. I . . .," Another nudge and a directed glance focused Rich's gaze to the end of the table where a pleasant faced man sat next to a well-proportioned woman.

"I understand that you . . .," Bahls looked as his notes, "the Professors Robinson, are working together on a study of faculty interaction in secondary schools. Am I correct?"

The two remaining Ed. Psych. faculty swiveled their heads, as if connected; from Bahls to face Rich. The woman spoke. "We are cultural anthropologists. That means we are looking for rituals and practices that shape thought and behavior."

The male Professor Robinson nodded. "We are especially interested in the informal interactions of the sexes and how the culture of the school promotes sexual freedom!"

Mrs. Professor Robinson's face glowed at this academic opportunity.

Jesus God! What am I gonna do with these fruitcakes? Rich gulped back several more appropriate comments and spoke to the faculty, "Well now, you have given me a sense of what you're about and I'll be looking forward to . . . some productive interaction." He was aware of prurient interest on the part of the female Professor Robinson and his voice gave out.

Bahls took the resulting silence as closure. "I want to thank you all for your time. I know that Dean Jessen is eager to help you work toward new leadership for this department." He stood, pulling Rich to his feet. "So, we'll leave it to Rich to arrange for sessions with each of you."

The faculty nodded at Bahls and Rich, but their eyes flicked among one another, looking for the wedges of advantage that the Acting Chair might offer.

Outside the meeting room, Rich mopped his forehead with a handkerchief. "I can't believe. . ."

"Cool it," Bahls hissed. "Let's go back to my office and plot some strategy."

When they were seated in the Dean's Office, Bahls slouched in his chair and scowled. "Wow! That was some meeting! I didn't realize just how far out that department had become."

"I couldn't agree more," Rich said. "Seems to me that I have an impossible task; nobody could lead that collection of wierdos."

"You're probably right, but they all have tenure and we need to find somebody to take on the task of shaping them up. Tell you what," Bahls sat up and spoke with Dean-like authority. "Meet with each of them and see if you can find any promising directions for the department, then give me a short report that I can use to help me make sense of the insensible."

Rich grunted. "Well, OK. But don't expect me to lead those birds. It's a total waste of time."

In the next weeks, Rich revisited his evaluation over and over again. *Why am I doing this?* He even reverted to his childhood subconscious. *God! Why me?*

Nevertheless, he forged ahead; a martyr carrying one cross at a time.

Actually, his first meeting involved two crosses – the Professors Robinson. They were on-time for their appointment.

"Good morning," Rich said. "Thank you for making some time for our visit. Please sit down and, if you will, share a more detailed description of your research with me."

"Glad to," Mrs. Robinson smiled. "But you needn't be so formal. I'm Evelyn and this," she clapped a hand on Mr. Robinson's shoulder, "is Marvin. May we call you Rich?"

Rich swallowed his customary off-putting response, "That would be fine . . . er . . . Evelyn."

"Now that we are on friendly terms," Evelyn said, "I think Marv can put you in the picture."

Familiarity and invasive good nature made Rich uneasy. This was one of the few times when he had the feeling that he wasn't in control.

Marv began, "A couple of years ago, Evy and I became aware that there is a sexual awakening among public school faculty. A high-pressure environment and physical proximity gives each faculty member a positive valence that is often transformed into sexual attraction."

"Yes," Evy added, "and the more that they talked about the sexual behavior of students, the more they thought about their own opportunities." She licked her lips and continued. "We've uncovered a whole sub-culture of adult behavior that defies conventional norms." She crossed her arms and sighed.

The dissertation went on with Marv and Evy sharing insights gained from their research. Rich followed as best he could, putting the offered findings into a pattern that made sense to him. *These kooks have the material for an entire conference!*

Marv noticed Rich's wandering interest and suggested, "Say! We are having several of our research subjects over for cocktails this Saturday. Would you be able to join us?"

A bolt from a clear sky! Rich was unprepared. "What? Well . . . I suppose it's possible. I'd need to check my calendar."

"Oh, please try to come," Evy pleaded. "And why don't you ask your colleague Professor Berland as well? I'm sure she would be interested in what our research has uncovered."

Rich couldn't imagine any topic of less interest to Felicity, but having her along would be a bright spot in what promised to be a very drab, dull evening. "She's very busy, but I'll ask her and let you know."

The Robinsons responded earnestly and emphasized the invitation as they left. "Now be sure to come," Marv said.

"We'll have a great time," Evy added.

When his office door had closed on the Robinsons, Rich slipped into a reverie where he stood outside himself and looked at his condition with pity. *Now I'm really in the soup!* Even reverie could not supply adjectives that described his view of the Robinsons. *Damn Bahls! Why's he doing this to me?* Similar observations rolled across his mind; Acting Chair Jessen, the Victim!

The problem created by the visit remained for the next several hours until Felicity knocked at the closed door.

Startled, Rich awoke. "What? . . . oh, come in please."

"Excuse me Rich. I didn't know what to make of your closed door. So I . . ."

"No problem," he interrupted. "I'm glad to see you. I just had an invitation to a dinner on Saturday and you're included."

"Really!" Felicity arranged her self on the chair opposite Rich's desk. "What sort of event might that be?"

"You know the Robinsons, in Ed. Psych.?"

"Yes, I guess so."

"Since I took on the Acting Chair position, I've been trying to meet the faculty and understand what they're about. These two invited me to a cocktail party and they included you."

Felicity frowned. "I wonder what made them do that. I've had virtually no contact with them, except on a couple of committees."

"That's interesting. They made a point of asking for you. What do you say to that?"

"Normally, I wouldn't go for that kind of invite, but so long as you're going I guess I can tag along."

Rich had a new, pleasant vision of himself and Felicity as the featured couple at the Robinsons. "I really appreciate that," he smiled. "They live across town and I can pick you up at your place, say around six on Saturday. OK?"

Felicity stood and stopped in the doorway. "Guess so. Just so long as I can get back at a reasonable time. There's plenty to do before Monday."

Anticipation gradually gained the upper hand over pity and the hours passed quickly. Saturday came and Rich parked his Mercedes in Felicity's drive. She came down her walk and slid into the car.

Rich filled his eyes with her vitality. He considered several comments. *You're looking great! Too adolescent! That's a fine dress! No – she wouldn't like that!* Eventually he said, "I hope that you'll enjoy the evening. Should be interesting."

"Why do you say that?"

Why did I say that? "Umm . . . well . . ." he gave undivided attention to getting underway while he searched for an answer.

Felicity stared, waiting for a response. "Rich, what makes you think I'd be interested in the Robinsons?"

"Oh, I was thinking about . . . their research!"

"Yes, I heard about that. Something about the sexual behaviors of high school teachers. Sounds pretty weird to me."

"That's kind of what I meant, they said that some of their subjects would be at this dinner too."

"Just a minute!' Felicity exclaimed. "That's spooky! I can't imagine spending an evening with a bunch of creepy research subjects!"

"Well, I have to go through with this. Maybe we can cut out early and . . ."

"Since we're committed," she said helpfully, "we'll have to make the best of it."

Rich sighed, "At least it'll give you the opportunity to see another side of academic administration; the social side that can't be avoided."

They continued to search their expectations for some way that each might benefit from what was likely to be a supremely dull evening. Neither could identify any possible benefits.

Felicity was silent for several blocks. Then she volunteered, "I've done an Internet search on the Robinson's. Not very impressive. Actually, kind of weird."

"That's the way they came across to me. Well, an hour or two at their place can't be too obnoxious."

Rich pulled into the Robinsons' drive and handed Felicity out of the Merc.

Marv Robinson answered the doorbell. "Good evening," he beamed. "Hello Rich and Professor Berland! We're so glad you could join us. Please come in."

Marv offered his arm to Felicity and led her into the Robinsons' living room. Rich trudged along. Evy Robinson came to his aid, "Oh Rich! Come along and meet our other guests!" She tucked her hand under his arm and pulled him toward a collection of chairs where two couples sat, drinks in hand.

While Marv fussed over Felicity, Evy used her hold on Rich to present him to the guests. "Here's Tommy and Alice Parsons from Harrison High. Tommy's in social studies and Alice is a counselor."

Tommy stood, a hulking brute with a scraggly goatee. "Glad to meetcha."

"Hello there," Alice gushed. "It's so nice to meet another real professor."

Evy turned Rich to the next couple. "Rich, this is Manny Fernandez and his friend Beth Schiller. He's the Assistant Principal at Foreman High and she's the Head of the Art Department.

Rich's eyes drifted from these two. Marv Robinson was leading Felicity toward the Parsons, holding her arm in a possessive grip.

"How do you do?" Manny's voice jerked Rich's attention back to the introduction.

"Just fine . . .," Rich mumbled, staring at a caricature of an Assistant Principal; chubby, thick glasses, rumpled suit – with a vest!

He shifted his gaze to Schiller and held out a hand. "Rich Jessen, Ms. Schiller."

A limp hand touched his as if waiting for a formal bow and – *MiGod!* – a kiss!

Rich dropped the clammy hand and forced a grin. "How do you do, Ms. Schiller?"

The hand slipped under his bicep and steered Rich toward a table of drinks and appetizers.

"What do you say to a glass of wine?" Ms. Schiller asked.

" I'll take . . . a red, thanks." Rich retrieved his arm and walked around the table, distancing himself from the clinging woman. As he moved toward the others, she pursued him, asking endless academic questions.

"What is your line of work at the U?" Ms. Schiller deftly switched her drink in order to free a hand to recapture her victim.

None of Rich's answers could stem the interrogation. In desperation, he herded her to a chair and used his captive arm to seat her.

Surveying the gathering, Rich could see that Felicity was trying to disengage from Marv Robinson's grip. He nodded to Ms. Schiller and moved to Felicity's side.

"You have been very kind to invite us," Rich lied as he took Felicity's free arm. By staring at Marv, Rich was able to win the tug of war and pull Felicity to his side.

"Think nothing of it,' Marv said. "We're delighted to have you folks here so that you can see what we're about in Ed. Psych."

"Yes," Evy cackled. "We, that is, the Ed. Psych. faculty, are forging ahead with some basic work on human sexuality."

The eyes of the seated high school contingent glowed at this pronouncement.

"That's right," Schiller said. "I just can't believe how much we've learned by working with you and Marv!"

"Same goes for me," Parsons growled. "I have a totally new perspective on my colleagues!" His eyes wandered over Ms. Schiller's slightly covered form.

The level of excitement grew along with discussion of intricate details of the Robinson's research. Professorial comments were tailored by psychspeak while the research subjects conversed in more earthy tones.

Rich and Felicity were largely observers. They gradually pulled back from the others, appalled at the graphic descriptions of high school faculty life.

"Another glass of wine?" Rich asked.

"Please," Felicity said as they put the drinks table between themselves and the discussion group.

Their movement caught the attention of Marv Robinson. "Don't you find our research design interesting Professor Berland?"

"Just what is that, Professor Robinson?" Felicity asked.

"It's really exciting!" Marv exclaimed. "We are engaged in an anthropological study of the sexual mores of teachers in local high schools."

"Is that so?" Felicity said, her hand wrenching at Rich's arm. "How are you approaching the study?"

"Well, my wife and I studied under Margaret Mead. We have a sound basis for our work. You may have heard of Dr. Mead's work in Samoa."

"Yes I have. But I wonder how you are making use of her work."

Marv gestured with his drink and began the lecture. "You probably recall that Mead lived among the Samoan people and was ultimately accepted as a member of their community. We found that we could use a similar approach by cultivating authentic friendships with our subjects. In fact, these four people," he waved the drink to include the other guests, "were the first we encountered. They have been invaluable informants as well as conduits that led us to our findings."

"And, what have you concluded from your study?" Felicity asked.

Evelyn Robinson answered, "We discovered a vibrant sexual sub-culture that supports Mead's notion of sexuality as an essential component of human interaction and personal pleasure. Through our interviews and observations, we have been able to weave the several strands of behavior into a single . . ."

"Woof!" barked Marv in a doglike baritone, ". . . that is, we now can create a complex canvas that uncovers the sex lives of teachers!"

"Oh! 'Uncovering' says it all!" blurted Alice Parsons. "Why . . . I . . . we . . . had no idea that there was so much going on . . ."

"And the level of wholesome enjoyment!" enthused her husband. "The Robinsons have changed all our lives!"

305

"It's awesome!" Alice bubbled. "Tommy and I attended a Sensate Workshop last weekend. You know, the one based on the work of Masters and Johnson. It was fantastic!"

"Betcha!" Tommy actually rubbed his hands.

Several minutes of joyous celebration followed during which the four secondary educators pulled their chairs together. Their conversation turned on salacious observations: "... her dress!" "... I'll bet he's ..." "... wonder if they ..."

Rich listened, fascinated at the emerging clinical level of the exchanges. It was as if he were a spectator at a junior high school sleep-over.

At his side, Felicity was engaged in a scholarly exchange with the Robinsons.

Rich heard her ask Evelyn, "What does all of this have to do with Margaret Mead?"

"It just goes to show that the human sexual force," Evelyn writhed, "shapes all of our lives."

"Sound more Freudian to me." Felicity said.

"Oh no! Sex isn't in the brain, it's right out in the open. Just like Mead found in Samoa!"

Felicity shot back, "As a Mead scholar, you are aware of Derek Freeman's criticism of Mead. He concludes that Samoan sex wasn't all 'play in the sunshine'; Mead was taken in by her subjects. What have you to say to that?"

Marv Robinson gulped a half-raised glass – along with a quantity of air. The resulting coughing projected a fine red spray toward Rich.

Ms. Robinson was at her husband's side instantly. "Oh Marv! Are you all right?" She patted him on the back with one hand and mopped wine with a handkerchief in the other.

The occupied Robinsons did not see Felicity turn Rich away. Nor did they hear her whisper, "We've got to get out of here! Now!"

"Huh?" Rich mumbled.

Felicity set her drink on a nearby table and stood directly in front of Rich. "I mean it! Get my coat and make whatever excuse you can think of! I'll meet you at the front door!" Her facial expression supplied the exclamation points as she turned away.

What's that about? Rich had never experienced this aspect of Felicity's personality; he was instantly under her control.

"Marv . . . ," Rich hesitated. "Professor Berland isn't . . . feeling well. I need to take her home." As he listened to himself, he gained confidence in the line of argument. "I'm sorry to have to cut this short, but you know how it is. We are both very grateful for your hospitality." He began to move toward the front door.

Evelyn Robinson raced to intercept him. "Oh! Please don't go! Felicity can use our spare bedroom. I'm sure she'll be all right soon." Eager hands tugged at Rich's coat.

Rich nearly gave in, but he could see Felicity standing at the door waiting – with no familiar welcoming smile. He pulled Evelyn along with him to the hall closet where he recovered Felicity's jacket.

Pleadings from the Robinsons, supported by the other educators, followed Rich and Felicity through the door and down the front walk. Rich held the passenger side door of the Mercedes for Felicity. It was jerked from his hand – a footman out of livery.

Rich slunk around the car and eased into the driver's seat. A perfunctory wave and a change of direction left the Robinsons standing at their door. Two blocks and a right turn put them on the road to the University.

"Stop here!" Felicity commanded. "Pull over! We need to talk!"

The Mercedes responded instantly; offside wheels bumping the curb.

Felicity snapped on the overhead light and glared at Rich. "What the hell's the idea of dragging me into this mess? Do you have any idea of what's going on back there? Well?"

Rich was stunned. "What's . . . the matter? What did I do?"

She stared at him for several seconds. "I can't believe that you could be so stupid! Can't you see that these . . .," she searched for a label, ". . . people . . . are into partner swapping?"

"You mean. . ."

"Damn right 'I mean'. Those high schoolers can't wait to get off with a new partner. And the Robinsons had us pegged for their next exchange! I've never been so insulted!"

"Are you sure? I didn't see anything wrong."

"You're probable right about not seeing anything. You may know University politics, but you haven't the foggiest about human behavior. You are badly in need of adult supervision! Now take me home." Felicity snapped off the light and retreated to the corner of her seat next to the door.

Rich realized that there was nothing he could say to cool her anger. He moved the Mercedes away from the curb and drove the two miles to Felicity's house in silence. He parked at her door and reached a hand toward the car key. However, Felicity had already opened her door and was swinging her legs out of the car.

"Think about what I said! We'll talk this over another time!" The door slammed and she stalked up her walk.

Rich sat like a teenage lover, lost in review of a confusing quarrel. *What the Hell was that all about?* He could find nothing in his behavior that warranted Felicity's anger. If there was any problem, it had to be the Robinsons and their 'subjects'. With a deep sigh, he turned away from the curb toward his empty house. How different it would be if she were . . .

Possibilities were reviewed throughout Rich's night. Every image of a compliant, sensual Felicity was terminated by a replay of her rejection. There was no rest and Rich left early for his office.

There was to be no refuge from the events of the previous night. Dean Bahls was also early to work; leaving his car as Rich pulled into his reserved parking place. Bahls gleamed with energy and enthusiasm, along with a quantum of obscene good cheer.

"Morning Rich. How'd it go with the Robinsons?"

Rich scowled. "Not so hot. Too many sexual innuendoes that I didn't catch."

They walked toward the elevator. "What do you mean?" Bahls asked.

"Well, the whole evening focused on the Robinson's research. You know, kind of a high school confidential. It got so bad that we left early."

"We? Who went with you?"

"Oh, I didn't tell you. The Robinsons invited Felicity Berland and she pulled the plug on the evening."

"Sounds exciting!" Bahls laughed as the entered the elevator. When the door closed he said, "I'll bet she had plenty to say about that!"

"No kidding! I'm really in the doghouse now. Can't figure out what to do. You have any ideas?"

They exited the elevator and Bahls drew Rich into an alcove, out of student traffic. "I think it's time you gave Carl Mertens a call. When he was chair of Ed. Psych. he told me a very similar story. Why don't you put your heads together and see what you can come up with?"

"Sounds like a plan," Rich said. "I'm beginning to see why Mertens left for the Business School."

Rich almost ran to his office, closed the door and reached for his phone. After several rings, Mertens answered.

"Carl Mertens here.'

"Carl. This is Rich Jessen. As you know, I'm Acting Chair of Ed. Psych. this term. Dean Bahls suggested I give you a call. I'd sure appreciate you insights into the workings of Ed. Paych.."

"Been expecting your call!" Mertens guffawed. "You having a fun time with my old colleagues?"

"That's just it," Rich pleaded. "I can't make any sense out of their work, nor can I see where the department's headed."

"Welcome to the club. I tried to manage those idiots for two years and ended up chasing my own tail. Sure, I'd be glad to visit. How's about the Faculty Club at noon today?"

Rich clutched at this straw. "You bet! Meet you in the Lounge?"

"Yep. See you then."

Rich hung up the receiver and sat, staring at the closed office door. Would Felicity ever come through it again? Was last night the end of his dream? *Adult supervision!* Felicity's parting shot repeated itself throughout the morning and it was a drained Dean Jessen that meandered toward the Faculty Club.

Mertens was waiting in the Lounge; his handshake and smile penetrated Rich's gloom. "Carl. Thanks so much for making time for me. I really need help."

"I can see that. Come, let's postpone lunch. We can talk in private here."

The found comfortable chairs in a corner of the Lounge, away from the few other faculty loungers.

"Now, tell me what's upsetting you," Mertens said.

Rich summarized his meetings with the Ed. Psych. faculty and the events of the Robinson's cocktail hour.

Mertens laughed. "Sounds like you got off easy. When Bev and I visited those perverts, we were treated to a porn video. And, they weren't so subtle with us. Old Marv actually took me aside and proposed a weekend swap. I nearly tore his head off!"

"You . . . he . . . actually propositioned you? I . . . can't believe that I," Rich groped for words, ". . . missed all the signals. It was Ms Berland that saw where things were going. She was angry with me for setting up a sexual deal." He shook his head. *Adult supervision needed!*

"Don't blame yourself," Mertens counseled. "The Robinsons have become serious experts in partner swapping. Hell, it's all over the university! That's the main reason I cut loose from the department. And that isn't all. That screwball Emmit is another problem. She had an apartment in the Faculty Commons, you know, the place where new faculty live 'til they find housing. Well, she was making a mess of the place so Central turned her out. When she left, she burned her garbage in the bathtub!"

"I just can't believe it!" Rich mourned. "Why, these . . . these . . . kooks must be the subject of all kinds of jokes!"

Mertens frowned. "It's much worse than that! Since I've been at the Business School, I've heard a lot of talk about the weak intellectual standards of the College – and criticism of Mike's leadership. If this thing isn't cleared up soon, Central will have to make some kind of response."

Response! Mike in trouble! All of Rich's careful political manipulation was at risk! "But what can I do? These people all have tenure and you know how difficult it is to get rid of a faculty member on moral grounds!"

Mertens took a pipe from his jacket pocket, filled it and lighted it slowly. "Yes, that's so. But what if the Department is disbanded? As you know, tenure in the University is located in the Department. Closing Ed. Psych. puts these problem people on the market. If they can find a place within the U, they might be able to preserve their tenure."

"I guess I knew that," Rich mused, "but what grounds can we find to put them out of business?"

"It's all in the numbers," Mertens sucked on his pipe. "Ed. Psych. has few students and fewer advisees. Put that in the context of the U's financial problems and you have a kind of 'financial exigency'."

"Hmmm . . . you may have something there. Mike could sure use some help." Rich reflected on the strategy he and Bahls had devised to divert the focus of the Graduate School with student tuition dollars. *Maybe I could do it again!*

Mertens took a fat folder from his briefcase. "Here. Take this. It's a record of enrollment and advisement in Ed. Psych. for the past three years along with faculty vitae. Interesting reading," He stood. "Now let's grab lunch and you can get to work."

Rich remained seated, the folder in his hands. "Carl. I don't know how to thank you." He rose and gripped Mertens' hand. "I think I'll skip lunch and get right to work on this. Thanks again!"

He nearly ran back across the Quad to Blewett Hall. The promise of a solution to his problem propelled him up the back stairs, two steps at a time. Dean Bahls' side door was closed and Rich took a few moments to recover his breath before he knocked.

"Come on in!" Bahls called.

Rich stood inside the office, panting and clutching Mertens' folder.

"Hey! You look like you've been running a marathon! What's on your mind?" Bahls asked.

"Just this," Rich dropped the folder on the Dean's desk. "I just met with Carl Mertens to talk about Ed. Psych. He says that the whole University is aware of what's going on with that faculty and they're talking about loose standards in our College!"

Bahls grimaced. "Now what could have brought that about? I wonder . . ."

"It's the crazy behavior of those people." Rich interrupted. "You remember that I told you about my experience at the Robinsons. Well, Professor Berland and I were clearly being set up for a partner swap."

"I can't believe that!" Bahls scoffed. "Sounds crazy to me!"

"I thought so too," Rich agreed, "but Mertens said the same thing happened to him and his wife. Evidently the Robinsons are famous for promiscuity."

"That's very bad news!" Bahls exclaimed. "If that gets to the President, we're in deep trouble. You know how moralistic he can be."

"Yes. We just got off Central's radar screen with our response to the External Review. Another big issue like this and we could be back on the chopping block!"

They were silent, considering the magnitude of the issue and the actions that might be taken to minimize the damage.

Bahls was the first to speak. "You know, I can't see any way out of this. We're stuck with those perverts and President Rose is sure to hear about them!"

"That's why I ran back here!" Rich said. "Mertens and I think there may be a way to get rid of the whole Ed. Psych. Department."

Bahls brightened at the prospect. " Let's hear about that!"

Rich outlined Mertens' plan to use the low performance of the department to declare 'financial exigency'.

"That way," Rich concluded, "we can shut down the whole works and rid ourselves of those problem faculty."

"I hear what you're saying," Bahls said. "However, as I understand it, exigency is a sort of university-wide issue. We can't single out a particular department under that approach."

"Well . . . you may be right," Rich's smile evaporated. "But you will agree that the objective performance of Ed. Psych. is way below expectations. Right?"

"Sure. They're absolutely rock bottom on all measures of enrollment and budget. I'd have no problem arguing closure, if there were a rationale for it."

Rich scooped up the Ed. Psych. folder and stood at the office door. "Let me work on this. I'll get back to you soonest!"

He left and walked across to his office. He mentally reviewed University policy. No ready solutions came to mind. All he could visualize was Felicity tormented by the advances of Marv Robinson.

Adult supervision!

CHAPTER SEVENTEEN

Queer Theory

"Queer theory today is one of the most important developments in social theory... precisely because it has so devastatingly completed the process of queering the most naïve assumptions of our most cherished traditions."

(S. Seidman: Queer Theory Sociology)

In the following weeks, Rich felt an increasing need for some yet-undefined stratagem to resolve the Ed.Psych. dilemma. Every option he considered led to a dead end, terminated in University regulations or in the canon of accepted practice. He knew that any attempt to close the department would founder on the rock of academic freedom. Clearly, retrenchment would not overcome these obstacles. The hours wasted as Acting Chair were a burden that increased daily.

Adult supervision! As it had many times since their visit to the Robinsons, Felicity's parting shot crossed his mental bow. Was there any way that he could re-establish their relationship? Each option he considered involved an apology; a novel action that was not a part of his behavioral repertoire. On the other hand, waiting for Felicity's call produced no results. Pride had to give way to contrition if he were to regain his adult status in her eyes.

He reached for his phone and entered the familiar number. Three rings and . . .

"Professor Berland."

"Felicity. This is Rich. I hope you will accept my apology for what happened at the Robinsons."

"Don't you think this is a little late? After all, our night out was a week ago."

"I know. I know. I guess I was so mortified. I just couldn't find the right words."

"OK. I'm willing to accept your apology."

There was a pause and Rich could picture the cradled phone between one of those beautiful shoulders and that lovely ear.

"Look, let's get together for a ..."

"I'm way to busy right now," Felicity barked. "Maybe sometime next week."

The phone hummed on an empty line.

Rich placed his phone on its cradle. *Now what?* He groaned in self-pity. He stared at an unopened folder on his desk. *Mertens' data?* He opened the folder and leafed through pages. These data were followed by several pages of notes where Mertens summarized his view of the Ed. Psych. problem prior to his leaving for the Business School. Rich read the final page aloud.

"Major Points: 1) history of under-performing; registrations, majors, graduates 2) reputation for bizarre sexual activities 3) publications of questionable scholarly relevance."

"OK. These are obvious. Now what does Mertens plan to do?" Rich read on.

"Action seems impossible: 1) no University policies apply to these issues 2) Department faculty regularly hide behind academic freedom."

So that's why Carl bailed out! The Business School must have looked like Paradise!

Rich assembled the papers and enclosed them in Mertens' folder. He sat back in his chair and reviewed his options.

He considered how Dean Bahls had responded to the external review of the College. In that case, the Dean had folded marginal departments into the newly labeled 'College of Human Science'. That move had silenced the reviewers and opened the door for retrenchment.

"Felicity sure got that one right!" he mumbled.

Had an observer looked in through Rich's office door, he/she would have seen a series of emotions displayed on the professor's face. Puzzlement – a frown; Despair – a blank countenance; Inspiration – a growing smile.

"That's it!" he exclaimed. "Felicity!" Here was an approach that might solve the administrative problem and reconnect Rich to his love interest. He recalled how Felicity had taken the measure of the external review and instantly conceived the strategy that saved the College. Rich realized that this problem was different. There was no alternative College home for Ed. Psych. In order for Felicity to help now, she'd need to find a way to free the U from these undesirables.

Rich swiveled his chair to and fro, gazing out on the usual noonday bustle of campus life. What he needed was an opening gambit that would excite Felicity's interest. More movement to and fro – to …. Suddenly he stopped, gripping the edge of his desk with both hands. *Mertens!* While Felicity wouldn't take direction from him, she'd surely listen to Mertens. Why, nearly everyone on the College faculty was envious of Mertens' move to the Business School and his success at applying the magic of psychology to corporate problems.

"Let's try . . ." he reached for his phone and punched in Mertens Business School number. "Hope he's in."

"Carl Mertens here."

"Carl, this is Rich Jessen. How's the new position?"

"Just great! It's amazing how little business folks know of their own psychology! My first two seminars were, believe it or not, standing room only! Anyway, what's up?"

Rich hesitated. "I guess that's what I need, a seminar on what to do with your old colleagues. I've looked over your notes and tend to agree that there aren't many options. So this is a kind of a call for help."

"I can imagine what you're up against. At least during my time there wasn't any pressure from the Dean's office. OK. Let's meet at Tubby's this afternoon. I've got a blank spot in my calendar. Five o'clock work for you?"

"Sure. And thanks." Rich hung up, and mentally crossed his fingers.

At four forty-five Rich was seated in a corner booth at Tubby's with Mertens' folder on the table next to two glasses of the house Merlot.

Mertens breezed in five minutes later. "Hi! I see that you're set up for the seminar. So let's get going." He sat down and sipped at the wine. He grimaced, "Gotta tell you that Business School wine is a hell of a lot better than this!"

A ripple of envy flicked over Rich's forehead. Mertens had moved up! And left him behind! Rich grunted and opened the folder. He took out Mertens' notes and handed them across the table. "Here. Take a look at your summary. I agree completely with your conclusions. Now, I'd like to know what you might have done if you were still in charge."

Mertens flipped through the notes. "Sure, I remember jotting these down last year. At that time, I concluded that there was nothing I could do. So far as I see it, the key is that your problem can't be solved at the College level. It has to be moved up the food chain to Central. That's the only place where there's the muscle needed."

"I guess I agree," Rich said. "But I'm at a loss as to how to proceed."

"Think about it this way," Mertens suggested. "We agree that there's no way you can focus on the behavior of these wierdos. That will only result in a debate about academic freedom, and you'll lose. What you need is first, to get the attention of the faculty power brokers in the other departments. Get them to back you on the issue of the quality of research and writing in Ed. Psych.. Second, shift the focus of your decision to the lack of Ed. Psych. faculty productivity. That's where my data will back you up." He jabbed a finger at the file.

They discussed these directions for the better part of an hour. Throughout, Mertens was able to provide Rich with insights into the psychology of the players.

"Think about the faculty in other departments. They all have traditional views of scholarship and are against any new ideas. Right!"

"Yess . . . but . . .,"

Mertens continued. "Now my old colleagues have found a new pathway to publication. Take a look on the Internet for 'Queer Theory' and see what you come up with."

Rich nearly tipped his wine glass. "Queer Theory," he sputtered. "What the hell's that?"

Mertens laughed. "It's a fancy label that covers all kinds of human sexuality and lends status to an emerging – and suspect – subject matter. If you can put this development in front of College faculty, I'll bet that they'll gather under the banner of academic integrity'"

Academic Integrity! Here was one of his familiar mantras! If there was such a thing as 'Queer Theory', College faculty would crucify the creeps!

Rich reached for Mertens' summary and penciled a heading 'Faculty Support – Queer Theory'. "That's the kind of advice I hoped for. I can think of several College faculty members who'll explode at this sort of thing!"

"Now," Mertens went on. "You'll need to move carefully with Waldo. He'll resonate to departmental productivity issues, but he won't want to get involved in the nitty-gritty of moving faculty or closing Ed. Psych.. If you're going to succeed, you'll need a compelling solution."

"Sounds like a plan," Rich agreed. "But isn't that just the approach you considered when you were Chair?"

"Sure, but now that Waldo is beginning to turn the screws on every low-productivity department, Central is involved. Remember how he jacked you around on Higher Ed.?"

Rich nodded. That had been a close call! And he had succeeded when he came up with a solution that focused on money. "Guess you're right. Suppose I can make that case, any chance those nuts will come up with an argument that might sway Waldo?"

Mertens chuckled. "Can't imagine what it could be. They haven't had a creative idea in the last ten years." He tossed off the remainder of his wine and stood. "Well, I gotta move along. Let me know how this comes out and how I might help."

When Mertens had left Tubby's, Rich sat for a long time, considering how he could do triple-duty with Mertens' suggestion. Get Felicity involved, get Mike's backing, and come up with another significant victory.

Eventually he stood, stretched, paid his tab and left Tubby's. He strolled back to the U and crossed the Quad to Blewett. After all, there was no hurry to rush home or to a meeting with Felicity.

Rich pushed his personal problem ahead of him into his office. All was quiet in the Dean's Office complex. He was alone with thoughts of Felicity – and Ed. Psych..

Tossing Mertens' folder on his desk, Rich sat and reflexively turned his computer on. The lighted screen drew his attention. He thought for a moment, then Googled "queer theory". It took only a moment of surfing to find that this topic had penetrated the American Educational Research Association. He printed the description of the Special Interest Group:

AERA Queer Studies SIG Home

The Queer Studies Special Interest Group (SIG) of the American Educational Research Association was formed for the specific purpose of encouraging empirical, interpretive, and critical educational research in education that considers an interdisciplinary discourse including queer theory, queer students and educators, curriculum and sexuality, issues of intersectionality, and other vital issues.

Rich read and reread this description. He knew that the SIG's in AERA were a locus for new directions in educational research – some of questionable relevance to the field. *I wonder...* He clicked the 'back' arrow on his browser and found a large number of references to queer theory. Read for a time, then closed the browser and opened his mind to the Felicity problem.

Call her? This option had little appeal given her anger about their visit to the Robinson party. *Email?* Here was a way to approach Felicity without risking a rebuff. *What should I say?* Rich knew that any further apologies would only rekindle her anger. He needed to focus her on ... *His problem! No, on Dean Bahls' problem!*

If Rich could convince Bahls that Ed. Psych. was more than a simple administrative issue, he might be able to bring Felicity on board. *Mertens?* If

Mertens could bring psychology to bear on management actions in industry, surely the same principles would apply in the academy.

Rich was actually a practicing psychologist when it came to analyzing his colleagues; although not formally trained, he was several levels above 'beginner'. He stood and began the pacing that facilitated a study of Bahls. Rich's customary approach to analysis required a one-word characterization of the subject. For Bahls this was simple. *Ambitious!* Mike's journey at Midwest was driven by ambition; head of the Policy Studies Academy, Dean of the College. Could the Ed. Psych. problem propel Bahls to a higher level in the U? How could this be arranged? The analyst cleared his desk and placed a yellow legal pad in the center of the protective blotter. Rich began to draw and mutter."

"Here's the issue." He drew a circle and labeled it 'Ed. Psych'. "Now, the key actors are . . .," Circles for 'Mike', 'Pearson', and 'Felicity' were connected to the central circle by solid lines. "The psychology here is . . .," Rich wrinkled his brow, looking for the key. "Gotta put myself in the picture ." The drawing was revised. 'Pearson' was elevated to a distant actor and 'Rich' was positioned between 'Mike', 'Felicity' and the 'Ed. Psych.' circle. "That's more like it!" He sat back and studied his drawing.

"Waldo has to be the key." The diagram made it clear that 'Pearson' had to be connected to 'Ed Psych' with 'Rich' as a key actor. 'Felicity' was his problem and couldn't be allowed to interfere with his plans for 'Mike'. Then, all at once, he saw the problem from a totally different perspective. "Wait a minute! This isn't a problem. It's an opportunity!" His focus shouldn't be on Ed. Psych. and the wierdos. Bahls and Pearson were the actors that demanded his attention. He took a clean sheet of yellow paper and redrew the figure.

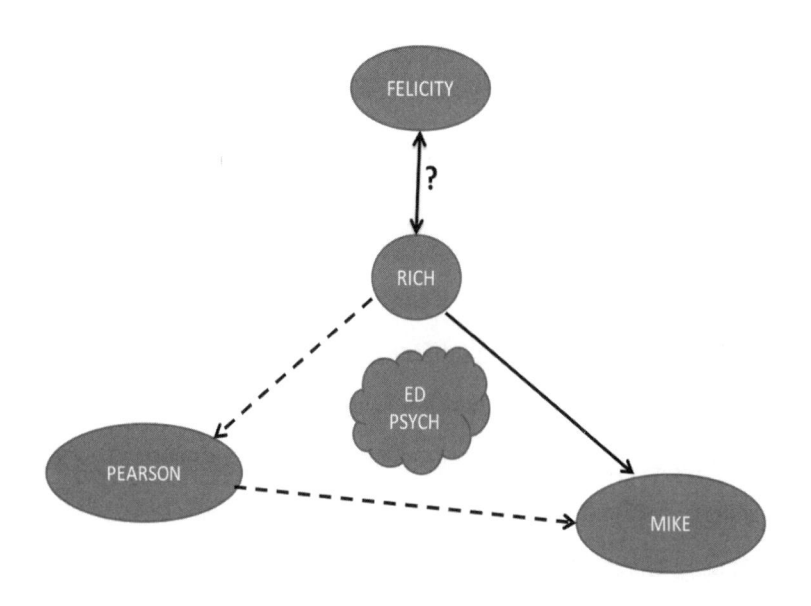

Arrows replaced lines to reflect influence and 'Rich' was at the center of the web of relationships. 'Mike' was clearly the objective of actions taken by 'Rich' and 'Pearson' – while 'Ed. Psych' was merely the cause of opportunity. Although 'Ed. Psych' remained at the center of the drawing, it was no longer connected. Instead, Rich placed it in a 'cloud' to reflect its move from 'problem' to 'opportunity', where 'opportunity' was found in how Rich and Pearson could influence Mike in creative directions.

Rich smoothed the drawing. *How can I make this thing work for Mike?* The answer was, of course, to be found in Bahls' drive for advancement. If Rich could make Ed. Psych. a problem for Central, and solve it, everyone (except the Ed. Psych. faculty) would come out a winner.

The drawing told Rich that he had to manage the interactions represented by the dotted arrows. He failed to see the arrogance of his position. This was understandable, given his history of political successes at Midwest; Semester Conversion, self-plagiarization, Legacy Fund, Dean Bahls, Annual Review. Like any master politician, Rich could identify opportunities for exercise of power and influence. This time, however, there was one important qualifier – Felicity. She had to be brought in as a 'player'; one who would buy into his agenda and benefit personally. So far, she was at the periphery of these interactions. The question mark next to the arrow connecting 'Felicity' to 'Rich' made that clear.

What's the hook for Felicity? Rich considered her character in this setting. Physical attributes aside, she had considerable intellectual skill. Her contribution had to focus on the academic issues involved. *The vitae!* He quickly searched through Mertens' Ed. Psych. file for faculty publication records.

"Just what I thought!" he crowed. "Plenty of off-beat journals; International Journal of Transgenderism, GaySource, Critical inQueeries, The Electronic Journal of Human Sexuality! For God sake!" Here was the hook. He assembled the faculty vitae and sped to the office copy machine. Aggressively, he pulled staples, fed sheets and collated output. The resulting packet was thrust into an inter-campus mail envelope. "Now all I need is a covering memo."

Back at his desk, Rich turned to his computer and composed his call for help.

To: Felicity.Berland@midU.mail.edu

From: Rich.Jessen@midU.mail.edu

Subject: Ed. Psych. Review

I hope you have forgiven my ignorance of our abortive session with the Ed. Psych. faculty. I'm asking you to make allowances for my confusion concerning this department. Frankly, I was so taken aback by their behavior that I failed to catch the signals you noticed.

This email is asking that we return to our previous working relationship and that we come together to address the problem that the Ed. Psych. department raises for the University. I have scheduled a meeting with Dean Bahls for next week and

I'd like to have your perspective on the academic quality of the work of Ed. Psych. faculty members. Hoping you will help me in this important task, I am sending copies of faculty vitae in campus mail.

Thanks for your understanding. Rich

He read the email several times. Satisfied, he clicked "Send". Then he placed the envelope containing the vitae in Campus Mail, turned off the office lights, and was about to leave when his mental review held him in check. *Wait! Why not send her the whole packet!* This would show Felicity that he was asking for a team-mate and not just for help. He flicked on the lights and returned to his desk. Assembling the contents of Mertens' folder, he fed the copy machine and collated the contents.

Ripping open the campus mail envelope, he added the new material, sealed, and mailed. With renewed confidence he once again turned out the lights and exited the Dean's Office.

Confidence jousted with confusion over the next week. 'When will she respond?' alternated with 'Why doesn't she call?' Hours were spent at his desk – moving papers – carrying out Deanly chores. Toward the end of the week, Dean Bahls breezed into Rich's office, coffee cup in hand.

"How's it goin' Rich," Bahls asked as he slouched into a chair. "Seems like you're pretty stressed. Deanin' too much for you?"

Rich hesitated. "It's like this," he began. "Remember, I told you that I asked Professor Berland to go with me to a cocktail party at the Robinsons a week ago."

"Yes, you told me that she bailed you out." Bahls said.

"Hardly! I didn't tell you, but Marv Robinson put a serious move on her!"

Bahls was suddenly alert. "You mean . . ."

"That's right! She was plenty angry. In fact, she hasn't spoken to me since."

325

"Rich, I'm truly sorry I got you into this. Have you any way out?"

"Let me tell you! I've studied this department and I can't believe what I found! Why, every member of that faculty is into off-beat studies of sexuality. There's not s single publication dealing directly with education! If other College faculty knew what was going on, there would be hell to pay!"

"Fill me in," the Dean spoke. "I need to know more!"

Rich nodded, summarized Carl Mertens' analysis and added an overview of the emerging 'scholarship of sex' that he had discovered.

"Wow!" Bahls frowned. "From what you say, we have a serious problem! Have you any ideas as to how we might proceed?"

"The way I see it, I have to be careful not to appear to punish the department for the Robinson's cocktail hour. We need to find a way to base our actions on standards that apply across the College. Otherwise, we'll have grievances and possible lawsuits on our hands."

"Couldn't agree more," Bahls paused, then stood to leave. "Well, let's keep in touch on this. I know you'll find a way." He left.

But the problem remained.

Several days passed with no solution in sight. Drawings, yellow sheets of options cascaded into Rich's wastebasket. He often sat at his desk late into the night, becoming more desperate day by day. He was alone with the problem, until – his phone rang long after the Dean's Office had closed. Usually, he did not answer these pleas for Deanly advice. When he answered the late calls, he was't 'Professor Jessen', he was just …,

"Rich"

"This is Felicity. Glad I caught you. I'd like to talk. May I drop by?"

Felicity! "Well. Sure! I'll unlock the outer door."

"See you!"

Ten minutes later Felicity glided into his office. "Rich, I'm glad you sent me the Ed. Psych. papers. I can see how you were confused by the Robinsons and I hope you will accept my apology. I came on too strong and . . .," she paused.

"Of course . . . you don't need to . . .,"

"Yes I do! And I'd like to get us back on track by working with you on solving your problem. Please let me help."

"Why, I surely need all the help I can get!"

"Good!" Felicity laid a file on Rich's desk. "Now, put me in the picture. OK?"

The picture Rich envisioned was one where Felicity was dressed in white, next to him at an altar. "I do!" he blurted. Her puzzled look brought him back to reality. He stammered, "Ummm . . . yes . . . here's where I think we are."

Rich continued. "The Dean agrees with Carl Mertens' outline of the problem. The Ed. Psych. faculty can probably hide behind Queer Theory – whatever that is."

"Yes," Felicity mused. "I agree. It's really too bad that the academic community let that one loose. However did they get a Special Interest Group in AERA?"

"The same way that all other SIG's came about. A group of members put the idea in front of the AERA Board and got the votes. Nobody pays any attention to these SIG proposals."

Felicity scowled. "Well, I guess we can't worry about that, but it's a shame that there is no evidence that academics police their craft. We just work on our own thing and let anything that looks like scholarship take on a life of its own."

Her pronouncement stifled conversation. Each paged aimlessly through Mertens' file, looking for guidance

"Here!" Felicity jabbed a finger at Mertens' final memo. "We haven't been following Carl's conclusion. Listen!" She read, "Point Number one - no University policies apply to these issues. What we need to do is drill down to find a policy lever and . . ."

"Hold it!" Rich nearly shouted. "Take a look at this!" He showed her his 'bubble drawing'. "What I was trying to do is to find a way to connect Central through Waldo Pearson. When I put your name in the picture, I was hoping that . . .,"

Felicity studied the drawing, her face reflecting surprise, puzzlement, and enlightenment. "I like the picture! If we can connect the Dean and Pearson . . .," Another minute passed. "Got it! The policy has to focus on departmental performance. You know, measures of productivity, fund raising, enrollment. Like Mertens says."

"Sure. We're on the same page. I've trolled through all University policies and can't find any hook that'll reel in Ed.Psych.."

"I imagine you're right. What I'm saying is that we need to come up with a new policy that builds on Waldo's concern for money. That's all he sees when he looks at departments and colleges."

"You're right about Waldo, but he usually gives the College a budget number and leaves it to the Dean to make the cuts."

Felicity raised a finger. "That's where a new policy comes in. Let's say that Dean Bahls goes to Waldo with a proposal for measuring department performance; a policy that cuts across the University. That would take the Dean off the hook and give Waldo budgetary leverage."

"And close Ed. Psych.," the Acting Chair said.

"It might even do more than that," Felicity added. "It could pave the way for Mike to move up. Maybe even into Central. See how you've connected the

Dean in your diagram?" She stood and leaned over the desk, hair swinging forward.

Rich was mesmerized by her beauty. *MiGod!*

"What was that?" she asked.

"Oh, I was just . . . kind of surprised at how you've given us a focus!"

"Focus! Hang on! I've got a report in my office that . . .," she sped out the door.

Report? Rich held his drawing at arm's length. He mentally traced the connections. No 'report' caught his attention. The question mark on the 'Rich' to 'Felicity' arrow remained.

A few minutes later, Felicity swept in the door, report in hand. "This is the Indiana University Report that fits our problem. Listen to this! 'RCM provides an environment in which deans and directors have the flexibility to make substantive and beneficial changes in their operations in a timely manner.'," She watched for Rich's reaction.

"Sounds good, but what's RCM?"

"That's the kicker! RCM stands for Responsibility Centered Management. What it means is that Central sets performance standards that each college and every department has to meet in order to justify budget numbers. It's absolutely fantastic!" Felicity smiled as she contemplated this management innovation. "And, RCM is catching on in major universities! All we need to do is to get the Dean to sell RCM to Waldo Pearson! Here!"

Rich reached for the report where Felicity had underlined the words, 'substantive and beneficial changes in their operations in a timely manner'. "Are you saying that these 'changes' involve program and departmental cuts?"

"You bet! RCM was cooked up to do just that. The language in the report is a smoke-screen for hatchet work!"

"I like that!" Rich gloated. "But where do we get the measures that drive RCM?"

"No problem! What we need to do is analyze all the College departments. You know, do the numbers. In fact, that's just what will silence any criticism."

"Don't see how," Rich frowned.

"Think!" Felicity commanded. "The educational research studies that are quoted and praised by the big boys and girls are the ones with methodological sophistication. You remember how our policy studies publication record exploded when we hooked into new research methods?"

Rich smiled. "Now I see where you're going. Methodology takes the heat off substance. Why our last paper, the one where we used 'multi method', was accepted by . . .,"

"Yes. Yes. That's what I'm saying. Here's our next step. I'll work through the U's data base on our College. I think I can come up with a method that will produce reliable rankings of departments."

"Sounds like a plan. How can I help?"

"You need to work on the Dean. Bring him up to speed on RCM so that he's ready to see the numbers."

"Isn't that too soon?" Rich worried. "What if . . ."

"There'll be no problem! All you need to do is Google RCM and get the language in hand. I'll do the rest." She reached across the desk and shook his hand. "It's great to be back together! Thank you so much for including me!"

Rich sank back in his chair – gaze fixated on the shape that turned in the office door – cheek ready for the blown kiss.

BOOK IV
MASTERY OF
THE ACADEMY

"... the ideals of scholarship are yielding ground, in an uncertain and varying degree before the pressure of businesslike exigencies."

(Thorstein Veblen: The Higher Learning in America)

CHAPTER EIGHTEEN

QFM

"Faculty lack . . . understanding of education quality and how to produce it at optimal cost levels, they don't know how to measure it, and their incentive system doesn't reward efforts to improve." (William Massy: Academic Quality Work)

Rich dedicated most of the next week to his assignment. He nearly became an expert on the administration of higher education with a special focus on Responsibility Centered Management. As a result, he concluded that the RCM movement was here to stay; countless leading universities had implemented some form of RCM where budgets were linked to academic productivity. These studies supplied him with both language and examples that he could lay on the Dean's table. He decided to open with the threat posed by the Ed. Psych. faculty.

"Mike," Rich said. "We must view our Ed. Psych. problem as an opportunity."

"How's that?" Bahls tipped back in his chair, visibly bored.

"Major universities have come up against just the sort of culture we have here. It's one that uses the traditional forms of scholarship and academic freedom as cover for behavior that increases public suspicion of the academy. I have two recent examples that prove my point. First, the University of Iowa recently permitted the showing of a pornographic film in the student union under the umbrella of 'academic freedom'. Second, and even more significant, a professor at Northwestern University permitted the demonstration of 'sex toys' by a couple engaged in 'kinky sex' to a class of undergraduates."

Bahls chair thumped to the floor. "You gotta be kidding!"

Rich shook his head. "No, I'm not kidding. Given the nature of the academy, it's incredibly easy for any action or point of view to be expressed in the open. That's why we see Ed. Psych. as a challenge and there's not much we can do about it."

"Then how is it that you think this obvious challenge is really an opportunity?"

"Here's how," Rich said earnestly. "It's clear that we can't make any headway by trying to confront these faculty creeps. What I'm proposing is that we enlist Pearson and Central in a university-wide initiative that makes it possible for us to close down this department."

"That sounds too good to be true and probably isn't."

"It certainly would be difficult if it weren't for some important new directions in higher education management. For the past week, Professor Berland and I have been studying Responsibility Centered Management. We . . ."

"What the hell's that?" Bahls interrupted. "Seems to me that managers ought to be responsible, and . . ."

"Wait! The beauty of RCM is that it puts the responsibility for budget and outcomes at the level of colleges and their departments. Here," Rich slid a bulging folder across the Dean's table. "Take a look as these papers; they show how RCM has changed the management landscape at several universities."

Bahls slid his glasses down from his forehead and paged through the file. "Hmmm. . . University of Indiana . . . University of Missouri . . . looks like this RCM has really caught on. But I don't see what that does for us."

"I believe Fel . . . Professor Berland and I will have a plan for you in the next couple of days," Rich paused. "Let's meet next Wednesday. That'll give you time to get a handle on RCM. What say?"

"I think . . .," Bahls glanced at his desk calendar. "Can do. Ten o'clock work for you?"

"We'll make it work!"

Rich's optimism carried him to his office. Once the door was closed and he was seated at his desk, the familiar pessimistic cloud descended. "What plan?" he asked himself. He realized that everything depended upon Felicity. Without her ideas, there would be no plan and Ed. Psych. would resume its status as a major challenge to Rich and to the Dean.

Rich's hand reached out from the fog of pessimism, picked up his phone and punched in Felicity's number.

"Professor Berland."

"This is Rich. I've just come from a meeting with the Dean and we're on for next Wednesday. I've convinced him as to the merits of RCM. Now all we need to do is come up with a plan for laying it on Central. Maybe I'm moving too fast?"

"No, I don't think so. In fact, I've developed a design for RCM that should work across the U. Why don't you come to my office and I'll show you."

Rich hung up the phone and shot out of his office. He ran up the multiple flights of stairs to the fourth floor. He paused outside Felicity's door to control his heart rate, then tapped at the half-opened door.

"Ok to come in?" he asked.

"Sure! Grab a chair and listen to this," she ordered.

When Rich was seated, Felicity leaned her elbows on her desk and began. "I think we were right in not confronting Ed.Psych. directly. Here's what I found out. I called Win and . . ."

"You mean Pyke?' Rich asked; alarmed at a connection he considered dead.

"Yep. Seems that his D.C. group has some of the same issues we're confronting. They wanted to close the door on off-beat research. And, like we surmised, their attorneys told them to forget any attempts to monitor that type of work."

"Just what I thought," Rich said. "But where does that lead us?"

"Here's the kicker! Win started to stack his proposal review committees with academic heavy hitters. No surprise. They axed nearly every proposal coming from the academic fringes. What we need to do is to find a way for main-line university professors to do our work for us. Remember how vicious the sciences were when we had that external review?" She stopped and gazed over Rich's shoulder at the promise of RCM.

"Yeah. I remember how tough Menes and Utoft were on the College. So, getting those kinds of folks to take care of Ed. Psych. would be great, but I still don't see. . ."

"It's academic quality!" Felicity blurted. "All we need to do is hook Central on the notion that academic quality improvement is number one and that RCM exists to channel resources to the most deserving colleges."

"Sounds like a pretty tough sell," Rich said skeptically.

"That's what I told Win. Then he clewed me in on AQIP."

"AQIP? Never heard of that."

"Me neither," Felicity admitted. "But a few minutes on the Internet and I found out that the Higher Learning Commission, you know, the group that accredits colleges and universities, has an accreditation pathway called the

Academic Quality Improvement Program. Just think! The U is coming up for an accreditation review and we have the option to go the AQIP way."

"So," Rich frowned, "you're saying that we convince Central to go with AQIP. Right?"

Felicity nodded, "Right."

"Then how does RCM come into the picture?"

"Here's how," she shoved a paper across her desk. "What I found is that the external review team we had year before last ranked the College departments along some sort of continuum of academic quality. And get this. Ed. Psych. was dead last!"

"No surprise there. What's that mean?"

"Just a minute! That's the key to our approach to the Dean - and to Central. Look at this Powerpoint."

Rich was always troubled by bullets and had stubbornly avoided Powerpoint in favor of chalk or, in his hi-tech moments, the overhead projector. He took the offered paper and studied it.

A NEW MANAGEMENT PLAN

- FOCUS ON QUALITY – AQIP ACCREDITATION
- MANAGING FOR QUALITY – COLLEGE LEVEL
- MAXIMIZING UNIVERSITY RESOURCES – RCM
- COLLEGE OF EDUCATION AS 'TEST BED'

While he was occupied with these topics, Felicity continued. "The way I see it, we need to convince Mike . . . er . . . Dean Bahls as to the wisdom of our approach. Given the widespread adoption of AQIP and RCM that should be easy. The hard part is the last point. He has to be convinced that the College should take the lead. If he agrees, we should be ready to go to Central."

This was moving too fast for Rich. "Wait a minute! Are you sure that we can make your 'test bed' idea work. Seems like that's taking a big risk."

"I've been working on this," Felicity grinned. "The weakness in all these initiatives is in the methodology. They take what is essentially a qualitative problem, academic quality is always a matter of qualitative judgment, and try to reduce it to numbers. It's very difficult to put numbers on programs or departments that will stand up to quantitative analysis."

Qualitative? Quantitative? Rich's bafflement was written large on his face. He admitted his ignorance. "What does that mean?"

"Just this. The College will need to demonstrate to Central that it's possible to translate academic quality into the measures that define RCM. Simple as that!"

This was getting far beyond Rich's depth. He was accustomed to leading his students while they fished in waters that he had already depleted. Now he was the one rowing behind Felicity. "Don't see that it's all that simple," he muttered.

Felicity flashed a brilliant smile. "Just leave it to me! Set up a meeting with the Dean for next week," she commanded, "and I'll lay our methodology on him. Can't miss!" She began to leaf through papers on her desk.

Rich followed orders and left Felicity to her work. He shuffled down the fourth-floor corridor. This time, there was no spring in his step and he took the elevator to the main floor of Blewett.

The appointment with the Dean was confirmed and Rich spent the balance of the week fixated on Felicity's Powerpoint. He could see that AQIP and RCM were the keys that might unlock Central. What he didn't understand is how Felicity could perform her magic to bridge the 'qualitative' – 'quantitative' divide. This remained a mystery and left Rich with a feeling of uncertainty when he and Felicity sat down in the Dean's conference room.

"Well," Bahls began. "Good to see you!" He was looking at Felicity. "Have we a solution to our problem?"

Felicity glanced at Rich, then began. "We think so." She passed the Powerpoint page across the desk to Bahls. "Here are the ingredients to our solution."

While the Dean studied the bullets, Felicity explained each in detail. Although Rich had heard these points previously, he was captivated by the clarity of her explanation and elegance of her person. Visions of their partnership distracted him. *Together we could . . .* Scenarios of Felicity and Rich studiously at work gave the future precedence over the present.

The Dean interrupted this reverie. "Well Rich, what do you think of all this?"

"Huh? . . . Oh . . .," Rich stumbled back to the present. "Well it's a big step, but we, Dr. Berland and I, feel that the College could and should take this opportunity to create a management system that meets the needs of the times." He sat erect, mindful of the power of the proposal.

"Hmmm," Bahls hesitated, "seems to me that we're taking a considerable risk; if Central buys this plan, the College will surely have to make some sacrifices."

"Yes," agreed Felicity, "but we have some pretty low-hanging fruit that Central can harvest without damaging the mission of the College. As Rich may have told you, I've run several statistical studies of our departments where I related departmental rankings given by our external review to the variables that make up RCM."

Bahls was immediately attentive. "What exactly did you do? You know, the methodology?"

Felicity smiled confidently. "I carried out a multiple discriminant analysis. It showed that RCM puts departments like Ed. Psych. on the chopping block. This means that we can give up a low-performing unit without hurting the College."

"You sure about this?" the Dean asked.

"Hundred percent! You can take it to the bank."

What's she saying? Rich was clearly uncomfortable with the way the conversation assumed that Central was a done deal. "Just a minute. Are we sure that we have an iron-clad case? Pearson can be a real inquisitor when anyone lays a new idea on him."

Felicity turned her considerable charm on Rich. "That's just where you come in."

What? Me?

She continued. "Pearson has to be convinced that our plan gives him control over all college budgets and that RCM will make it possible for the U to meet its financial challenges. You're just the person who can give Waldo an historical perspective where RCM is the natural evolution of university management. Remember how we scored with the Legacy Fund."

Bahls was clearly lost in contemplation of the possible outcomes of the plan. "Maybe," Mike ruminated, "it would be better if we made this a team effort. Suppose we prepare a written plan for Pearson, one where Dr. Berland's four bullets are fully developed. Rich, you can write the Executive Summary of our plan. I'll hand carry it to Waldo and explain the benefits. How's that sound?"

"Brilliant!" Felicity enthused. "Rich can have the Executive Summary on your desk by tomorrow afternoon. Right Rich?"

Executive Summary! Rich found it very difficult to frame a coherent answer to Felicity's question. "I guess I can do that . . .," His intake of breath signaled more comments, but none was forthcoming.

The meeting was over. Rich remained seated as Bahls walked Felicity out of the Dean's Office. An Associate Dean in a supporting role! Rich's drawing was changing shape. Now he was no longer at the center of influence. Bahls had moved him to the periphery where he was merely a team player. This would require some serious thinking if he was to have any part in the College Test Bed Plan. Now his only opportunity was to engage university politics in a way that manipulated both Pearson and Bahls!

A few minutes later, Bahls strode back into the office and clapped Rich on the shoulder. "Well done Rich! You've shown me how we can shift our focus from Ed. Psych. to a significant policy initiative for the U."

Although credit wasn't due, Rich accepted praise. "Thanks. However, there's a lot more to do. So I'd better get going." He gathered his paperwork, nodded to Bahls and slipped into his office.

Seated at his desk, Rich considered how he might regain control over the plan. He realized that Felicity's four-part approach and her calculations were essential elements that he couldn't claim as his contributions. Instead, he would need some sort of lever to shift University policy. His pencil guided his thoughts.

'RCM' 'AQIP' 'Discriminant Analysis' "How about something like, Quality Improvement Management? No, that doesn't sound quite right," he mumbled. "How about – 'QIM' – now, that's better. But not good enough." Rich put down the pencil and studied his notes. He knew that three letters were testing the limit of administrative attention span. "Maybe," he picked up the pencil and wrote, 'QFM'. "Quality Focused Management." He read the phrase aloud several times. It began to roll off his tongue. Rich could almost hear Waldo Pearson enunciating a new edict. This image drew him to his computer and a new QFM policy document began taking shape.

As often in the past, Rich's turn of phrase captivated his audience at the next meeting in the Dean's Office.

"You've done it again!" Bahls hoisted Rich's document as if it were a manifesto. "Waldo will buy this in a minute!"

"I'll say!" Felicity said. "You've captured all our ideas and put them in a form that will appeal to the faculty as well as to Central. Congratulations!"

"OK. OK," Rich dissembled. "Now, let's talk about exactly what we want Waldo to do. It's not enough just to lay this on him. We need to make sure that the plan is implemented and that there's evidence that academic quality is improved and that Central gets its arms around the money."

Bahl's enthusiasm became hidden behind his raised coffee cup. His eyes wandered over the rim of the cup to ravish Felicity and attention followed desire.

Rich caught the glance. "What you must do Dean, is to decide whether you're ready to make a move to Central."

The cup thumped to the table and Bahls sat upright. "What do you mean? Central?"

That's better! "The success of the plan depends on leadership at Central. Since we're proposing QFM across the University, Central will need a responsible leader with supporting staff. I believe we should propose that you move to Central and make QFM your portfolio."

Felicity was also surprised by Rich's idea. "I don't see . . ." she began, ". . . yes, that's a very interesting idea. In fact, it's exactly what Central needs to do. Why, with the Mike's leadership there's no chance that the plan might fail!"

Bahls was caught! Visions of a top-level administrative position and University-wide acclaim swept caution aside. "I do believe you two are right. But," he hesitated, "where does that leave the College? If I move up, who will lead QFM in the College?"

"Rich is the obvious choice!" Felicity offered. "He's already Associate Dean and he knows the plan."

"No," Rich shook his head. "That won't do. I've given this a lot of thought and have concluded that Hank Loras would be the best choice to lead the College."

"Hank, hmmm . . .," Felicity mused, "could work."

"Well, now . . . ," Bahls said, "I agree that Hank could do the job. But would he want it?"

"If we agree, that's our next step," Rich advised. "What say we go for it?"

There was silent consideration of the 'step'. Three faces reflected emotions of: interest – Felicity; ambition – Bahls; determination – Rich. Then . . .

"I recommend we go ahead," Felicity decided. "An opportunity like this doesn't come along very often."

Her support removed any hesitation Bahls had. "If you say so," he said. "I had no plans to move on, but you're right, this is too good to pass up."

"OK," Rich said. "So here's my suggestion. First, Dean, you need to see if Hank is on board. Next, Felicity, I hope you will lay out your methodology in a form that Pearson can follow. Finally, I'll take the lead with Waldo. I'm confident that he'll go along with the plan; provided that we have all our ducks in order. All right with you two?"

Everyone, including Rich, nodded. He was back in charge! And giving his co-conspirators their marching orders!

Bahls was the first to report. Two days later, he came into Rich's office and closed the door. "Hank's on board!" he exulted. "When we worked through the plan, he could see that it could strengthen the College. You know, prune the deadwood."

They grinned at the prospective demise of Ed. Psych. and the power that Dean Loras would wield under the plan.

"The other thing," Bahls went on, "Hank hopes that you'll stay on as Associate Dean."

"I thought Hank would see it that way, Rich said. "And, I hope that I'll be able to connect with you in Central to make the College an example for the University."

Bahls offered a hand. "Absolutely! Now I guess it's up to you to convince Pearson as to the merits of the plan."

This was the assignment that Rich had devised and desired. He reflected again at his drawing of the players, where he was once again firmly positioned at the center of the plan. QFM would go forward under his direction, along with the benefits that only University politics could provide. All that remained to be done was to plant the magic word of 'quality' in the lexicon of Central.

"You gotta appointment?" Pearson's secretary growled.

Rich marveled at Waldo's patience with this crone. "Yes. Please tell the Vice President that Dean Jessen is here."

The crone wasn't impressed by a mere Dean. Nevertheless, she ushered him into Waldo's office.

"Hello Rich. Long time." Pearson came around his desk, hand outstretched. "Here, have a chair." When they were seated, Waldo asked, "What brings you over this way?"

"Remember when you and I had that discussion about closure of the College?" Rich asked. Waldo nodded and Rich continued. "Well, we went round and round that issue and we could find no common ground."

"You can say that again! It's always the same. I try to get the colleges to shape up. Invariably, I run up against a stone wall called 'academic freedom'."

"Exactly! What I'd like to show you is a way that Central might crack that wall and put the University on a more productive track. Interested?"

"Yes . . . I guess so. What have you in mind?"

Rich paused. He knew that he had to position 'quality' and the plan within QFM if these ideas were to captivate Pearson and other key actors in Central. He began, "We are proposing that the University initiate a Quality Focused Management system based on performance data linked to college and department budgets."

"Sounds good, but how does it work?"

"As you say, the academic wall must be penetrated. QFM can do that. Performance indicators such as student enrollment, faculty publications and research grants become the measures of department and college quality. They are one side of the QFM system. The other takes a comprehensive view of costs within the University budget."

"What you're saying is that we inaugurate a QFM program. That right?"

"Yes. And, we propose to use our College as a kind of 'test bed'. We've done the basic research and know that we can make this go. In fact, we have identified at least one department that lags on all performance indicators. If the University goes with QFM, Dean Bahls will guarantee a successful example that academicians will not be able to criticize."

Rich could almost hear the synapses in Pearson's brain. Felicity was right! Waldo was following her Powerpoint and assimilating the mantra of QFM. When Rich saw evidence of agreement in Pearson's eyes, he took the next step.

"There's more," he said. "When the College Test Bed example is completed, we propose that Dean Bahls move to a position in Central where he can direct QFM across the University."

"Well now," Waldo considered. "QFM would be a significant policy change in University management. Let me think about your proposal. I'll also share your ideas with President Rose. As I'm sure you realize, the President will need to come out in total support of QFM."

"Of course," Rich intoned as he handed Waldo several QFM packets. "Here we have assembled the case for QFM. If either you or President Rose has any questions, please give me a call."

Pearson's parting handshake was damp. Normally, Rich would wipe his hand after such an experience. This time, he preserved Waldo's sweaty approval – a signal that QFM had been seeded in fertile soil.

"How'd it go?" Bahls asked as Rich returned to the Dean's Office.

"I think pretty well. Pearson was interested in the plan and I think he caught on to QFM."

"Good! What's next?"

"Pearson is taking our idea to President Rose. My guess is that he'll buy it. What we must do is position your transition as a centerpiece of the plan."

"Still seems like a big order," Bahls said hesitatingly.

"Sure. But so long as we can keep everyone talking about QFM, I think it'll go."

Rich was correct. The mantra of 'quality' and the magic of QFM drove Central in the direction set out in the plan.

It was only a week later that Pearson called Rich. "Rich. I pleased to report that President Rose liked QFM very much. He'd like to meet with you and Dean Bahls as soon as possible. Please work with my secretary to set this up."

"That's very good news," Rich said. "However, QFM is far too important to release to our secretaries. Instead, give me a date when you and the President are available and I'll coordinate with Dean Bahls."

"Guess you're right. I'll do my part. QFM is on the way!" Pearson hung up.

So did Rich. He sighed and smiled. The University was about to be driven by the mantra of 'quality'. The many handshakes of the past several weeks were memories worth preserving.

CHAPTER NINETEEN

The Prince

"Nothing makes a prince so much esteemed as great enterprises and setting a fine example."
(Nicolo Machiavelli:The Prince)

Bahls wasn't the only one interested in Rich's meeting with Pearson. "How'd it go?" Felicity asked as she slid into the chair across from Rich's desk.

"Pretty good. Pearson bought QFM and is arranging for a meeting with the President, Bahls and himself." Rich carefully omitted the fact that he was to be included.

"My! That's great!" Felicity beamed. "Why, that means we can look forward to working with Central!"

"I think so," Rich considered her enthusiasm. "But there's work to be done now. The Dean needs to be fully aware of all aspects of the plan, especially your research approach. If you can find the time, it'd probably be a good idea to have a session or two with him."

Felicity nodded. "You're right. He'll need to be able to bring the President up to speed and make the case for QFM. I'll get right on it!" She jumped up and swept out of Rich's office.

"Wait! Wait!" Rich called out to the empty room. He now had second thoughts as to the wisdom of Felicity educating the Dean. Visions of the two; closeted in the Dean's Office after hours overpowered his interest in the plan.

"Why did I do that?" he asked aloud, shaking his head. He changed his thoughts with difficulty. "Well, better make sure that Hank is on board." Rich lifted his phone and punched in Loras' number.

"Hank Loras. Who's calling?"

"This is Rich. Gotta minute?"

"Sure. Shoot!"

Rich considered his approach for a moment, then said, "The way things look, Bahls is positioned to move up to Central. That'd work, but only if you're ready to take over as Dean. Mike says you're interested. That right?"

"Well . . .," Loras hesitated, I did say so, but it's not exactly what I'd planned. However, I think it might be a good move – if you're gonna stay as Associate Dean."

This was an option that Rich had been mulling over for some time. On the one hand, moving to Central along with Bahls had the allure of big-time university administration. It also had the disadvantage of constraints on his freedom. *I'd probably do better on the outside.* Rich put this conclusion into his answer. "Yes. I think we could work together to integrate the Center into College operations. That would give us leverage with the Feds and take the faculty off our backs."

"About what I figured," Loras said. "You can count on me for the Dean's spot."

They continued talking and plotting a strategy to increase their influence over the working of the College and their access to federal grants. It was a political arrangement with no downsides to either Rich or Loras.

Rich used Loras' decision as the opener for his next meeting with Bahls. Once the meeting was scheduled, Rich reconsidered his intention to be involved when Bahls approached Central. He realized that the combination of Bahls, Pearson and Rose was at a level above his own position and he ruefully concluded that he would be an outsider. However, he could still manipulate the meeting!

When he was seated in Bahls' office, Rich said, "Dean." He used Bahls' title to give weight to his proposal. "You should know that Hank Loras is in agreement with our plans. He's ready to move to this office when you've found a place in Central. By the way, when do you feel ready to lay our proposal on the President?"

"I'd say sometime next week. Fel . . . I mean . . . Dr. Berland has educated me on the mysteries of QFM and I believe that I can convince the President of the merits of our approach."

"Great!" Rich enthused. "Would you like me to set up a meeting? Actually, I'd suggest that you let Pearson carry the water on this. You know, just the three of you together. Then you can lead the discussion of QFM. How does that sound?"

"Sounds good! Go for it!"

Rich 'went for it'. Pearson was eager to accommodate the plan and the President appeared to be looking forward to a briefing on QFM. Now it was all up to Bahls!

The transition worked beautifully. Rose appointed Bahls to a new role of Provost; Loras became Dean of the College; Felicity consulted with all University units on implementation of QFM. Rich was the beneficiary of these developments; he was adviser to each of the major players and the backstage director of political machinations.

Along with his new level of importance, Rich received the customary reward given to academic politicians – a second office in Conant! Dual offices were a sort of 'coin of the realm'. They gave their incumbents podia from which pronouncements and summons could be issued. Also, a second office gave the political reptile almost total freedom, since the office-holder was always 'at the other office' or 'enroute' – while actually at Tabbacy's or at home. Rich was ready-made for his new role as adviser to the Provost and he slithered between Central and the Dean's Office.

One of his first days at Central, he was gliding down the second-floor corridor in the Conant Administration Building when a familiar voice called to him.

"Hey Rich! Welcome to Central. C'mon in and tell me all about your move!" Ex-Dean Merton Dunkard beckoned from a side office.

Dunkard! Forgot about him! "Well, sure . . . good see you Mert," he turned into the door marked 'Legacy Fund Office'. His confusion was understandable; Dunkard had been moved up from Dean of the College of Education and Home Economics to Central - as Director of the Legacy Fund. At the time, Rich saw this move as a dead end for Dunkard; a Rich reward for the removal of an obstacle.

Dunkard seized Rich's hand and drew him into the Legacy Office. "Rich! Rich! I'm glad to see you! You know, I wouldn't be here if it weren't for your suggestion. Why, the Legacy Fund was made for me!" Dunkard pointed to a graph on the office wall. "Look! We've doubled the size of the Fund and there's no end in sight!"

These data were almost a physical blow to Rich. He had supposed that Dunkard would fade into oblivion like other cast-off deans. Instead, he was a success!

"Sure looks good," Rich gritted. "Congratulations."

"Thanks. Now tell me what you're up to."

Rich inhaled deeply, and exhaled a verbal smoke screen. "Oh, just a short-term appointment as an adviser to the Provost. He's working on a new management system and needs somebody with a bit of perspective on higher education administration."

"I've heard the rumors," Dunkard said. "I hope you'll keep me informed so that I can share the Provost's innovation with alumni. They'll bite on any new idea and write the checks."

That got Rich's attention. "Just how much is in the Fund?" he asked.

Dunkard turned to look at his computer screen. "Let's see," he typed a few commands. "Yesterday we had just about . . . two hundred fifty million. That's up nearly a hundred-fifty million since I took over."

Rich's envy subdivided and the millions caused his head to slouch forward. ". . . why . . . I can't believe." And he couldn't. All those millions! Why, he and Hank Loras only raised five million the last two years! Rich's eyes nearly crossed at the transformation of 'the drunkard' into the 'master fund raiser'.

The balance of the time in the Legacy Office was a blur of additional data that proved that the Fund was a tremendous success. A half-hour of Dunkard boasts – followed by mumbled faint praises from Rich – ground away the luster of Rich's appointment at Central. It was a humbled Associate Dean that finally escaped to his own lair to lick his wounded pride.

Rich assuaged his frustration by working with Bahls, Felicity and Loras to make the College the 'test bed' for QFM. The three realized that Central's support for QFM depended upon a successful demonstration in the College. While Rich enjoyed working the machinations of QFM, he had moments of anxiety that he shared with Felicity; culminating in the final assessment of Ed. Psych..

"Well," Rich said as he finished Felicity's Ed. Psych. "Quality Profile". "This looks pretty convincing. Think the College faculty will agree with your conclusion?"

"A walk in the park!" Felicity grinned. "I've shared this with the faculty politicians and they're all on board! Especially the chairs of other departments low on the quality indicators. They're our best advocates, so long as their departments aren't on the chopping block!"

She was correct. Ed. Psych. was disbanded. The Robinsons, Emmit, and Singer were terminated; Klein was – oddly enough – offered a position in the Department of Psychology. And, the key College faculty reacted with support and verbal applause. The 'test bed' worked!

At the same time, QFM gave the new Provost University-wide visibility. Gradually, Bahls became the public face of the University. Handsome, slender, articulate Bahls replaced jolly, portly, pancake-flipping Rose. Rich discerned this shift in leadership from conversations with Bahls; references to comments by Trustees, legislators and other public figures told of the Provost's growing influence. In fact, Bahls was often the initiator of new policies at Trustee meetings and the one who not only announced new directions; he was usually at the center of implementation.

Bahls' ascendency was accompanied by a gradual fading of the persona of President Rose. The empty Presidential space was filled by Bahls and his minions; Rich and Felicity. Rich provided political advice and Felicity's research supported Central's new directions.

Rich was aware that this conspiracy had to deal with President Rose, else it risked a Trustee-level confrontation. There had to be a way! Rich gnawed at this bone for months, until he was given a tour of the Presidential Mansion. Rose had virtually retreated to the sanctuary of the Mansion. His wife Rita made that retreat less appealing as Rich soon discovered when he accompanied Bahls to a Presidential reception.

"Hello Mrs. Rose. I'm Professor Richard Jessen," Rich said. "It's a great honor to be invited to the Mansion."

"Melvin has spoken of you often," Rita twittered. "I do wish we could receive you in more pleasant surroundings." She waved a dismissive hand at the tawdry furnishings in the parlor. Rita continued on this theme as she took Rich's arm and led him around the room. "Look!" she commanded. "These old wall coverings are original. And they look it!"

Rich nearly agreed. "Yes they are clearly antique, but they offer a relaxed environment where . . ."

"Relaxed!" Rita snorted. "Why I'm continually embarrassed by this place. Come! Let me show you the kitchen."

After a half-hour tour of antiquated appliances and musty rooms, Rich was ready to agree with Mrs. Rose. The place was not suitable for a Presidential Residence!

President Rose and Bahls were waiting in the parlor. They both looked uncomfortable in the heat and odors of the Mansion.

"Ah ha!" exclaimed The President. "I see that Rita has been giving you the Grand Tour. What do you think of the place?"

Rich was caught! *Tell the truth!* This unfamiliar conscience command caused him to give a faltering response. "Well, to tell the truth. The Mansion could use a bit of an overhaul."

"Couldn't agree more," Bahls confirmed. "A Presidential Mansion has to come up to the same standards of quality that we're seeking in QFM."

"Of course," Rose said ruefully. "But there isn't enough money in our facility funds to take on a project of this scope."

"Oh Mel!" Rita exclaimed. "That's what you always say. Seems to me that the President should find the money to bring this place up to date!"

"Take it easy Rita," Rose consoled. "I'm looking!"

So he's looking! Rich and Bahls were also looking – at each other – mutually searching for the funds and opportunities that might be associated with remodeling of The Mansion.

Conversation over dinner continued to focus on the Mansion. Bahls' wife, Beth, contributed her perspective. She summed up at the end of the meal. "I have to agree with Rita. Something must be done to bring the Mansion up to the level one would expect at a Research I university."

Research I! Here was a mantra that Rich could understand.

Evidently, Bahls agreed. "Beth's right!" he glanced at the President. "In fact, I've been thinking that Rich and I might be of help to you and Rita. If you'd like, we can put out heads together and get back to you."

An offer that summarized Presidential needs; the Roses accepted enthusiastically.

As Rich and Bahls walked back to the Campus, Beth asked, "Were you serious Mike? I mean, where's the beef?"

Bahls turned the procession aside to a bench at the entrance to the campus. They sat and he served up a cut. "I think Rich and I can dig up the cash. That'll put the President in debt. And, we can sure count on Rita to be our cheerleader!

"You're right about that!" Beth said. "She calls the signals for life at the Mansion!"

They considered life with Rita for several moments, then Rich said, "Let's go ahead with this. A big remodeling project will occupy the President and we can proceded with QFM without his criticism. Mike, you and I can see if we can find the money and it would be great Beth, if you'd be willing to encourage Rita. Deal?"

Agreement was universal and each set about the assigned task. Beth was the first to report when they met in Rich's office two week later. "No problem with Rita," Beth said. " I've spent the past week paging through architectural magazines. She's totally committed!"

Mike gestured helplessly, "Can't say that I've anything good to report. There doesn't seem to be any surplus cash anywhere in the U."

"That's bad news," Rich grumbled. "I've combed through all the college budgets, no joy there. There's only one pot of money that isn't committed and that's under Dunkard's thumb."

"Tell us about that," Bahls ordered.

"According to Dunkard, the Legacy Fund has around three hundred million in the bank. Remember how we wrote the Fund Charter; only the interest can be used. Also, expenditures have to go to improving the academic environment at the U by supporting innovation."

"Sounds like a dead end," Beth observed. "The Mansion hasn't much to do with academics, and certainly no innovation is involved."

"Wait a minute!" Mike exclaimed. "Remember how the President lit up when we suggested that an updated Mansion would help him move the U into Research I?"

"Sure," Rich recalled. "But that sounds pretty wide of the mark so far as the Legacy Fund goes."

"Nono!" Mike said. "The key is Research I. I think we can make the case for improvement of the Mansion as something that has to be done to foster academics at Midwest."

It didn't take long for the three to conclude that Dunkard was the banker and Research I the key to the vault. There was, however, a serious problem that required strategic thinking. Bahls outlined the issue.

"We gotta remember," Bahls said. "Dunkard is still plenty pissed off at me for moving him out of the College. He even avoids me when he sees me coming down the hall in Conant. There's no way I can put this argument to him."

Two pairs of eyes flicked over to Rich. "OK. OK. You two are telling me that Dunkard is my assignment," Rich paused, "I'll give it a try."

The conspirators adjourned , leaving Rich in deep thought. He ambled back to his office where he sat at his desk reviewing ways he might liberate Legacy Fund monies. Mumbled options were posited and rejected. 'The President could appeal . . . no, Rose can't get in front of this.' Rich sat, hands folded on his desk. 'There might be an alumn . . . ?' No outside actor came to mind. Time passed. 'I think the only way is to see if Dunkard is still on the sauce. If so, I might be able to make an appeal for the Mansion.' Rich recoiled at the prospect of a long evening at Tubby's with 'The Drunkard'. "Better give it a try," he spoke aloud as he reached for his phone and punched in the number for the Legacy Fund.

"Hello. This is Merton Dunkard. How can I help you?"

"Mert. This is Rich. I've heard something that might interest you. Any chance we could get together at Tubby's?"

"Let me see . . .," sounds of calendar pages turning. "Sure. How's tomorrow?"

The next efternoon they met at Tubby's. Dunkard was seated, a half-empty Manhattan in hand, when Rich arrived.

"Hi Rich! Thanks for the invite!" Dunkard raised the glass and emptied it in one gulp.

Half in the bag! "Hello Mert. Let me get this one." Rich beckoned to the bartender and two fresh drinks arrived.

Dunkard drank deeply and asked, "So. What's this you have in mind?"

"Just this. The President is moving to lift the U to Research I. And . . ."

"Great idea!" Dunkard interrupted.

"But, here's the kicker. You'll probably agree that the Mansion isn't much to look at. What it needs is a major overhaul to make in a place the President can use to entertain the bigwigs who'll determine whether the U gets into Research I."

"SSure," Dunkard slurred. "SSoo what?"

"Well, I figure the Mansion needs something like three to five million to put it into shape. You know there's nothing like that kind of money floating around the U. What I wondering; is this the kind of project the Legacy Fund might be interested in?"

". . . don't see how . . .," Dunkard seemed confused. ". . . the Fund . . ." he stopped and gazed at Rich.

Hope he's not too far gone! "Tell you what," Rich said. "Let's you and I meet with President Rose and explore options. I'll bet this is exactly the kind of thing the Fund should support. What say?"

Dunkard peered owlishly through his alcoholic haze. ". . .maybe . . . good . . . idea . . . still gotta bring the alumni along . . ." He looked around Tubby's – but no alumni materialized.

Rich chaperoned Dunkard for the next hour, then deposited him at the door of Dunkard's house. "I'll be in touch Mert!" he called as he drove away. Dunkard stood staring after the departing car.

This has to be Rose's plan! Somehow, the President would have to make the case for a 'Research I' investment by the Fund. *Mike's job!* Rich made the call.

"Mike. Rich. I think Dunkard's ready. What he needs now is an invitation from Rose to discuss plans for the Mansion. Can you set this up?"

"That's great! And I'm sure that I can line up Rose. Should you be there? You know that I can't get involved with Dunkard."

Rich thought for a moment. "No, I don't that that's wise. The pressure on Dunkard is much stronger if it comes from Rose. Beth might help here by planting the idea of Legacy funding with Rita. Possible?"

"Good idea! I'll take care of it!"

Nobody ever knew exactly what transpired at 'the meeting'. No notes were kept and there were no email exchanges between Dunkard and Rose. Nevertheless, substantial appropriations of LegacyFund resources were transferred to a 'Mansion Renewal Account' controlled by the President. The Mansion was restored to its 1930's look along with a new Prairie Lodge replete with conference room, guest quarters and technological infrastructure. The total cost was never calculated, but estimates ran as high as ten million dollars.

While restoration was in progress, Rich and Bahls were set free to build the political foundation for control over University operations. Bahls developed Trustee meeting agendas and shaped the work of University governing committees. Rose was the symbolic President; Bahls was President In Fact.

This realignment of University power fascinated Rich and he took considerable pleasure for the role he had played in support of Bahls. From time to time, he did wonder just where Bahls' journey might end. *President Bahls?* The image of Bahls as the leader of the U recurred with increasing frequency and Rich considered how Mike's elevation might come about.

Felicity was, once again, the catalyst that precipitated the solution for Rich. One day, when he happened to be in his office in Blewett, Felicity floated in and closed the door. "Rich. I have something we need to talk about."

"By all means," he said. "Where do we go from here?"

She evaded the implications of that question. "I've been following the agendas of the Trustee Finance Committee. Ed Ryan, you know, the guy from Farmers Bank, is raising questions about the Legacy Fund. He's proposing a full Board session where they're going to put Dunkard on the hot seat!"

"What for?" Rich puzzled. "Dunkard's pulling in plenty of money..."

"That's not it! The Board wants an accounting of where money is being spent. You see, Ryan believes that Dunkard is using money from the principal of the Legacy Fund to renovate the Mansion. That's a violation of the Charter of the Fund and could cost Dunkard his job!"

"Holy sh... excuse me! That could go all the way to the President! He's the one who cooked up the renovation!"

Felicity wagged a finger. "Let's get real! You and Mike set this one up. What I need to know is, are you in the clear?"

Rich's brow moistened. *In the clear?* "I think so... all we... I... did was to suggest that Dunkard talk to the President about Rose's idea of making the U a Research I institution."

"I'm glad to hear that," Felicity sighed. "I've been plenty worried. Ryan is going to make a case for misuse of Legacy Funds and I think he's got an iron-clad case, given the Fund Charter. Heads are going to roll!"

Rich calmed down at this news. Here was what he had been looking for! He assumed his Professorial manner. "You're probably right. The President may also be at risk. I can imagine that he put considerable pressure on Dunkard. You know how weak Mert is." Rich realized that he had, somewhat subconsciously, arranged for realignment of University administration.

"Yes," Felicity smiled. "And I'll bet you and Mike set Beth on Mrs. Rose. She's the one who's been beating the drum for renovation. Right?"

Rich cleared his throat and assumed he most engaging manner. "You're right!" he chuckled. "The three of us visited with the Rose's several months ago. Rita showed us around the Mansion and rolled out the case for renovation. But it was the President's mention of Research I that got us thinking. It was my idea to connect Dunkard. All I needed to do was to buy a couple of drinks at Tubby's. Rita and the President did the rest."

"Wonderful! Now, am I also correct when I say that the big plan is for this issue to result in Rose moving on and Mike becoming President?"

"Well . . .," Rich pursued his lips, "we haven't actually discussed that. I guess I figured that the President would be preoccupied with the renovation and Mike would continue to take on more of the presidential role. I confess that I hadn't actually thought of . . .," his voice trailed off as he considered. . . *Mike as President! Well – whaddya know!*

They looked at one another, contemplating the advantages a Bahls Presidency might confirm. After a moment, both talked at once.

"Well . . ." Felicity said.

"This means . . .," Rich blurted.

They laughed.

Felicity was back in Rich's office a couple of days later to suggest an approach to the Trustees.

"Rich," she began. "I think we'll need to help the Trustees get a grip on the issue of Presidential leadership."

"That'd probably be a good idea, but I don't see how we can be a part of Trustee discussions."

"Just look a bit deeper. Think about how Ryan has the rest of the Trustees in his pocket. All we need to do is shape his thinking along the lines we've discussed."

"Sure. That would be great," Rich shook his head – negating optimism, "but Ryan isn't the kind of guy to listen very closely to what we might say."

"You got that right! But you're still not thinking deeply. Ryan depends on his daughter – Sugar, he calls her – to set up his agendas and do the background research."

"Guess I've heard that. So what?"

"Well, I play tennis with Shug!" The name slid off Felicity's tongue. "And, I know that I can get her to think along our lines. What say to that?"

Rich frowned. Working the back channels was nothing new to him, but this was serious as they would be connecting with Ryan without the President's knowledge. He posed the question, "Are you sure that we won't be too visible?"

"Yes . . . you're right to worry," Felicity stroked her chin, a slight frown indicating her concern. "Maybe what I'd need to do is give Shug some language – like, talk about Research I and QFM."

"Can't see the harm in that," Rich stretched and leaned back in his chair, arms folded across his chest. "If Ryan could pick up on a link between Research I and QFM, that would give us a sound foundation for contrasting the President's leadership skills with those of Bahls."

Felicity shook her head. "Something's wrong with that. It's too much edspeak. Kind of hard for folks like Ryan to understand. What we need is an idea that's in the national news . . .," her voice faded as she thought of options. "Got it! Let's promote the Malcolm Baldrige Quality Award."

"Hell's that?" Rich blurted. "Never heard of it!"

"It's a competitive award that up and coming universities covet. Gives them instant credibility." The prospect of a Baldrige Award for Midwest animated her conversation. "Why, I'll bet that Shug will . . .,"

"Sounds too much like more of the same. Just like QFM. How do you think Ryan will get a grip on the Award?"

"Here!" she reached across Rich's desk. "Turn your computer this way. Let me show you what Baldrige is all about."

Rich followed orders and Felicity took several minutes to find the Baldrige website and the specifics of the Education Quality Award. "Now," she commanded, "take a look at this!"

The computer was returned to Rich. Its screen displayed a collage of circles and boxes with thick arrows linking all the boxes to "Results". He was confused. "But!" he protested. "There's nothing here. Just words we've heard before! Strategic Planning! For God's sake, that's been in the mix for years. And, Customer Focus – I suppose that means students. I don't see . . ."

"Just a minute!" Felicity cut in. "You're missing the point! The weakness of all so –called quality awards is that they require what I'd call 'symbolic efforts'. That is, universities only have to demonstrate that they do 'Strategic Planning' and pay attention to "Customer Focus' – along with the other requirements. There's no auditing function on the part of Baldrige. The U can just spin the language."

Rich frowned and studied the web page. "If you're right, all we need to do is to get Ryan to speak the language of Baldrige. Then he'll likely see that Mike is the one to land the Award. It's just like the accreditation reviews we do – a bunch of our buddies visit for a couple of days – then the go away and write a glowing report. Right?"

"Right!" Felicity clapped her hands. "It's beautiful!"

"Forgive me for saying so, but it's bullshit!"

"Of course," Felicity chuckled. "But it's our bullshit and I'll bet it can put Mike in the driver's seat!"

As Felicity predicted, Shug and her father were taken by the national status that accompanied a Baldrige Award. They also saw that Melvin Rose wasn't the person to raise the University to the heights of quality.

All that remained to be done was to hit upon a tactic that would assist the Trustees in taking the necessary actions. Again, it was Felicity that identified the approach. She tested her idea on Rich.

"You know Rich," she said a week later in Rich's office. "I'd like to run an idea about the Trustees by you. Here's what I've been thinking. Suppose the Trustees decide to run an audit on University finances with a special focus on the Legacy Fund and the Mansion. Wouldn't that raise the right issues?"

Rich thought for nearly a minute. "Say! I think I get it! The audit would lay out exactly how much was spent on the Mansion and where the money came from. That'd put the President on the spot! I like it!"

"Thought you would," Felicity beamed. "Now all we need to do is sell it to Ryan. I'll bet a couple of tennis games with Shug will do it."

And – it did. Ryan easily persuaded the Trustees to approve the audit; which turned out to be simple to complete. The results where as Felicity and Rich predicted. The President had approved nearly ten million dollars of expenditure on Mansion renovation and construction of the Prairie Lodge. Dunkard had carried out Rose's directives and released Legacy funds – in contravention of the provisions of Legacy.

Felicity and Rich were interested bystanders watching the Trustees fume over the duplicity of the President, who was also blamed for Dunkard's behavior. The resignation of Rose and retirement of Dunkard occurred simultaneously.

CHAPTER TWENTY

Research I

"Gallant audacity is never out of countenance." (Gabriel Harvey: Marginalia)

Chancellor Bahls became President-elect Bahls in the kind of back-room decision making that frequently characterized leadership succession in higher education. Chairman Ryan appointed a Selection Committee made up of Trustees and faculty members charging them with the task of identifying Rose's replacement. Only a few meetings were needed for the Committee to discover that they had the ideal candidate in hand – Dr. Michael Bahls. No national search was required!

When the announcement of the Selection Committee's decision was made, there was general support within the University community; only a few questioned the integrity of the 'search'. The conspirators – Rich, Felicity and Hank – were overjoyed at the prospect of a Bahls presidency.

The President-to-be looked forward to implementing the ideas of Rich and Felicity. He seized on the juxtaposition of QFM, Baldridge, and Research I. So much so, that he planned to weave these concepts into his inaugural address. "I'm indebted to you two," Bahls admitted. "My speech will light a fire under the faculty!"

"Yes," Rich pursed his lips. "Better be careful though, each of these terms involves substantial changes in the way the University works. You could end up making some enemies."

"I suppose so," Bahls said dismissively. "Can't move this place ahead without some opposition."

"I agree," Felicity said. "The trick will be to persuade the majority that QFM and Baldrige are the best ways to make this a Research I institution."

"How's about this?" Rich offered. "You know how there's always a collection of faculty and administrators seated behind the speaker at events like this. Well, let's be selective as to who gets to sit on stage."

"Not bad," Bahls pronounced. "Will you two work up invitations?"

"Sure," Felicity nodded. "And, let's have the stage group parade down the aisle in the auditorium – led by Ryan and Mike."

They imagined the pageantry; state, University and American flags! Multicolored academic robes! Martial music! A Midwestern Third Reich!

Felicity and Rich approached the selection of the stage party with enthusiasm. When they had chosen approximately half of the favored, Rich noticed a problem.

"You know Felicity, most of the ones we've named are from law, medicine, the Business School and the sciences."

"Yes, that's right. So what?"

"Think about who's left out. The humanities and social sciences. Take that along with 'Research I' and we'll have some ready-made opposition to the President's agenda."

"Hadn't thought of it that way," Felicity frowned.

They recalculated and tried to fill the stage seats with a cross-section of the University 'family'. It didn't work. When the professions and the sciences were appropriately represented, there were only a half-dozen seats for what was becoming 'the opposition'.

Finally, Felicity sighed. "We'll just have to go with this," she waved their final draft.

On Inauguration Day, robed dignitaries marched into the Auditorium and filled the seats on stage. When all were seated and invocations pronounced, Chairman Ryan called the assembly to order.

"It is my great pleasure to welcome all the members of the Midwest community to the inauguration of the 30th president of this University. Over the years . . ."

Seated in the top row of the faculty 'family' next to Hank Loras, Rich half-listened to Trustee Ryan's enumeration of the accomplishments of President-elect Bahls.

". . . building on his impressive record at the Department of Health and Human Services, Dr. Bahls has energized our University during his tenure as Dean of the College of Human Science. You are all aware of his seminal work as Provost, when he . . ."

Ryan plowed on and Rich surveyed his colleagues from his lofty perch. In this instance, height was a measure of unimportance; revered faculty were seated immediately behind the podium on the lowest row of the risers that elevated lesser academics. Sciences in the first row, professions in the second, and the sprinkling of those at risk in Rich's row.

The risers were usually employed to position the members of the University Chorus, whose youth enabled them to cope with the narrow platforms that barely accommodated a folding chair. Unconsciously, Rich glanced at the back legs of his chair to make sure that the top riser had a two-inch high ridge to prevent slumbering faculty from tumbling backwards to the stage floor. He was relieved to see that the precaution had been taken and that several layers of gymnastic mats were positioned on the floor to catch faculty tumblers. He yawned.

As he inventoried the positions of his colleagues, Rich became increasingly upset. Why was he banished to the top layer? Hadn't he been the political strategist who had raised Bahls to the Presidency? His eyes ranged over the heads in the front row. Bobbed dark hair under a rakish mortarboard – Felicity! How did she? He puzzled over this seating arrangement for the balance of Ryan's remarks.

". . . please join me in extending a warm Midwest welcome to Dr. Michael Bahls, the 30th President . . ."

Halfheartedly, Rich joined the assembly in extending warmth; then relaxed, ready to hear the inaugural address of the new President.

After some short opening remarks, Bahls embarked on a definition of a 'New Midwest' to be forged in the crucible of his presidency. "I envision a new Midwest University that will take its place among the leading institutions of higher learning in America!"

Eager faces brightened in the audience; enthralled by this announcement and mesmerized by the stature of the 30th President.

Bahls continued. "It is my intention to assist the members of the Midwest community in elevating this University to membership in the august intellectual company of other Research I institutions." He paused, savoring the excited murmur that this announcement produced.

Rich could see Felicity's head bobbing in support of Bahls' agenda. He caught himself nodding agreement along with others in his row.

"Sounds like he's gonna go for it," Hank whispered. "Hope us peons will get a piece of the action."

"No problem," Rich muttered.

Bahls turned a page of notes. "Getting to Research I will involve Quality Focused Management across the University. We've made great strides already, but there's much more to do . . ."

Scanning the audience, Rich could see scowls of disagreement. He recognized several humanities professors who were whispering to one another. Nearly audible remarks were being exchanged in the social science seats. Here were the problems they had tried to avoid.

Bahls drowned these grumbles by raising his voice, ". . . building on QFM, the University will compete for the Malcolm Baldrige Education Quality Award – and I'm confident we'll be successful."

These themes were interwoven in a verbal tapestry that enabled listeners to picture the 'New Midwest'. Rich dozed his way through the balance of Bahls' speech – attempting to visualize how he and Felicity might be involved.

"In closing," Bahls said. "Let me invite all of you to join with me as we rekindle the lamp of learning at Midwest. Thank you!"

There was a standing ovation; accompanied by the toppling of several chairs from the upper riser. Fortunately, none of Rich's colleagues followed the cascade of chairs down to the protective matting. Evidently, lower-status academics were accustomed to this sort of finale.

"Well," Hank said. "Ain't that something! Research I and Malcolm Baldrige! Pretty big talk. Think he can do it?"

"I sure hope so," Rich responded. "There'll be some bumps in the road and we'll have to be ready to help Mike along."

"You bet!" Hank stepped to the next lower riser and looked back up at Rich. "I assume you're gonna hit the reception?"

Rich stood and looked around for Felicity, she was nowhere to be seen.

They followed the other members of the stage party out of the Auditorium where a bus was waiting to transport the elect to Prairie Lodge.

"C'mon," Hank said. "Let's take my car. Even a short bus trip with our esteemed colleagues is too much."

"You can say that again!"

When they entered Prairie Lodge, they were stunned by the opulence of President Rose's creation. Oaken beams bridged a wide area where thick rugs led the eye to a massive fireplace – ablaze with a crackling fire.

"Holy Toledo!" Hank exclaimed. "Sure beats the old Mansion!"

"You got that right!" Rich's head swiveled from side to side. So this is what Rita cooked up! And now Bahls was possessed of the luxury that was, in effect, Rose's legacy. On one edge of his vision, Rich saw Felicity. She was seated at a table which was draped with an ornate cover emblazoned with the University seal. She was offering name tags to attendees.

Seeing his gaze, Felicity beckoned. When Hank and Rich were at her table, Felicity held out two name tags. "Here, pin these on," she said, then added in a lower voice. "You two have to be proud of what you've done!" She held out her champagne glass for a toast.

Three glasses were touching when President Bahls arrived. "What are you three celebrating? May I join in?" He offered his glass.

"Of course!" Felicity invited. "We're just celebrating the New Midwest!"

"Yes," Rich said. "That was a great idea! It sure caught the attention of the faculty!"

"Second that! Here's to the New Midwest," Hank saluted with his glass.

There were now four glasses in contact, all four enveloped in the aura of the New Midwest.

Bahls broke the spell. "Rich, there's somebody I'd like you to meet." He took hold of Rich's arm and led him across the Lodge to an assembled group in a far corner.

Rich recognized the group as Medical School faculty, who had all been seated in the first row of the stage party. These were serious academics whose research and teaching actually affected lives outside the University. They were also rival political actors who Rich avoided whenever possible.

"Dr. Ramsborn," Bahls got the attention of a distinguished middle-aged man with a mane of silver hair. "This is Professor Rich Jessen, the architect of the Legacy Fund."

"How do you do, Professor Jessen."

Rich looked into deep blue eyes that were set approximately an inch above his line of vision. He had the uncomfortable sensation of a patient at a pre-operation consult. This was a real 'doctor'! "Umm. . . hello," Rich shook the manicured hand. "Pleased to meet you."

Ramsborn held Rich's hand and gently led him aside. "Come. I'd welcome the opportunity to have a short visit with you about the Legacy Fund."

Legacy Fund! What. . .? Rich followed the Doctor to two leather chairs in what the architect of the Lodge called a 'conversation alcove'. Ramsborn beckoned to a chair for Rich and seated himself, crossing well-creased trousers; exposing what were obviously new Gucci loafers. Rich was appalled! New Guccis! He hid his Second Life versions.

"As President Bahls may have told you," Ramsborn said. "I've been released from the Medical School to head up the Legacy Fund and I need to know what I've taken on." He looked at Rich appealingly.

This was a jaw-dropper for Rich! *Head up! Fund!* Here was Dunkard's replacement. Gone was the chubby drunk! "Why, I'm . . . well . . . no, President Bahls hadn't told me," he stopped in confusion.

"Please excuse me," Ramsborn said in a professional voice. "Would you rather continue our talk at another time ?"

"No . . . I think . . . now is as good a time as any."

"Good! Given the situation, I want to be absolutely clear as to the charter of the Fund. I understand that you were the person who developed the Fund. Am I correct?"

"I guess that's so," Rich admitted. "What can I tell you about the Legacy?"

Ramsborn re-crossed his legs. "What I'd like to know is how the Tofte gift was obtained and how it was developed into the Fund."

Rich considered how to address this question. Should he go into the details – no – better to make Tofte a part of 'the strategy'. "Well," he said. "Our strong relationship to the Tofte family and the work we were doing in support of handicapped citizens made for a convincing appeal. Once that gift was aboard, it was relatively easy to encourage other alumni to invest."

"Just as I thought," Ramsborn mused. "That's exactly how I plan to proceed as the new Director. You see," he added. "We can draw a similar connection between training of medical doctors and gifts to the Fund. What's more important, is that our graduates touch the lives of countless patients, many of whom have the capacity to add to the Fund."

Here it was! Rich could see that the Fund was evolving from its narrow political agenda to an instrument that was clearly intended for inclusion among the organizational tools of the Medical School. Rich was impressed by Ramsborn's proposed use of the 'Tofte caper', and by the cleverness of the President in moving the fund from its base in the College of Human Sciences to the Medical School.

371

After all, the supply of ready money among College alumni could not compare with the mountains of cash among doctors and their patients!

Ramsborn and Rich continued to explore new horizons for the Legacy for some time. As their mutual understanding grew, Rich began to visualize the Doctor as an emerging political insider – a person to cultivate and, in the long run, a possible fellow conspirator.

On their drive back to campus, Rich painted this vision for Hank. "So," he concluded. "The Fund pool will be bottomless and we can have a say in how that money is spent!"

"Don't fool yourself, Old Buddy," Hank warned. "We'll be bottom feeders in that pool. The Med School will siphon off the trophy catches and we'll be lucky to collect what sinks to the bottom."

For a moment, Rich smiled at the metaphor, then he confronted Hank's analysis. "Hmmm, I guess you're right. If so, why did Mike make the shift."

"That's got me plenty worried. Think about what he said in his speech, you know, about Research I. The Med School is Research I already. By adding the Legacy, he's increasing its financial muscle. I'd say he's already thinking of ways he can marginalize other units of the University."

Marginalize! "You mean us?" Rich was horrified at this possibility.

"Not just yet!" Hank smiled. "We're pretty tight with Mike and we'll ride along with this trend. We just gotta be careful and cut loose from the marginal units of the University."

It took only a few months for Hank's prediction to be tested. The President scheduled Rich, Hank and Felicity for a meeting at Conant Hall. His opening statement dispelled any confusion they may have had concerning the agenda of this meeting.

"What I want to talk about is my plan to close the Open College," Bahls sat back with a smile. "What do you think of that?"

The three evidently thought a good deal as nearly a minute of silence passed. Everyone knew that the Open College was the principal pathway whereby community college graduates entered the upper division of the University. The 'OC' – as it was called – was based on the land-grant foundations of the University and the source of legions of students who followed this path to the baccalaureate.

Rich broke the silence. "Close the OC? Are you serious?"

"Yes. I am taking this action to better position the U as a Research I institution. Having the Open College reduces the academic quality of our undergraduate program and taking this action will send a strong message to faculty and major donors."

"I'll say it'll send a message," Hank snorted. "Why that'll make enemies of most of the liberal arts faculty. Have you thought of that?"

"I have and am willing to take the risk," Bahls looked at Felicity. "Professor Berland, you haven't spoken. What's your reaction?"

"I agree with what Rich and Hank are saying. Closing OC is taking a big risk. However, I think the key concern has to do with the Trustees. Are they on board? And what about the legislature? We've used the land-grant argument with them for years."

"I know. I know," Bahls ran fingers through his hair. "I must confess that I worry about the legislature. Every land-grant university . . ."

Rich interrupted, "Exactly! We' have to come up with a whole new language! That won't be easy with our rural legislators!" This was his turf! He continually pontificated about the Morrill Act of 1862 and how the original grants of land to universities were in support of 'agriculture and the mechanic arts'. That history had help cement relationships between the University and rural legislators.

Felicity took up this challenge. "I think the President's right. The composition of the legislature is changing and the land-grant is meaningless to the urban representatives who will gravitate to Research I."

"My reasoning exactly!" Bahls said. "I think the political decision makers can be aligned to make this possible. You two agree?" He looked at Hank and Rich.

"I guess it's OK so far as I'm concerned," Hank shrugged. "I think I can bring most of our faculty on board. Just so long as our College is not on the chopping block."

"How about you Rich?" Bahls asked in an unfamiliar, commanding voice.

Better go along! "Could work, depending on the way the decision comes across. Are you thinking about using QFM to show why the Open College is being closed?"

"You've got something there!" Bahls praised. "Yes, QFM could provide the rationale. How's about that Professor Berland?"

Professor Berland? Why so formal? Rich was puzzled by the wedge Bahls was driving among the four conspirators.

"Of course," Felicity answered. " If QFM data can be made to show the OC as an outlier, and I think it can, you could . . .," Felicity paused, waiting for her thoughts to crystallize. "The way I'd do it would be to form a faculty committee – heavy on the sciences - to conduct a University-wide review of all units. Then QFM data would identify targets for action."

Bahls brightened. "I knew this group could help me focus on the OC. Now, how's about the three of you putting some language around Professor Berland's QFM approach?"

"OK, but just remember to keep my College out of it," Hank said.

"I'd be happy to work with Professor Berland on the QFM angle," Rich beamed at Felicity. "After all, we were the ones who came up with that idea."

"Great!" Bahls said. "Get back to me as soon as possible. Oh Professor Berland, please stay a moment so I can review some of my suggestions as to who should be on the faculty team."

Hank and Rich were excused. On their way out of Conant Hall, they reviewed the results of the meeting.

"I think we've been rolled!" Hank said. "All Mike wanted from us is help to close OC."

"More than that I bet," Rich grumbled. "He's really got Research I on his mind. Another thing that bothers me is that he's putting you and me at the margin of this effort. And what about that 'Professor Berland' thing?"

"Wondered if you caught that," Hank observed. "I, for one, am not comfortable with Mike and Felicity having their heads together. She's showing a bit more political savvy than I like."

Rich was dismayed to hear his most-feared emotion expressed in so few words. He had to take every opportunity to keep her in his personal political nest. Now, the only way that would be possible is to insert himself in the President's agenda.

It wasn't all that hard. Felicity took every opportunity to consult with Rich and Hank. She also made sure that Rich had a significant measure of what he came to view as 'quality time'; QFM time that included intense interaction with Felicity.

Events moved speedily to the desired conclusion. The Open College was 'discontinued' not 'closed'. The strong support of the sciences effectively silenced faculty opposition; those who disagreed with the closure were careful not to be too visible. It was clear that QFM could strike at will!

Rich marveled at the power of the quantitative approach to university management. His sessions with Felicity converted him from one who merely spoke the language of quality to an advocate of QFM. He was surfing the wave of Presidential power!

However, he was conscious of a loss of balance when Hank confided in him in mid winter.

The Associate Dean's phone rang early one morning. "Rich, this is Hank. Can you come over for a moment?"

"Sure. On my way."

Hank was seated at the Dean's conference table, absently shuffling a sheaf of papers.

"Say! This looks serious," Rich observed.

"I guess so. Better sit down."

Rich sat and Hank arranged papers into a neat pile. "It's both good news and bad news. First, the bad news; I can't handle both the College and the Center. There's too much administration involved and some of our grants are not being properly managed."

"I'd agree that's bad news," Rich said. "So what's the good news?"

Hank cleared his throat. "I'd like for you to take on the Center full time. That means that you'd have to give up being Associate Dean."

Give up! "But," Rich protested, "that's not very good news! It would take me out of QFM and . . .," He paused, alarmed at the consequences. Fewer Presidential huddles! Less time with Felicity!

"I can see that this isn't totally good news. I was afraid that you might not like the idea. So let me see if I can help you see the bright side. You'd have your hands on real money for a change. That gives you the opportunity to reward people here and cement connections to the national research community. So far, you've been at the periphery of the money flow. Believe me, it can give you leverage that will make you powerful as well as invulnerable in the University."

Rich considered these inducements. "Put that way, I can see the good news side. I guess I'd go along with your proposal if you could give me an example of how the change might work."

"Been thinking about that. There's a new federal initiative directed at the quality of life of handicapped individuals. If I were in charge of the Center, I'd go for this one."

Rich folded his arms across his chest. "Suppose you tell me just how I could take this on. I have no experience with that sort of research."

"Oh, but you do. Take your work on QFM. There you took a problem that was mostly talk and put some numbers on it. Seems to me that you could repeat that on quality of life."

"Well now," Rich was interested. "You mean take a sample of handicapped people and have experts rate the quality of their lives. Then look at,' Rich paused, "I mean, look for . . . numbers to describe . . . might work."

"I know it would," Hank slid his bundle of papers across the table. "I've done some preliminary grant writing that you can use to develop the proposal. All you need to do is describe the QFM methodology and put some numbers on the project. What say?"

Rich leafed through Hanks papers. The quality of life issue was outlined with references to policy, practice, and related research. "Looks quite complete and I see your point. Yes, I could spin this into a research proposal."

"So give it a try. You can count on me to help position the Center at the front of the quality of life movement."

Hank could indeed be 'counted on'. Rich moved into a spacious new office in the Tofte Center where he completed the Quality of Life proposal. With Hank's help, the proposal was passed through federal funding channels. As the money flowed into the Center, Rich discovered that control over money was even more rewarding than political manipulation. He foresaw a new dimension to life at Midwest. Felicity, too, was impressed at the use to which her methodology was put. Quality now described the life of Professor-Director Jessen.

Nevertheless, University politics was ever-present and Rich was constantly drawn into its web. In the spring of the President's first year, Rich was at his Center desk . . .

Now who? Rich pressed the blinking button on his desk phone. "Hello. Dr. Jessen speaking."

"Hi Rich! This is Carl Mertens. Remember me?"

"Of course! It's been a long time since we spoke. How're things with you?"

"That's why I'm calling. I'd like to buy you a drink at Tubby's. We have a lot to talk about."

"Why . . . sure," Rich said hesitatingly. "How's about . . ." he consulted his PDA calendar, " I'm open this afternoon, say around 5 at Tubby's. That work for you?"

"Absolutely! See you there."

Rich held the phone, open line signal in his ear. *What's that all about?* He hadn't talked with Mertens for several months. "Can't imagine what's up with Carl," he muttered as he hung up the phone.

At five o'clock, Rich was seated in a back corner booth at Tubby's, a glass of the house red in hand. Mertens breezed in along with the first sip.

"Rich! Good to see you!" Mertens slid into the opposite bench, held up two fingers at a waitress and folded his hands on the table. "Thanks for making time for me. I know how busy you must be."

Rich shook his head. "You can say that again. Why President Bahls comes up with a new idea that I've got to . . ."

Mertens interrupted. "Exactly what I want to talk about. When old Mike closed the Open College, it was a wake-up call for many of us. We finally realized that this guy is plenty dangerous and we need to look to our powder!"

Rich smiled at the metaphor. "Isn't that kind of strong? After all, Bahls is just trying to make the University run more smoothly. Don't you agree that QFM is working?"

"Tell me," Mertens twirled his wineglass, then looked at Rich, "wasn't that your idea?"

"Well . . . yes," Rich said deprecatingly. "QFM seemed to me to connect academics to Central and . . ."

"Connect!" Mertens snorted. "I'll say! Just ask the Open College faculty how they feel about that 'connection'."

"Sure," Rich agreed. "But OC just wasn't efficient; it was the lowest of all colleges on QFM measures."

"That's just it! Can't you see? Bahls is picking off the University units with the lowest performance. And, he's reaching into the colleges to force them to prune departments."

"You're right about that!" Rich exaulted. "QFM is really shaping up the University!"

Mertens studied Rich skeptically. "I suppose you have to say that. Anyway, what I'm about to tell you has to be way off the record. Do I have your word?"

"Absolutely! Fire away."

"Well, the Business School has decided to change its relationship to the University. It will no longer be connected financially, but will continue to offer courses and degrees through the U."

Rich was stunned! "Wait a minute!" he exploded. "Are you sure? Never heard of such a thing!"

"I knew I'd get your attention. We've had enough of Central's meddling in our programs. When Bahls closed our overseas MBA, faculty and students were ready to march on Conant Hall. Well, we found out that there's a growing movement across higher education for law schools and business schools to go their own way."

"But . . . but . . .," Rich made a motor-like protest, "you can't . . . where'll you get the money to . . .?"

"We've figured that we can raise corporate money along with alumni giving to replace University funding. This past year, the U only provided about fifteen percent of our operating money. We can easily double that on our own. There's one more thing. I've been watching the ways the Med School uses the Legacy Fund and I know that we can repeat their success with our alumni – to say nothing of the businesses that will give us financial support."

Rich followed Mertens' argument to its conclusion. There was probably more money in business than the medical school could access! And Mertens had plans to tap into that reservoir. "I see your point," he said. "I imagine you're on to something, but have you thought what this might do to the University?"

Mertens swirled the wine in his glass, then looked up at Rich. "That's why I'm talking to you. Something has to be done to focus the President on what's really happening to this University. He's only been in charge for six months and he's already made enough enemies to last for his whole presidency. If he's going to survive, he must lead the U in a positive direction."

Enemies! Survive! Rich was incredulous! "Are you serious? And won't your plan for the Business School just make things worse?"

"Yes, it will – unless the President backs off QFM."

"That's impossible!" Rich barked. "He's tied his presidency to QFM. Remember what he said in his inaugural speech?"

Mertens nodded. "I've studied the transcript of his speech and it seems to me that he could easily shift his focus from QFM to Baldrige. That way, he'd stay on the quality issue while, at the same time, turning quality into something positive for the U."

"You may have something there," Rich considered. "Baldrige would give the President something to use, you know, to solicit faculty support. There's plenty of room for maneuver in Baldrige."

"That's what we concluded. The President could engage in University-wide strategic planning to create opportunities for colleges and professional schools to invent a new future. Then, the Business School could come to the table with our proposal."

So that's it! Mertens had come to Tubby's with more than the Business School plan. He was offering Rich the opportunity to shape Bahls' presidency in what 'biz-speak' would call a 'win-win' direction. Rich assumed a tone reflective of his considerable academic wisdom. "Carl, you've convinced me that this is a problem requiring careful study. Let me think about it."

Mertens drank the last of his wine and stood to leave. "Don't take too long," he warned.

Rich remained seated, sipping at his half-full glass, eyes boring into the depths of the wine. Images of Felicity advocating Baldrige. He could almost hear her say, 'But it's our bullshit!' Yes! It was theirs to shovel.

381

CHAPTER TWENTY-ONE

Forty-Love

"...if the player who is serving has a score of 40-love, the player has a triple game point... as the player has three consecutive chances to win the game."

And shovel they did. It proved to be easy for Rich to convince Felicity that Baldrige should be the signature venture of the Bahls Presidency. When the two brought Bahls into the conversation there was instant agreement. Actually, it was Felicity who convinced Mike to make Baldrige the watchword for all presidential activity. Rich was impressed with her ability to construct a Presidential agenda on what was clearly a weak foundation; it was, as Carl Mertens predicted, the Business School proposal that 'made the sale'.

As spring turned into summer, Felicity balanced Baldrige with an increasing involvement in tennis. Although the change interested Rich at first, he came to dread her invitations 'for a game' – and the embarrassing lessons that ensued. Athletic pursuits were of little interest to Rich, unless they led to connections with the powerful; any activity that involved physical exercise usually had little call on his time.

Nevertheless, tennis became for Rich, a necessary part of his life with Felicity. It was the only opportunity he had to view her as a lithe, sensual being. When she bent to retrieve a ball, he was transfixed by her silhouette; Rich felt a stirring of sexuality penetrated his scholarly reserve. These moments were, however, fleeting snapshots in the blur of lessons.

"C'mon Rich!" she would call. "You need to anticipate my shot, not wait to see where it's going. Here, let me show you." An easy lob: a lumbering lunge, flailing racquet, and the 'plop' of the ball striking the net. "Nonono!" Felicity admonished. "You aren't keeping your eyes on the ball! Try this! Just bounce the ball on the court and hit it when it's at its highest!"

Lessons like this were repeated, endlessly Rich thought, throughout the spring. Dollops of praise were laid on the struggling novice to shape his play. He was never good enough to satisfy Felicity. New dimensions were added to the game and the mystery of the serve was dissected.

By midsummer, Rich was able to engage his mentor in a passable game. Felicity was careful to limit her play so that Rich could win points and a game now and then. Even though he knew that she was holding back, he found that he enjoyed his occasional victories. He actually found himself using tennis terms in his interaction with his staff at the Center. "Let me lob one over to you. That's really out of bounds! We're facing match point here."

Rich's immersion in the world of tennis puzzled Hank Loras, who finally had to ask, "Say Rich, what's all this tennis stuff? I thought you'd given all that up for Lent."

"Just a way to get in shape," Rich patted his ever-leaner stomach. "You should take up the game. Do you good!"

"No way that I'm chasing balls when I can sit in the shade with a gin and tonic!"

They considered the two images. Sweltering heat beat on green asphalt. Cool shade appeared in the corner of a green lawn. Gatoraide took a distant second to gin.

Rich recalled these contrasts throughout a hot summer of tennis. Felicity was impervious to heat. She actually looked as cool as a gin and tonic! He cherished visions of a future life when Felicity would be his life-mate. Tennis was, he hoped, a step on the path toward this objective.

Rich was going through his usual office-closing ritual on a Friday in mid-September when Felicity looked in.

"Are you busy tomorrow Rich?" she asked.

"Nothing on my calendar," he beamed his anticipation.

"Great! Mike and Beth have invited us to The Mansion for a game of doubles. Doesn't that sound like fun!"

It didn't sound like fun to Rich. Instead several scenarios flashed across his mind. The Presidential setting would be a reminder of the meteoric rise of Bahls. Beth would flash looks of disapproval at the team of Felicity and Rich. And, Mike and Beth were seeded first in this doubles competition.

"I'm not sure that my tennis elbow has recovered sufficiently to stand the test of a full match. Why . . ."

"Oh, don't worry!" Felicity interrupted. "I can cover your weak side and we'll do fine!"

Rich couldn't resist her evident enthusiasm for the match. "Well. OK . . . I guess."

"That's great," she enthused. "We're supposed to join the Bahls for a drink at the Mansion around eleven. Then we'll play a set or two on their court. Doesn't that sound fantastic?"

It did indeed. Worse than Rich had imagined. *Lunch! The Mansion! A set or two! Shit!* "Why, that's . . . wonderful . . .," he grumbled.

There was no sleep for Rich that night. He played endless games of tennis against a grinning Mike. Beth sat on the judges chair at the net and called Rich for one fault after another. Felicity sat dejectedly in the spectator's seats, her expression becoming increasingly gloomy with his every mistake.

Rich's television timer followed the metronome of dream tennis. To and fro throughout the night.

"Good Morning America!" The television blared. Rich bolted upright in bed. *What the hell?* It wasn't a good morning for Rich. Tired and stiff from the virtual tennis he played during the night, he creaked his way out of bed and loosened his muscles in a hot shower. Somewhat recovered, he began to visualize various probable scenarios for the upcoming tournament.

The most appealing possibility was a leisurely volleying on a shady court. Plenty of cooling drinks were provided by the President's waiters – who applauded the graceful strokes of Professor Jessen. What an appealing setting for the life he and Felicity would lead!

Rich actually enjoyed dressing in his tennis costume. White shorts terminated six inches above athletic socks (striped in University colors). New white shoes added sparkle to the lower half of Professor Jessen. The upper half was sheathed in a varsity tennis shirt, accented by a colorful sweater – arms tied across his chest. He was ready!

This satisfactory image persisted until Felicity drove into Rich's driveway in her Corvette with the top down. Dark hair was lightly ruffled in the winds of passage and her fantastic shoulders gleamed, accented by her golden sleeveless blouse. She was magnificent!

"Hi Rich! Hop in!" Felicity reached over and opened the passenger side door. "Say! You look like a real tennis pro!"

He slipped his tennis racquet behind the seat and tentatively raised a foot as if to step into the Corvette. It was too low! Rich changed his approach and began to shape his body to match the seating of the car. Muscles couldn't cooperate and he felt an electric twinge in his lower back.

"Uhhh!" he cried. "Can't bend that way!"

"What's the matter, Rich. Are you OK?"

". . . just . . . a little muscle spasm. I'll . . .," Rich swiveled and slid, backside first, into the car, an old man's way of entering an automobile. His sweater caught on the doorframe, jerking his head painfully – requiring a major sartorial adjustment. The tennis image was simply too complex for Rich.

"All set?" Felicity asked in a solicitous tone.

"I guess . . . let's go."

The Corvette lurched backward into the street. Felicity slammed the car into first gear and accelerated. Rich's head snapped back against the seat.

"Hey! Easy does it!" he blurted.

Felicity laughed - a vision in designer sunglasses. "Gotta hurry! Can't be late for the President!" They raced down the street, wind roaring in Rich's ears. Felicity treated him to wrenching corners and competitive freeway driving on their way to The Mansion.

By the time Felicity jerked to a stop in Bahls' drive, Rich was soaked in perspiration as if he had just completed a tennis match. "Wheeew," he puffed. "That was some trip! You always drive like that?"

"Sure! There's no other way. Corvettes don't like to be pampered!" She glided out of the car and swung her hair into place. "C'mon Rich! Now the real fun begins!"

Rich struggled out of the car and slowly straightened, one hand on the shooting pain in his back. Ramrod straight, he gingerly reached for his tennis racquet and sweater. He was no longer the sophisticated player. His wrinkled clothes and shuffling gait marked him as a tennis wannabe.

Bahls was at the door of the Mansion. "Hi Felicity! Hello Rich! Welcome to the tennis match!" Mike's clothes and athletic frame spoke of tennis prowess. When taken together with the background of Prairie Lodge, Bahls was the model advertisers sought.

Felicity ran up the walk and fell into the welcoming embrace of Bahls. It seemed to Rich that the encounter was a little too friendly and lasted a bit too long. When they parted, Bahls arm continued to circle Felicity's waist – the complete advertisement.

"Rich!" Bahls waved. "Come round the house. Beth's got the drinks poured!"

Rich stumbled after the pair, his eyes on Felicity's hips. The undulating motion seemed to be guided by Bahls' hand.

At the rear of the Mansion, Beth was seated at a glass-topped table where a central umbrella protected a frosted pitcher. "Hello Rich . . . and . . . Felicity. Please find a chair and let me pour you a refresher before the big game."

Margaritas were handed around and Bahls offered a toast. "Here's to friends and frolic!"

They drank in agreement and exchanged opinions and observations concerning University life.

"So how's life in the new Mansion Beth?" Rich asked.

She scowled. "I have to say that I liked our old place. This seems artificial to me."

"Oh! I'm surprised to hear that!" Felicity said. "Why this place is perfect! Where else would we have a setting like this?" She waved a hand at a velvet lawn, swimming pool and tennis court.

"Yes," Beth said. "It has all the trappings of the good life, but it can come up empty at times."

"Just takes getting used to," Mike pronounced. "I'm starting to feel at home."

"It's just lovely!" Felicity gushed. "It's the kind of place we faculty members dream about!"

Rich could agree. The Mansion was exactly the setting where he would like to spend the rest of his life – with Felicity.

"Well, we better get the game under way," Mike stood. "Let's warm up with a doubles match. Beth and I will take on our guests."

Rich levered himself out of his chair and bent to retrieve his racquet. Another shooting pain lanced into his back. *I'm not ready for this!* He limped after the others – into a glaring sun – onto a baking asphalt court.

"How's about a few warm-ups?" Beth asked.

"Good idea," Mike replied. "Let's pair off. You and I will take on Rich and Felicity. OK everyone?"

Felicity nodded, arms stretched overhead as she swiveled her upper body. Rich simply mumbled agreement.

Lobs and strokes began and continued for several minutes before Mike called a halt.

"What's it to be? Couple games? Full tournament?"

Beth answered. "Let's make it one game. It's so hot!"

"Good idea," added Rich.

The game began with Beth serving to Rich. They were well-matched, each served successfully, but lost points when Felicity and Mike intervened with sharp exchanges. A few more serves and Rich was unable to continue.

"Sorry. I can't go on. Must have pulled a muscle in my back."

"Oh! Poor Rich!" Felicity patted him on the shoulder. "Why don't you take a breather? You'll feel better sitting in the shade."

"Yes Rich," Beth agreed. "Come with me and we'll share a cool drink." She took his elbow and led him to the shaded table.

"Sorry to spoil the game," Rich called over his shoulder.

"Oh, don't worry!" Felicity replied. "The two of us can wind this up, right Mike?"

Bahls wiped the sweat from his forehead and squinted into the sun. "Sure . . . I guess so. Whose serve?"

"Yours," Felicity said, taking the defensive position.

The rhythmic 'thwock' – 'thwock' gave Rich a mental picture of the contest he was leaving behind. When Beth had him seated in relative comfort, drink in hand, he was able to focus on the match. At first, it was merely a blur of action; later he could identify the different styles. Bahls was a power player who relied on his serve. Felicity was a masterful position player whose strokes kept Mike moving all over the court.

"Pretty interesting game," Beth said. "Wonder how it'll turn out, you know how Mike hates to lose."

I hope the bastard is whipped! "Umm . . . yes, I suppose you're right." He sipped his margarita, relaxing in the contrast of shaded comfort vs hectic heat.

"Say! She's playing with him!" Beth exclaimed. "Watch how she's got him running from one side of the court to the other!"

Rich watched for two sets. The first was taken by Bahls with a cannonball serve, the second by Felicity with cleverly placed shots. "Wonder what the score is?"

"I think it's forty-love," Beth observed. "Game point's coming up now."

Bahls stood, toe on the service line – bent – bounced the ball and tossed it high in the air. He rose to his full height and sent a bullet that nearly grazed the net.

"She'll never . . .," Rich stated. But he was wrong. Felicity took the missal with a two-handed stroke that whipped over the net. Bahls was ready. However his return was a shade weaker than his serve. Felicity pounced and, at the last moment, popped a sky-high lob that seemed to baffle Bahls.

The lob caught Bahls running toward the net. An abrupt reverse of direction – right foot caught the left – and he crumpled to the asphalt. He lay in a fetal position, clutching his knee.

"Ohhh . . . my knee . . . I think I've . . ."

Beth stood and started toward the court, then stopped. She wasn't needed.

Felicity sped around the net and kneeled over Bahls. "Mike! Are you OK? I'm so sorry!" She mopped his forehead and smoothed his hair. "Where does it hurt?"

"Not your fault . . . clumsy . . . caught my foot . . . twisted my knee . . . God! It hurts like hell!"

Rich watched Felicity help Bahls stand – right leg hanging with knee bent – right arm over Felicity's shoulder. They tried to move, but Felicity couldn't support his weight.

Now Beth was needed. "Beth! Can you help? We need to get him out of the sun!"

The threesome made their way slowly to the table and Mike eased himself into a chair next to Rich. "Hell of a note ain't it! Two old crocks sidelined by a tennis match! Hard to believe!"

"Don't be so hard on yourself!' Felicity advised. "What you need is an ice pack on that knee. Do you have something that would do the job Beth?"

It was clear to Rich that Felicity was in charge. Beth ran across the lawn and disappeared into the house.

For the balance of the afternoon, Bahls was the center of attention. Each woman tried to outdo the other in providing comfort and condolence. Rich was a bystander whose advice was ignored. In fact, he was one of the 'walking wounded' – his old metaphor come to life.

Rich's attempts at conversation became ever more plaintive, a voice that begged for attention.

"Oh Rich!" Felicity said in exasperation. "Stop complaining! Get in the car and I'll run you home!"

He was stunned! Ordered around like a kid! *What does she think I am? A dog?* Rich hung his head in an approved obedience school manner and slunk to the Corvette. There was no help for this invalid. Painful grunts and stoic effort placed him in his seat, ready to return to his kennel.

During their return trip, Felicity was preoccupied with Mike's injury. Rich could hear her murmuring over road noise. "Hope it's not too serious!" "Wonder if Beth knows what to do?" "How will he get to the office?" All of his attempts at conversation were ignored.

At the end of the trip, Felicity pulled up to the curb in front of Rich's house. No driveway delivery this time! The Corvette's engine was left running as Felicity waited for Rich to exit. He was on his own!

He continued to be on his own for the next several weeks. Felicity was remarkably absent from Blewett Hall. Rich would make several trips past her office on Fourth Blewett each day. Her door remained closed.

Rich's weekends were similarly empty. Each Saturday he dressed for tennis: white slacks, cotton sweater and appropriate footgear. The phone never rang, as it had all spring. He was disappointed, and mystified. Where was she? He had always respected her privacy by not calling her, but this was too much!

Eventually, on a Saturday in late summer, Rich decided to look for her. He drove past her house. The garage door was open and her Corvette gone. *Tennis courts!* He wheeled the Mercedes to the University courts. There was no trace of Felicity among those at play. Where was she? *Blewett Hall?*

He flashed his key card at the gate for the underground parking ramp at Blewett. The doors opened and he scanned the few cars ahead. There it was! The Corvette! She was in her office! Rich fumbled at the handle of the car door and swung out, anticipation driving his movements. His usual fastidiousness was forgotten as he failed to lock the Mercedes and to give the car its customary caresses.

Rich raced up the five flights of stairs from the basement parking lot to Fourth Blewett - no back pains now. At the top of his climb, he stopped, out of breath, lightly sweating. There! He could see a light in Felicity's office and hear her radio tuned to the University classical music station. He crept along the hall and peered into her office.

Felicity was kneeling on the floor, sorting books from a lower shelf into a cardboard box. He opened his mouth as if to announce himself, but the outlines of her body prevented speech. This was the woman he wanted as his companion! Sexuality actually penetrated Rich's political persona – he sweated profusely.

The vision continued its movements, oblivious to Rich's presence. He watched for a half-minute, then backed quietly into the hallway. After another half-minute, he knocked on the wall next to the open door.

"Hello Felicity. You in there?" He walked in.

She remained kneeling. "Oh! Hi Rich! You gave me a start! I thought there was nobody else in Blewett!"

"Sorry," he apologized. "I was . . ." *Doing what?* ". . . just going to pick up some papers from my old office and I thought I heard noises up here."

"I'm so glad you found me!" Felicity beamed. "I've been waiting to tell you the good news! Guess what's happened!"

"I can't imagine."

"President Bahls wants me to take charge of his Baldrige project. I'm to be his Special Assistant! Isn't that just grand!" She jumped to her feet and embraced Rich. "And, it's all possible because of you!" He received a brush-kiss of gratitude.

The doorway seemed to press in on him. *Special Assistant! What about . . ?* The thought forced its way into speech. "But . . . what about the Center? And all our research?"

"I know. I know," she gazed at him sympathetically. "I won't actually be leaving my appointment. Mike . . . I mean President Bahls has assured me that I'll be able to continue to work with you and Hank. I'm so excited!"

Her excitement was obvious. She was flushed and agitated. "Just look at this mess! I have to get it all together for a move to your old office in Conant Hall. By Monday! Here Rich, take this box down to my car. You can use the elevator." Felicity thrust a heavy box of books into his arms and returned to her work.

Here Rich! That dog order again! The anger quickly passed. It was impossible for Rich to do any other than admire his love object. He staggered to the Blewett Hall elevator with his burden.

"Just a minute!" Felicity called. "You'll need to key to the 'Vette. Here!" She tossed a ring of keys that fell at Rich's feet. "The red one's for the trunk!"

He held the box of books against the wall with one hand while the other groped for the keys. An impossible balancing act; the box tipped and books cascaded across the hallway. Fortunately, Felicity didn't see his clumsiness and he was alone in recovery. When the box was refilled, he was able to punch the elevator call button with an extended finger. He entered and his spirits sank along with the elevator.

Inside the garage, Felicity's key popped the trunk of the 'Vette. Rich tucked the box of books on the edge of the trunk. Two gym bags nearly filled the space and he balanced the box with one hand while the other shifted the bags. *Two bags?* There was a name tag on the larger bag; "Michael Bahls – University City". *Mike's bag! What??* He slid the books into the trunk and zipped open Mike's bag. *Overnight stuff! What's she doing?* Rich consoled himself. "Hauling Mike's clothes for him. Guess his knee's still giving him trouble." He zipped the bag and slammed the trunk.

The ride up in the elevator didn't lift his spirits. When he exited at Fourth Blewett, he decided that he'd had enough of office moving. Rich stood in Felicity's door and handed her the keys. "Well, gotta be going. Hope the move goes OK."

"Huh? Sure . . . thanks," she took the keys.

Their eyes met for only a short moment. Then Felicity tossed the keys on her desk and resumed sorting books.

Rich remained in the doorway for a half-minute; looking at a vision that seemed to be fading.

That image remained with him for the balance of the weekend. He wandered aimlessly around his house where other well-crafted images of Felicity seemed also to fade. For the first time in his life, he felt lonely; actually in need of another person.

On Monday, he slept late and arrived at his office just before noon. There was a voice mail message from Hank Loras.

'Rich. This is Hank. Give me a call as soon as you get in.'

He picked up the receiver and punched in the Dean's private number.

"This is Hank. That you Rich?"

"Yes. What's on your mind?"

"You and I need to talk about Felicity's move. Can I come over?"

About Felicity! "Sure. Anytime."

The line went dead as Hank hung up. Two minutes later he came into Rich's office and closed the door.

"You know about Felicity?" Hank asked.

"Yes. I ran into her on Saturday. She was moving her office. Quite a surprise."

"You can say that again. When Mike called me on Friday, I couldn't believe what he said. Moving her to his office put a spoke in the wheels of the Center. I let him know how we'd be hurting without her help. Guess what he said."

"Can't imagine. Probably something like 'you'll manage somehow'."

"Worse than that!" Loras exclaimed. "He's bringing back your old grad student – Winslow Pyke!"

Pyke! That sonofabitch! "But . . . you don't have to take him. We can set up a search . . ."

395

"Nothing doing!" Loras barked. "Bahls is using the same dodge we used to get Mike here in the first place. A Presidential appointment! And that ain't all. Pyke's built himself a hell of record in DC – got a three-pound vita – and connections to the money spigot! With Mike's help, he'll probably take over the Center!"

Rich sank back in his chair. *First Felicity! Then Pyke!* "But . . . can't we count on Mike to make this work for us?"

Loras sank into a chair across from Rich. "Don't hardly think so. I'm beginning to think that he's off on a whole new agenda. The only thing going for us is that Pyke can't get here 'til early next year. Gives us some time to come up with a plan."

They sat for several minutes, waiting for the ignition of a lightbulb of plan.

Rich flipped though several mental scenarios. *Set a new direction for the Center? Shut it down? Just be a professor?* These ideas deepened his growing depression. There seemed to be no way to recover the life – and power – he had constructed.

Loras stood and sighed. "I can see by watching your face that you don't have any solutions to our problems at the moment. Neither do I, so let's continue to work on this. All we need to do is to make sure that we have something in the works by the time Pyke arrives."

"OK by me," Rich grunted. "I'm in no shape right now to think clearly."

They continued to explore options throughout the fall semester, with no concrete result. Loras and Rich were able to land two small grants without Bahls' help, but they neither strengthened the Center nor advanced its reputation. It became clear that Bahls was the key to their future success.

Loras and Rich met in Rich's office in early December.

"I'm not giving up yet," Loras announced. "The way I see it now is that we should lay in the weeds and see what Pyke brings. I'll bet he has a line on some federal bucks. Maybe we can get a piece of the pie. What say?"

"I suppose you're right," Rich mumbled. "Can't say as I have any better strategy."

They left it at that. And it fell to Rich to welcome Pyke when the latter appeared at Rich's office door in early January.

"Hi Prof!" Pyke shouted. "Man! Am I glad to be back! It'll be great working with you again! You can't imagine what a favor you did me when you greased the skids for me to slide to DC! I've made some unbelievable connections that'll put the Center in the number one slot for policy studies!"

Unbelievable was the word! How could this little shit usurp his role as the academic godfather! Rich was unable to respond to Pyke. Instead, he stood and reached out for a handshake.

"Good to have you back Winslow. Have you made arrangements for a place to live?"

"Not yet. I think I'll look up some old friends and see what's possible," Pyke leered.

Not Felicity again! This guy was not only an academic competitor, he was obviously planning on cutting in on Felicity!

Rich changed the subject. "Come! Let me show you an office we have in mind. It's on Fourth Blewett."

They walked toward the elevator.

"Isn't that where Professor Berland has her space?"

"Yes, that was the case. However, she has moved to Conant Hall. It looks as if her appointment as Special Assistant to the President is permanent."

"I'm sorry to hear that," Pyke's face was a caricature of tragedy. "I was looking forward to working with her."

More likely hiting on her! "You can probably find her in the President's office, but she's been very busy lately."

In the months ahead, Pyke tried to re-establish himself with Felicity – with no success. She was, as Rich had expected, 'busy with the President's agenda'.

During Spring Break, Rich discovered a critical element in 'the President's agenda'. One Friday afternoon, he received a call from Beth Bahls.

"Rich? This is Beth. I'd like to talk with you as soon as possible. Might you be free for dinner this evening? Mike is away and our cook can do for two as well as one."

This was a surprise! Beth hadn't spoken with him since the tennis fiasco last summer. "Why. . . Beth . . . good to hear from you. There's nothing much on my calendar and I'd be happy to join you. What time would work?"

"Good! Let's say seven o'clock. OK?"

"It's a deal." Rich hung up. *I wonder what that means?* Beth was never one to confide in others. The social conventions of the University were the only things that brought them together.

Dinner was very pleasant. Beth was the perfect Presidential hostess and the cook at the Mansion was one of the best in University City. When they had finished dessert, Beth took Rich's arm and led him into the adjoining study where a coffee service was ready. When they were seated and coffee poured, Beth put down her cup and studied Rich for a moment.

"Rich," she began, "you and I, we have a problem."

"I can't imagine what that could be," he said.

"It's Mike and Felicity. Haven't you noticed how close they are?"

"Well sure, but they have to work together. Probably no more than that," he reasoned unconvincingly.

"I'm sure there's more to it," Beth stated. "They work late. Why Mike is frequently is away most of the night and there's often a perfume odor on his clothes."

"He was always fond of after shave," Rich observed.

"Rich! Please listen!" Beth waved a finger. "They travel together. In fact, both Felicity and Mike are attending the higher education research conference in San Francisco this weekend!"

"Don't jump to conclusions, Beth! That's a convention they both need to be at. Why . . ."

"Rich Jessen! I'd say that you have your head up your ass! These two are having an affair. It's my husband and the woman you'd like to have for a wife. Can you get that through your brain?"

Affair! His Felicity! And Mike! He stared at Beth. "Are . . . you sure . . .?" he mumbled.

"Damn right!" Beth was red with anger. "That bitch has stolen Mike. Why, he can't even hold a conversation with me. His mind's on her! What I want to know is; what are you and I going to do about it?"

Mike's gym bag! The tennis match! Special Presidential Assistant! The pieces of a horrible puzzle snapped together. *Traveling together!* He ruminated on this unpleasant cud.

"Well!" Beth exclaimed. "That's better. I can see that I've gotten through to you. Now, back to my question. What are we going to do about it?"

This was a question much like the one posed by Hank Loras. He was confronted with a problem which no familiar solution could address. "I . . . don't . . . know," he stammered.

"I was afraid of that!" Beth said, her hands gripping the arms of her chair. "Let me tell you what I'm going to do. As of tomorrow, I'm moving out of this place! Mike and the bitch can have the run of the Mansion. And he can deal with my lawyer!"

Rich was stunned. "Mike won't like that! That kind of situation will be all over City papers!"

"I surely hope so!" Beth stood. "Maybe that will help him come to his senses! Imagine, a sixty-year old man chasing after a thirty-something! Makes me sick!"

The sickness was catching. Rich felt an emptiness in his stomach – a void that replaced a dwindling reservoir of delusion. Was all this really true? He slouched in his chair.

Beth walked over and put a hand on his shoulder. "You really didn't know, did you? I'm sorry to have broken the news this way, but you'll have to come to terms with the fact that your woman isn't yours anymore."

Rich bowed his head. "Why? Why?" There were tears in the corners of his eyes. This was a new and powerful emotion for the confident Professor.

"There is no 'why'," Beth said. "Youth and beauty are just too much for a man like Mike. Remember what I said when I came to Midwest? I warned you about his ambition. He always gets what he wants. And now he wants Felicity."

Rich stood and they walked together toward the door of Edgewood – an old man and an angry woman.

CHAPTER TWENTY-TWO

Big Cigars

"We want to build a university of which the football team can be proud." (George Cross: President, University of Oklahoma)

The passing of the spring term was marked by the rituals of academic life that made it possible for Rich to maintain a precarious emotional balance. There were, however, instances when he was reminded of Beth's warnings. At his shaving mirror, he caught himself looking to see if his head was really on his shoulders and not where Beth said it was. Class meetings, for the few that he attended, were taken up by student reports and lackluster discussions. For the most part, he thought only of Felicity – and Mike!

One day, toward the end of April, Rich received a call from the President's secretary.

"Professor Jessen? This is President Bahls' secretary. He's asked me to call you to see if you can come to his office later today. Would that be possible?"

"Why. . . ?" *Now what?* Rich's surprise was mixed with anger. "I guess so. When?"

"Let's see," there was a calendar-checking pause. "How about three o'clock?"

"Well . . . OK." Rich hung up the phone and swiveled his chair to look out an office window. A newly-leaved branch waved against the glass, a reminder of how the year had passed. It was the first time in months that Rich had heard from Mike. The daily exchanges had diminished, first to weekly, then monthly. Conspiracy had morphed into bureaucratic distance.

At two-thirty, Rich closed his office and made his way across the Quad toward the Conant Hall. The Greek Captain that navigated Bahls' accession to the Presidency was now a simple sailor. The ships bearing federal loot were unloaded at other ports in the University and Rich received only a seaman's share of the spoils. He no longer needed the Greek Sailor's Cap for this venture to Conant Hall.

The climb up the outside steps of Conant Hall reminded Rich of his trip to Athens years ago. In a similar manner, he huffed his way upward to this Midwest Acropolis. Brass-studded double doors responded as Rich tugged at the handles. The doors were now power-assisted and swung open with an immediate force that nearly overbalanced him. As he stumbled in, the doors closed, propelling him into a long hallway, floored with newly-laid marble slabs, leading between administrative offices, toward huge glass doors at the far end.

Halfway down the hall, where the University crest was once inlaid in the floor, there was a new logo. Rich stopped, transfixed by a giant tornado-like figure that seemed to be sweeping down a football field. He stooped to read the slogan, 'Blow 'em away!'

Rich straightened. *MiGod!* His eyes swivelled to photos on the walls of the corridor. Grant Wood and Thomas Hart Benton were gone. Instead, lighted pictures portrayed University athletes in dramatic poses – dominating unfortunate opponents. He walked from picture to picture, overwhelmed by the drama of sport.

"How do you like it?" Felicity appeared in the doorway of an office near the glass doors. "I call it Tornado Alley. It's my idea of a new image for the U."

"Is all this," he waved a hand, "really your doing?"

"You bet!" Felicity took his arm and walked him along the far wall. "See! Here's the touchdown that beat Missouri Central last fall! And, how's about that shot of Will-I-Am Brown? That was taken at the NIT Quarter Finals."

Rich was speechless, overcome by the gross athleticism on display - and by a changed Felicity. The serious scholar had become a cheerleader! Was this what association with Bahls had done to her?

"Is this . . ." he struggled for words, "the direction that Mike wants to take the University? I thought he was going for Research One."

"Oh!" she laughed. "President Bahls has a new vision for the U. He wants it to be number one in everything. He wants to start by driving it to first place in athletics. Isn't it exciting?"

It was appalling! Academics had given way to athletics and Research One had taken second place to Conference Champion.

"I guess . . .," Rich mumbled as they turned to face the glass doors at the far end of Tornado Alley. There, a grinning Bahls beckoned to them.

"Hang on to your hat! Don't let the Tornado tip you over!" he cackled. "C'mon in Rich. Good to see you!"

Bahls held one door open. As Rich approached, he noticed that each door had a Tornado cartoon etched in the glass. The faces on the cartoons were drawn to strike fear into Tornado opponents.

"Where did you get these guys?" Rich asked. "They look like a version of the old Plymouth Duster figures."

"Exactly!" Bahls crowed. "Felicity got the idea and negotiated the use of the trademark with Chrysler. They were plenty happy to put their label on a winner!"

Felicity smiled demurely as she traced one of the figures with her fingers. "Aren't they cute!"

So far as Rich was concerned, they were more weird than cute. He nodded a reluctant endorsement.

"Here!" Bahls took Rich's arm. "I have something to show you!" He steered Rich through the glass doors to another set of double doors – these elegantly molded in shining oak. Inside, a long table and plush chairs told of high policy - the home of the University Trustees.

"Felicity has probably told you of our plans concerning University athletics. Right?"

"Umm . . . yes . . . she showed me around Tornado Alley. Most impressive."

"That's just the beginning!" Bahls boasted. "I called an audible at the spring meeting and convinced the Trustees that we need to develop an athletic complex that's second to none! Let me show you what we have in mind." He stepped to the first of several architectural drawings posted on the conference room walls.

"This perspective shows how the U will look when the project is completed. We're going to use the old Arboretum grounds. We'll be removing the trees and filling in the ponds this spring. That'll give us nearly forty acres to work with!"

Rich had never been interested in the Arboretum, however, he often walked through the shady wilderness to escape from the boredom of Blewett Hall. So far as the architects were concerned, only a few of the larger trees would survive Bahls' plan. There were curving drives that connected several huge arenas labeled: 'Basketball', 'Football', 'Tennis', 'Swimming', 'Hockey'.

"What this about 'Hockey'?" Rich asked. "We don't have a team, do we?"

"Not yet," Felicity said. "It sounds like a Hail Mary Pass, but Mike. . . I mean President Bahls is convinced that hockey is the coming sport. Why, even girls are competing at the collegiate level!"

"So what's first in line?" Rich asked.

Bahls stepped to the next drawing. "Here! It's Tornado Stadium! Seats sixty thousand! Twelve skyboxes! Ain't she a beaut!"

"Sixty thousand!' Rich look at Bahls. "Why that's about double our enrollment! Who'll fill those seats?"

"When we have a NFL coach who can recruit top-flight players the fans will be knocking at the gates!"

Felicity's face shown at the word-picture Bahls was constructing.

Metaphors of sport permeated the conversational environment confusing Rich. He shook his head. "What's the point? Those coaches don't come cheap and it'll cost a bundle to build that thing!"

"Don't worry," Bahls patted Rich's shoulder. "When we've got a winner, the whole thing will come together. Here's the way it works. I've got the stadium paid for by Farmers State Bank. They were the winners when I asked for interest in naming rights. Then, the alumni came on board. Felicity calls them 'the Big Cigars'. They contributed about twenty million as a start on our Tornado Legacy."

"And that isn't all," Felicity chirped. "Why we've already been selling season tickets! On a lottery system!"

"What's that?" Rich looked puzzled. "Lottery?"

"We've made it appear that seats are scarce," Bahls explained. "The way it works is that we've sent out letters to all the alumni telling them to call in at a specific time when their lottery number is coming up. Then they actually bid for a chance at premium seats!"

"Isn't that a beaut!" Felicity said. "For the best seats, we've attached a Tornado Legacy gift requirement. Ten grand for a lifetime reservation! And even bigger bucks for access to one of the Cloud Boxes!"

"What's a Cloud Box?" Rich was inundated by the flood of marketing ploys.

"Oh, there are a dozen enclosed suites at the top level of the Stadium. They're likely to go for something like ten grand a year. It's already clear that corporations will bid against the super-rich for these seats. Isn't it wonderful!"

Rich was still skeptical. "Maybe it'll work, but what about the other buildings? Who's going to pay for them?"

Felicity beckoned to the next drawing. "Basketball is already in the net!" She laughed at yet another metaphor. "We've got an investor who's agreed to pay for the whole thing! You may have heard of Max McGinnis; you know, the all-American here about twenty years ago. He's made it big in Las Vegas."

"That's the guy!" Bahls exclaimed. "Last fall he came in and dropped a check on my desk. This time, he covered both the building and the operating endowment. He's the biggest Cigar yet!"

The tour continued. Naming rights for tennis would be going to a big sportswear manufacturer. Hockey was paid for by alumni whose nostalgia for the old outdoor rink opened their wallets. Rich was dazzled by the impossibly large sums of money; transfixed by Felicity's enthusiasm; awed by Mike's confidence.

"What's all this got to do with me?" Rich asked.

Bahls folded himself into a chair at the conference table. He indicated a seat for Rich. "What you see is a part of a bigger plan the Trustees have for the University. They want to make similar changes in academics to position the University for the 21st century. As a senior faculty member, you have a strong interest in their plan. Here's the basics," Bahls handed a slim folder to Rich. "Take a look at the bullets on page one. They summarize the new direction."

Rich opened the folder. Page one was titled 'Executive Summary':
- Strike a strategic balance between athletics and academics.
- Focus academics on science and medicine.
- Limit access to tenure.
- Increase the use of non-regular faculty.
- Market graduate programs through non-traditional delivery systems.

Rich closed the folder and looked up at Bahls. "This is all very interesting, but it doesn't answer my original question. What's all this got to do with me?"

"I'll let Felicity explain the bullets; then we can address your question."

Felicity opened her laptop and began to speak. This was a new Felicity; a professional administrator! She was no longer Rich's graduate student, love interest, fellow conspirator – she was . . .

"When I made our presentation to the Trustees," she said. "I showed them this graph." Felicity projected a complex graph on a screen at the end of the room.

MIDWEST UNIVERSITY REVENUE STREAMS (%)

FOR 1990 (1): 2000 (2): 2010 (3)

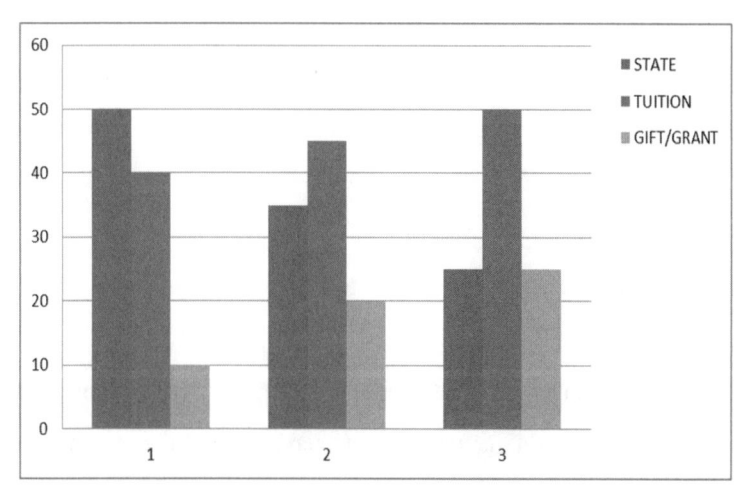

Year	STATE	TUITION	GIFT/GRANT
1 (1990)	50	40	10
2 (2000)	35	45	20
3 (2010)	25	50	25

The graph confused Rich; it looked too much like the output of the mathematical models in Felicity's dissertation. "Well . . . looks like you're talking about the University budget."

"Right on!" Bahls exclaimed. "What we have here, is a picture of where the money comes from and how income stacks up against our expenses. You see," he paused, "when I came on board and looked at our revenue streams, I was stunned by the challenge."

"Yes," Felicity added. "The point is – legislative appropriations are sinking rapidly and we must increase tuition each year. But that's not enough. The result is a serious deficit; which will grow exponentially in the out years unless we take drastic action!"

"Is that where your 'bullets' come in?" Rich asked.

"Yes. What the graph shows is that legislative support makes up about twenty-five percent of income, while tuition roughly covers about fifty percent today. In the near future, the legislative portion will decrease to twenty percent. And, worse news, the State may ultimately pay something like ten percent of our operating costs unless we can persuade them to hold at a higher level. That means that tuition will need to increase drastically unless other sources of revenue can be found. As the graph shows, gifts and grants already make up a significant part of the total. The only way forward is for us to develop a new academic model. That's our challenge."

Bahls took up the presentation. "The way we're going to address this issue is four-fold. First, we'll focus on building the Tornado image and the athletic 'branding' of the University. Then, the U will be re-positioned from a land-grant institution toward a world-class research university in the sciences and medicine.

Next, we'll take a leading position in the non-traditional and on-line market, with a special emphasis on graduate degrees. Then . . ."

"Wait a minute," Rich cut in. "This University was built on the land-grant model. Our biggest client is the state. We can't neglect that! And, graduate degrees don't come cheap. You'll just lose money if you go that route. Besides, we all know that the market is flooded with colleges and universities who're delivering low-quality degrees. Remember how upset we were when Prairie University was accredited?"

The mention of Prairie University – or PU as it was known in University circles – halted their exchange for a moment. When this for-profit 'university' opened its doors in Midwest City, the U had scoffed at the competition. Later, when it had been accredited by the North Central Association – Higher Learning Commission, traditional academics began to realize that the market for degrees had been transformed and moved out from under the umbrella of academic standards.

Bahls shook his head, as if to dispel the fumes of PU. "Let me take this one at a time. First, the future of this state isn't in the boonies! It's in our three metro areas, where science and technology take the place of agriculture. Second, with the U's label, we can scoop the on-line market. Students will turn to us to get a measure of the quality the others can't offer."

"But won't that just drive up your costs?" Rich asked.

"No!" Felicity interjected. "By using adjunct faculty, we can keep costs in line. We have to recognize that all universities have been turning out countless doctorates for positions that don't exist. These well-qualified graduates are eager to get any kind of academic position."

This was an analysis that Rich had been ignoring for several years. His graduate students rarely landed tenure-track appointments. When he thought of their plight, which wasn't often, his economic training forced the conclusion that he and his colleagues were obsolete! Rich visibly shrank in his chair.

Rich's standby mantras; 'academic integrity', 'incredibly high standards', 'basic research', were now to be replaced with new phrases; 'adjunct faculty' and 'on-line degrees'. These management devices would enable the U to 'scoop the market'. Rich recognized the vacuity of his view of life in the academy; he gritted his teeth for what was to come.

Felicity didn't notice. She continued, "Finally, we'll have to make significant reductions in our operating budget. It will be necessary to take a close look at unproductive subject matters and departments. I'm setting up a Balanced Score Card that will make it possible for us to assess the performance of colleges, departments, and individual faculty members. We'll be able to determine where to prune the dead wood."

Unproductive departments! Rich did the mental arithmetic on his output. Three graduates in the last four years! But both Pyke and Felicity had real jobs! Wasn't three enough?

"I can see that this hits close to home," Bahls turned in his chair. "Felicity, would you bring me the red folder that's on my desk?"

She nodded and left the room. It was obvious to Rich that a private talk was in the offing and he was about to be taken to the academic woodshed for some special treatment. *So here's what this visit is all about!*

Bahls stood and walked to the coffee bar. "How's about a refill?" he asked.

Rich picked up his cup and walked over to the coffee service. "OK. Just a half cup."

When the coffee had been poured, they resumed their seats.

Bahls took a long sip, put the cup carefully in front of him and began, "I need to make headway on the changes I've proposed. That means I need to initiate actions that are highly visible to the University community. As a senior faculty member, I value your opinion on some critical decisions."

"Fair enough," Rich said, relieved at the change of focus – from him to the 'community'.

"You've seen Tornado Alley and my athletic plans. How will the faculty react?"

Rich considered for a moment. "Well . . . they won't rush to buy tickets, but they'll probably be impressed with the show."

"Hmmm . . .," Bahls rubbed his chin. "I'd like them to be enthusiastic. Any ideas?"

"That's a tough one." Rich glanced at the plans for the athletic complex. "The only thing I can think of is the increase in visibility of the U that you have in mind. If you can convince the faculty that the Big Cigars are a source of new money, they might buy it."

"OK. That's a done deal. But is it enough?"

Rich moved his coffee cup in circles on the burnished table. "No, I don't think so. What you'll have to do is make the 'branding' you spoke of an integral part of the whole design."

"Say more," Bahls commanded.

"This is way out of my league," Rich said. "You'll need more positive signs of your design than athletics. For instance, where is the Baldrige Award? I haven't heard much about it in recent months."

"I have to be honest with you, Baldrige is no more than a smoke screen to cover our athletic program. We'll keep key faculty involved in Baldrige committees; when Tornado Stadium is in place, they'll forget about Baldrige."

Smoke screen! "So . . . it's really some version of 'bait and switch'. You lay on academic quality – and build. Kind of like a tornado. Right"

"I see. I see," Bahls furrowed his brow. "Well, how's this. I'll lay out the funding picture to get faculty support. Then show how the design is going to be paid for. For instance, the shift from land-grant to world-class research needs money. Athletics will play a key role in our future cash flow."

"Maybe," Rich mused, "but how can junking land-grant status bring in any money?"

"Simple. You know the Walden Campus – the one out in the boonies where we focus on agriculture research and education. Well, I'm planning to close that campus."

"That'll save a few bucks for a year or two," Rich scoffed. "Where's the beef?"

"You made a joke," Bahls chuckled. "But it's no joke. When I close Walden, the Legislature will eat it up! They'll see this as a serious attempt to focus the U on the future. My guess is that they'll hold our state funding around twenty-five percent. The faculty will understand that, won't they?"

"Possibly," Rich conceded.

"But that isn't all. I'm dickering with the federal Bureau of Prisons; looks like they might come up with 40 million or so for the Walden Campus. Hell, it already looks like a prison! All it needs is a fence!" Bahls guffawed at the image.

Walden a prison! "Are you sure you want to do this?" Rich asked.

"Absolutely! As Fel . . . Dr. Berland said dead branches have to be pruned. That's where you've been a great help."

"What do you mean by that?"

"You heard Dr. Berland indicate that we'll need to close unproductive units of the University. When you took over Ed. Psych. a couple of years ago, you showed how a financial argument could be used to close it down. I owe you big time for that."

Yes that was a good idea! Rich did not remember that it was Felicity's idea – he was only the messenger. "Yes, that was a useful tactic. But I don't see how it can work across the University. When you closed the Open College, you made plenty of enemies. And, won't tenure get in the way of any such cost-cutting move?"

Bahls smiled. "It would if I hadn't got the Trustees to connect tenure to operating units. In effect, individual faculty members are tenured to their department or college – not to the University. So, if I want to close, say, a college, everyone on that faculty is out of luck. They haven't a legal leg to stand on."

Rich had to admire the devious ploy. He knew that this approach had worked with Ed. Psych. In that instance, tenure was connected to departments. Now Bahls was raising the bar to connect tenure to the colleges that might be at risk of closure.

He could imagine how faculty in several hated departments would react to their pink slips. He actually chuckled, "Now that's real tree surgery!"

"That's not the end," Bahls swirled the coffee in his cup. "Remember the bullet that said 'Increase the use of non-tenured faculty'?"

"Sure, but you're already gone pretty far down that road with the steps you've outlined."

Bahls picked up on the metaphor. "Rich, we're only on the first lap. What we must do is encourage he retirement of senior faculty in the surviving departments so that they can be replaced by non-tenured recent graduates. Tenured faculty now make up about half of our instructional staff. That has to change. Adjunct faculty can increase our presence on the Internet and staff high-enrollment undergraduate courses at lower cost. That'll put us close to my target of one-third tenured faculty.

Rich considered the plan. It did make sense. There was a lot of deadwood at the University, and it was high-priced. If some of his colleagues . . . "You have a point. I can think of several in the College who are past retirement age. I guess I'd help in any way I can to make this happen." Rich was forgetting his own vulnerability; he was soon to be reminded.

"I'm glad to hear that," Bahls leered. "If you took early retirement and made the case for others, I know of at least twenty College faculty who would follow your example!"

Early retirement! Rich had never considered that his professorial time was limited. He had envisioned countless years when he and Felicity would be at the center of national attention. How could Mike even talk about retirement? Rich stared at Bahls. It was returned with a steady gaze not unlike the look that Rich had often used to terminate unwanted students.

". . . you can't be serious! Why, I'm at the top of my game!"

"That's just the point! We must get senior faculty to leave when they are at the peak of their careers. We can't support decline. Not that it's the case where you're concerned."

He's greasing the skids! Rich's whole career flashed across his mind: graduate school with Mike, Beth and Muriel; his first appointment at the University; Associate Dean with Dunkard; tenure; full professor; the Center; Hank, Mike and Felicity. All that wonderful journey was coming to an end! *No way!*

Rich shook away the memories, "I don't see why I should . . ."

Bahls held up a hand. "I didn't mean to come on so strong. What I can offer is a very attractive retirement package; one that I'm sure you will find appealing. You see, I know how valuable you are to the College and the Center. What I want to do is to create a future for you that takes away all the mundane responsibilities of faculty life."

"Just what does that mean?"

"Here's the deal."

Rich could almost see the order pad and the salesman's pencil.

"If you decide to do early retirement, I can guarantee full salary and benefits for three years. That'll take you to around sixty three. With your University pension and later, social security, you'll end up making more than you would as a regular faculty."

Rich did the mental arithmetic. He could see that Bahls was probably right. The money was there. Why, with Muriel's money and their investments he would be in the clover. "Well, maybe . . . I'll need. . ."

"Wait a minute! There's more. I have in mind some sort of continuing consulting arrangement. We can't afford to lose your knowledge of the U."

"This has come on pretty fast," Rich stood. "I better think about it."

Bahls led the way out of the conference room. "You do that and I'll confirm our talk with a formal letter," Bahls stood at the double glass doors. "But we have an informal understanding as to future opportunities. Right?"

Rich glanced at Bahls; then stared down the long hallway. At his side, the Tornado characters seemed to be grinning at the change from 'Professor' to 'Emeritus'. He turned his head back to Bahls. "Yes . . . I guess that'll be OK . . ."

"Great!" Bahls said. "Well, I gotta get back to work. See you later." He wheeled into his office – leaving Rich alone.

Rich walked slowly down Tornado Alley, the photos a blur of change. He carefully detoured around the Tornado mosaic and opened the massive outer doors of Conant Hall. Outside, he walked to one of the metal tables on the paved courtyard and sat – looking across the Quad at an unfamiliar landscape. *She never came back!* There probably wasn't any 'red folder'; merely a plan for Mike to set him up!

He sat for nearly a half-hour watching the diminishing flow of late-afternoon students. Finally, he sighed and walked to the Plaza railing where he overlooked the circular drive that gave access to the lower level of Conant Hall. Cars came and went, picking up the many functionaries leaving for the day.

The door to the underground garage opened. A burble of exhaust resonated in the canyon of the up-ramp. A yellow Corvette emerged. *Felicity!*

The Vette swung around the traffic circle and stopped at the entry to Conant Hall. Bahls emerged; immaculate, distinguished, a slim briefcase in hand. He leaned over, tossed the briefcase into the car, straightened and lit a cigar. He tossed his match in the direction of a nearby smoker's receptacle. Then he bent into the passenger seat of the 'Vette. Bahls leaned across to brush Felicity' cheek with a kiss.

The engine's burble gradually increased to a competitive roar. Squealing tires emphasized the transformation of promise into the depression of reality.

Big Cigars! And motorcars!

CHAPTER TWENTY-THREE

Master of the Academy

"The art o' the court is as hard to leave as keep, whose top to climb is certain falling. . ."
(Shakespeare: Cymbeline)

The promised letter from President Bahls arrived in Rich's Campus Mail box the next week, just as the University was completing its spring term. It was a thin Presidential envelope addressed to Dr. Richard Jessen, Professor Emeritus, with the University crest in the upper left-hand corner. Rich held it gingerly at arm's length as if it were warm to the touch. He carried it into his office and closed the door.

Seated at his desk, he opened the envelope and read.

Dr. Richard Jessen
Professor Emeritus
Tofte Hall, Campus

    Dear Rich:

        It is a great honor for me to formalize our recent conversation. I am hereby appointing you Professor Emeritus in recognition of the many contributions you have made during your long tenure at this University. I know that I speak for all your colleagues and the many students who have benefited from your advisement when I say, Congratulations Professor Jessen.

Sincerely,

Michael Bahls

President

Rich placed the letter in the center of his desk blotter and stared at it for several minutes. The words began to run together – another blurred summary of his career. It was over!

There was a second paper in the envelope. Rich drew it out and unfolded it. This paper summarized his status as 'Professor Emeritus' in a series of bullets.

PROFESSOR EMERITUS
STATUS AND BENEFITS

- Free admission to all University events (except for conference football and basketball games).
- Lifetime free parking in a University lot.
- Full library privileges (excepting reserve materials).
- Open invitation to attend faculty Senate meetings (non-voting).
- Use of University letterhead for personal correspondence (two-year limit).
- Full participation in the University Health Plan (1 year limit).
- Faculty office space (shared with other retirees).

Rich read no further. He had a sufficiency of these petty benefits. *What a come down! Sharing an office!* He nearly wept as he looked around the space that he had so carefully created. His imagination peopled it with fellow political plotters; Hank Loras, Mike Bahls, and Felicity. No! She was different! Rich recalled the times she had sat next to his desk, gazing at him, admiration written on her face. Then there were the days when she seemed to be reaching out to him for a personal relationship.

He knew that Felicity was truly his creation. A consummate political actress whose meteoric rise was testimony to the efficacy of the example he had set for her. She had learned how to use the levers of power and when and how to terminate those who might be competing with her for a grasp on the controls of the University. She had eased him out of the presidential circle; as completely as the U's basketball team had fared in last year's NIT. *One loss and you're out!*

Out indeed! Within a week, Hank Loras dropped by to define 'Emeritus' in concrete terms.

Rich looked up from his desk. "Hello Hank. Surprise! I haven't seen you for quite a while!"

Loras closed the door. "Rich, I'm sorry to bring you bad news. Mike has offered tenure to Winslow Pyke. I was out of the loop on that. Apparently Pyke fits into Mike's plans for the Center. He told me that Pyke will be the new Director."

"What!" Rich exploded. "Why, that . . . that . . . guy! How can he . . . I thought we were all in this together!"

"Me too," Loras nodded. "But Bahls is cutting us both out of the Center. He evidently has big plans for new federal funding initiatives. Wants to make the Center a University-level organization."

"Anything we can do?"

"Nothing that I can think of. So, what I'm here for is to ask you to switch offices. I need to open yours for Pyke."

"Switch! What the fuck! Why?" Rich spluttered.

"I know how you feel and I want you to know that this is Mike's idea, not mine."

Rich hung his head. "When?"

"First part of next week. The university movers will do the heavy lifting. They'll have your stuff out of Tofte and into Blewett 104 by Wednesday."

"104? That's in the basement!"

"I know. I know. But it ain't so bad. Got windows on two sides and you'll be away from Pyke."

"Well . . . I suppose I've got to give in. At least I won't be sharing my office with other retirees like it says in the official University policy."

"Look Rich," Loras folded his arms and leaned forward. "I can guarantee that office space for the summer and I'll try to hang on to it as long as I can."

"What does that mean?"

"I have no final say on office space. If somebody can make a case with Central Administration, you'd have to move along."

"What a crock of shit! Thirty-five years at this place and I end up like a first year instructor!"

The picture of Richard Jessen as 'Instructor' was jarring to both Rich and Hank. Each shook his head at this image.

The move to Blewett 104 went forward as Loras predicted. By the end of the following week, Rich was unlocking the door to his new office. Loras was right about the windows, however he hadn't mention that the space was only about ten feet wide and fifteen long; less that half the size of Rich's office in Tofte Hall. File cabinets took up the far wall with Rich's desk under a set of windows. Since this was a basement office, all Rich could see were the legs of co-eds as they passed on the sidewalk.

A few of Rich's books were arranged on rickety shelves. The balance of his collection was stored in official university moving boxes in the far corner. When

Rich was seated at his desk, his head barely cleared the lowest of the bookshelves. Several painful collisions taught him to arise carefully.

The first weeks in the office were a time for self-pity – followed by anger at Bahls and the University. Blewett 104 was punishment that he avoided by staying away from the U.

Although he could shelter at his house, it was hardly a respite from the consequences of 'Emeritus' status. Muriel was gone! He had eliminated all traces of her life. Only furniture defined their years together. When he could no longer tolerate the silence of the house, he would take the Mercedes and drive aimlessly around University City, taking care to avoid the campus.

Later that summer, he turned the Merc north for a visit to Moland, Iowa. Rich hadn't visited the town where he grew up for at least twenty years. It was a place to escape from; not a location for solace. Main Street was recognizable only because the abandoned high school building was still standing. Strand Drugs was a vacant lot. His family Our Own Hardware was gradually sinking into Iowa loam; seeking a more comfortable position to withstand the heat of summer.

The house where he had lived with Aunt Tillie and his Mother had been updated with a glassed-in front porch. The old tool shed was gone, replaced with a three-car garage. Rich drove past these landmarks, looking for a familiar name or a face from the past. It was clear that virtually everyone was now 'outta here!'.

When Rich returned to University City, he found the usual collection of catalogs and advertisements in his mail box. There was only one personal letter. It was from Hank Loras.

Office of the Dean

College of Human Science

    Dear Rich:

Your friends at the University are planning a retirement party for you. It will be held in Blewett 307 on August 26, prior to the opening of classes. Please give me a call and let me know that you'll be able to attend.

Your friend;

Hank Loras

    What the hell do I want with that? Similar emotions occupied his thoughts for several days. He considered excuses for not attending. When he recited them, they sounded like the whining school child of his Moland years. Finally, the loneliness of the house overcame his reluctance and he confirmed the invitation.

    On the day of the party Rich dressed carefully in the Second Life clothes he collected when he was anticipating a full social life with Felicity. The (relatively) new Gucci shoes still had their factory shine and his trousers held their sharp crease. At least he could go out in style!

    "Might as well take the Merc," he mumbled as he triggered the garage door opener, letting the sun caress the gleaming finish of the car. The Mercedes was a prop for the life story of Rich and Felicity. Now it was simply transportation for the Professor Emeritus.

    Rich drove slowly to the U and headed down the inclined ramp to his spot in the underground garage next to Blewett Hall. He motored down the window and held his parking pass against the card reader. Nothing happened! *What the hell!* He rubbed the pass on his coat and tried again. The door to the garage remained closed. Behind him, a frustrated fellow parker blew several horn blasts. Rich seethed!

With an exasperated heave, Rich swung out of the Merc and strode up the ramp to the horn honker.

"What's up?" the woman leaned out of her car window.

"My parking pass doesn't seem to work," Rich growled. "If you'll back up, I'll get out of your way."

"Sure. No problem," the woman closed her window and reversed the car.

Rich followed and pulled to one side of the street leading to the ramp. *Now what?* "Well, better find out what I can do." He opened the cover on his cell phone and keyed in the number for University Information.

"University Central. How can I help you?"

"Connect me to Parking Services!" Rich ordered.

A momentary pause, then, "Parking Services."

"This is Professor Jessen. I have a parking space in the Blewett Hall Garage. My pass doesn't seem to work."

"Lemme check." There was a pause of several minutes. "That pass no longer works for Blewett. It's been reassigned to the Fairgrounds Lot. Over on the Ag Campus."

"The Ag Campus!" Rich exploded. "Listen here! I'm a retired Professor and am supposed to have lifetime free parking! I demand . . ."

"Just a moment," the voice interrupted. "University parking policy does provide for lifetime privileges, but all retired personnel are assigned to Fairgrounds."

"Well, you can change me back to Blewett! I've an appointment at the College and need to get into the Garage!"

"Sorry. Can't do it. You can pick up a Campus Shuttle bus at Fairgrounds. It stops at Blewett." The voice hung up.

Rich pounded the steering wheel with his fist. He hung his head and gritted his teeth. His past experiences with University bureaucracy held no hope for special treatment.

The Mercedes leapt forward around the Blewett parking circle and took off for Fairgrounds, tires squealing. Rich raced the three miles to Fairgrounds lot and held his pass against the card reader. The gate raised and he roved the rows of cars looking for an opening. *Not even an assigned spot!* Finally, a student in a beat-up Ford vacated a spot and Rich positioned the Mercedes in the exact center of the space. "Please don't let these cretins scratch . . ."

A light rain was falling as Rich stepped out of the car. He reached into the rear seat for his leather-covered umbrella. Slipping it out of its case, he unfurled another of his image-building trademarks. The few puddles in the parking lot were easily avoided and he trudged up the inclined sidewalk toward the Ag Campus.

The sidewalk was bordered by a collection of farm buildings – the experiment station for Animal Husbandry. A towering pile of winter-generated manure crowded the chain link fence, waiting to be spread on nearby fields. "Just like Moland," Rich said aloud. "Shit everywhere!"

At the top of the hill, a bus shelter was crammed with students, chattering and jostling one another. Rich stood outside under his umbrella, avoiding contact with the rabble. Rain increased in intensity, splashing Gucci's and trousers.

Soon he was jostled by a phalanx of co-eds, all soaking wet. Their chatter told him that these were leading contestants in the Tornado Wet T-shirt Contest. Each shirt boasted two Tornado characters – strategically placed. For a moment, Rich was transfixed by the display of youthful charm. Then his age and distain took over. *Dumb bitches!*

When the inter-campus bus finally arrived, Rich attempted to furl his umbrella. The few moments this required, placed him at the end of the boarding line – no seats remained. He forced his way down the center aisle past the Tornado candidates. A reflexive grab of the overhead handrail and the press of their bodies kept him upright as the bus accelerated.

Rich was a half-hour late for his retirement party when he dismounted at Blewett Hall. Inside, he made superficial repairs to his appearance and climbed the stairs to the third-floor. The party was well under way in the conference room. President Bahls was standing, talking to ex-Legacy Director Dunkard. Hank Loras and Waldo Pearson were sipping coffee and laughing about some shared joke. Felicity was looking out a rain-streaked window.

In a corner Winslow Pyke was talking to a small group of graduate students – all attentive to his lecture.

"Rich!" Bahls shouted. "We've been waiting for you! Come in, Guest of Honor!" Mike held out both hands in welcome.

Felicity turned from the window and smiled. The room was alive with light!

Hank beckoned Rich to a seat at the head of a new oak conference table. "Take a look at the inscription!"

Rich leaned forward and read from an inlaid brass plaque.

Midwest Legacy

Professor Richard Jessen

Distinguished Scholar and Leader

1975 - 2010

"It's my personal gift to you and the College," Bahls said. "In meetings and dissertation defenses to come, everyone will remember your contributions to the academic enterprise at Midwest University!"

Applause covered Rich's mumbled response.

As far as Rich was concerned, the party was a confusion of conversations involving cameos of people from his University past. ExDean Dunkard looked at least ten years older. The effects of alcohol were clearly exhibited in the veined nose and red eyes. Waldo Pearson showed a little of his old good humor; it seemed to Rich that he was covering up some personal tragedy. Loras was sociable, but thoughtful, as if he were confronting some particularly challenging problem. Pyke was chattering continually in the clipped accent he had acquired in DC, occasionally interrupted by penetrating glances at the President.

Bahls was the only one who evidenced a party spirit. He worked the room – once a Presidential candidate – now elected. Felicity continued to beam her smile on the assembled. She did not, however, make any effort to share her luminosity with Rich.

Rich simply endured, responding only when required. He was a participant-observer, with the emphasis on the latter. Looking around the room, Rich noted a few surprises among the attendees. There was Dr. Ramsborn, the Director of Midwest Legacy. *Probably delivered the plate for the table!* The Three Old Buffaloes had evidently left their retirement stalls to welcome a new arrival. Rich was stunned to see Roxanne Graves, his ally in the Solvig caper. *Must be doing a study of university retirement practices!*

Like all retirement parties, this one came to an end. One by one, the participants came up to Rich, shook his hand, and mouthed familiar congratulations.

"Good job!"

"We'll sure miss you!"

"Won't be the same place without you!"

Roxanne Graves made a special point to corner Rich as the party wound down. "Rich," she said, "I'm told that you were the person who designed the College of Human Science. I want you to know that my faculty is much impressed by your leadership and we all wish you a productive retirement." She wrung his hand in a manly grip and moved to the door. *What was that all about?*

Ramsborn, too, make a personal connection. "Professor Jessen. I must say that your vision of the Legacy was an inspired creation. It has proven to be a compelling approach that has unlocked philanthropy among our alumni! You have my personal congratulations on your achievement, and my very best wishes!" He held Rich's hand for a long moment.

Finally, only his fellow conspirators remained: Loras, Bahls, and Felicity. Theirs was an awkward leave taking

Bahls was first to speak. "I owe you big time! There's no way I could have made the move from D.C. to the U without your help. I'll never forget what you've done for me."

The magnitude of this endorsement rendered Rich speechless. All the bitter comments that came to mind were submerged by the tide of gratitude. *Am I hearing this right?*

"Aw c'mon Rich," Bahls said clutching Rich's shoulder. "This isn't the end. Why, we'll come up with some new schemes that require your input. Bet on it!"

As far as Rich was concerned, all bets were off. He knew that his days as Mike's confidant were ended. He had nothing to contribute to the regime of the Academic Emperor!

Bahls stood back, smiled and moved toward the door. Felicity came up to Rich, hugged him, and kissed him on the cheek.

"Oh Rich!" she whispered. "I owe you my life! Without your advice and help, I would be just another junior faculty member. And, your friendship and support has made the journey a pleasure!" She stood back, holding his hands and smiling.

Here was the image that he saw in the airport so many years ago! Intellect! Beauty! Promise! The Holy Grail he had sought – and lost. He tried to speak, but no words were forthcoming.

Felicity sighed. "I know how you feel and I'll do everything I can to make this an easy time for you. Let's always be friends." She released his hands and moved away.

Rich took a step as if to follow her. *Please! Come back!* But she went on to where Bahls was waiting.

Winslow Pyke appeared; Bahls' black raincoat on a hanger! The capo Mafioso, being served by his spear-carrier!

Bahls shrugged into Pyke's coat-embrace and stood, framed in the doorway. Felicity stood on tiptoe and kissed Bahls. Then, arm-in-arm they disappeared down the stairway.

Hank was last, the fellow originator of the University politics.

"Sure was good run, Old Buddy. We kind of shook up the place. I hope I can carry on without you."

Rich instantly replayed the phone calls that began their 'run'. "I guess you're right. We did indeed find ways around the system."

Loras closed the door and sat at the table. "You better sit down. We need to talk."

The conspiratorial tone forced Rich into a facing chair. "What do you mean?"

"There have been some big changes while you were away this summer. Changes you ain't gonna like."

"Such as?"

"Lemme ask you this. Did you notice that long face on Waldo Pearson?"

"Now that you mention it, he did seem a bit sad. Why?"

"Well, Mike's given him the axe. He's been asked to retire. Just like you."

"I can't believe that! Why Pearson is a big player in bargaining with the Legislature. Mike can't be serious!"

"He's plenty serious," Loras grimaced. "Here's the hammer! Mike's appointed Felicity to replace him!"

"You gotta be joking! Why . . ." Rich rubbed a hand through his hair. ". . . she hasn't . . ."

"That ain't all. Mike and Felicity were married last week. Beth is out and Felicity is in!"

Rich was overwhelmed. *Felicity! His girl! Mike! His friend!* "That sonofabitch!" he snarled. "Who does he think he is?"

"He's the President of this fucking place!" Loras stated. "And, he's tied the can on me too. I've been given the same kind of 'Emeritus' line that he handed you. We're both outta here as of this fall."

Mike and Felicity! All that remained of the group that set the U on its path to national prominence. All that work! Wasted!

"There's more," Loras said. "Mike's gonna close the College! He's using the same approach that you discovered when you axed Ed. Psych.. It's a part of his Big Plan. With Pyke in charge of the Center, there's damn little that the College has to offer. In fact, he's moving parts of the College to the Freud Building and combining them with Psychology. Roxanne Graves will be the new Dean of the 'reinvented' College of Human Science. What do you think of that?"

So that's why Graves was here! "Guess you're right," Rich gulped. "I'll bet that there won't be anything for us in that."

"You got it!" Loras gritted. "We have to accept the fact that this guy's only for himself and that he'll use anything to look out for number one. Mike dangled the bait in front of our noses to get the retirements. You can be sure that we're out in the cold!"

Rich nearly sobbed. "What can we do?"

"Well, I think I'm set for a move to Missouri State. I'll do my best to see if I can connect to you when I'm up and running."

"Sure. Sure," Rich fumbled for a handkerchief and blew his nose. ". . . be good thing . . ."

Loras stood. "Tell you what. I'll give you a call sometime next week and we can hoist one and give Mike the finger!" He left.

Rich was alone with the wreckage of his party. Cups, napkins and paper plates of cookie crumbs littered the shiny table. He stepped to the head of the table, sat down and took a napkin to restore the glitter of the brass plate.

Midwest Legacy

Professor Richard Jessen

Distinguished Scholar and Leader

1975- 2010.

Thirty –five years! Just a fucking brass plate! Rich stared at the Legacy Plate. He calculated that it, along with the conference table, had cost some donor less than five thousand dollars. Since it did not cross the Legacy threshold, there was no donor naming rights.

Gradually, Loras' news sank in. *Mike and Felicity! Married!* There was no way that Bahls would find a place for him in the future. With Loras gone, Rich had no support – Winslow Pyke would replace him.

"Felicity!" Rich sighed. "How could. . ." He stood and ran his fingers over the brass plate. He slowly stood and turned his back on the room and his career.

The bus ride back to the Ag Campus was a repeat of the earlier hassle. Now, it was raining harder and the interior of the bus was fogged with suspended moisture. He sat crammed into a side seat, umbrella between his knees. On his arrival at the Ag Campus, he was the last off the bus.

"Hell of a storm!" the driver remarked. "You watch yourself crossin' the street Oldtimer!"

Oldtimer! How could this peasant insult Professor Jessen? Rich clamped his teeth, holding in the retort. On the sidewalk, windblown rain pressed his umbrella against his body and spatters of moisture penetrated its fabric.

Rich struggled against a wind that drove sheets of water across the sidewalk. Past the Animal Husbandry Building rain pounded the pile of manure, soaking its essence into a waterfall of filth that coursed over Rich's shoes. *Sonofabitch!* Gucci never intended their product for serious farmwork. Rich's socks became sodden and he squished his way across the street into the Fairgrounds lot.

The Mercedes was nearly alone, standing in a pool of storm water. Rich pressed the remote entry keypad and struggled to furl his umbrella, without success. A gust of wind caught it, ripping it from his hands. The umbrella cartwheeled across the parking lot. *Shit!*

He bent himself into the car and began to lift his legs. "Can't have that crap in here!" Rich kicked off the soiled shoes, leaving them outside the car. He closed the door.

Rain continued to hammer on the Mercedes. Rich did not start the engine. Instead, he sat behind the wheel and stared out the windshield at the distorted image of the Ag Campus. So this was how it all turned out! Exiled to the barnyard! Tenure and trappings of academic power – gone!

The few passing students glanced at Rich's face in the window. They did not, of course, know that they were looking at Professor Richard Jessen, Master of the Academy.

UNSUSTAINABLE

"Don't try to play the game better, try to figure out when the game is over."
George Soros

The thesis of this book is that 'the game is over'. An unsustainable model of higher education has been put in place by actors like Rich Jessen as they have pursued personal objectives. Hunting for personal advantage has largely obscured the original missions of colleges and universities, replacing value by ephemeral promises. Midwest University embodies most of the features of the unsustainable model: a highly-charged political environment, depletion of the humanities, entertainment through sport, and enrichment of faculty and administrators at student and public expense.

Clearly, a new higher education model is called for. Here are the major features such a model must incorporate.

- Cost Reduction: The acceleration of college and university tuition prices must be halted and significant cuts put in place – beginning with (at least) a fifty percent cut in administrative expenditures. Further, bloated student services must be optional and billed only to those who make use of them. The most difficult issue in Cost Reduction will have to do with over-built, unnecessary structures. This 'edifice complex' will require therapeutic intervention in the deliberations of trustees, administrators and donors.

- Accreditation: *"The goal of accreditation is to ensure that education provided by institutions of higher education meets acceptable levels of quality." (U.S.Department of Education)* Proliferation of accredited institutions has resulted in a market where many degrees have become suspect. The goal of 'quality' has been trampled in the rush of institutions to feed at the buffet of federally-guaranteed student loans. Liberal arts colleges have become Doctoral-granting universities with no research foundation; educators have been replaced by recruiters whose assignment is to enroll the gullible. A new generation of academic leadership must reform accreditation to guarantee the promise of quality and drive the unethical profit-takers from the academic market place.

- Teaching and Learning: *"Our goal is to see teaching equally valued with research as a professional commitment of faculty and teaching assistants and to provide the training and resources to make excellent teaching possible." (Center for Teaching and Learning: Stanford University)* It is fair to say that teaching is an 'art' – supported by little science. Education is the only profession where practitioners have such a limited understanding of how learning takes place and how it is to be enabled by effective teaching. Recognizing that teaching and research are both essential to the health of the academy is an essential first step toward promoting learning. In most colleges and universities, this means that teaching/learning must take first place in claims on institutional resources.

- Staffing the Academy: Faculty tenure – originally instituted to protect academic freedom – has produced a small, highly paid cadre of 'professors for life'; and a large mass of adjunct faculty who do the bulk of undergraduate teaching. These dynamics describe the core of the 'unsustainable model' of higher education. Resources and prestige go to the few while the many – and their students – conduct the academic enterprise at a subsistence level. The only hope for correcting this problem is for abolishing tenure and redirecting resources to support teaching and learning.

- Truth in Packaging: Higher education must open itself to the realities of the intellectual marketplace. The subject matters have conspired with administrators to continue to produce graduates who have little opportunity to apply their knowledge. In response, the academy retreats behind the smokescreen of 'learning for learning's sake'; a promise that defies definition.

- Entertainment: The case against the deification of sport in higher education does not need to be made here; instead, the complex webpages of Division I universities make the concluding argument. See, for example: www.MGoblue.com where the array of athletic offerings of the University of Michigan makes one wonder whether UM engages in any teaching and learning activities at all. Seeing oneself as a 'Wolverine', 'Hawkeye, and even 'Gopher', has captivated the imagination of faculty, students, and administrators - and diminished the international standing of American higher education.

- *GAME OVER!* The game may be over; however, it is still being 'gamed' by the powerful. Upon his retirement, the president of the University of Minnesota signed sweetheart deals for his associates worth nearly three million dollars. He also awarded himself a half-million dollar one-year 'leave' along with a 'professor for life' position – at three hundred fifty thousand dollars a year. (Minneapolis Star Tribune: February, 2012) Clearly 'referees' are needed to control these unsustainable games!